THE DECISION

THE DECISION

WILLIAM BOSWORTH

TATE PUBLISHING
AND ENTERPRISES, LLC

Published by Tate Publishing & Enterprises, LLC
127 E. Trade Center Terrace | Mustang, Oklahoma 73064 USA
1.888.361.9473 | www.tatepublishing.com

Tate Publishing is committed to excellence in the publishing industry. The company reflects the philosophy established by the founders, based on Psalm 68:11,
"The Lord gave the word and great was the company of those who published it."

Published in the United States of America

ISBN: 978-1-63063-804-7
1. Fiction / Christian / General
2. Fiction / Religious
14.03.11

DEDICATION

To my beloved son.

ACKNOWLEDGMENTS

A sincere thank you to my wife, Judy, for her support and tolerance. Many thanks to my daughter, Lisa, her husband, John Kelley, and my beautiful granddaughters, Alex and Brianna, for their help in editing and bringing this story to reality.

CHAPTER ONE

Mary O'Leary walked up to the ornate front door of the cardinal's residence as she had done on so many days before and fumbled with the key as she had done on so many days before. She thought to herself that it would continue to remain a mystery why she always had trouble opening the door, even though it was a task she had performed every morning, with the exception of days off, for over twenty-five years.

With her brief struggle behind her, she entered the hallway, hung up her coat in the convenient closet, and assumed her command position in the residence.

Cardinal Harold Farley had been up for an hour already and was presently in the Lady chapel of the cathedral celebrating Mass. He would return to the residence in about another thirty minutes. This allowed Mary enough time to have breakfast ready and also present the cardinal with his morning paper. She always had time to think while preparing breakfast, since over the years the task had become so routine. This morning she thought about the former resident of the mansion, Cardinal Thomas Fitzpatrick, and the contrast between him and Farley.

Fitzpatrick had hired her and she had worked for him for about twenty years. *What a wonderful man*, she thought, *a saint*. She continued to think about his lack of complaining and how he had always treated her as an equal and never let her be subject to the oppressive employer-employee relationship. When she turned sixty-five five years ago, he had talked with her about retirement.

She explained to him how lonely she would be since she really had no family, having only one sister who had died ten years ago. She actually enjoyed coming to work each day as it made her feel useful and wanted. Fitzpatrick told her that her pension and her social security would be adequate; she would have no financial problems. But she remembered how at that time she would hear none of it and how Fitzpatrick had leaned back in his chair, smiled, and said, "I was secretly hoping you'd want to stay here."

Mary thought about how Fitzpatrick was a priest's priest, a deeply religious man. She often thought the church hierarchy sort of snubbed him. *Not intellectual enough*, she thought. That was just fine with her because she knew then and knew now that Fitzpatrick was always side by side with the Lord. *After all, wasn't that all that mattered?*

Shortly after they had agreed on her continued duties at the residence, Fitzpatrick contracted cancer. He was dead in seven months. Mary was consoled by the fact that he didn't suffer long. *He deserved at least that.*

Archbishop Farley succeeded Fitzpatrick and was elevated to cardinal two years ago by Pope Clement XV, the successor to Pope Matthew. Clement also happened to be a friend of Farley's.

Clement became pope within weeks of Matthew's death, and so for Mary, who was a deeply religious woman, her sixty-sixth year was riddled with sorrow—the passing of Fitzpatrick followed shortly by the passing of her beloved Matthew.

She remained in thought as she removed the bacon from the pan and placed it on the paper towel to allow it to drain. She remembered her first meeting with Farley and how pleasant he was, but his mannerisms seemed rather contrived. Perhaps she was still mourning Fitzpatrick. *It's unfair for me to judge too quickly. I must give him a chance*, she had thought. He was always very mannerly, but aloof. Admittedly, he was extremely intelligent and able to remember details on matters no one else considered to be of the slightest importance. *I guess he's a very private person*, she pondered. Although Farley had told her that he would prefer her to remain at the residence when he was appointed successor to Fitzpatrick, and he was always polite and courteous to her, she always felt on guard around him.

Two years ago, just after her sixty-eighth birthday, Clement XV announced that Farley would receive the red hat symbolic of the College of Cardinals. She had congratulated him on hearing the news and they had sat and talked awhile; she recalled those few moments as being the only time she ever felt close to Farley. She never forgot about being absent from the reception for Farley after receiving the red hat. She didn't really expect to be invited, but she couldn't live with the fact that she wasn't.

Mary's days off were Thursdays and Sundays. She often wondered what Farley did on Thursdays, which were his days off. She knew he frequently visited the Lincrofts from his former parish. But that was all she knew. She remembered Fitzpatrick went to his little cabin up by the lake every time he could. He liked the solitude of the country to "meditate" as he would often tell her. She knew, however, that he was a dedicated fisherman and the proximity of his cabin to the lake caused him no end of torment of the decision to "meditate" or hook the big one. Fitzpatrick would always laugh when, on occasion, he would return from the lake with his catch and ask Mary to clean and prepare it for him. His reason for laughter was her usual vehement refusal. "You can fire me if you want to, but I don't clean and prepare fish." It amazed her even more that he would then clean the catch himself and even enjoy preparing it. She would never tell him that once in a while he was in her way in the kitchen. She would never try to upset the good Cardinal Fitzpatrick.

She got back to her original train of thought. *What did Farley do on Thursdays? Just sit with the Lincrofts? Did he play golf? Did he go to shows?* He certainly didn't have a cabin that she knew of. She would have to come up with a clever way to inquire about his days off and assuage her nosiness.

She timed it perfectly. Breakfast was ready and she placed the morning paper on the table. She had barely turned from the table, when she heard Farley walking toward the kitchen.

Cardinal Farley entered the kitchen doorway. A strikingly handsome man, he was in his midfifties and possessed a thick mane of gray hair. Just under six feet tall, he had no hint of a paunch. Mary often thought that with him and so many other priests, not getting married was more of a hardship on the women than the priests. His only outward sign of aging was his need for glasses to read the fine print. They did, however, add a touch of class when he put them on to read the fine print in the morning paper.

"Good morning, Mary, and how's Mary this morning?"

"Just fine, couldn't be better," she replied, though she was hiding some aches and pains from him. *He's always pleasant to me*, she thought. *But I still feel an aloofness. He remains a mystery.*

"Everything looks good, Mary. You make the waking hours bearable," he said to her while he glanced at the headlines in the morning paper. "The paper says rain tomorrow. That's too bad as the Lincrofts and I were planning on dinner and a show tomorrow night, as well as a leisurely lunch in the afternoon."

Well, I didn't have to ask him. He volunteered that much information on his own. Maybe I was being too hasty in thinking he was secretive. I've worked for him so long to know now that if I don't ask, he won't tell. I don't know why I'm thinking about it so much after these years. Truthfully, I've been here four years with him and that's the most he's ever spoken to me about the Lincrofts. She boldly spoke up. "I've never met the Lincrofts."

He placed the paper down and replied, "Well, I'll have to remedy that." He picked up his coffee to take a sip. "I intend to have them here some evening soon to see how the good people live," he said jokingly. He then added, "And you should be here. I'll introduce you to them and I'm sure you'll like them. I have no family, Mary, so they have been like family to me."

"Tell me about it," she interrupted sarcastically.

He continued. "The Lincrofts have been my family and I love them dearly. They have a special place in my heart and I know the good Lord will bless them because they are also very good to him."

Changing the subject, he looked at Mary and inquired as to what she might be doing tomorrow on her day off.

Then it hit her. *All this time I thought that he was being evasive, but maybe I've been less than overflowing with personal information myself. He doesn't know that much about me either.* She answered, "I'll get some shopping done and catch up on some reading."

"Do you ever get to any of the shows?"

"I'd love to go but I never seem to get the chance."

"Well maybe we'll have to remedy that too."

What's gotten into him? Here I am thinking all morning about how evasive he is and what I can do to find out more about him; and in one short morning, he's become a veritable fount of information. She continued to luxuriate in the new relationship she seemed to be developing with Farley, and thought that maybe the Lord had listened to her thoughts and agreed with her that she had been in the dark too long.

She opened the door to the pantry where a box of dish detergent rested on the bottom shelf in the corner. She picked it up to use in the new dishwasher. She so loved that dishwasher. She felt it added years to her life. It was that good.

Farley continued to enjoy his breakfast and peruse the morning paper. He put the paper down and looked at Mary. "Yes, I've made up my mind. When I'm with the Lincrofts tomorrow, we'll arrange a definite date for them to come here. I'll invite some of their friends, whom I have met over the years and who have been very gracious to me. It will be a fine evening. You will definitely be there."

"Thank you. I'm already looking forward to it," she replied. She wondered if this was going to entail much work on her part.

She loved planning an event like this, but she also felt she was not quite up to it. She remembered when Farley was installed as cardinal; all she did was call the catering hall. She wasn't feeling strong about her ability to create and host a festive occasion in the large dining/reception room at the residence.

Farley interrupted her thought. "Call Johnson's Caterers and give them the necessary information when I give you the date. Johnson has been good to the diocese, so I'm sure he'll do the usual bang-up job."

"That he will," was all she could muster as a reply. *Could he also read minds?* she thought.

Farley finished his coffee and took the paper into his office to allow Mary to clean up the kitchen and finish her chores there. He contemplated on the fact that he just told Mary he had no family and the thought struck him as frightening.

He was born fifty-four years ago, the only child of Harold and Jane Farley. They were an upper middle income suburban family and Harold, Jr. never really wanted for anything. He attended the best private schools and in his fourth year of college made up his mind to be a priest.

After receiving his degree, he entered the seminary to begin his priestly studies. Some of those studies in his later years were done in Rome. After his ordination, he continued his education while also serving in his first parish. He eventually received a master's and a doctorate.

At the age of thirty-eight, he was assigned pastor of St. Bartholomew's church in Rosewood, a well-to-do suburb. His knowledge of canon law and his favor with the people made him a popular man of sorts. While people liked him, he seemed to maintain an air about him that stopped people short of loving him. It was during this time in his priestly career that both his mother and his father, who were in their forties when Farley was born, passed away within a year of each other. Farley had some cousins but none he was very close to, and this left him virtually a man without a family.

He developed a close relationship with a couple in his parish: Ann and Charles Lincroft. Charles was a successful president of a bank started by his family, and Ann was his very attractive wife. Their relationship developed into a major friendship. Farley had found himself a family.

At the young age of forty-four, the title Right Reverend Monsignor was bestowed on him. Due to his many good works and his knowledge of church law, he was again recognized by Pope Matthew and made an auxiliary bishop of his diocese. While an auxiliary, he remained at St. Bartholomew's.

Four years ago, in Farley's fiftieth year, Cardinal Fitzpatrick, the archbishop of the diocese, passed away and the administrative duties fell on Farley. Within months after Fitzpatrick's death, Pope Matthew again honored Farley by making him successor to Fitzpatrick as archbishop. He left St. Bartholomew's and took up residence at the cathedral.

Some months later, the shocking news of the unexpected death of Matthew reverberated throughout the world. Farley flew to Rome to attend the funeral. Following the funeral, he remained in Rome to meet with some of his former classmates with whom he had studied so many years before. One of those classmates was a cardinal in the Curia by the name of Guiseppe Francone. Although Farley would not be involved in the election of a new pope, he was partial to Francone. Francone was only five years his senior, but he was in the tradition of Matthew and the beloved John Paul II. Farley felt the church needed to continue the tradition. But he was Italian. Would the church return the papacy to an Italian? Not since John Paul I had an Italian been elected to the papacy considering the stranglehold they held on that position for so many years. Farley felt that, Italian or not, Francone was the man to succeed Matthew. He met quite a few times with Francone prior to the conclave and they continued to nurture their mutual respect for each other.

Farley returned to the United States before the papal election began and was overjoyed a few days later when the white smoke from the Sistine Chapel announced the election of a new pope. The new pontiff was announced as Giuseppe Cardinal Francone who would take the name Clement. He would be the fifteenth pope to take that name. Two years later, Clement appointed Archbishop Farley to the College of Cardinals. Farley would remain archbishop of his diocese.

Mary knocked on the door of Farley's office, interrupting his thoughts about his past life. She told him she would be leaving the building for awhile as she needed some things for lunch. Farley jokingly told her not to buy anything fattening and then assured her he would be in good hands. He was expecting his secretary, Karen Michaels, at any minute.

No sooner had Mary closed the door when Farley heard it open again. He heard the staccato of high heels heading toward the outer office and that was as good as an announcement that Karen, his efficient secretary from the days of St. Bart's, had arrived.

Karen was not an outstanding looking woman but she made the most of what she was given. Her hair was coiffed in a current style, her clothing showed good taste, and she knew how to make up her ordinary face and transform it to a more attractive face. Karen, in her early thirties, had a slightly long nose that held a pair of stylish glasses which she was forced to wear while working. She was a pleasant person and always made a good appearance as the archbishop's secretary.

Farley welcomed her on the intercom and bid her good morning. He also asked what was on the agenda for today and also for Friday. "I have some letters that must go out today, plus further rough copies of my pastoral letter," he said over the intercom.

Karen responded with a pleasant good morning and began to perform the tasks she had been assigned.

Mary peered at the beautiful things in the store windows as she made her way to the market. As she gazed at the beautiful clothes, she started to think what it would have been like to have been married and to have been able to raise a family. *I can't say I haven't enjoyed life, but really what have I done? I'm seventy years old and I guess all I do now is wait for the grim reaper.* But she insisted to herself that she must be positive and stop those useless grim thoughts. *I've always had enough money; I love to read and I always have enough time for that, so why should I complain?* Nevertheless the more she saw of the good life as exhibited in the store window, the more remorseful she became concerning her twilight years. *God has a reason for each life, and each life has its purpose and mine was to take care of the worldly needs of his holy priests so that they would have the time to minister to his people.* That thought consoled her and she took a jauntier step as she headed toward the market.

Karen could keep it a secret no longer. She must ask the cardinal for advice. She had gone to her parish priest who could do nothing for her, and so she felt, *Why not go to the top?* She thought about Farley's aloofness and she wondered how he would take the news, but her courage won out, and she left her chores to go to his office.

"Can I interrupt you for a second, Your Eminence?" she asked as she stood in the doorway of his office.

"I'm sure I can find time for you, Karen. What is it?"

"It's a personal matter that I've already discussed with Father Jablonski at my church, but he says he can't do anything for me, and so I thought I'd come to you."

"Sit down," he said as he motioned toward the large leather chair across from his desk. "How serious is this? You didn't murder someone, did you?" he questioned with an air of levity. He was trying to ease the now obvious tension that had injected itself into his office.

Karen's thirty-one years started to become obvious as she wrinkled her face and squirmed in her chair before she told Farley that she wanted to marry her boyfriend of the past year, one Thomas Kiely. Before he could interrupt with congratulations, she informed him that there were some religious problems involved.

"Relax and tell me all about it," Farley said as he looked at her with a blank stare.

She informed him that Kiely had been married before, was five years her senior, and that he had two children from his previous marriage, which, to make matters worse, took place at a Catholic ceremony. She had met him last year after his divorce became final and she had dated him ever since. "I realize my position as the archbishop's secretary could lead to scandal for your office, Excellency, but I truly love Tom and I intend to marry him with or without the church's consent."

"Why did you want to see me then? You've obviously made up your mind."

"Is there anything that can be done so that we may marry in the good graces of the church?" she implored.

"My offhand answer has to be a painfully honest no. However, there is a slight chance that his first marriage was somehow contracted invalidly, and he and his wife could have their marriage annulled."

"No," she interrupted. "Check with the Matrimonial Court and you'll see that his case was rejected."

"Then I am powerless to help you, Karen. While I feel for you, I think you must realize that to contract this marriage with Tom Kiely would be against the church."

"Then there is nothing that can be done?" she asked in a final tone.

"Karen, I feel so helpless but the answer is no. Church law is perfectly clear on this and there is nothing I can do. Please let your conscience guide you in making your decision. Don't ever underestimate God's love for you and do what you think is right. What a beautiful thing love is that brings two total strangers together in a lifetime relationship. However, it is my opinion that sometimes love and infatuation are confused and this is what leads to the high divorce rate. The church can in no way lessen the severity of the marriage contract or the resulting family unit. In her infinite wisdom, therefore, the church has adamantly stood against the divorce concept. While it allows two people to divorce, it does not permit remarriage while one of the partners is still alive. And for you to marry a man who has been married before, you would be cutting yourself from the grace of the church. Father Jablonski is right, Karen, there is nothing anyone can do for you except to continue to pray for you."

"What about my position here?"

"Let's cross that bridge when we get to it," he replied with a smile. "Do me a favor, Karen. Allow the Holy Spirit to enter your life and ask him to help you make the right decision. Don't rush into this. Check with me from time to time so I can hear of your progress. Oh, and by the way, have you set a date for the wedding?"

"Not exactly, but we had planned within the next year. Tom has some financial obligations to clear up first."

"And he may always carry obligations to his first family. That's something you should think about."

"Thank you, Eminence, for your time."

"Don't ever hesitate to come to me if you have a problem, Karen, but bear in mind I may not have all the answers or at least the ones you want to hear, but I think it does one good to talk over with someone else what's bothering them."

She thanked him again and presented him with the day's agenda and returned to her office.

She loved Tom Kiely but she also loved the church. Working for the cardinal kept her close to the church. While it made her feel better to talk to Farley, she still brooded over what to do. *I may have just complicated matters*, she thought as she removed the rough drafts of Farley's pastoral letter from the files. *I've finally found a man who loves me, and I care so much for him too.*

She started to type on her keyboard, but it became oppressive to try to work with the thoughts of her "illegal" upcoming marriage locked into her mind. It was a good thing Karen was efficient, or the time would have been ripe for mistakes. That could lead to the loss of her job even more quickly then her upcoming marriage might.

She restocked the printer with a fresh supply of paper and continued her work on the pastoral letter.

Farley glanced at his agenda and noticed that he had a meeting with the housing Commissioner of the city at three that afternoon. He was involved with a clergy group in a new minority housing project. Religious leaders of all faiths were represented but Farley was the chairman. Today would be a must-attend.

He actually did dwell some on the anguish his secretary must be going through, but he knew he must remain firm.

His stomach began to growl prematurely for lunch. He awaited Mary O'Leary's return and her preparation of lunch. It was still too early. As he continued to fine-tune his thoughts for the meeting, he also continued to be annoyed by thoughts concerning the plight of his secretary. He said a quick prayer that the Lord would guide her and also guide him in being able to assist her in any way that he could. He knew that as one of the highest church officials, he could not bend. His unbending posture would certainly haunt his future life. He just didn't know it at that time.

CHAPTER TWO

Ann Lincroft walked out of Greyson's Department Store and headed toward McMurty's Restaurant. The sun shone beautifully on the city streets, and suddenly the city didn't seem so oppressive.

Ann was a particularly stunning woman who carried her forty-eight years handsomely. Her hair, beautifully dark when she was younger, now held the nicest shade of gray. Her facial features and her skin were flawless. Her large blue eyes gave her a look of innocence that belied her age. Her childlike face and slim figure made her among the most beautiful of the high society set.

Her jaunty walk carried her closer to her destination which was lunch with her husband of twenty-three years. As she neared McMurty's, however, there were two department store windows that caused her to detour and thus delay her arrival at the eatery.

Charles Lincroft, or Charlie to his friends, looked at his watch. He had arrived somewhat early and anxiously anticipated the arrival of his wife. He ordered a martini and held a brief but inane conversation with the waiter. He then stared into space and gave some thought to the transactions that he would be working on that afternoon. Lincroft was president of the New American Bank and was a wealthy man, not only by virtue of his position, but also by virtue of his ancestry. His father had started the bank and when he retired, Charles took over.

Charles was a slightly balding but handsome man. He was tall and that lent itself to his lean look even though he sported the slightest paunch. He attributed that to his sedentary job.

He looked at his watch again and began to grow impatient.

Mary O'Leary noticed the attractive woman walking towards her. She only noticed her for an instant because it was then that everything happened so fast. She saw the car mount the curb and the woman get knocked aside by the car. She then saw the car slam into the storefront. Her first instinct was to feel relieved that had she left the rectory a few seconds later, or it could have been her as the victim. After that fleeting thought, instinct told her to help. At her age, running was out of the question, but since the distance was so short, walking sufficed. She walked past the car and peered inside to view what appeared to be an intoxicated driver who needed very little help. She walked over to the woman and knelt alongside her. The woman appeared to be in great pain. Mary comforted her until the police arrived. By now, a crowd had gathered, and so at the arrival of the police, the crowd was pushed back. One officer went to the driver's aid, while the other officer aided the struck woman. He thanked Mary for comforting the woman and told her he could take care of things now. As she walked away, shaken by what had happened, she didn't hear the woman tell the officer her name was Ann Lincroft.

Charles sipped the near final draft of his second martini and looked askance at it. "It's usual for Ann to be late, but never this late." Then he chuckled to himself. "If I order another martini, I'll be smashed before she arrives."

The waiter walked over to the table and asked Lincroft if he cared for another drink, but he resisted the urge to take another drink and told the waiter of his plight. He then tried to assure himself, as well as the waiter, that Ann would be along shortly.

The medical assistants and police helped Ann Lincroft into the ambulance. She was in great pain and not fully coherent. She mumbled to the police officer in the ambulance to notify her husband who was waiting for her at McMurtry's. The officer told her not to talk and to remain calm, and he would take care of notifications when they got to the hospital.

Mary O'Leary picked a few items from the shelf of the market but could not drive the thoughts of recent events from her mind. What she had just witnessed had left her just short of trembling. She shopped for what she had to buy, keeping in mind that she wasn't about to do any extra shopping. She brought her order to the checkout lane, paid the young lady there, and began the trek back to the rectory.

Charlie Lincroft began to worry. He gave in to the thirst for another martini and started to exercise his thought processes in the search mode for possible answers to the whereabouts of his beloved Ann. *She said she had some shopping to do and then she would come directly here. Then we were going to talk about spending the day tomorrow with Father Harold. I've already made reservations at La Palais for dinner and at the Center City Palace hotel for lunch. I'll call the office and see if maybe she called there to tell me of a delay. At times like this, I wish she would carry a cell phone. She absolutely refuses. But she knew I would be waiting here, so why didn't she find someway to contact me. I better call home.* Lincroft extracted his cell phone from his pocket and called his home in suburban Rosewood.

Their housekeeper, Marie, answered the phone and confirmed Lincroft's fear. "Your wife said she was meeting you for lunch after some shopping. The limo picked her up shortly after nine thirty this morning."

"Call me if you hear anything," he replied. He took a deep breath and sipped the last of his second drink. It was a larger-than-usual sip. He called the waiter over and acknowledged with some bravado that he had been stood up and then meekly asked for the check. He promptly paid and headed to the office. As he left McMurtry's, he looked down the street and at a distance of almost two blocks, he saw flashing red lights, a crowd of people, and what appeared to be a car resting partway in a store window. He turned and headed in the opposite direction thinking to himself, *Just another afternoon in the city.*

Cardinal Farley continued to work on his pastoral letter and awaited the return of Mary and the ensuing lunch bell. He didn't want to eat too late as he had that appointment this afternoon at three o'clock with the city housing commissioner. It was important because Farley was in the forefront of better advantages in housing for minority groups. This was a stance that managed to cause problems for him with more politically conservative people. He also gave thought to an answer for Karen's plight, but was convinced that his duty, as he saw it, was to try to talk Karen out of that marriage. He continued with his work, consoled by the fact that Mary would be returning soon.

Ann was removed from the stretcher to a table in the emergency room at Mercy Hospital. A tall, black nurse who presented a commanding presence took over the activities of the room and comforted Ann. She told Ann that they would clean her wounds and then prep her for X-ray and minced no words regarding the extent of her injuries. She told Ann that it appeared as though she had a broken leg.

Ann replied weakly, "I hope that's all I have. The pain in my ribs is also severe." Then she closed her eyes and tried to relax, hoping that by relaxing she could alleviate some of the pain.

Officer Williams, who accompanied Ann to the hospital, phoned the New American Bank and asked for Charles Lincroft. The receptionist at the bank said he was out to lunch and asked if anyone else could help. Williams said it was a matter of urgency for Lincroft only. He asked her to have Lincroft call the Mercy Hospital Emergency Room as soon as he returned from lunch. His wife had had an accident and she was there now.

The receptionist thanked Williams and then wondered why she did, as she pondered how she was going to relay this awful information to the president of the bank.

Mary O'Leary returned to the rectory and greeted Karen Michaels. She saw that Karen was busy and so went directly to the kitchen, passing Farley's office and noticing that he too was busy. Once back in the natural habitat of her kitchen, she began the preparations for lunch.

Karen picked up the phone on the third ring and answered her usual, "Good morning, Holy Cross Cathedral, Cardinal Farley's office."

"Oh, yes, Your Eminence, I'll connect you right away." She pushed the number two button and Farley answered. Karen told him it was Cardinal Spencer, the Apostolic Delegate to the United States.

Farley replied, "Let's not keep the brass waiting," and immediately picked up the line.

No sooner had he picked up than the phone rang again in Karen's office. In this instance, however, the caller was only of great importance to Karen. It was Tom Kiely.

"Have you spoken to Farley yet?" he asked after the usual preliminaries of "How do you do?"

"Yes, but he's not very encouraging."

"I didn't think he would be. I wish I could make things easier for you, but if we can't get Farley to help us…well…I guess it's a lost cause."

"Tom, I love you," she whispered, "and we'll talk about it some more tonight. I want so much to have the blessing of the church on this marriage, but if it's not to be, we'll have to work around it somehow."

"I'll pick you up tonight at five, okay?"

"Fine, and thanks for calling, Tom."

"I love you," she said, and before she replaced the receiver of the phone, he replied the same.

Lincroft walked into the bank lobby; he felt nervous and just a slight bit dizzy. *Never should have had that extra martini,* he thought.

The receptionist stopped him and gave him a written note that ordered him to call Mercy Hospital; his wife had had an accident. He blanched when he read the note and rushed to the elevator and his private office. He never even acknowledged the receptionist. Arriving in his office, he tried to compose himself as his stomach turned and his insides felt like they would be expelled from his body with little persuasion. He used his private line and trembled as he pushed the buttons on the phone that would connect him to Mercy Hospital.

Upon reaching the emergency room, the nurse on the phone assured him that while Ann was in a great deal of pain, she was in stable condition, and was currently in X-ray. She was to be admitted, and he should come to the hospital. The nurse told him that Ann had been hit by a car in a freak accident, but she had no other details.

"My God," he mumbled to himself, "my poor Ann having to suffer like this." He told his secretary of his wife's accident and told her to cancel all appointments until further notice. Appointments that couldn't wait could be handled by John Martin, a vice president. Charlie gave no thought to his next day with Cardinal Farley. That was the furthest thing from his mind.

After a quiet lunch, Mary could contain herself no longer and told Farley of the morning's events. He sympathized with her for having to witness such a horrible incident and asked for the details. She explained everything to him. He assured her that she did everything she could have under the circumstances, and perhaps if she would pray for the victim, as well as the driver, it would probably make her feel better. He returned to his office.

Karen had returned from lunch also and as she settled herself in for the work of the afternoon, the unmerciful ring of the phone disturbed her for what seemed like the millionth time today. She answered in her usual gracious manner, although forced, and transferred the call to Farley.

"Eminence, this is Charlie."

Farley detected the alarming tone in Lincroft's voice, but before he could say a word, Licroft explained that Ann had been taken to Mercy Hospital and that he didn't know any of the details yet. When did he think he could come to the hospital?

Farley answered that he would stop on his way to city hall. He had an important meeting at three that he had to attend. "However, if Ann is serious, I'll cancel everything."

Lincroft assured him that Ann was stable and that it did not appear to be a matter of life or death.

Farley comforted Lincroft and told him that as long as Ann was in stable condition, she would eventually be all right.

After feeling more assured from his phone conversation with Farley, Lincroft rushed to the hospital and Ann's bedside. She was more coherent by the time Charlie arrived, and she greeted him warmly and tenderly. She clutched him and began to cry. The nurse standing by informed him that she had been heavily sedated and would probably fall asleep soon.

Before she fell asleep, she gave Charlie all the details. As he listened, it suddenly hit him like a freight train. The accident he had seen from a distance as he left McMurtry's was not just another passing scene in the daily drama of life in the city. Ann was the victim in that particular accident. Charlie felt awful to think that his wife had lain in the street, the victim of an accident, and he was only two blocks away, yet he had turned away from the scene and ignored it. He became inconsolable.

Farley rushed into the kitchen and told Mary that the pleasant day he had been planning for tomorrow was not to be. He had just received a call that Ann Lincroft was in the hospital, the victim of an accident, but Charles Lincroft was unable to give him any details.

Mary thought, *I wonder if…*, then stopped. *No, it couldn't be.*

Farley told Mary he was on his way to the hospital, then to the meeting, and he would be returning at about six thirty that evening. He repeated all this information to Karen on his way out the door. As he picked up his briefcase and looked at Karen, he was distracted for a moment. Very unlike his seemingly standoffish manner, he casted a friendly glance at her and smiled. "Chin up."

⸎

Lincroft met Farley as Farley entered the hospital lobby.

"So good of you to come so quickly."

"Why wouldn't I for my favorite people? What's the latest on Ann?"

Lincroft told Farley that Ann was now sleeping and that she was in a stable condition. He then blurted out all the details of the accident as Ann had told him. He cowed his head and looked away from Farley as he explained to him about avoiding the accident when he was leaving McMurtrys and his resulting self-recrimination.

"Let's not be harsh on ourselves, huh?" Farley commanded in a friendly tone. "You had no idea that it was Ann in that accident, and besides, the police had already arrived and this matter was theirs to handle. So stop whipping yourself and get on with the business of supporting Ann."

They entered the tiny private room, and Farley gazed on Ann as she lay in deep slumber. He knew it was the wrong time to think about such things but he couldn't help but notice how innocent and beautiful her face looked even with her body in casts and bandages. He walked over to the bedside, said a brief prayer, and then turned to converse with Charlie.

Charlie snapped his fingers as he remembered all the reservations he had made for tomorrow as well as the theater tickets. "Why don't you go to the show anyway?" he asked Farley.

"Not alone and not without you people either."

"We can't let them to go waste," Charlie implored.

Farley thought of Mary O'Leary and how she had never been to a show. He then assured Lincroft they would be put to good use. While thinking of Mary, he recounted what she had told him at lunch and it hit him that Mary had finally met Ann, but in a most bizarre introduction.

Farley grabbed Lincroft's hand and said he would be available if needed in any way. Charlie thanked him for coming and for being so reassuring. Then Farley left the room and headed for the meeting.

As he arrived at city hall, he requested a phone and called the residence. After Karen answered, he asked her how she would enjoy going to the theater tomorrow evening. He said he had three tickets he was no longer going to use and that he would be pleased if she and Tom would use them. "And would you do me a favor?" he added. "Take Mary. She's never had the chance to go to a show and I know she'd enjoy it." Farley had some reservations concerning what he had just done. *I'm promoting Karen's relationship with Tom instead of trying to push her in other directions. But if it will get Mary to the theater and provide her with some happiness, I guess I can look in the other direction for a special occasion.*

Karen thanked him and informed him that they would be pleased to take Mary and hung up the phone. She rushed into the kitchen to tell Mary and all Mary could do was argue and say, "No. You and Tom enjoy the show. You don't want to take an old lady with you."

Mary knew of Karen's dating Tom, but she wasn't aware that Tom had been married before. Her thoughts concerning their dating were that they made a nice couple.

"We won't take no for an answer," Karen replied. "We'll pick you up at four tomorrow afternoon. We'll go to dinner and then the show."

Before Mary could continue her argument, Karen was out of the kitchen and back in her office. She phoned Tom and he had no objections. The idea of Farley giving the tickets to Karen struck him as a possible softening of his stand against the marriage. Tom would find out that Farley was a lot more unwavering than he was giving him credit for.

Farley returned from his meeting at city hall just at the time he said he would. Mary had dinner ready and thanked him for the opportunity that she was going to see her first show.

"I hope you enjoy it." He smiled at her. "By the way, Mary, you met Ann Lincroft today. She was the victim at that accident scene." Mary's legs began to weaken, and she grabbed a chair.

"Ann told her husband how helpful some woman was to her just by being there. It gave her much comfort."

Mary then confessed to him, "I thought maybe it was her when you told me about the phone call, but since this happens every day in the city, I just ruled it out as being too coincidental."

Farley then assured her that Ann was coming along well but had to contend with a broken leg and bruised ribs.

Since the thoughts of that morning still caused her some anguish, Mary changed the subject. "How was the meeting?" she inquired uninterestingly.

"We seemed to accomplish a great deal in a small amount of time," he answered. "The mayor and the housing commissioner seem to be very committed to this new program and that pleases me. They both seem to be very sincere individuals."

He then quickly changed the subject again and said, "I almost forgot something. I received a call from Cardinal Spencer, the apostolic delegate. He wants me to visit him in Washington on Monday. I better leave a note with Karen for tomorrow to make sure that it's on my agenda. What with this afternoon's events, I almost forgot. It wouldn't be too good for my résumé if I missed a meeting with him, would it?" he asked Mary humorously.

Mary thought to herself that he still presented that aloofness even when he was apparently trying to be funny. *I've got to get the message to him somehow that he's too uptight. Loosen up! Be natural!*

You're a likeable person. Don't try so hard. All this was easy to think about but to convey this in words to Farley would require herculean effort on her part.

Karen noticed the note on her desk in the morning and phoned the travel agent for plane reservations for Monday morning. She went through her daily routine, knowing she was leaving early today for dinner and a show.

Farley stayed closeted in his office for his day off, trying to conclude some work before his trip to Washington. He left his office in the afternoon, however, to visit Ann Lincroft.

He stood at her bedside and noticed a big improvement in her condition. She even joked about the great day they would have been enjoying, had she not stopped to gaze at a store window in front of a moving car. She also thought about her bad decision to be let off by her limo a block away from her destination to purposely go window shopping. Farley bantered with her. "Yes, but the odds were strongly in your favor since most cars remain in the street."

"So I defied the odds," she replied. "I wish I could be that lucky in Vegas."

Farley and the Lincrofts, after so many years as friends, had agreed to drop many formalities. No fancy titles. So it surprised Farley when Ann said sarcastically, "By the way, Eminence, how about easing the mind of that husband of mine regarding my accident?"

"I tried to but I think he'll have to work it out himself, and just between you and I, he'll do that very quickly." He proceeded to tell her of his upcoming trip to Washington, and she inquired as to its nature. He told her he had no idea, but when Spencer calls, all answer the call. He reminded her that Spencer was the pope's representative in this country. He said all Spencer conveyed to him was that it was a matter of extreme importance and that he would like Farley to be in Washington on Monday.

After other conversations of little note, Farley told Ann that he had to return to the office. He walked over to the bedside and held her hand. He liked Ann immensely, and for a fleeting second, her grasp sent a jolt through him unlike anything he had experienced before. He quickly pushed the pleasurable feeling from his mind. He whispered a prayer and gave her his blessing. He felt guilty as he left her by herself in the hospital room. *These people have been wonderful to me all my priestly life*, he thought. *I feel guilty leaving her in that room.* He returned to his office and its demanding pace.

He returned to an empty residence. Karen had left early to get ready for the show, and Mary was enjoying her day off and presumably also getting ready for the show. He called Auxiliary Bishop James Reynolds and informed him that he would be out of the diocese for a while. He desired that Reynolds take over while he was away. Reynolds jokingly told him his shoes would be big ones to fill. "About a size 13EEE." He laughed. Then in a more serious vein, he asked if Farley knew what the visit to Spencer was about. Farley said that he hadn't the slightest idea but he would find out on Monday.

Farley continued to work at his desk and then called his friend and spiritual advisor, Monsignor Beardsley, to ask him out to dinner. Beardsley accepted and they agreed to meet at a little restaurant only blocks from the Cathedral.

Karen and Tom were dressed to the nines and couldn't get over how nice Mary looked when they picked her up. All were in such high spirits that neither Karen nor Tom gave much thought to the church's impediments on their upcoming marriage. Mary proved to be excellent company and all three enjoyed the evening.

Beardsley and Farley conversed at their dinner and speculated on Farley's upcoming meeting with Spencer. "You have a good relationship with the Holy Father," Beardsley reminded Farley and proffered that this might be a major appointment by Clement. Farley dismissed that conjecture but couldn't offer any other ideas.

Charlie Lincroft stayed by Ann's bedside. Ann told him of Farley's trip to Washington. They speculated also as to what the significance of the meeting might mean for their friend. Ann began to yawn and was fast growing tired even to the point of dozing off. Charlie held her hand and stayed with her.

CHAPTER THREE

Farley awoke early on Monday and celebrated his usual early morning Mass. He had been out of the office over the weekend on a pastoral visit, so he had no time to hear about Mary's and Karen's evening at the show. He literally ran through the kitchen, acknowledging Mary with a fast good morning, grabbing a bun from the table, and telling her he had to get a cab to the airport. She had already prepared a full breakfast for him even though she knew he was leaving for Washington that morning. She didn't know he would be rushing out so early and now she worried about what to do with his breakfast. She would not be able to eat it and Karen wouldn't be in for awhile, so she knew it was going to the garbage. *What a total waste*, she thought.

"I want to know how your evening at the theater was, but I'm running short of time. I want a full report when I return." He called a taxi and one arrived in less than five minutes. He carried his suitcase outside, and Mary wondered how he did his packing.

On this particular occasion, Lincroft's limousine was not available. Farley, with an eye toward finances, declined the use of a hired limousine. *Too much unnecessary expense*, he thought with a mixture of sincerity and levity that the church hierarchy should display some humility.

Although Farley was present at Cardinal Spencer's installation as delegate to the United States, he had spoken very little to him in the past year. He was looking forward to spending some quality time with the delegate.

The drizzle that had been falling in the city at departure time had developed into a steady rain as Farley stepped off the plane in Washington. As he left the terminal building, he hid from the downpour under a canopy and hailed a cab. Traffic was surprisingly light, and in almost no time, he arrived at Cardinal Spencer's residence.

A well-groomed receptionist announced Farley's arrival to Spencer. Spencer replied through the usual garbled tones of the intercom that he would see Farley right away. She brought Farley into Spencer's office and Farley made himself as comfortable as possible in an overgrown chair. Spencer was an imposing man and his mere presence commanded attention.

A little heavy on the pasta, Farley mused to himself.

With cordialities completed, Spencer looked at Farley and began to explain his reasoning for summoning Farley to the office of the apostolic delegate.

"Do you mind if I call you Harold?" Spencer asked.

"Only if I can call you John," Farley returned somewhat bravely.

"By all means," Spencer replied. "Anyway, Harold, I received a communiqué from Clement regarding a commission he wants to organize to investigate the church's laws and customs regarding marriage. He's recommended that you be the ranking member of the United States delegation—"

"What is he doing? Having someone from every country serve on this commission?" Farley interrupted.

"Maybe I should read the communiqué to you first. That should fairly well explain what's going on."

My dear brother in Christ,
I write to you today as my heart grieves at the loss of so many people from the bosom of Holy Mother the church due to divorce and remarriage. My heart aches for these people of good faith who can no longer live together as husband and wife, and then, once that decision is made, they also cannot live within the church as full partaking

members. It is time we reached out to these people to find a way to return them to our bosom. How can we bring divorced and remarried Catholics back into the stronghold of the church?

We cannot strip matrimony of its sacramental status or permit divorce and remarriage. Yet we can no longer sit idly by as thousands of Catholics divorce and remarry for what they feel are the best reasons and then allow themselves to be cut off from the state of grace.

During the tenure of our beloved John Paul II, this offense was reduced from excommunication. So we are asking these people to stay in the church and, at the same time, telling them that they cannot partake of its full life. While they are no longer excommunicated, they are not in the state of grace and not full members of the Mystical Body. This is obviously the condition if they partake in marital relations and refuse to deny the new partnership.

These people must be reached by our church. This is a task for which I am asking for help from around the world. I look particularly at the United States since it is not only a world leader, but it also sadly possesses a high divorce rate.

I propose a worldwide commission of thirty-seven members of which five delegates will be from your country. I would like Cardinal Harold Farley to head the US delegation. I have the utmost confidence in his knowledge of canon law to feel comfortable with him as head of the US delegation. I ask you also to contact Cardinals Feeney and Josephson, and Archbishops Carson and Carnavale.

It is my intention that these appointed prelates meet together and then prepare to come to Rome when notified. I will then set forth to the entire commission their tasks and obligations.

I ask that you pray with me for the success of this commission, so that we may once again embrace all Catholics within the full Mystical Body of Christ's church.

Hoping you are in good health and keeping you and all the people of the United States in my prayers, I remain.

Sincerely yours in Christ,
Clement XV

"There you have it," Spencer quipped.

Although Farley's first instinct was to be awed, and he was that, he managed to criticize. "So he thinks the US is in the forefront of bad marriages."

Spencer looked argumentatively at Farley and retorted, "I don't feel that's the meaning he's trying to convey. I think he feels that because of the number of people in the United States, especially Catholics, that we would naturally have a higher rate of anything. He feels that with you and your expertise and the expertise of the other members of the American contingent, you would have major influence in decision making."

Farley grinned and replied, "I really didn't mean that to be anything other than an idle comment. Of course, I'll accept the position and will be hearing soon from His Holiness regarding the first meeting, I trust."

"As stated in the letter," Spencer said, "you will be notified." Spencer then inquired of Farley if he would care for lunch. Farley thought that to be a good idea since he wanted to continue to talk with Spencer. They adjourned to the dining area and while it was not yet noon, Spencer felt it was close enough to have a drink. A uniformed staff member of the household proceeded to make drinks for both of them and they sat down and began to chat.

Spencer took a sip of his drink and directed the talk to Farley. "I think from the tone of that letter that Clement is a fan of yours."

"Well, we met years ago in Rome and we've been friends for years. Through the years prior to his papacy and whenever I was in Rome, we would get together. Since his papacy, obviously, there has not been much contact. When I received the red hat, we got together but very briefly. I have a great deal of respect for the man and knew he would be Matthew's successor."

"For obvious reasons," Spencer interjected. Then he continued, "You know the consensus of opinion appears to be that you, yourself, Harold, could be a successor to the papacy."

"I beg to differ with you, John, and I don't mean to sound humble, but I know others of the college that are far better qualified than I."

Spencer took another sip of his drink and replied, "But Clement has given you a very important task and between you and me, if you maintain your present conservative thinking, you would find great favor with the Curia. We all know how important they are."

Farley looked into his half-empty glass and contemplated his next remark to Spencer. "John, please don't think me rude, but are you trying to direct my efforts on this matter? It sounds that way to me. I believe in laying all the cards on the table and I feel that you are putting pressure on me to push this upcoming meeting in a certain direction."

"Harold, I'm not trying to direct you, just guide you. We have a responsibility to God and to his people to maintain order in our society and religion. Clement obviously thinks you can provide him with answers to the marriage and divorce problems, and I don't think you can, without some very radical changes in church law and policy. As a priest, I feel that radical change would lead to further instability in marriage and in the family. This could ruin the human race. We must maintain the present laws to the greatest extent possible. If we loosen up, we create a carte blanche situation of easy divorce and a mockery of the sacrament of matrimony. By the way, let's not forget that in the Catholic church, marriage is a sacrament. We must continue to make divorce and separation an undesirable thing and try to return stability to the family unit, the basic structure of the human race."

"I couldn't agree with you more, John, but it's not that simple. Obviously Clement knows that it's a complicated issue and has asked for help. I am conservative, but I intend to look into all aspects of this matter and hopefully ease the burden on our church and its priests and more importantly, its people, by coming to some conclusions that will help stabilize the family unit as well as ease the pain of those who are unhappy in their marriage for one reason or another, and yet want to be active members of our church. I think that about sums it up."

They were called to the lunch table and each lifted his unfinished drink and directed themselves to the dining area.

As they sat down, Spencer informed Farley that he would be meeting with the four other prelates of the United States picked by Clement, and he expressed his favor with Clement's choices including Farley. Spencer thought Farley to be independent and unwavering and was hoping Farley would continue on a conservative path.

In order to lighten the mood for lunch, Spencer leaned toward Farley and repeated his statement about Farley's being a possible papal successor.

Farley returned a look to Spencer and replied lightheartedly, "Francone is but a few years older than I and I'm sure he will outlive me, so I give no thought to my being pope. Besides, the Curia still has strong feelings for an Italian and would love to see the papacy stay in the hands of one of their own. Francone is the first Italian in the Vatican Palace since John Paul I. I don't think they would look at an outsider again."

They both laughed and Spencer retorted, "But all of the Cardinals vote, not just the Curia." But he lowered his head, and after a quick thought, reminded himself aloud, "But then again they wield a tremendous amount of influence."

Farley dipped his spoon in the mushroom soup and practically inhaled the first spoonful. It was delicious. "Great chef," he interjected. He placed the spoon down and began to tell Spencer of the plight of his secretary. "John, this appointment comes at a rather opportune time. Just last week my secretary, who happens to be a wonderful young woman and a good Catholic, I might add, asked me if there were anything I could do for her. You see she's seeing a young man who is divorced. He is also Catholic. I know nothing of the reason for his divorce, but I do know of Karen's love for him. She is in agony over a decision to marry him and leave the church or forget him. I told her what church law was, and I was always comfortable with church law. But this situation is striking close to home. I have no real family, so my familiarity with people is through friends. This girl has worked for me for a number of years and I feel for her. We are going to lose her from the faith. I am anxiously looking forward to serving on this commission and hopefully coming up with a solution."

"I hate to be redundant," Spencer interrupted, "but I think I've already expressed the fact that you've been stuck with an insurmountable problem. We can never lessen the seriousness of a sacrament, and matrimony is a sacrament."

"But don't we relieve priests and sisters of vows when necessary?" Farley inquired. He continued his question. "Why can't we find a way to release two people from marriage vows when necessary?"

Spencer replied testily, "I've been over that, Harold. We can't allow the breakup of the family unit. What about the children? Shouldn't they be considered? And we all know that children do, in fact, suffer from a divorce."

Farley returned his attention to lunch and after a pause smiled at Spencer. "I guess we do have a task ahead of us. Carnavale and Feeney are conservative, but Josephson and Carson will certainly lend some debate to the meetings with their liberal views. By the way, John, when do you think the pontiff will summon us to Rome for our first meetings?"

Spencer replied, "I absolutely don't know. As it says in the letter, you will be notified. Naturally, I'll communicate to His

Holiness your acceptances after I've talked to all of you." He then added, "Now to change the subject, how about a tour of DC this afternoon and a round of golf tomorrow?"

"Sounds good to me, but I'm not a great golfer."

"That makes two of us, so we can give each other pointers."

Farley enjoyed the rest of his lunch and put some concentration toward the upcoming marriage commission. He also gave some thought to Karen and her anguish. He had to concede that Spencer was right. The task was near impossible. He also thought about Ann and decided he would place a call to Charlie tonight to ask about her condition. He looked up at Spencer and questioned, "Where do we begin the tour?"

"I have an open pass to the White House, so we can start there."

They enjoyed the rest of their lunch.

CHAPTER FOUR

Farley returned to the city Wednesday afternoon and went straight to the residence. The cab driver who took him in from the airport had recognized him, but his attempts to strike up a conversation met with quiet stubbornness. Farley limited everything to pleasantries.

Upon arrival at the residence, he greeted Karen, who was finishing up her duties for the day, and went to his office. He looked at the stack of mail on his desk and couldn't believe he was gone only two days. He had some fresh ideas in mind regarding the commission, and he was anxious to put them to paper so he could organize the meeting that was to be the first of the contingent from the United States. Again, gazing at the desk reminded him of some unfinished business on the housing program for minorities. His first instinct was to get away, and he did exactly that, but not far away. He walked down the hall to the kitchen.

He greeted Mary and told her he would appreciate a drink in about half an hour. She inquired of him as to his trip and he exclaimed that it was very informative.

Here we go again, she thought, *very informative doesn't tell me much.*

Hoping to block further inquisitiveness by Mary, Farley asked her to tell him about her evening at the show.

She replied, "How do I begin to thank you for the tickets. The whole evening was marvelous. You missed a really great show and Karen and Tom were great company. A real enjoyable evening."

"By the way," she added, "that Tom Kiely is a charmer. Karen's picked herself a good man. If I were a few years younger…" she said, with eyes raised.

Farley decided it best not to reveal anything to Mary regarding Tom and Karen. He felt that Karen would tell Mary in her own good time.

Farley returned to his office and asked Karen to get him Mercy Hospital. He was connected to Ann's room and asked Ann how she was progressing.

"Oh, Father, I'm so sick of being cooped up in here that I could scream."

Farley knew she was feeling better. "You've only been in there a week. Enjoy the relaxation. Obviously you're feeling better."

She asked how his meeting with Spencer went, and Farley explained some of the details to her. He added, "I'll tell you and Charlie all about it when I see you."

"The pope is high on you," Ann said emphatically.

"Apparently," Farley fumbled, trying to sound humble. "But we've had many discussions and dinners together, prior to his election, and I think he feels as though he knows me very well. I wouldn't attach any more significance to it."

"Let's not be modest," Ann retorted. "Charlie and I will have to buy a plane to get to Rome to see you."

"I'll tell you what I told Spencer. I give it no thought. Spencer even went so far as to say that I had a shot at the papacy."

That's what I'm leading to," Ann interrupted, then added, "He seems to be grooming you for his successor."

Farley chuckled. "The Holy Father has but a few years on me and if he has as much unfinished business to attend to as I do, I think he can expect enough years at the Vatican so that both of us will be too old to get out of a chair."

Farley hated to put Ann off, but he told her he would see her tomorrow and there was so much he had to do. She thanked him politely for calling, and as he hung up the phone, he realized that he really didn't want to. A feeling unknown to him coursed through his body. He dismissed it quietly and got down to business.

Although the minority housing program was staring him in the face, he, being a true priest, knew his first obligation was to his immediate flock and so he had to check with Bishop Reynolds.

He called Reynolds and inquired humorously if there had been any great insurrections in the diocese while he was away.

Reynolds, playing the game, quipped, "Yeah, I decided to squash the celibacy rule for priests in this diocese. A funny thing happened. There was no insurrection, just a rush on to book wedding days. Seriously, Harold, how did the meeting go?"

You almost hit it on the head," Farley retorted. "The meeting concerned only the loyal and legal connubial rights of the married." Then in an attempt to play along with Reynolds, he added, "not the illegal connubial rights of the Catholic clergy. I just rescinded your celibacy rebellion. To be truthful though, Spencer received a letter from Clement asking myself and four other prelates of the United States to be on a worldwide commission to study the divorce problem within the Catholic church. We'll be notified about our first world meeting and in the meantime, the head of each delegation representing each country will hold an organizational meeting within his own country in preparation. The Holy Father will send along the details as soon as he has received the acceptances."

Reynolds became serious for a second and advised Farley that it appeared as though he had a difficult task on his hands.

"I'm aware of that," Farley said, "and I'd like to talk to you and Frank Beardsley about it. I admire you men, and I feel that your advice on this whole matter would be beneficial to say the least."

"You flatter me," Reynolds replied. "I'll do whatever I can, Harold."

"I'll be calling you again, Jim, and thanks for sitting in. By the way, were there any problems?"

"No. Everything was quiet, Harold."

They hung up the phone, and Harold called Karen on the intercom to tell her to contact Monsignor Frank Beardsley for him, but he received no answer. A look at his watch told him that not only had Karen left for the day, but she had never even said goodbye. Thinking only the best of Karen, he assumed that she had thought him too busy and so she left quietly.

Mary announced that his drink was ready. Although earlier than anticipated, it was a good excuse to put off the call to Beardsley. He took up a quick residence in the dining room and sipped at his cocktail. He would call Beardsley later.

He thought about Ann and why it bothered him to cut off their conversation. He also felt pangs of guilt about not seeing her until the next day. He had never felt that way about Ann before, and the more he tried to push thoughts of her from his mind, the more they reappeared. *This is absurd*, he thought. *I am a cardinal in the Roman Catholic church and Ann is a close and dear friend and a married woman. Can this longing for her be a temptation? I guess the answer is yes. Could I possibly have stronger feelings for Ann than just friendly feelings? My God! I've got to get a grip on myself because the problems I could be running into are insurmountable. I'm a priest and Ann is a married woman. Besides, I've known Ann for years and why would this hit suddenly? If I am feeling love for Ann, I'm defiling the very concept of love. I'm corrupting love by turning it into a temptation for which the only outcome can be sin. How can something as beautiful as love be at any time, a sin?*

He continued in thought. *I must stop toying with this nonsensical idea. If this is a temptation, I'll have to avoid Ann. Now how in God's name am I going to do that? I can't admit the truth that I have strong feelings for Ann, and therefore don't intend to see her again. That's unthinkable. But I can't continue to be even in the proximity of Ann. I can't be falling in love. What about Charlie? What would this do to him? Ah, there it is. Imagine me thinking myself so pompous that Ann would even think of requiting my love. Just because I think I love her doesn't necessarily mean she loves me or that she would leave Charlie and fly away with a defrocked priest.* He thought that his thinking was starting to border on juvenile, and he immediately took a sip of his drink. He relaxed and began to pray. He prayed that the Lord would show him the way out of this dilemma. He knew that he was going to have to spend more time at his priestly duties. He had to avoid Ann in any way he could. If he admitted anything, his relationship with the Lincrofts would come to an end. The most gnawing thought of all was why these intense feelings had developed so suddenly. He'd known Ann for years.

He picked up the paper, unread since that morning, and tried to put his mind on other things. Perusing the paper was a poor substitute for thoughts of Ann. Again he thought, *Why all of a sudden?* He fought with himself to concentrate on the paper and took another sip of his drink.

Mary's voice, cracking from the kitchen, startled him back to reality. "Dinner's almost ready!" she announced. She then added, "I'll clean up quickly and head home if you don't mind. I don't feel too well. Maybe it's coming down from the high of the other evening at the show."

Farley looked at her and noticed her pallid appearance and asked her if she was well enough to get home.

"Why? Do I look that terrible?"

"Well, let's just say a little blue around the gills. Let me call you a cab and I'll finish up tonight. And nothing further from you as a protest either. I insist. In fact, I order you."

"What can I say?" Mary asked.

Farley was concerned because it was unlike Mary to give up so easily, but he also knew her age was beginning to make itself noticeable.

"Mary, it's your day off tomorrow. Give me a call if you need anything. Do you hear me?"

"I'm just a little tired. I'll be fine in the morning."

Farley assisted Mary into the cab and tipped the driver so that he would see Mary safely home.

He returned to the rectory and finished his drink. After finishing his supper, he proceeded with the cleanup process. *Hell of a life, this bachelor life,* he thought as he applied liquid detergent to the dishes. *I wonder why the dishwasher can't do the whole job. I was always told you have to rinse the dishes first. Well, at least it gets my mind off more mundane things.*

He finished up the chores as quickly as possible and called Monsignor Beardsley.

"How you doing, Frank? This is Harold."

"Glad you're safely back. Anything I should know about?"

"Plenty. As my confessor, do you want to hear my personal problems first or about my visit with Spencer?"

"Are you serious, Harold? You don't have any personal problems. You're always sailing smoothly. Truthfully, as your confessor, personal problems always come first. But I must admit that I'm anxiously awaiting the cause of your being summoned by the apostolic delegate."

"Frank, can you come over tonight?"

"Sure. I'll be over in a half hour or so. Is this serious, Harold?"

"I've got a lot to talk to you about and I'll let you know everything when you arrive."

Beardsley smiled and asked humorously if he should bring a sleeping bag in case Farley was too long-winded.

Farley, in his usually serious manner, sort of brushed the remark aside, but he snickered dutifully. "See you in a half hour, Frank."

"See you," Frank replied.

After hanging up the phone, Farley went to the living room. He picked up the paper again. Thoughts of Ann returned as he stared at the paper blankly. *I'm making an ass of myself. Wait till Beardsley hears this. The poor guy will have a coronary.* He started to read the business page with intensity to distract himself and it appeared to work.

At the hospital, Ann talked with her husband. "I'm dying to find out what Father Harold and Cardinal Spencer discussed in Washington."

Charlie stared at her. "You must be getting much better. You're starting to sound a little nosy to me. I suggest we not tempt Father Harold to tell us anything about it. Let him volunteer. It could be sensitive."

"He said he'd tell us about it when he talked to me on the phone today."

"Well, right now, I'd like to talk about your being discharged from this hospital. Doctor Lang tells me only one more weekend here and then you can go home early next week." Charlie explained to Ann his idea for a welcome-home party. He knew any excuse would be a good excuse for a party. He was so delighted to have Ann come home from the hospital that he was planning a gala affair at their duplex in the city. Ann was also thrilled with the idea, but she wondered why Charlie wouldn't want to have the party at their home in Rosewood. Charlie explained to her that the travel time for most of their friends would be prohibitive and since they had the apartment in the city, why not make it convenient for everyone?

Ann closed her eyes in thought and sighed. "I'm getting enthused about the idea now. Planning the affair will give me something to do while I spend my last days at this health resort."

Charlie chided her. "Now, Ann, you're getting the best of care. Be grateful." He looked at her and had to admit that even with all the impediments to a ravishing appearance that a hospital patient is confronted with, Ann somehow presented herself as radiant. He leaned over the bed and kissed her.

"I really do love you," he said in a manner which didn't sound serious but nevertheless expressed itself to Ann as sincere.

"I love you, too," she replied. "And thank you for all you've done for me, honey."

He thought about the day of Ann's accident and how he ignored the accident at the time. Rather than agonize over the thought again, he suppressed it and finally drove it successfully from his mind. He stared at Ann for a while as she took a sip of water and he knew she would continue to be his greatest joy. No matter how successful he had become both financially and personally, she was his shining light.

Ann was told early in their marriage that she could never bear children. When they received this news, they were devastated. Charlie never let Ann know how immensely devastated he really was. Since Ann took the news so badly, he decided he would be stoic and give her the support she needed. He truly loved her. In a curious manner, this situation seemed to bring them closer together.

Ann began to nod and Charlie knew she was tired; so as not to cause her undue exertion, he volunteered to leave her alone for the night. He again leaned over the bed and hugged and kissed her and told her he couldn't wait until she came home. She returned his affection with a smile and a kiss and she blew him a final kiss as he went out the door.

Monsignor Frank Beardsley entered the cardinal's residence, made his way to the lounge, and sat his corpulent self in the most comfortable chair in that room.

Farley greeted him with a terse, "No drinks, no refreshments. I've got a serious problem and I've got to talk to you about it and I think we should both be stone-cold sober."

"Harold, I don't believe this. Were matters in Washington that severe? Are you bullshitting me?"

Farley looked at Beardsley sternly and commanded, "Watch your language for right now, Frank, as this is a matter between my confessor and me."

Beardsley apologized and immediately reached for his stole. He kissed the stole and placed it around his neck with the proper prayers.

Farley blurted out to his confessor all that had crossed his mind that evening concerning Ann. Beardsley, in the sanctity of the penitential sacrament, allowed no emotion to show.

"As your confessor, Harold, I must advise you that you are on a dangerous course and, as I see it, only you will be able to steer from the obstacle. This woman is your friend as is her husband. You have taken a vow of chastity and any carnal desires for this woman could become violations of that sacred vow. What makes this even more intolerable is that this woman is married. You will be in the company of this woman quite often for the rest of your life unless you decide to ostracize yourself from your friends, which isn't too likely. Only you will have to muster the strength it takes to avoid the temptation.

"My opinion is that you're reacting to Ann's accident in a fatherly manner, and that you are confusing this fatherly love with true love. You admitted to me that you thought the whole thing was childish and I agree. If you would seriously agree to that self-evaluation, I'm sure you would see how ridiculous you have been. Once your mind accepts that, then you will be able to resume normal relations with the Lincrofts and continue your good work in the priesthood.

"Work on your assignment from His Holiness, whatever that may be, and bear in mind that the Lord is with you and will give you strength.

"You have been given a task by our civil leaders concerning housing for minorities. Channel your love in their direction. Get involved in this program and contribute your talents through your priesthood to this endeavor and pray for help. It's all up to you and God. He will help you. You must help you. My penance to you is to pray the rosary tonight to ask our Blessed Lady to be at your side so that these temptations, with her help, will be cast aside."

Farley said the Act of Contrition while Beardsley performed the penitential blessing over him. Beardsley removed the stole and folded it away. He sighed and looked intently at Farley and said, "Let's change the subject as much as possible. Tell me about your visit with Spencer."

Farley explained to Beardsley about the formation of the marriage commission.

When he had finished the report of his visit with Spencer, Beardsley couldn't help but snicker. "Some change of subject."

Farley just sat in his chair looking uncomfortable.

Beardsley said, "I must add some advice to that I just gave you. Work diligently on this assignment given to you by the Holy Father. He has great faith in you in that he who is the successor to Saint Peter has chosen you from many to help those of his church who are in need. While the subject of the commission is marriage, bear in mind that the Lord is with you and will give you strength. Don't let your personal feelings cloud any decisions you might make while on the commission. The task will be difficult enough as it is, without burdening yourself with personal problems with a married woman. Pray, Harold. I know you can conquer the temptation with God's help."

With this matter temporarily out of the way, Farley figured it was time for a tension breaker and offered Beardsley a drink. He accepted and they spent another hour talking about the seemingly impossible task ahead for Harold Farley on the marriage commission.

Upon retiring for the night, but before saying the rosary that Beardsley had given to him for penance, Farley thought about Beardsley's advice. It was good advice. He would begin to concentrate on how juvenile and useless his seeming love for Ann was, and concentrate positively on contributing to his church and community as a priest, something he had been overwhelmingly successful at until today. Farley picked up his rosary and began the recitation.

CHAPTER FIVE

arley stopped on his way to the hospital to pick up a flower arrangement for Ann. He left the florist and walked the remaining blocks to the Mercy Hospital complex. While walking, he gave some thought to his confession to Beardsley last night. He knew he had to face this issue square on and he was determined to overcome his longing for Ann.

He entered the hospital and the girl at the front desk sent him to Ann's room. Charlie and Ann were conversing as Farley came through the doorway with the flower arrangement in hand. Ann's leg was in a cast and would continue to be for some time, but she looked as glamorous as ever. Farley presented the flowers to Ann, then leaned over and kissed her on the forehead, and finally turned to Charlie and greeted him.

Charlie returned the greeting cordially and then added humorously, "If you weren't a priest and a close friend, I'd say that you were trying to romance my wife with that beautiful floral piece."

As Ann and Charlie chuckled at the remark, Farley forced himself to smile while conflicting thoughts streaked through his mind. It seemed to take an eternity to come up with a clever remark. It was funny that while he himself realized how dangerous his thoughts of Ann were, her husband, through an innocent playful remark, could hit so close to home. He thought about the destruction of his friendship, his priesthood, and eventually, his life if these cravings for Ann continued. He began to see not just the impracticality of his thoughts, but the sheer stupidity of them.

"Since Ann is coming out of the hospital this week, we're having a welcome home party," Charlie announced. "By the way, you're invited, Father Harold. And just for the convenience of the guests, so that we have a big turnout, we're having it here in the city at our apartment."

Farley replied hesitantly, "I wouldn't dream of missing the occasion."

"I'm planning an extravaganza," Ann quipped.

"It will be that if you're there," Farley braved, trying to act in a normal fashion. Charlie, of course, echoed his sentiments.

The happy talk of the upcoming party was interrupted in Farley's mind by another thought. This time, his mind turned to his faithful housekeeper, Mary O'Leary. She had been coming to work but not really looking well and he was concerned. He then thought about her meeting with Ann and spoke up.

"Not to change the subject, folks, but as we are well aware my housekeeper, Mary O'Leary, was the woman who helped you, Ann, on the day of your accident."

Ann explained how dazed she was and how little memory she had of the accident, but she did remember a helpful woman in her more lucid moments.

"She was a big help to me," Ann said. "But what made you think about her?" she asked immediately.

Farley replied, "I guess my being in the hospital atmosphere reminded me that she hasn't been feeling well and I was wondering if you would consider having her at your party. She enjoyed the theater so much and it was her first night out in years. I think she could use some variety in her life to get her mind off a rather dull existence. I honestly feel it makes her feel better."

"It shall be done," Charlie quipped. Now it was his turn to suffer a torturous thought as he remembered how Mary O'Leary ministered to his wife while he walked away from the scene of

Ann's accident. He had pangs of guilt all over again. "Mary is welcome in our home anytime," he added.

"It just occurred to me," Farley interrupted, "that I had been planning a party myself. What do you say?"

"In the rectory?" asked a surprised Charlie.

"Isn't that against the rules?" Ann added.

"No. We have celebrations there many times. Did you forget the celebration when I received the red hat?"

"Despite that, I won't hear of it," Charlie commanded. "You just bring yourself and Mary to our apartment and save yourselves the worry. Besides it will save the church some money," he added with a smile.

With a look of acceptance on his face, Farley turned away and thought of a topic to change the subject gracefully. He then explained to Ann and Charlie his meeting with Cardinal Spencer. He said he should be hearing from Spencer again soon when the other prelates of the United States gave their consent to be on the commission.

The Lincrofts conversed with Farley about the seeming impossibility of the commission to change any policies in the light of present church law.

"I'm anxious to get started," Farley said, "and I'm hopeful that some good will come from this commission."

After talking about the possibilities of the commission for near an hour, Farley announced that it was time for him to leave so that the lovebirds could have some time for themselves. He leaned toward Ann and looked at her face. She thanked him again profusely for the flowers, and then he leaned over and kissed her on the forehead. He knew that fighting this feeling he had for Ann would be a more monumental task then the work of his marriage commission. He shook Charlie's hand and turned back towards Ann and gave her his blessing.

Ann looked at him as he left the room and said, "Next time I see you at least I won't be here. Better times are coming."

Farley smiled and said, "I'm looking forward to the party."

Farley arose at five thirty in the morning and said his morning prayers. He quickly took a shower and dressed. Since he was a little behind schedule that morning, he used the electric shaver, although he got a much closer shave with his old safety razor.

He went over to the Lady chapel of the cathedral to offer Mass. He would say a special thanksgiving prayer for Ann's recovery.

Mary was in the kitchen when he returned to the rectory and she looked surprisingly well.

He commented, "I guess you needed some rest, Mary. You look terrific today."

"Thank you. I feel much better. Maybe it was just the excitement of the other evening."

"You better get used to it, Mary, because we're invited to a party at Lincroft's next week."

"But I thought we were having a party here," she said.

"Charlie Lincroft talked me out of it. Besides, this will be a chance for you to see their penthouse," Farley responded. He then added, "They want you to be there, especially because you were so helpful to Ann."

"That's so nice of them," was all Mary could muster. She then found herself able to add, "I'll never forget that day. It gave me the shakes. All my life in the city and I had never been witness to anything like that before."

Mary continued her chores while Farley read the paper. She had convinced herself that she felt better and it worked. She could even convince others. Oh, she did feel somewhat better, but not as well as she should. But if she could psyche herself, why not?

After breakfast, Farley went to his office to start his workday. His five-point plan on better housing was still in its preliminary draft form and he had a deadline to meet. *Must get to that*, he thought.

Karen arrived and went to Farley's office door. She peered in and wished him a good morning. Before she could return to her own office, Farley called her in.

"How's Tom?" he stuttered.

"Fine," she answered. "We're going out tonight. Dinner."

"How are you feeling, Eminence?" she questioned in an obvious attempt to steer Farley clear of her personal life.

"I'm doing just great, but I'm worried about Mary. She looks terrific today but I don't think she's been feeling well lately."

"I've noticed that, too," Karen said. "I'll keep an eye on her."

"I'd appreciate that," Farley said, relieved.

She left Farley's office and he thought that it appeared relations between him and Karen were strained, to say the least.

I wish I could do something for her. Possibly she could find another boyfriend. Tom seems like a hell of a good man and Karen is great, but they have to realize that they can't marry within the church. I hope she doesn't take it out on me. There's good theological and moral reasoning involved in the laws of the church. I'll have to think of a sensible way to explain this to her soon. Once she's married, it's too late.

Farley got to work on the housing program first, saving the after lunch hours for further study of the "marriage problems issue" as he called it.

Karen called him on the intercom with his first interruption of the day. She informed him that Cardinal Spencer was on the phone. Farley immediately picked up the reciver.

Spencer's voice boomed from inside his cavernous body and came across the phone wires as if from next door.

"How's the golf game, Harold?"

"Not too good. You see I don't get enough time. Only when I visit dignitaries such as yourself do I find the extra time," quipped Farley.

After the traditional jousting of vagaries, Spencer explained the reason for his call, but Farley had anticipated it anyway. He explained that the other American prelates had accepted their positions on the marriage commission. He had notified Pope Clement of their acceptances. It was now up to Farley to get together with the other American prelates. After that they would be notified by Clement concerning the first meeting in Rome.

Farley understood the instructions and now felt that he couldn't wait to get started. Marriage problems had been hitting him to close to home and he was hopeful that the commission would find a solution to the problem.

Ann shouted instructions to Marie, her housekeeper, from a wheelchair in the living room of her apartment. "I think that floral arrangement looks better on that small table over there. Just move that lamp a slight bit to the right," she ordered. Preparations were feverishly underway for her hastily concocted "welcome home" party.

Charlie was putting in some time at the bank as he felt he had been neglecting his duties there with so many visits to Ann. She anticipated his arrival momentarily, and hopefully, they would have some time to relax before the festivities.

Charlie had invited approximately twenty couples, their best friends, fellow officers at the bank as well as Cardinal Farley and Mary O'Leary. Ann and Charlie had purchased a gift certificate for Mary at Grayson's. They didn't want to embarrass Mary by making a ceremony of their gift, so they decided to present her with the certificate off to the side and very unceremoniously.

Later and with all the preparations made, the guests started to arrive. Mr. and Mrs. John Martin, Charlie's bank vice president, Mr. and Mrs. Hebert Downey, Mr. and Mrs. John Costman, and their neighborhood friend and widower, Carl Winstead and his guest. They kept arriving as though orchestrated, one couple every few minutes.

In one of those intervals arrived Cardinal Harold Farley and his guest, Mary O'Leary. Mary looked magnificent. She appeared a bit nervous but that was to be expected as this was her first journey into high society. Charlie walked up to her and took her by the hand. He started to introduce her to those already assembled. Farley, in turn, knew most of those present and also started to roam the room and greet people. There were some new faces though.

After introductions, Mary asked for a light drink then stared in awe at the magnificent scene before her, the Lincroft penthouse. Charlie noticed her awed and curious look and piped up, "Mary, how about the grand tour?" She felt honored and nodded her assent.

The living room with its glass doors looking out to the skyline and the terrace outside running the full length of the living room looked like something from magazines Mary had seen. It was almost unbelievable. The two bedrooms off the balcony from the living room were furnished to the point where estimating their value was impossible. Mary couldn't help but think to herself that there couldn't be this much money in the world. The kitchen was huge and appeared almost as a restaurant kitchen. The two dining rooms were indescribable. The small dining room for intimate dinners also had a glass door to the terrace. The large dining room could host twenty for dinner with ease. This room was an interior room with a huge chandelier of crystal with crystal sconces on the surrounding walls.

Tonight's party was buffet style and was being held entirely in the living room. But even with forty-five or so people, it didn't appear crowded.

Mary thought to herself, *What a way to live. And this is just their apartment. What does their home in Rosewood look like? Now I know why His Eminence is with the Lincrofts on his days off. What a life.*

Mary rejoined the cardinal and thanked him for bringing her to the party. She enjoyed the tour of the apartment and especially enjoyed all the nice people she was meeting. At this point,

Charlie asked Mary to step aside with him and he quietly gave her the certificate.

"I wouldn't dream of accepting anything," she protested. "What I did was a human act of kindness and I would hope someone would do the same for me someday if the situation were reversed."

Charlie, however, insisted and told Mary they felt fortunate to have met her and besides their best friend, Cardinal Farley, thought the world of her and that was a good endorsement.

Mary's thoughts raced back a few weeks to her comparison between Farley and Cardinal Fitzpatrick. Farley's days off with the aristocratic Lincrofts and Fitzpatrick's bungalow in the country for his days off. There was the difference. But she had to admit that while she was in the twilight of her life, she could get real used to high society. She felt ashamed of her rash judgment. She never considered Farley as giving her much thought. In his own style, he was proving himself to be as thoughtful a man as Fitzpatrick. He just had a different manner about exhibiting his feelings.

Mary also remembered passing Grayson's on that fateful day of Ann's accident and her longing for that one dress that would make her feel young again. A quick glance at the certificate indicated to Mary that the figure was enough to make her dream come true.

She bounced back to reality, thanking Charles Lincroft for his gift but restating that it wasn't necessary.

The party lingered until the early morning hours, and Farley walked over to Mary who was busily engaged in conversation with the Costmans. He announced that it was the witching hour and he would be taking her home. She protested little, as she knew the hour was late. She bade fond farewells to those that remained and especially to the Lincrofts. Farley took her hand and announced that Charlie was providing them with a limousine to deliver them both to their residences.

Mary had a beautiful evening. She changed to her bedclothes, got into bed, and nodded off to sleep easily. Her mind was relaxed about her new relationship with the "mysterious" Lincrofts, and more particularly, about her new perception of Cardinal Harold Farley.

At the rectory, Farley laid awake trying to drive thoughts of Ann from his mind. He felt as though he was having some success. He had little but conversational contact with Ann all evening. He seemed more concerned about Mary. That was good. He was conquering the temptations. He did admit to himself that Ann looked beautiful as usual, even in a wheelchair. But he remembered praying fervently for help before the party. He felt his prayers were answered. He went to sleep with the knowledge that he was succeeding in his efforts to drive Ann from his carnal desires. But for how long?

CHAPTER SIX

The day started cloudy and damp as Farley was preparing to leave for Chicago. He thought, *Just once I'd like to fly on a clear day so I could see this country of ours. I'm always forced to read the dull pages of the airlines magazine or look out the windows at the clouds.*

He had contacted the four other United States prelates serving on the marriage commission and it was agreed that a central meeting place for all involved would be the most convenient. Although Cardinal Michael Mayfield was not on the commission, he agreed to host the commission members and allow them the space for their meeting.

Farley bade farewell to Mary and Karen and told them to help Bishop Reynolds man the stronghold. Both smiled. He felt the coolness of Karen and the worry of Mary regarding her health. But there was work to do and he had to pursue it. He turned at the doorway and gave them his blessing and descended the steps of the rectory to the waiting cab.

The plane arose gently at first, bounced through the cloud layers, and finally broke through to the brightness of the waiting sun that had been hiding from the world below. Farley couldn't see much of the country below through the cover of clouds, so he took his prayer book and began to read.

It seemed as though time had passed rapidly, and he heard the lowering of the landing gear signaling the imminent landing of the jet at O'Hare Field in Chicago. The stewardess leaned over him and informed him that he should report to the United Airlines desk at the airport where he would receive transportation to the cardinals' residence in Chicago. He thanked the stewardess and proceeded to prepare for the landing.

Farley settled himself in the limousine for the one-hour ride to the cardinals' residence. He picked up the heavy briefcase he had been carrying and began to rummage through the rather disorderly papers that were carried therein. He picked up the papers on the city minority housing project and devoted some thought to that. Thoughts started to come like lightning, and he swiftly wrote them down. The hour passed rapidly and the chauffer announced that they had arrived. Farley quickly returned the papers to the briefcase and in so doing, proceeded to enlarge the disarray present within the case.

He stepped lively from the car, and the chauffer opened the trunk and picked up Farley's suitcase. They proceeded to the front door and were greeted by Mayfield himself.

Mayfield and Farley had met several times before but never had visited each other or been with each other over any extended time period. They walked together to the large reception room where Farley noticed to his surprise that he was the last of the commission members to arrive.

It was Cardinal Frederick Josephson who quipped, "The best is always saved for last. Welcome!" Farley extended his hand and greeted each prelate who stood around him individually.

Archbishop Frank Carnavale then volunteered, "We've already agreed, honorable chairman, to have our first meeting tomorrow morning at nine. How do you feel about that?"

"What can I say?" Farley replied. "After all, I'm only the chairman. I'm as anxious as you are to get started. Where are we going to meet?"

Mayfield announced that they would be welcome to meet right where they were now standing, in the large reception room.

He assured them that they would have complete privacy. Farley was agreeable to that arrangement.

"Right now, I'd like to freshen up a bit and then return to this good group and get better acquainted," Farley said. Mayfield accepted the hint and steered Farley to his accommodations that would be home for the week.

After a quick shower and a change of clothes, Farley returned downstairs and joined the other prelates, whom he now realized he would be seeing a lot of in the next year. They began to converse and as the afternoon wore on, they became more engrossed in conversation. All, however, carefully avoided the topic of marriage as they knew when they entered that arena the next morning it would be for keeps.

Mayfield interrupted the conversation and announced a personal tour of the cathedral. Even though Archbishop Carson was the only prelate who had never been inside the cathedral in Chicago, all present thought it would be a good idea to see the cathedral first hand with Mayfield.

As his first day in Chicago drew near to an end, Farley retired to his room to prepare some notes for the next morning's meeting. He wrestled with thoughts of Ann as his mind turned to the subject of marriage. He said a quick but fervent prayer, and a small miracle seemed to take place. He was able to concentrate on the topic at hand and clear his mind of Ann. He struggled an hour or so with his notes and felt the overpowering desire to sleep.

The unyielding ring of the alarm was prompt at five thirty in the morning. Farley was so used to getting up at this hour that he sometimes wondered what the purpose of the alarm was. He was scheduled, at his own request, to say a 6:00 a.m. Mass at the cathedral at the Altar of Our Lady. Farley prayed during the Mass for her assistance in his commission's endeavors.

He strolled into the dining area and joined his fellow prelates for breakfast. Archbishop Frank Carnavale seemed to lead the discussion at the table. His sense of humor was appreciated, as he seemed to elicit the most laughs from the group. The levity did much to ease the apparent tension related to the matter at hand and made it tolerable to enter the reception room and close the door behind them to begin discussion.

After all had assigned themselves to a position around the table, the secretary closed the doors behind them. She was supplied by Cardinal Mayfield to take notes. The hour was at hand. Carnavale jumped from his seat to retrieve an ash tray from a distant table and brought it over to the conference table. He then lit the largest cigar Farley had ever seen. Archbishop William Carson commented on the rather unpleasant aroma of cigars but that did not deter Carnavale. He picked up his ash tray and moved closer to a ventilation fan that just happened to be in the room.

"I guess we can be casual," Farley said, as he tried to regain what he felt was lost control of the situation. "Let's begin with a prayer," he announced. Carnavale put his cigar on the edge of the ash tray and arose with the others as Farley began the prayer.

Each prelate in attendance was to read a prepared statement on his ideas surrounding the issue at hand. As expected, Carson and Josephson were liberal in their thinking, advocating drastic changes in the current attitude of the church toward divorce and remarriage. Carnavale and Cardinal Brendan "Ed" Feeney were conservative, advocating no change at all.

Farley now came to the realization that this task was nearing insurmountable. His advisors had forewarned him. It now appeared that he would be casting a deciding vote for this group from the United States. After the statements were read, Farley opened the meeting to general discussion.

Carnavale, in his usual humorous manner aimed at trying to break the air of tension in the room, said, "I don't see any major discussion on the issue at all. marriage is a sacrament. How can we allow two people, who have been bound together via the sacramental vehicle, to separate and remarry under the veil of a sacrament again? You demean and mock the sacrament. As far as I am concerned—case closed."

Cardinal Josephson interjected, "What about the human element, Frank? We can always be released from our priestly vows under certain circumstances. I realize our Holy Orders are permanent, but we can still be released from the priesthood. Has Holy Orders been demeaned? If two people can no longer live together, why not allow them, under special circumstances, to separate and still allow them another chance at contracting a marriage?"

It was now apparent to all present that the issue was complicated and certainly deserved the attention that Pope Clement wanted to give it.

After four days of meetings, Farley told the group that they should prepare a statement for him to present at the inaugural meeting in Rome. Farley knew that the statement would take at least a day to prepare. At the conclusion of the meetings, the group was divided evenly, conservative and liberal, with Farley being the deciding vote. He was keeping an open mind, but gently leaning toward status quo.

Back at Holy Cross Cathedral, Mary O'Leary went about her daily tasks, but with consistently less vigor. Karen had noticed and left her desk to go to the kitchen and talk to Mary.

She hesitated. "How are you feeling, Mary?"

"Not up to snuff. I can't explain it. I just don't feel like myself."

"Sit down and let's talk. The boss is away so the mice will play," Karen quipped. She then looked directly at Mary and added, "I think you ought to get to your doctor." Mary protested, "No. No. I don't believe in doctors."

"But Mary, just get a check up. Might only be high blood pressure which can be easily treated. The doctor will prescribe the proper medication and you'll feel like a million dollars. Why persist in feeling badly?"

It started to make sense to Mary, and after more convincing from Karen, she called Doctor Lang who was the physician for the cardinal as well as the Lincrofts. She made the appointment.

A much- relieved Karen remarked, "Now in a few days I guarantee you'll be feeling better."

"I guess I should thank you." Mary hesitated. "But I'll save that for after my checkup."

"Mary, don't be pessimistic," Karen commented. "When I set a date for the wedding, I want you there so get with it."

Both thought at that moment about Farley's meeting in Chicago and both thought that maybe, just possibly, a breakthrough in the church's marriage laws would be forthcoming. Mary particularly felt anxious for personal reasons that she never previously discussed with anyone. As for Karen, it appeared as though she was destined to marry outside the church. They smiled at each other and returned each to their own tasks.

In Chicago the next morning, Farley called the final session to order. They were to prepare a statement summing up their activities. Also, the secretary had gathered together reams of minutes of meetings that would accompany Farley to Rome.

At about four in the afternoon, the doors of the conference room swung open and the prelates and secretary emerged. Farley went directly to Mayfield to thank him for his hospitality. Mayfield convinced Farley to remain the night and leave the next day as he had some ideas he wanted to discuss with the cardinal. The other prelates had all made reservations to depart immediately.

Farley consented to stay an extra night but told Mayfield the discussions and results of the meetings were confidential until

Clement XV would announce the final results of the commission. That appeared to be quite a distance into the future.

Mayfield said he wanted to discuss with Farley some ideas on marriage, but certainly wouldn't delve into anything discussed at the meeting.

Farley and Mayfield bid farewell to the other prelates, and Farley told them he would keep in touch with them on the progress of the worldwide commission. He also notified them that their local group would most assuredly be getting together again. With thank yous and farewells having been said, Mayfield and Farley adjourned to the lounge for cocktails and conversation.

Mayfield lit a cigarette and offered one to Farley, who graciously refused. He didn't like to make a great deal over the fact that he didn't smoke.

"I'm going to say it and get it over with," Mayfield intoned. "I very simply think your commission has nowhere to go and thus will have to rule on a status quo posture."

"You said a mouthful," Farley replied. "We can't lessen or cheapen the sacramental value of marriage, but we've got to come up with a system of reconciling Catholics in bad marriages. No matter what we do to ease that burden, do we open the floodgates to abuse? I feel we'll be locked into this commission for some time to come, but I am hopeful that somewhere along the line, a compromise will be reached. We've simply got to find a solution."

Mayfield chuckled and admitted he was seldom joyful at ducking any issue, but this was one issue he was glad to be out of.

Farley warned, "You may not be out of it altogether as it is our intention to gather information from other prelates throughout the country. I feel confident we will be knocking on your door, Mike."

Farley made his reservations for the plane trip home and spent the remainder of the day with Mayfield going over issues of mutual interest. When Farley retired for a few hours of sleep before his early morning trip home, he went to sleep almost immediately. In his last moment of consciousness, he noted that he had given nary a thought to Ann all day. He was thankful that it now appeared his affection for Ann was just a fleeting thought and that he was fast returning to the task at hand, that of being a good priest.

CHAPTER SEVEN

The letter arrived in the morning mail. Karen looked at the postage stamp issued by the Vatican City State and thought for an instant about how bureaucratic this church of hers was. She thought, *Imagine the money spent on designing and issuing your own postage stamps from a country a little larger than a few city blocks*. She dutifully brought the mail to Farley's desk although he had not as yet arrived at his office. On her way back to her office, she chided herself for even thinking her church to be worldly.

Mary bumped into Karen in the hall and informed her of the recent medical exam she underwent. With her head down, she stammered to Karen, "I've got to go to the hospital for a more thorough exam. I told you I didn't like going to doctors. For some reason or other, you always wind up in the hospital." She raised her eyes and stared at Karen. "He found something that needs further attention. Now who's going to look after Cardinal Farley while I'm in the hospital?"

Karen answered, "Don't worry about him. He'll be taken care of. You just take care of yourself. Please don't worry, Mary, as I'm sure the major checkup will reveal that all is fine. Don't forget that you admitted you haven't had a check up in years, so you're just catching up on some neglect."

"I have to go in next week," Mary volunteered.

"Please don't worry," Karen reassured her.

Mary returned to the kitchen and Karen heard Farley enter his office. It seemed as though all had returned to their respective duties as if on cue.

71

Farley opened the letter from the Vatican addressed to him by Cardinal Fiorvante, the Dean of the College of Cardinals. He was Pope Clement's right hand and some cynics called him the power behind the throne. In substance, the letter was a call to Rome by the pope to organize the embryonic marriage commission. To this particular meeting, only the heads of each country's delegation would be invited. Goals of the commission would be determined and an agenda drawn. Farley should be ready to leave for Rome within the next two weeks. He should allow for a stay in Rome of at least one week.

He immediately started to get his papers together on the American's group meeting held in Chicago so he could report their findings at the first world meeting. He also spent time on the housing report so he could finish his initial report prior to his leaving for Rome.

Mary, while feeling better then she had been, was still not herself. She busily engaged herself in her routine chores and thought about how she was going to break the news to Farley about her upcoming hospital stay. This would make him a bachelor, and things like that worried Mary. She felt an overwhelming mother complex toward her "family," as she called it. She also thought about the gift certificate she received from the Lincrofts. Even though she thought the purchase of that certain dress at Grayson's would make her feel years younger, she also knew that the fountain of youth was an imaginary fountain. She would always be Mary O'Leary. She made up her mind to give the certificate to Karen. She wouldn't let on to Farley because she surmised that he would tell the Lincroft's what she had done and she didn't want them to be offended.

Lunchtime arrived quickly and Karen scooted out the door for lunch with Tom while Farley walked across to the dining room. While having lunch, Mary dropped the bomb about her hospital stay. She would stay mum on the gift certificate, and she hoped Karen would do the same. Farley was surprised but felt compelled to offer Mary assurances that everything would be all right. "Are you concerned about my welfare?" he inquired. "Worry about yourself, Mary, please. I may not be the most adept bachelor around, but I'll just have to manage, won't I?"

"I just hate to leave you."

"Well, how long are you anticipating being in the hospital?"

"I haven't the slightest idea. If they find something that needs attention, I could be a while."

Farley stared at her and assured her that everything would be fine and that he would be at her side as often as he could manage it. He was hoping she would try to relax. As he continued in thought, however, he knew that Mary's age was against her and he was seriously concerned. He convinced himself that his primary task at this time concerning Mary was to keep up her morale.

"Don't worry about me, Mary. I'm going to Rome shortly and they will take care of me. So just worry about yourself. In fact, I feel guiltier than you, since I may be leaving before you're out of the hospital. But you're always in my heart, Mary O'Leary."

After lunch, he returned to his office and immersed himself in work. It wasn't long before his work was interrupted by the ringing of line two. It was Charles Lincroft. Charlie informed the cardinal that his presence was requested at dinner on Thursday, and Ann and he would accept no refusals. Farley gave him no argument, and after a brief conversation, he thanked Charlie and returned to his work.

Supper at the Lincroft's was the usual gourmet event. Farley mused as to how it was a mystery, albeit a pleasant mystery, that he didn't seem to gain weight from these extravagant repasts. Ann was still in a wheelchair, but she assured Farley that before long she would be up and about. Progress was slow but still gradually improving, according to her doctor.

Their conversation continued in a light vein and Farley was pleased that it remained that way as it kept his mind off other things. Ann was beautiful. Her beauty was starting to overpower Farley. The light conversation that he was maintaining kept the inner tension, which was his to bear, to a minimum. At one point, however, he did question himself with what was starting to become his tranquilizer when around Ann: *Why am I acting like a schoolboy instead of a priest?* It seemed to work because the oversimplification of the problem made him feel overly simple. This worked for a short period of time, but when he gazed at Ann, he was in trouble. He also thought about Charlie. Both Ann and Charlie, as a couple, had been good to him as an individual and had also been good to the church. He was aware that his emotional interest in Ann could only lead to disaster for his priesthood and his friendship with the Lincrofts.

He broke the news to the Lincrofts of his upcoming trip to Rome by telling them he had made reservations to leave very soon. He also informed them of Mary's upcoming stay in the hospital for a major checkup. He was relieved when Ann said that if Mary were to remain in the hospital, she would be happy to visit her and care for her.

Farley looked at Ann and said, "That's a load off my mind. Mary is a wonderful person, but there is no way I can postpone my trip to Rome. I'm confident that she will be out of the hospital before I leave, but in case she isn't, I'm glad to know that you will pitch in, Ann. It means a great deal to me."

As the evening ended and Charlie helped Farley on with his coat, he informed him that he would take care of his transportation to the airport for the start of his journey to Rome. Farley appropriately thanked him for his offer and also for the pleasant evening. He leaned over to kiss Ann as she sat in the wheelchair and as their hands grasped each other and their lips met, excitement soared through Farley's body. The firm grasp they maintained was one of friendship in Ann's mind. To Farley's mind, it was magnetism of an unbelievable nature. It was so strong that he could barely pull his hand away. The brief moment of the kiss and the accompanying hand clasp passed in a matter of seconds, but Harold Farley felt all the emotions of desire, love, and possession surge through his body like nothing he had ever experienced. He walked out the door firmly convinced that this situation with Ann was hopeless. He muttered a quick prayer. "Lord, give me strength."

Farley's preparations for his trip were underway. His initial report on housing was completed and mailed to the mayor's office.

It was Mary's last day before entering the hospital. She seemed to be in good spirits and both Karen and Farley did all that was possible to keep her morale high. Farley assured her that if, for any reason, she was detained in the hospital and he had to leave for Rome, Ann Lincroft would see that her needs were met. Mary thought about feeling guilty in the matter of the gift certificate, but she vowed not to tell Farley or the Lincrofts about what she had done. She just hoped that Ann Lincroft wouldn't ask her anything about it, because if she did, she would be forced to come up with a good story.

Mary reported to Mercy Hospital, and Karen stayed by her side during the admissions procedure. After securing Mary at the hospital, Karen returned to the cardinal's residence to work.

Some hours later, Karen brought Farley his flight information, and as she placed it on his desk, she hesitated and then bravely burst forth. "May I be so bold as to ask if there will be any hope for people in my dilemma through this commission that you will be serving on, Eminence?"

Farley laughed and replied, "I admire your spunk, Karen, and the answer is I hope so. But the problem is so vast that you should be aware that I can't draw any conclusions at this time. Be patient. You have your whole life ahead of you."

"But Eminence, I don't. Life is flying by. I love my job here, but complete fulfillment for me is a person who cares for me and for whom I care for, and sharing life with that person with all its problems, and better, its happiness. I beg you not to deprive me of that."

"Karen, it isn't me who's depriving you. No one is depriving you. Unfortunately, the person you want to spend life with is unavailable by church law. You have to make a decision. Be careful to understand I'm not judging Tom, since I think he's a very fine man, but canon law is specific regarding the sacrament of matrimony, and it says that people in Kiely's circumstances are not available to be marriage partners to practicing Catholics."

Seeing that the plea was going nowhere, Karen interjected, "Well, I'll still hope for assistance from my dilemma through your commission, but I can't wait too long."

Farley laughed again and grabbed her hand. "Karen, this is going to take months, but maybe I can advise you better when I return from Rome. Don't run off and get married now, promise?"

I promise," she said with downcast eyes and she started to walk out of the office.

"What about Mary?" Farley asked.

Karen turned abruptly and answered with all the details of Mary's admission to the hospital and explained to Farley that she comforted Mary as best she could, but Mary remained apprehensive. Farley brought his finger to his chin and rubbed the barely visible stubble on his chin which indicated to Karen that he was worried. He told Karen that he was pleased with all she was doing for Mary and that she was showing herself to be a good Christian.

She looked at Farley and said sarcastically, "I guess I need all the points I can get on the good side of the ledger."

Farley knew she was going to persist on the marriage situation and knew she was going to be difficult to deal with as she was looking for an easy answer where none could be found. He smiled at Karen as she retuned to her office.

Farley was booked on a flight that would arrive in Rome at an early morning hour, and so he called Monsignor Beardsley to ask him to handle the arrangements for transportation from the airport to the Vatican. His room arrangements were already made. He contemplated momentarily on the trip that he would be making in a few days.

That evening, it was arranged that Farley and the Lincroft's would visit Mary at the hospital. Farley met Ann in the lobby, and she announced that Charlie was detained at the bank and couldn't make it. Her chauffeur waited outside as Farley pushed Ann's wheelchair into the elevator.

When they entered Mary's room, Doctor Meyner, the cancer specialist recommended by Doctor Lang, the Lincroft family physician and Farley's as well, was entering information on the chart. Meyner recognized Farley and immediately rose from the chair at the foot of Mary's bed and greeted him.

"Do you always work this late, Doctor?" Farley asked.

"Only on my special patients, Eminence."

Ann introduced herself to Doctor Meyner, and he said that as a friend of her doctor, he had been consulted by Doctor Lang during her recent stay at the hospital. "Mind you," he said to Ann, "it had nothing to do with anything serious." He didn't want to mention the *C* word in front of Mary. "It was just to see if I agreed with his diagnosis and treatment, and I must say that you wear a wheelchair rather well, Mrs. Lincroft."

"Hopefully, I'll be out of it soon," she said. "I really don't care for the fashion."

Meyner explained that he had to be going and that there was more testing to be done on Mary, so he was not informational at this point. Meyner did tell the cardinal, however, that Mary would remain in the hospital for a while. Farley concluded from this that he would be on his way to Rome before Mary was released. Meyner explained that it had been a pleasure to have met him and Ann and left the room.

Farley went over to Mary's side and kissed her and then said with a smile, "I feel as though I've been a patient here myself with my friends spending so much time here."

Mary looked up and said, "Believe me, I'm the first one who would rather be meeting with this group in a more joyful atmosphere, but to be truthful, this place isn't as bad as I thought it would be. Doctor Meyner tells me he should have some news for me tomorrow. Hopefully they can find out what's giving me the blahs and prescribe some medication."

"That's the spirit," Ann chimed. "You'll be back on your feet quicker than me since I have a week or two left in this chair before I graduate to crutches."

Farley returned to the residence in Ann's limousine, and she went from there to the bank to pick up Charlie. Farley noted that his proximity to Ann without the presence of Charlie had posed no threat to him tonight and he felt good about that.

The plane tickets told the story of Farley's flight itinerary, and they clearly stated that his plane was taking off Sunday. The Lincrofts insisted on his having dinner with them Saturday night after they visited Mary at the hospital.

Farley and the Lincrofts lifted their glasses for a toast as well as a Godspeed for the journey the Cardinal was about to undertake.

"Mary was certainly in good spirits tonight," Ann said and the cardinal and Charlie nodded in agreement.

"She'll pull through this. The woman is amazing," Farley said, trying to hide the obvious worry on his face. "I hate to be leaving at a time like this, but I know she'll be in good hands with you people. Thank you again for caring."

The relaxing mood was broken by the unrelenting ring of the phone. Charlie was called to the phone by Marie, the housekeeper, consequently putting Cardinal Farley in a one-on-one position with Ann.

He stared at Ann for what seemed an inordinate amount of time. He uttered, "Ann, you look more beautiful each time I see you."

She sipped at her cocktail and said in a joking tone, "I think you're trying to flirt with me."

Farley was dumbfounded. He felt foolish and said to himself, "What an ass I can make of myself when I want to."

Ann added in all innocence, "Sometimes I wonder about handsome priests like yourself. You know, aren't you ever lonely for a woman?"

He thought the repartee could soon become juvenile and pressed himself to change the subject as continuance of the conversation could only lead to disaster.

Charlie entered the room and provided him with the break he needed. "Well tomorrow is planned," Charlie said. "That was Martin at the bank on Saturday night of all nights. I have to go to the bank tomorrow regarding an investment account that needs some attention."

Ann butted in, "You're leaving me on Sundays now?"

"C'mon, Ann. It's only for a few hours."

Ann laughed and chided Charlie, "That's all I'm going to give you is a few hours." They chuckled and proceeded to the dining room for dinner.

After dinner and cordials and much conversation, the evening drew to a close. Farley bade farewell to the Lincrofts. He kissed Ann and knew as he gazed on her that he wouldn't see her for at least a week and possibly longer. His mind reeled at the diverging thoughts that were crossing it at this time. They were good and bad. It was good that he would be separated from temptation for a week or more, and it was bad that he would be separated from

Ann for that same period of time. He also thought about his love for Charles Lincroft, and he knew that his attention to Ann could lead to the destruction of three lives—not only his, but the innocent Lincrofts as well. He didn't feel as though he wanted to be instrumental in that. The Lincrofts wished him well, and he said he would do his best to stay in touch.

Farley said the early morning Mass at the Cathedral and contacted Reynolds at his parish to inform him that he would have to administer confirmation at St. Andrew's Parish in Lexington. He told Reynolds that he was to do this particular confirmation but had no inclination he would be summoned to Rome. Reynolds told him he had some duties penciled in for Tuesday but all could be moved to another day. He told Farley there was no problem.

As he hung up, he saw Karen suddenly appear in his office. "What brings you here on a Sunday morning?" he curiously asked.

She looked at him beseechingly and pleaded, "Before you go to Rome and begin your deliberations on a look at the annulment procedures, please think of me and all those in my position. We want so much to stay a vital part of our church. We want to stay as full participants."

He smiled at her and placed her hand in his and said, "I will do that, Karen. You also pray for me." She also smiled, "Thank you."

"And don't forget Mary. Tell her I'm praying for her also."

He contemplated on these things as he left the residence and entered the luxurious limousine provided by the Lincrofts. He was on the first leg of his journey to Rome.

CHAPTER EIGHT

The arrangements made by Frank Beardsley in conjunction with Karen were the usual perfection. As Farley sat bleary eyed in the limousine, he could see the dome of St. Peter's in the distance. The rising sun cast a golden glow over the entire scene. It was as though Michelangelo had painted a canvas exclusively for him.

Upon arrival at the Vatican State, Farley was greeted by a young seminarian studying in Rome. He was an American who introduced himself as Bill Armstrong. He placed the lonely suitcase of Farley's on a cart, and he led Farley away from the Vatican area a small distance through the streets of Rome. At this time the streets were fairly well deserted. While walking, Armstrong said to him, "While you are here, your wish is my command."

Farley chuckled, looked at him, and replied, "So you're stuck with me. Well, I promise I'll be easy with you and try not to give you too much trouble."

Armstrong perceived him to be a little stiff and thought to himself, *Certainly not a good sense of humor.* He then turned to Farley with the cart still dragging behind him and said, "I promise you I won't be in your way. I'll be your so-called errand boy and 'gopher' for the next week or so. I'm only acting under orders."

Farley laughed, "Don't take me too seriously, son. Whether you know it or not, I spent some time here myself and even pulled the same duty once. In fact, so did Clement while we both studied here."

That seemed to relieve Armstrong somewhat and he performed his assignment well by bringing Farley's luggage up the stairs and showing him to his room. The room was located in the North American College and when Farley looked the room over, he noted that the place was basically the same as when he had studied there. A basic bed with a wooden frame was thrust into one corner of the tiny room. Next to the bed was a simple nightstand with a small inadequate lamp. There wasn't even room in the nightstand for more then a Bible and a set of rosaries. The sliver of a window which faced away from the warmth and light of the sun let in barely a micron of daylight. This gave the strong impression of a prison cell to Farley. On the wall opposite the bed was a picture of Jesus and next to the wall below the picture was a prie-dieu. A small closet was inserted in the wall behind the doorway. The brown tile floor added all the warmth of an Eskimo igloo. Farley continued to gaze upon the room. He looked at Armstrong and in a sarcastic tone muttered, "Well, it's home for the next week. I guess I rate these first-class accommodations. Thank you for your help, Mr. Armstrong."

"You're welcome," Armstrong replied, not knowing how to take Farley. "I'll be available to assist you if you merely dial Monsignor Rinaldi at Extension 11. He will contact me to take care of your needs."

"Thank you," Farley said, wondering whether or not he had noticed a phone in the room. As Armstrong walked down the hall, Farley turned back into his room, or cell as he preferred to call it, and sure enough on the wall next to the closet was a somewhat outdated wall phone. The bathroom was several steps down the hall and Farley would use it to shower and prepare for the day. He noticed a small pitcher and basin on the floor next to the nightstand, but it seemed as though he would have to obtain the water himself from the bathroom. He quickly wrote that off as useless since he could take care of his washing chore in the bathroom anyway

Farley unpacked and proceeded down the hall to the bathroom to take a desired shower. While in the shower, Armstrong must have left a note on his door because when he returned the note was affixed to his door. He was to contact Monsignor Rinaldi. He changed his clothes and then picked up the antiquated phone and dialed Rinaldi.

"Welcome, Eminence!" Rinaldi blurted when he picked up the phone. "It is my pleasure to inform you that His Holiness, Pope Clement, wishes to dine with you at noon."

Farley was speechless. He always thought himself to be in control at all times, but he was in awe. Even though Francone and he had been classmates and friends while they were being educated in Rome, this was different. Francone was pope and Farley was being asked to dine with him. "Will the others from the commission be dining with His Holiness?" questioned Farley.

"No, Eminence. It appears only you and the Holy Father will be dining. Bill Armstrong will escort you to the papal apartment."

Farley wasn't given a chance to say no. He did laugh to himself though, "Now just who would refuse an invitation like that?" He figured he should relax and realized that he was just having lunch with an old friend. He knew, however, that try as he might, he couldn't convince himself of that. Giuseppe Francone was His Holiness, Pope Clement XV.

In a short while, Armstrong knocked on Farley's door to escort him to the papal apartment. The day shone bright and the sun was warm, but Farley didn't know it until he stepped outside. His room was so dark and slightly dingy. They traversed the streets and walked into the beautiful Vatican grounds. They entered the Vatican Palace and took the elevator up to the papal apartment. Upon arriving at the apartment, Armstrong delivered Farley to

Monsignor Bella, the Prefect of the Pontifical Household. Bella introduced himself and opened the door to the residence of the pope. Francone walked over to Farley and embraced him. They were just old friends.

Francone was not a striking man as Farley was. He was thin and wore glasses which were held up by a very Roman nose. He vaguely resembled Pius XII. He was tall and had gray hair and was very slightly balding. It was the opinion of the world, however, that what he lacked in physical appearance, he made up for in intellect and spirituality. He was a well-loved man and his interest in trying to do something with the marriage situation within the church was indicative of his concern and sincerity, and above all, his love of all people. Farley was proud to be his friend. He was never prouder than that moment when he, of all prelates in Rome at that time, was chosen by Clement to chat informally and enjoy a repast.

In broken, but very understandable English, the pope looked at Farley and addressed him, "Harold, how good it is to see you again."

"I never dreamed I would have this privilege, Holiness."

"You mean you never thought of your friend, Francone, as pope?"

Realizing what he had blundered into, Farley tried to salvage himself with, "Holiness, I knew all the time that you would eventually be our Supreme Pontiff, but I never thought with your busy schedule that you would remember me and ask me to break bread with you."

Clement laughed and Farley relaxed, assured that he had salvaged himself. Clement chuckled again. "By the way, Harold, call me Frank as you did in our younger days. We're still friends, so when we're together there's no need for formality."

Farley could not get over how much Clement put him at ease. He still felt awkward, though, about calling the pope, Frank, as he had years ago. Frank was short for Francone and Farley felt that if he were going to call the pope by any nickname, it should at least be his first name. He felt assured, though, that the pontiff would feel no disrespect if he addressed him as Frank.

Ann Lincroft wielded her new crutches and ungracefully walked out of Mary's hospital room with Doctor Meyner. She had managed to extricate herself from the wheelchair much sooner then expected and now wondered if that was a good choice. When outside the room, Meyner looked at Ann pensively and asked, "Has she family?"

Ann replied, "Not to my knowledge. The Catholic church and the residents of the cardinal's home were her life and her family. Why do you ask, Doctor?"

"Mrs. Lincroft, Mary has cancer and without going into great medical detail, the prognosis is not good at all. Mind you, all we have at this time are a few test results, but they indicate that the cancer is spreading rapidly. Miss O'Leary has very little time left. I hate to be so brutally cold and blunt about it, but I must tell you the truth."

"From the short time that I've known her, I never heard her complain," Ann worriedly declared.

"That's remarkable," Meyner said. "This has been with her for some time, and I cannot imagine her not complaining about this until recently." Then he added, "Before I go into any more medical details and treatments, we will need to establish who her guardian is. You're sure she has no family?"

"None that I'm aware of. But if she needs a guardian, Charles and I will make ourselves responsible."

"I'll check her records and even ask her personally, but once we establish that you are guardians, I will release all pertinent information to you. It's a wonderful thing you are doing for this woman."

"It's absolutely the least I can do for that woman who gave me such great comfort when I needed it." Ann had only known Mary O'Leary for a short time, but this news made her upset. Meyner assured her that he would do everything in his power to make her final days as comfortable as possible.

Ann felt awkward thanking Doctor Meyner, but she convinced herself that he was doing everything possible to help Mary. "Charles and I will help in whatever way possible. Do you suggest we tell her?"

"No," Meyner said emphatically. "That is my job and I will not shirk it. She's a strong woman and she can handle it. I know it."

Ann excused herself from Meyner and returned to Mary's room.

Mary looked at her with a twinkle in her eye and remarked, "Wait till Karen comes to see me, I'll give her the devil. She convinced me to get a check up and I told her no good ever comes of these checkups." She paused, sighed, and looked at Ann. "I know things aren't good. I've got what Cardinal Fitzpatrick had, don't I? I'm going to die soon."

Ann held her hand and very tactfully explained to Mary, "Doctor Meyner will be in to see you tomorrow. He will explain everything to you. In the meantime, don't worry and keep your chin up."

The ringing of the phone startled both Ann and Mary, and Ann didn't know whether to be thankful for the change of subject it might provide or resentful at the idea that it would ring while tensions within her were strung to the breaking point. Ann picked up the phone and gave it to Mary who answered with a quick hello.

"Yes, she is here, Mr. Lincroft. I'll put her on."

Ann smiled and took the phone from Mary. "What's new, love?" she inquired while thinking of the insanity of such a question.

"I figured you would be at the hospital so I thought I'd call to let you know that we'll go to dinner tonight since I will be leaving for the coast tomorrow. That investment account that I've been working on with Martin on Sundays, no less, requires that I go to Los Angeles. This deal needs my tender loving care and it won't wait any longer. I'll be gone only a day or two."

"Charles, I miss you so much when you're away, but I guess I'll have to make the sacrifice for the sake of business."

"I miss you too, sweetheart, but true love survives," Charles said humorously. "I've got to go, hon, but I'll pick you up at the apartment tonight and we'll discuss things at dinner."

"See you later," Ann said and then hung up the phone.

"I'm sorry, Mary, for the interruption."

"Don't even think about it," Mary said consolingly. "You've been so nice to stay here with me and keep me company."

Ann placed her hand on Mary's wrist and assured her that things would be all right. "Don't think negatively, Mary. The Lord is with you."

Mary told Ann that she had been praying to Cardinal Fitzpatrick who, she was convinced, was a saint. She also was thinking about Cardinal Farley in Rome. "How I hope his marriage commission can do something positive for Catholics with marriage problems. You know, Ann, I happen to know that Tom Kiely, Karen's friend, is a divorced Catholic. He's a fine man and Karen is a wonderful woman. Karen confided to me that she is definitely going to marry him. I feel for her and you can't imagine how much I do. I also realize the pressure on Cardinal Farley, but he's got to push that commission to a more realistic attitude. His own secretary could be marrying outside the church."

Ann listened but decided to cut Mary short when she realized Mary's tone was beginning to sound agitated. "Relax, Mary. Karen will have to work out her own problems."

"I must be going now," Ann advised, and then she added, "I've also got to get used to these crutches."

Ann handled the crutches clumsily and thought about how much easier the wheelchair was. She looked at Mary and said she would return tomorrow and that Karen would probably drop by tonight.

Mary lay back, assured that she did have friends who cared and that thought enabled her to nod off to sleep. Before she succumbed to sleep, however, she grew troubled at the thought of her castigation of Farley's aloofness and distance for so many years, and she realized that she had contributed heavily to the aloofness. Here, in a few short weeks, she felt that he and his lifestyle had now become an important part of her life. "Why did I waste all those years? Now I lie near death, and I realize the distance between Farley and me was largely my doing." Sleep gradually overtook her.

Ann wrestled as best she could with the crutches, so it was with great relief that she found a limousine waiting for her at the door. In her continuing clumsiness with the crutches, the assistance of the limousine driver was most welcome. She was comfortable with Jason since he had driven her and Charlie on so many other occasions.

Traffic in the city was unusually heavy tonight, so Ann kept talk at a minimum and allowed Jason to handle his driving duties. She thought about Mary and was obviously disturbed at the diagnosis and prognosis. What would Mary do when the terrible news was given to her? Ann would definitely call Cardinal Farley in Rome to make him aware of the serious condition of Mary. She had a fleeting thought to tell Mary herself the bad news, but she quickly realized that Dr. Meyner had the credentials to fulfill this awful duty in a more professional manner.

Cardinal Farley prayed in his room before retiring for the evening. He again sought help for his work on the marriage commission and also sought relief from his thoughts and desires for Ann. His luncheon with and conversation with the pope this afternoon had worked successfully to keep his mind off Ann. Hopefully, his working on the commission would continue to do the same for him. He blessed himself and climbed into bed. His mind began to wander and he rehashed his day with the pope

He and Clement had what he considered an uplifting conversation ranging from the marriage commission and its work to even mundane topics such as wine and recreation. Farley thought it was a shame that people never really saw the human side of the papacy. He was amazed at how much at ease he was with Clement. He was the same person as when they were schoolmates in Rome so many years ago. His opinion of Clement rose to new levels and he thanked God that His church was in such capable and loving hands.

Farley was to meet with many of the other leading members present for the opening proceedings of the marriage commission. He was looking forward to the morning and those meetings and laying the groundwork for the opening meeting with all the delegates present. He gave some thought to the minority housing program in his own diocese knowing that his obligation had been met with the submission of his preliminary report. He knew that his liberal stance would create some waves in the secular faction and with the more conservative members of the diocesan staff, including Beardsley. He nevertheless felt secure in knowing what he had done was the right thing.

As the sun rose and shone through the window of the Lincroft apartment, Charles was already preparing himself for his departure for the coast.

Ann rose with the sun and breakfasted with Charles. "I'll call Father Harold today and let him know the awful truth about Mary," she said.

"That's a task I don't envy you," Charlie commented.

Later, as Ann handed Charlie his briefcase while he stood by the door, he drew her close to him and clutched her. As she enjoyed the closeness with which he held her, they kissed passionately.

"I love you and I will miss you, honey," Ann said, teary eyed.

"I'm only leaving for a couple of days, hon. I'll be back in no time." With that, Charles was on his way to the airport and then to Los Angeles. Upon his arrival in Los Angeles, he phoned Ann to let her know of his safe arrival. He advised her to call Rome shortly as it would be about eleven in the evening there, and he felt sure Father Harold would not be engaged in any meetings at that time.

Ann was thankful for Charles's safe arrival and then prepared herself for the phone call to inform the cardinal of Mary's impending death.

The phone rang in Farley's room and its shrillness echoed throughout the Vatican night.

"Monsignor Rinaldi here, Eminence. A phone call from the United States. Ann Lincroft. Her name was on the list you submitted to us for phone calls you would accept."

"Thank you," Farley replied, wondering what would possess Ann to call Rome.

"Father Harold," Ann implored, whose voice came through the wire like someone at the end of a tunnel. "I'm so sorry to disturb you, but I have rather bad news that I thought you should be aware of. Mary O'Leary has been diagnosed with cancer and Doctor Meyner says the prognosis is not good. Several months to a year at most."

Farley replied, "May God have mercy on her. I knew she hadn't been feeling well but I never suspected anything of this magnitude. I implore you, Ann, to help her in any way that you can. Ask Charlie to help also and even Karen. Of course you know that I'm stuck here for another few days and only a grave reason could free me. It's not that this isn't grave, but it's not critical at the present time. Keep me informed as best as possible since phone contact is extremely limited. Ensure Mary that I will be returning as soon as possible and that while I am here, she will be in my prayers. How is everyone else holding up?"

"Very well. Charles is in Los Angeles for a day or two and I'm okay, a little depressed about Mary but otherwise fine."

"Take care of yourself, Ann, and thank you for calling."

"Bye," Ann said as she completed the very brief exchange. She did remember, however, that Farley told her that while he was in Rome, phone calls to him had to be as brief as possible.

Farley knelt in his room before the picture of Jesus. The phone call brought disturbing news and he knew that at times like these, prayer came first. He prayed fervently for Mary O'Leary.

Doctor Meyner entered Mary's hospital room as the sun shone brightly through the window. "Good morning," he said with a smile and then quickly picked up the chart at the foot of her bed. He fumbled with the chart and wrote several entries on it. He then clipped the pen back into his pocket after several attempts and sat down in the chair. He was uncomfortable. "Mary…" He stammered.

But she interrupted with a smile on her face. "If you're calling me Mary instead of Miss O'Leary, then I know you're trying to soften the blow of bad news."

Meyner's turn to interrupt came and he said, "Wait, Mary. Let me tell you the complete story as I know it at this moment."

"No, Doctor. Let me talk first."

"If you insist," Meyner replied as he sat back a little more comfortably in the chair.

Mary began, "I have cancer and I'm going to die. For years, I've dreaded this moment but now that it has arrived, my outlook has changed. All those years waiting for the inevitable moment and here it is. The worrying was needless. It always was and always will be in God's hands. I have led a long life and for that I am grateful, but I still grieve over never having been able to have my own family. Apparently that was not in God's plan. When Cardinal Farley returns and before I leave this world, I do want to talk to him about something near to my heart, and it will be the first time I have ever offered an opinion on a religious matter to either Fitzpatrick or Farley, both of whom I have worked for. They were my family but I could never be as close as I wanted to. It was always just a job. If I have several months left, Doctor, I'll be happy as it won't take much longer than that to prepare for the next world. I stand ready to do whatever I must to assist you in helping me to make my last days comfortable. Don't get me wrong now, it's not that I'm looking forward to dying, no, I'm just accepting what is to be."

Meyner sat back dumbfounded. In all his years in the medical profession, he had never had a patient quite like Mary O'Leary. He got up from the chair and walked to the side of the bed.

"Mary, nothing is definite yet, but being realistic, I would have to say the prognosis is not good. Six months to a year is all I can promise. Try to be optimistic. Maybe a breakthrough will occur. Above all, maintain your beautiful attitude. In all my years in the medical profession, I never saw anyone in your position with such a marvelous outlook."

Meyner then picked up the chart and entered some more notations. He then proceeded to get into all the medical terms surrounding Mary's type of cancer as well as what methods he would be using to keep her comfortable.

In Rome, the day's meeting of the marriage commission was in high gear. It was Cardinal Farley's turn to address the group. Clement, himself, was in attendance at the meeting. He wanted to listen in on the preliminary summations from each group. Farley had gathered his notes from the Chicago discussions and had prepared a summation to be read at this time.

Farley was an eloquent speaker and his presentation held all in rapt attention. The summary included a mixture of some new methods of handling bad marriages, but with a general trend toward no changes by the church toward the divorced and remarried.

It was obvious to those listening that the American group was split down the middle with Farley's opinion weighing the scale in favor of a conservative outlook. As Farley finished his oration, he glanced at Clement who was expressionless. Perhaps Farley was looking for either approval or disapproval, but if he was, he was disappointed. Clement was not about to tip his hand. The commission was going to arrive at a decision on their own.

Karen fought back the tears at Mary's bedside for she didn't want to upset Mary. She was amazed at Mary's attitude. She and Mary talked about Farley's meetings in Rome and both were in agreement with a confident attitude concerning the outcome. They were positive that because of the changing times, the church would ease the annulment procedures.

Ann replaced the phone on the receiver and was overjoyed. Charlie was returning home. He was boarding a plane the next morning and would be home late in the afternoon.

Farley readied himself for bed at the end of still another day. He recalled the various reactions to his talk at the meeting, and he recalled the evening banquet at which Pope Clement addressed all the delegates of the commission. He asked God's blessings on the commission and on his friends and fell peacefully to sleep.

The next morning arrived, swiftly interrupting Farley's enjoyable and peaceful sleep. He prepared for another day of meetings. This afternoon, after the second session, he was to get a special complete tour of the Vatican state and even a peek at some of the behind-the-scene apparatus and people. He was looking forward to that.

Charles Lincroft boarded the plane and sat down in the first class section. He read some business papers to pass the time as he was used to the long waits between boarding and actual takeoff. Finally the plane taxied to the runway to prepare for its ascent. The huge plane rumbled down the runway, picking up speed with each passing second, and in moments was airborne.

Charles put down his paper and a chill coursed through his body. Something was wrong. He could sense it. His flying experience told him the altitude of the plane was off. The plane, now barely airborne, began to shudder violently. No warnings were given. Charles prayed. It was over in a matter of seconds. The plane impacted on a farm field and no one on board had a chance as it exploded on impact.

While Ann enjoyed her lunch at her Rosewood home, from the den she suddenly heard an unearthly scream. Her housekeeper, Marie, was sobbing. She dropped her cup on the table and ran to the den only to see, in large letters, looming across the television screen, the word *Bulletin*. The announcer was saying, "As we just said, there appear to be no survivors of this crash which took place just outside Los Angeles."

The housekeeper continued to cry as she sat at the edge of one of the chairs. Ann suddenly felt sick. She looked at Marie and asked in a trembling voice, "Was that Charles's plane?"

Marie looked up at Ann, her cheeks streaming with tears, and said, "Oh my God, I don't believe it."

Ann shouted and grabbed Marie by the shoulders. "Tell me it wasn't Charlie. Please, God, I love him so much. Please, I beg you, not Charles."

Feeling sick and sobbing, but still hanging on to a slim thread of hope, she dialed the airline. The message on the phone advised her to call at a later time since the phone lines were extremely busy. She had barely hung up when the phone rang. She quickly picked it up and the voice of John Martin, Charles' vice president, was on the line.

"Ann, I'm so sorry. Is there anything I can do?"

Ann was inconsolable, and she told Martin to call her later. She replaced the phone and cried out loudly, "I refuse to believe Charlie is dead. I refuse to believe I'll never see him again."

Marie stood up and hugged Ann and advised, "Let's wait until we call the airline to verify it. Maybe Mr. Lincroft didn't get on that plane."

Ann looked at Marie and actually felt somewhat relieved and began to resent John Martin's call to her if none of them were sure that Charles was on that plane. She picked up the phone and was able to get the airline on this attempt. Her feeling of euphoria was short-lived as the news was bad. The woman on the phone verified that Charles Lincroft's name was listed on the flight manifest. He was listed as missing since verification of those dead at the scene had not, as yet, been ascertained. The woman expressed her sorrow.

Ann hung up the phone and completely broke down. Her world was at an end. The impossible was now reality. Charles Lincroft was dead.

〜

At the evening meal, Farley conversed with several other prelates, and one mentioned the plane crash back in the States. Farley knew that Charles was in Los Angeles on business, but he never gave a thought to the possibility of Charles being on that particular plane. After the meal, he inquired of Rinaldi the details of the plane crash in the United States that killed so many people. Rinaldi said he would contact the Vatican radio and would have details for Farley in the morning.

After a night of fitful sleep, Farley received, through Bill Armstrong, a complete media report on the American plane crash. The name of Charles Lincroft stood out on the page and emblazoned itself into Farley's consciousness.

What's happening? he thought. His knees buckled as he looked at the list of the dead again. It would not go away. The name Charles Lincroft was on the list. The plane was flying from Los Angeles to the east and Charles was, in fact, in Los Angeles. It had to be him.

"May God have mercy," he whispered. He then broke down and wept openly. His family was disintegrating. His closest friend was dead and his housekeeper was dying. He continued to weep bitterly and to pray.

CHAPTER NINE

Harold Cardinal Farley would have to get through his meetings as best as he could. He was barely functional and in a daze of disbelief. It would be noon before he dared call Ann. What would he say?

After a long morning, the noon bells peeled throughout the Vatican and Rome, and Farley obtained the use of a private phone and hesitantly dialed Ann Lincroft in the United States.

Marie picked up the phone and said Ann was awake and hadn't really been to sleep all night. She said she would get her to the phone.

Ann managed a weak hello.

"Ann, nothing I can say or do is adequate to let you know how truly sorry I am for your loss."

"Father Harold, please come home to be with me. I won't bury my Charles unless you are here with me and offer to celebrate his funeral Mass. I know I must be resigned to God's will, but you don't spend all these years with someone you love and who loves you and not feel completely and utterly sorrowful and helpless. I keep asking God for one more chance for Charles, maybe hoping there will be a miracle, but I know that's not God's way. Please help me, Father. I need you so much."

"The meetings are only introductory, Ann, so I'll probably be able to leave a little early but not before next week. Clement is very high on our American group and wants the introductory report completed."

"That will be fine, Father, as they still have to ship the body here from Los Angeles."

Farley told Ann to pray as she never prayed before and try to understand God's will and keep herself together until he returned.

"It's so good just to hear your voice, Father. I need you."

After she dropped the phone, Ann picked up the morning newspaper. Two glaring headlines reinforced her feelings of loss. One headline regarding the plane wreck and the other noting that prominent banker Charles Lincroft had passed away. Ann threw the paper down and cried again, bitterly.

Farley toured the Vatican state and tried to be gracious to his hosts, but today was going to be written off as a lost cause.

Before retiring he thought about the awful reality of Charles' death. He stared at the reality of his affection for Ann and an overpowering feeling of guilt was gnawing away at him. He thought, *Ann needs me now more than ever. Can I sublimate my affection for her through this immense crisis in her life? Am I resentful of Charles's death because he was my friend, or because his death forces me into a closer relationship with a person that better judgment dictates I should refrain from? Do I feel guilty now about my feelings for Ann, of which Charles was never aware? And also, now that he is dead, is he sort of "out of the way"?*

He continued in thought. *God Almighty, help me! I loved Charles Lincroft like a brother and I would never have done anything to make him unhappy. Forgive me, Father in heaven, for the terrible thoughts Satan is planting in my mind. Oh God, make me strong so that I can be an island for Ann in her sea of misery. I want to be a good priest, Lord. Help me and forgive me. Have mercy on the soul of the best man I ever knew.*

Farley blessed himself and fell off into a fitful sleep.

As the sunrise announced another day, Farley quickly arose to begin the day's activities.

First on the agenda was a desired visit with Clement to discuss the past few days' events and his particular desire to leave Rome early and offer a Mass of the resurrection for his best friend. He was delighted to hear that Clement would not only see him but wished to breakfast with him.

Farley greeted Monsignor Bella and entered the pope's dining chamber. A broad smile on the face of His Holiness announced a cheerful welcome to Cardinal Farley.

"I want to tell you how much I admired your talk on the findings of the American group, Harold."

Farley uttered a quick "thank you," recalling with puzzlement the expressionless face of the pontiff after he had delivered his oration.

Clement continued. "I'm hoping that at our next session here, when the entire commission meets, through the dialog of the church intelligentsia, we can somehow find a way to solve the problem. Your talk the other day presented some diverse but interesting views. I was also interested in the talk by Cardinal Tessier and the European group. I'm confident we're on the right track and if I accomplish nothing else in my papacy, I will be happy with the idea of establishing the marriage commission."

Not sure that Clement was finished, Farley interrupted. "I'm also confident that the commission will be fruitful." Deep inside, Farley harbored doubts. Yet he found that while listening to Clement, he was affected by the latter's enthusiasm.

Farley sipped his coffee and asked, "May I seek a favor, Frank?"

"Certainly."

"Charles Lincroft, a dear friend of mine was killed in that plane crash back in the States, and his wife has requested that I say the funeral Mass. I would like permission to leave Rome as soon as possible."

Clement responded, "I am truly sorry, Harold. Of course, there is no problem. The major work of this initial gathering of the group, to organize the marriage commission, has been completed. I have no problem with your leaving as soon as possible."

Farley managed a smile and offered thanks to the pontiff.

Clement and Farley continued their discourse while finishing their breakfast. Before they parted and Farley bid farewell, Clement reiterated to Farley the seriousness of his assignment and how close the commission was to his heart. Farley assured Clement of his loyalty and dedication to the commission.

The plane landed smoothly and taxied to the awaiting crowds eager to greet their loved ones. Farley disembarked and was whisked through customs and to a waiting limousine which Ann had arranged for him. He was taken directly to the Lincroft home in Rosewood.

He had no sooner reached the front door when Ann threw her arms around him and sobbed uncontrollably. "Father Harold, I loved him so much. I can't see how I will ever get over this. Please help me."

She pulled away and apologized for crying on his suit, but Farley laughed—not only because he thought the remark to be so distant from the subject at hand, but also because he thought it might ease the tension.

"Ann, dear, how will I get back to the residence in the city? My suitcase is still in the limo."

"Don't worry. The limo is available to return you to the city tonight, but I need you here now to help me. The body arrived today and I made the arrangements yesterday, so I need a little time alone with you for some consolation."

Farley was thankful that he was not tempted at this crucial time. Nevertheless, he was puzzled as to how easily one's sexual desires were so easily sublimated in a time of crisis. Nature seemed to take care of humans very well. He uttered a quick prayer of thanks and a plea to help him understand and deal with Ann's terrible situation. Because of all that happened in the last few days, he barely noticed that Ann was now walking without assistance, albeit with a pronounced limp.

Marie hastily prepared an early supper and at the table, Farley inquired of Ann how Mary was. His purpose was twofold. He genuinely wanted to find out about Mary's condition, but more importantly, he wanted to sway Ann's mind away from constant thoughts of Charles.

"She is in slight remission, but it is only temporary," Ann answered while sipping a cup of tea and leaving most of her meal uneaten. "Doctor Meyner said she is still terminal and it's still only a matter of time. I obtained a private duty nurse so she could be at home. Obviously, she won't be going back to work."

Farley chimed in, "Her going back to work doesn't concern me now, but I will need someone soon. I will do whatever I can to make her last days as peaceful as possible. And thank you, Ann, for caring for her. You are a true Christian."

If Farley thought he had moved Ann's mind away from Charles, he could forget it now. That last remark brought out a fury in Ann that he had never seen before.

She shouted, "Being a true Christian has done a lot for me, hasn't it? While I'm being a true Christian, God takes my husband from me."

Farley frowned. "Now, just calm down, Ann. I thought I told you that you must accept God's will. The fact that you were helping Mary O'Leary wasn't a remote cause of your husband's death. His death is a shock to all of us, dear, but we have no choice other than to accept it. Will turning against God and your fellow man bring Charles back? You need God more than ever now so don't condemn him. Pray to him and his mother for guidance. I will help all I can here, but you need him for your spiritual needs. I'm sure there are so many who care deeply about Charles' death and they are also finding this hard to accept, but let's not all get angry with God about it. Don't ever forget one thing. God saw his Son, Jesus, go to a horrible death for all of us. Our sins killed him. God certainly has feelings or he would not have given us our sensibilities. Since God has feelings, he has them to perfection. How do you think we would have fared had he condemned us to our sinfulness? Instead, he watched his Son die a truly horrible death for us and still did not allow his anguish to destroy his love for us. Because of that, you can be sure that Charles is with him now, and one day you will also be with him and will see Charles again. God's love is so much more then you can imagine. He is right now wrapping his arms around Charles and also around you. He knows what you are feeling and he wants to offer you comfort. Please accept it."

Ann sobbed again and apologized. It wasn't like Father Harold to chastise as he had just done, but Ann knew he was right. She continued to sob and she still longed for just one more moment with her husband.

That night, Farley returned to his residence and unpacked his belongings. He quickly got ready for bed but sleep for him would be delayed. He too was grappling with Charles' death. He prayed fervently to guide Ann properly and to help him also in his grieving.

The arrangements for Charles' funeral were completed and Ann did not wish a viewing at the funeral home. Firstly, the body was in such deplorable condition that there was nothing in the embalming arts that would permit decent restoration. Secondly, Ann was not comfortable with the idea of a procession of the "curious" gathering to view the body of her husband and then shake her hand with promises of help that would never be honored. Farley had advised her to do as she wished, but he was not content with her attitude. It was coming across to him that Ann was accepting the death as some kind of punishment to her by God for some imperceptible deed she committed. It certainly did not seem as though she was accepting it as God's divine plan. She did, however, invite friends to attend the funeral Mass and then to gather at the apartment.

Although Farley had celebrated many Masses of the resurrection, none would touch him as this Mass would. The casket making its way down the aisle of the cathedral belonged to not only a prominent banker, but also to a close friend—a man who was like a brother to him. For an instant, Farley understood Ann's attitude as he asked, "Why?" He knew he would have to compose himself for the body in the casket belonged to his best friend. This Mass would be difficult, and the eulogy would be the supreme test.

In a little over an hour, the Mass was over and Farley breathed a little easier. He made it through the eulogy while cracking only once. He became assured when he saw Ann being escorted by her sister's husband. He knew Ann was not very close to her family, and he saw the first signs of something positive resulting from the tragedy of Charles Lincroft's death.

The prayers at the cemetery were over in fifteen minutes. The wind blew briskly. Those who had come to the cemetery for Charles's burial hoped the wind wouldn't blow their solitary rose away before it would come to rest on the casket. All returned to the Lincroft apartment for lunch.

When all had paid their final respects to Charles and spoke their words of comfort to Ann, only Cardinal Farley remained at the apartment. Ann returned to the living room and completely broke down. "I don't know what I'm going to do. I feel so down and so hopeless."

Farley stayed with her to comfort her as best he could, but he was beginning to wonder if Ann was ever going to come to grips with this so she could take care of all the things that needed to be done with her personal life. Farley realized she had an immense problem.

Marie assured Farley he could return to the residence and that she would look after Ann. Farley told Ann that he would call in the morning. He kissed her on her now wet cheek and reminded her that she still had to go on living, and that she could always go to him for help.

The next morning, Karen politely greeted the cardinal upon his return to his desk, and while he did not see her at the funeral Mass, she nevertheless informed him that she was in attendance. She also brought him up to date on Mary's condition. He replied that he would make time to visit her.

The phone rang and after Karen answered it, she handed it to Farley. It was Monsignor Beardsley.

"Welcome home and please accept my condolences on the death of your dear friend." Beardsley had waited a few days to contact Farley because he was aware of the pain he was going through over the loss of his friend, and he wanted no part in adding to that pain. Beardsley contemplated on the fact that Farley was always secretive about the Lincrofts. He was not asked to concelebrate the funeral Mass. He was always slightly uncomfortable about Farley's closed mouth position on the Lincrofts, but he was beginning to understand a little more clearly as a result of Farley's last confession. He had to block that from his mind, however, due to the confessional seal. "I've got some news for you, Harold."

"What would that be?"

"Did you know that your preliminary report to the Mayor on the minority housing program has raised the hackles of the politicos downtown? Plain and simple, Harold, they don't like it. Too liberal. One comment made by one of our leading

Catholics downtown was, 'How can anyone who is such a church conservative be such a political liberal?' Of course, you know, that attitude started a war with all the minority support groups. So, needless to say, things are jumping."

"How do you feel about it?"

"The paper isn't publishing the full text until tomorrow. I'll let you know then."

"How did these political hacks get their hands on it then?"

"The mayor let them read it. He's all for it, and you know why, Harold. Gets him votes. Stays in power. But frankly, from what I hear, you're not going to make too many upper middle and upper income whites or blacks very happy."

"That's too bad, Frank, but I'll take my chances doing what I think is right and suffer the consequences."

"C'mon, Harold! We have to look at the whole issue with clear glasses. I think we can find a way to these issues through many avenues while trying to make everyone happy. Why should we zero in on a target that benefits one group of society at the expense of others?"

"Frank, I don't believe you. You sound like you have no sensitivity to the needs of the poor. Remember your confessional advice—put all my effort in the preparation of the report. Well, I did and I don't intend to change it because some insensitive politicians downtown can't accept it."

"Harold, I don't expect you to change the report and I'm certainly glad that you gave it your all. I'm trying to inform you as to why some of the people are upset. I personally feel for the majority of people who go to work each day and live by the golden rule. They educate their children in our schools at great expense and sacrifice. They give to the church and many of them leave very little for themselves. Besides championing the cause for the poor, you are their leader and champion too. What you're saying in effect to these people is, 'You haven't done enough. I'm recommending that you support my plan for affordable housing for minority groups by digging deeper into your pockets to pay the extra taxes it will take to implement the construction of new housing for the poor. In fact, the people who pay these taxes will soon be poor and by that time there will be no room left in this housing to accommodate all the newcomers. Where do we go from there—more housing with even less people paying for it. Don't chastise me, Harold, but consider these views."

Harold sighed. He didn't feel as though he wanted to debate at that time, so he advised Beardsley to read the full preliminary report in the paper and then they could discuss it further. He asked Beardsley for an update on the condition of the diocese.

Beardsley replied, "Reynolds played Cardinal while you were away, but he had an easy time of it. In other words, everything is okay."

"Thanks, Frank, for keeping me informed. I've got to run. I'll call you tomorrow." He hung up the phone and headed for Mary's apartment. He thought on the way about his mounting problems. Beardsley had a point. More than anything, he didn't want to disturb his flock and he hoped he hadn't done that, but tomorrow's paper would clarify that.

Mary's apartment looked neat and clean, and it was obvious that Ann had provided the best help she could get. Mary looked as well as could be expected considering her illness. She was extremely distraught over Charles Lincroft's death and her inability to help Ann, who was doing and had done so much for her.

It was difficult for the cardinal to console Mary, but he felt he had done his best reassuring her that Ann owed her life to her. But Mary was a stubborn woman of Irish heritage who insisted on frustrating herself over not being able to do anything for Ann Lincroft in her time of need. Farley felt assured that Mary's tenacity would give the angel of death a fight. She was a wonderful woman.

The walk home from Mary's apartment caused Farley's mind to work overtime. He thought almost in wonderment how Mary made this trip every day at her age, while he felt just the beginnings of the aches and pains of advanced years setting in. It was almost humorous to compare his "advanced" years to Mary's advanced years. Mary was getting along, but it was depressing to him to see her in her present condition. He was thankful that Ann had provided a nurse for her.

Upon his return to the residence, the afternoon paper was on his desk. The release of his report would not have to wait until tomorrow after all. The evening paper had scooped the morning paper and in it was the full text of Farley's report. He practically knew it by heart so he avoided the temptation to see how it looked in print. How he hoped that everyone would read it completely before the more conservative sheep of the flock would tear it apart. It bothered Harold Farley to have any of his sheep disturbed.

On his desk was also a message to call Ann Lincroft, which he did immediately. Ann answered the phone and advised Farley of a call she received from her attorney advising her to appear in court on the matter of her accident. It seems the driver was pleading innocent on the charges of drunken driving citing a medical condition. "I just can't be bothered with this, Father Harold," Ann intoned. She added, "Not at this time."

He told her to get back to her attorney to see just how much participation was needed by her. It was obvious the man was under the influence, and hopefully this matter could be adjudicated as quickly as possible and with as little participation as possible on her part. She thanked Farley for his advice and realized how distraught she was when it became so difficult for her to solve a problem as simply as Farley had. He then reminded Ann that he was accepting her dinner invitation for Thursday night.

At Ann's house for dinner, Farley told her that he had an inkling that he would be getting a call from Spencer regarding the next meeting of the marriage commission. He sensed that the Holy Father wanted to keep the momentum established by the initial meeting. At the next meeting, all the prelates would be asked to be in attendance. Then he laughed and said, "I hope they can find me better living conditions. That prison cell I had the last time was...let's just say small." He resisted the old cliché about a room being so small you had to step outside to change your mind.

After dinner, Ann asked for some advice on personal affairs. It wasn't that she didn't trust her attorneys; it was probably more because she was searching for someone to lean on. She was looking for a substitute for Charles. When Charles was around, he made all the decisions and Ann didn't have a worry in the world. Although Charles protected her by making her financially independent of the bank, she still had to cope with matters that were totally unfamiliar to her.

Ann sipped her after-dinner drink and looked at Farley. "You seem to have all the answers. I just can't seem to function without Charles. Do you think I'll ever get on with my life, or is this cloud going to remain over my head forever?"

Farley managed a smile, "You'll never forget Charlie. He was half of your life for a very long time, but you must go on living. Eventually you will find things falling into place. You'll never get over Charles; you will just learn to adapt."

"Leave it to you to oversimplify the problem."

"Oh, Ann, try to pull yourself together and realize that you must resume living until it's your turn to answer the Lord's call. You're a young woman yet and you've got a lot of living to do. You have so much to contribute yet. I'll help you all I can, but you will have to help yourself."

Farley was adept at changing the subject—probably a habit obtained from meetings with politicians—so he cashed in on his talent and turned Ann around to discussions of happy times. In the midst of conversation, Ann placed her hand on his and it immediately rekindled the glowing embers into a fire. Again, and as usual, Ann looked beautiful. Once again the blood rushed through Farley's body so fast that he thought his face must be a glowing red. *It's not time*, he thought. *Too soon.* Then in quick succession, more thoughts raced through his mind. *I sincerely hope she doesn't recognize my arousal*, and, *What am I going to do about this situation now that Charles is dead?*

Ann continued the conversation and removed her hand from Farley's. It appeared that his blushing went unnoticed by her. He felt extremely depressed when she moved her hand away.

Ann carefully stood up and announced she was getting refills. She didn't ask Farley whether or not he cared for one. He didn't say no.

She limped into the kitchen and while she tended the bar, Farley asked himself, *Why should I continue to fight this? I enjoy this woman's company and I find her to be the most beautiful creature on earth.* His conscience came to the fore, however, and interrupted, *You're a priest and you took a vow of celibacy. Except for friendship, this woman is out-of-bounds. You better get yourself together, Farley, while you're so busy telling this woman to get herself together.*

Ann emerged from the kitchen with two drinks. Even with her awkward attempts at trying to walk normally, she was just as radiant and handsome a human being as anyone could imagine.

Farley blurted out, "I still say you're beautiful, Ann."

She returned with, "And I still say you're flirting with me."

Besides making Farley uncomfortable, the thought had the positive result of forcing a smile to Ann's face and consequently lessening her anguish.

He spent the rest of the evening warding off temptation by talking to Ann only of her problems in adjusting to her new role of widow. At various times, he touched Ann by placing his hand on hers with reassurances to her of her ability to cope. Ann accepted it with a deeper meaning than just physical touching. In fact, her thoughts now were that she may be leaning on Farley too much. After all, she couldn't expect him to substitute for Charles. No, she would have to learn to be independent; and besides, frequent meetings with Farley could lead somewhere else.

In spite of these thoughts on both of their minds, Ann requested Farley to join her out at the marina next Thursday and check the boat with her. Farley loved that boat, so of course, the invitation could not be refused.

He kissed Ann good night and knew that their relationship was going to cause him no end of trouble. It was just as impossible to cease this relationship as it was to continue it.

Ann closed the door behind him and asked herself what had happened to her new resolve to be independent. She tried to decipher her mixed emotions—her extreme sense of the loss of her husband and her extreme reliability on Cardinal Harold Farley. She was definitely feeling an urge to have a stronger relationship with him. She tried to ascertain her feelings. She enjoyed his company and, after all, she needed his friendship and help. He was a most interesting man and he was a class above the stodgy men she was forced to be friends with for the betterment of her husband's bank. Ann knew she would continue to need Farley's help. Her resolve of only moments ago to be independent was now out the window.

After Mass, Farley went to the kitchen where a substitute housekeeper, Marcia Jenkins, fumbled to make him breakfast. He had to ask for the paper, something he never had to do while Mary was on duty, but he couldn't fault the woman as she was probably nervous. She had been recommended for the job by the cathedral rector through one of his relatives. She needed the money.

The cardinal read the editorial page where his preliminary report on housing for the minority groups received a halfhearted endorsement from the paper. Two other articles on his report appeared as well. The conservative writer, John Henley, panned the report by asking, "How can someone so conservative on church matters be so liberal on worldly matters? This report is a disaster for the already overburdened taxpayers."

Mark Lovett, the liberal reporter, gave it four stars. "We should back our bishop one hundred percent. We must give the minority groups decent housing so decent lives can be nurtured within decent homes. Cardinal Farley has a keen sense of human dignity and how to obtain it."

After reading the rest of his paper and adjourning to his office, he patiently awaited the phone calls from his priestly cohorts on both sides of the issue. They never came. In fact he had so few interruptions that he had time to sneak out of the office and pay a visit to Mary O'Leary.

Bundled up against an unusual chilly wind, he hugged his body as he walked up the street. He thought it was odd that not one call came to his office about the housing report considering the publicity it received in today's paper. "Are they annoyed with me? Don't they care? I'll call Beardsley and Reynolds when I return. Something must be wrong."

Ann Lincroft received a call from her attorney advising her that she simply had no choice but to go to court. "Mrs. Lincroft, we have to get these types off the roads or someone else will get injured or worse, killed. We need your testimony in the courtroom." Ann had no choice so she reluctantly agreed. The court date was the following day at ten thirty in the morning.

The chilly wind of the previous day developed into a major rainfall. The rain outside was relentless as Farley made his way to the kitchen from the chapel for breakfast. He forced indigestion on himself with thoughts of never making his promised phone calls to Beardsley and Reynolds and their possible disagreements with him. Now that Beardsley had an opportunity to read the entire text of the preliminary report on housing, it might be possible that his thinking may have changed. He thought about Ann and her morning in court, but a fast call yesterday to her attorney left him assured that her appearance in court would be brief and painless. His visit to Mary yesterday was fruitful, and he left her in high spirits. He rose from the table and headed to his office to spend the day tackling some of the paperwork of the diocese.

Thursday dawned as a much improved day from the past two days. As a matter of fact, it was a beautiful day and perfect for boating on the lake. Farley arrived at Ann's house in Rosewood late in the morning. She then drove with him to the small marina just a few miles from her home. On the way, Ann assured him that the day in court was, in fact, painless and she felt good about taking another bad driver off the road. They brought a sufficient supply of food and beverage for an enjoyable afternoon on the large lake.

They unloaded the car and walked the supplies over to the boat that Farley thought was a little too big for use on the lake. But it was a beautiful boat and it was a large enough lake. After loading the supplies on the boat, Ann laughed at Farley's attempts at being a sailor. He fumbled with the lines. When Ann saw him, she playfully tossed Charlie's old sailor hat at him. "You'll have to trade in your red hat for that old 'Barnacle Bill' relic of Charlie's," she joked. Farley was glad that she seemed in such good spirits and hoped that his spending time with her was lessening her pain. That would surely justify his spending time with her.

Farley piloted the boat out onto the lake from the cove that housed the marina. As the boat picked up speed, he saw the wind blow against Ann's face. He couldn't get over her beauty; it was like something from a magazine. Her face set into the wind caused her beautiful hair to blow back from her face and she appeared like an angel. She turned away from the wind and her hair blew toward the front of her face and formed a frame around a majestic work of art. Although her hair was speckled with a tiny bit of gray, it certainly did not detract from her appearance. She walked up next to him and held his arm. "You really enjoy this little putt-putt, huh!"

Farley replied, "Always did. It just seems a shame that Charlie didn't enjoy it as much as he should have." He hoped he hadn't touched off a soft spot with Ann regarding Charlie, as it was his idea to try and keep her mind off that subject.

She continued to hold Farley's arm, and he made no effort to remove her hand but instead covered her hand with his. There was an intensity growing between them and Farley could sense it. He thought quickly, *Could this be desperation on Ann's part due to loneliness, or a genuine affection developing? Regardless, I'm enjoying this. The love of a man and woman is good. Imagine two strangers one day finally find each other and two become one. It's a miracle so why should I fight it?*

The moment arrived. Ann reached up and kissed him on the cheek. "Thank you for being here when I need you."

The mind of Harold Cardinal Farley, a priest, now reeled with a myriad of conflicting thoughts. He managed a weak, "Don't mention it, Ann. What are friends for?" But he thought, *I am a priest and I took a vow of celibacy, but I am also a man in love. This woman may possibly be falling in love with me and I don't want to fight it anymore.*

Ann interrupted his thoughts. "Why so quiet? Never been kissed?"

The remark broke the tension of the situation, and he decided to let things take their natural course for the remainder of the afternoon.

He walked over to the bar to make drinks for Ann and himself, and Ann took over as captain of the vessel. She brought the boat to a stop and they remained drifting on the somewhat choppy lake while the afternoon sun beat down on them.

Harold Farley decided that he would tell Ann of his true feelings. He realized that it might be too soon after Charles's death and that she might react favorably due only to loneliness and not true love, but it was a chance he would take. He could never recall being so nervous and for an important world prelate, that had to be an affirmation of just how serious he thought this situation was.

"Ann, dear, I'm very nervous about saying what I have to say, but I feel it must be said. My affection for you has grown over the years and at the risk of our friendship, I must say the affection has reached the point where it could threaten my priesthood. This may be inappropriate in light of recent events, but I love you."

Ann looked surprised and answered, "Of course you do. I never doubted that over all these years, and I love you, too." She almost appeared to chuckle and this angered Farley as he thought she was being condescending.

"I mean real human sexual as well as spiritual love. I've felt this way for some time."

"Wow…" Ann stammered. "That's too heavy for me right now. I mean a priest and all…wow!"

"Maybe we should just leave it at that for now and…" Farley said, in a quandary as to how to finish the statement.

"No way," Ann interrupted. "How can we drop a subject like this and continue to remain on this boat together, or much more, remain as friends for the rest of our lives? Let's talk about it."

She began to cry and she placed her glass on the bar and walked across the stern of the boat to a waiting seat. She placed her head in her hands and then looked up, teary eyed. As she wiped her cheeks with her hand, she sobbed. "I feel so guilty. I certainly feel that I could love you too, but I'm too confused now. First of all, I'm certainly not over Charles's death and secondly, cardinals just don't quit the priesthood to get married. I always felt that Charlie and I had a beautiful marriage. I loved him tremendously and miss him terribly. But these past few weeks, I've come to rely so much on you that I feel an intimate special love developing as opposed to the normal love of one friend for another. I've been pushing it from my mind, however, as a reaction to Charles' death and my subsequent loneliness. Help me, Harold!"

Farley felt very uneasy especially when Ann did not preface Harold with the usual "Father." He put his hand on her shoulder while she sat and sobbed. "Forgive me, Ann," he said. "This was supposed to be a pleasant afternoon on the high seas and I've ruined it. Let's get ourselves together and try to enjoy the rest of the day. What do you say, huh?"

Ann continued to cry. "Do you think it's safe for both of us to be here with the feelings we have for each other? Maybe we should just turn around and head in. No. Forget I said that. Let's face this thing square on. We're just the victims of circumstance. I'm vulnerable and I'm reaching out to you. You want to help me and the result is a deeper love for each other which if left unchecked, could get out of control."

Ann stopped crying and dried her eyes, and they proceeded to the cabin to get lunch ready.

"How's your appetite, Father Harold?"

"Not good, but what the hell, let's enjoy what has been prepared."

Ann prepared the table in the cabin while Harold Farley poured further liquid refreshment. Both minds were busy with confusing thoughts. Both were fighting temptation. As Ann dished out a small salad on the plates, Farley placed the drinks on the table and again put his arms around Ann and this time drew her to him. In a split second that seemed like an eternity for each to make a decision, their lips met. Ann presented no resistance. Farley had never experienced the euphoria that surrounded his physical body and aroused his mind. Their lips parted and they stared at each other. Farley's conscience said, *Enough!* They parted and sat to partake of the repast Ann had prepared.

Lunch was virtually silent as each sat with his own thoughts. Ann was feeling guilty over the recent death of her husband and wondering if this attraction for another man was as sudden as it seemed or if it had been building for awhile. This, of course, led to more guilt.

Farley also felt guilty as he thought of his friend Charles. But even more difficult to deal with were his thoughts of his rank in the church and the many duties he was still to perform as a priest. If he were to decide to change his life for a life with this woman whom he was certain he was in love with, it would mean an enormous change in his life as he knew he could not remain a priest. If only Ann would not accept his love. It was becoming more apparent that she felt a love for him also, and this would prove to be disastrous to his priesthood, or so he thought.

Harold Farley and Ann Lincroft enjoyed the remainder of the lunch, but the feelings between the two of them were so intense that they both felt it showed better presence of mind to try to remain as far apart as possible. They remained cordial, however, for the rest of the afternoon, and after tying up the boat and seeing Ann home, they parted with a friendly kiss. It seemed a vast understatement and almost humorous, but Ann's parting words were, "I guess Father Harold is no longer appropriate."

Upon return to his residence, Farley called his confessor. He knew it would be a long session with Frank Beardsley.

This time Beardsley was tipped off in advance by Farley's phone call, so upon arrival at the cardinal's residence, Beardsley immediately proceeded to Farley's office. Upon arriving there, he removed his stole, kissed it, and placed it around his neck with the appropriate prayer.

"Bless me, Father, for I have sinned," Farley intoned in the same manner as he had heard those words in the confessional from so many penitents. "I enjoyed the feelings of sexual arousal and did nothing to stop those feelings and instead justified them as love. I feel as though I have violated my vow of chastity in thought, and my love of God is so great that I cannot possibly know why, in a split second, that love became secondary to the earthly love of another human being. I am truly in love with this woman, but I also love God and in an effort to offend him no more, I will seek release from my priestly vows. But please know that I am sorry for violating those vows."

Frank Beardsley had heard thousands of confessions in his years as a priest, but none that compared to this. He silently asked the Lord for help in advising his penitent.

He hesitatingly began, "Harold, you must make a resolve to avoid the occasion of sin. You are in a predicament. First of all, the love of man and woman is sacred as you have said, but you are corrupting it because you as a partner in any love relationship involving sexuality is a violation of a promise you made before God at your ordination. We all love women and feel as thought they are the crowning glory of God's creation, but we have sacrificed intimacy with them to deprive ourselves and humble ourselves and thus bring us closer to God. Besides all of this," Beardsley said with his voice somewhat raised, "any sexual love between two people who are not married to each other is also forbidden. If your love is true to this woman, then you must seek a release from your vows and turn your back on the priesthood, but as your friend and a fellow priest, I ask you to think long and hard about the decision. We need men like you to guide our church,

Harold, and it's my feeling that God needs you in his church. My advice to you is to avoid this woman as diplomatically as possible, at least for a time, so that you have time for yourself and your thoughts. Immerse yourself in your continuing good work for the church and in preparation for your next meeting in Rome. Give yourself time, Harold."

Beardsley gave the cardinal his penance, and after Farley prayed, Beardsley removed his stole and sighed. "What would you do if you were not a priest?"

"I haven't given it any thought, Frank."

"Well, that's beautiful," Beardsley chortled sarcastically. "Come on, Harold; give yourself time to see how childish this thing could get to be. You may be an intelligent man but how easy do you think it's going to be to just assimilate yourself into the business world? It's crueler now than you think out there. The diocese needs you, the city needs you in your present position, and the church needs you. Why not continue your life with those who need you, than quit and not even know how else you can contribute to society?"

"But Frank, what if she needs me, too?"

"You're out-of-bounds, Harold. You can certainly help her, but you can't be her lover."

Farley quickly arose from behind his desk and cried out, "God help me!"

It was easy for Beardsley to see Farley's frustration, but he got up and looked at Farley and steered him to the dining room. He then sat him down and fixed drinks for the two of them. It would be a long night. The more they talked, the more frustrated Beardsley became.

As the evening wore on, Beardsley became angrier, and forgetting the compassionate tone of his confessional admonition to Farley, his anger was now borne out in words strictly off the cuff. "Harold, what the hell is the matter with you? You're serving on a commission appointed by the Holy Father himself to study the problems of the divorced and remarried, and you have the gall to be hypocritical enough to take the stand that you have taken so far. Don't you remember that this infatuation started prior to this woman's husband's death? That would have put you in the same position you're posturing against now when it looks as though the church is looking for a way out for these people."

Beardsley's voice grew even louder. "Besides, Harold, you're a priest and a damn good one at that and a noted leader of the church. You can't give that up. Now get yourself together and come back to earth. She's out-of-bounds and your priesthood is in jeopardy, and if you want her then have the guts to go to Clement and tell him to get you off the commission and out of the priesthood."

His face now red and his blood pressure obviously up, Beardsley walked over to the side table. Farley looked at him and said, "You are right, Frank, but it's so difficult to shake this thing."

"I'm sorry, Harold, for blowing up but you're a good priest and the church can't lose you. I respect your position as archbishop and I shouldn't have lost my temper. I have a weakness in that I am strongly against people destroying themselves, especially people who are good at what they do."

"Pray for me, Frank."

"I will. You build up some fighting reserve and through your prayers and mine, God will help."

While taking a piece of candy from the dish on the table, Beardsley adroitly changed the subject. He asked Farley if he thought it was odd that no one had called him to comment on his preliminary report of the clergy minority housing committee.

"Yes, come to think of it, I was surprised."

"I spoke with Reynolds and some of the other powers that-be to give you some breathing room. There would be an appropriate time to discuss it later."

"Thanks, Frank, but it goes with the territory that I have to take stands on social issues and suffer the consequences. So you can tell Reynolds and the others that I'm ready to talk about it at any time." Farley contemplated that he really had more serious problems to work out now and he hoped that Reynolds would hold off for a while longer.

CHAPTER TEN

The phone in the Cardinal's office rang relentlessly while Farley tried to put the finishing touches on a pastoral letter to the diocese. Since the letter was concerned with the closing of some parishes in the diocese, he was giving a lot of attention to wording the letter precisely.

Karen informed him that the latest call to the office was from Cardinal Spencer. "Good morning, Harold. Spencer here."

"Good morning, John. How are you?"

"Just great, Harold, but you may not be when you hear the news."

"Try me!"

"Well, Clement was so impressed with the progress of the organizational meeting of the marriage commission, that he is anxious to proceed to the next level: a general meeting. He doesn't want to impede the momentum. He's calling for the entire commission to meet in Rome, and he desires strongly that all should be in Rome in two weeks."

Farley was not surprised as he had anticipated the phone call. "I guess I have no choice, do I? At least not when the commander in chief gives an order."

They continued their conversation and closed it out with promises of getting together some day soon. When Farley hung up the phone, he thought about the strange ways of the Lord. Just when he needed to get away, a good excuse happened to come his way. He hopped on it and viewed it as his passport to renew his commitment to the priesthood. He would become busy with preparations for his trip. This would leave little or no time for Ann.

He walked over to Karen's office and asked her to coordinate with Monsignor Beardsley to arrange his next trip to Rome. Beardsley was in charge of transportation arrangements through the Vatican in relation to all transportation for Farley when he arrived in Rome. Karen would handle the domestic arrangements and air travel. She asked Farley if she could talk to him after lunch. She didn't want to disrupt his work day. He put her at ease by telling her that he always could spare time for his favorite secretary.

It was her desire to again plead with him to look at her life and the thousands of others like hers and to find a way to change the remarriage laws of the church.

"I'm keeping an open mind," he said, as he looked at her in an almost sympathetic way. "If I don't convince you of anything else, please allow me to convince you that I will do all in my power to keep an open mind, but that I will not violate basic church law. My mind is not made up, Karen, because if it were, I wouldn't be sitting on this commission. You must be patient and pray to the Holy Spirit to guide us in our efforts to do God's will."

"Thank you, Eminence, but allow me to convince you of how deeply in love I am with Tom Kiely and how much I love God; and the terrible position I'm in with relation to his church. I think you will have to admit that it's difficult at best for a celibate person to understand the strength of physical love."

Farley always resented remarks like that, but he was forced to hold back his anger as he thought for an instant about his love for Ann. *If only Karen knew*, he thought.

"Karen, just because I took a vow of celibacy doesn't mean that I'm not physically attracted to women. If I weren't, then the vow wouldn't require much of a sacrifice, would it? I'm going to be brutally frank with you. I don't see any change in the church's stand on the divorced and remarried under present conditions. However, the commission will leave no stone unturned in its efforts to ameliorate the problems of those people. Whatever we do will take time, so you'll have to be patient."

"I'm only human, Eminence. I can wait, but not forever," Karen warned.

Farley sensed another stalemate with his secretary, so he backed out of the situation quickly. "Keep praying, Karen, and realize the seriousness of your situation."

She turned away from him and went to a file cabinet. She sighed and said in a low, annoyed voice, "Thank you."

Farley dismissed it and walked away. He then began to think about his own dilemma. Maybe his love for Ann was a reaction to much of the recent negative happenings in his worldly life. His only light seemed to be the spiritual side of his earthly life, his priesthood. He needed both loves, however. He was forcing himself to make a self-inflicted choice between physical love characterized by Ann, and spiritual love exemplified by his priesthood. He must continue to pray.

The nurse admitted Farley to Mary's apartment. Mary had awoken from a nap and, despite being drowsy, was obviously uplifted by his visit. They bantered about different topics with Farley apparently enjoying this as much as she, particularly her reminiscing of Cardinal Fitzpatrick. He related to her his upcoming trip to Rome and how the marriage commission was being accelerated. She stated her hope that his marriage commission would be fruitful. When he left her, he felt better about the fact that she was getting excellent care and would surely be there upon his return from Rome.

Upon his return to the residence, he thought about Mary's interest in the marriage commission and dwelled also on Karen's appeal for him to do his best to come up with some solution to the marriage problem within the church. He wondered about Mary's interest. After all, hadn't she elected to be single?

After pouring through some papers, Farley decided to call Ann. Before he could pick up his phone, it began to ring. Farley picked it up and the voice belonged to Bishop Jim Reynolds.

"It's about time I heard from you." Farley chuckled. "Okay, I'll take the criticism straight, Jim."

"Harold, you're entitled to your opinion and I respect your opinion, but beyond all that, I think you're right. We can't abandon the poor. Maybe we'll never ease the situation, but we can't stop trying. I'm with you. My only problem is funding."

Farley was dumbfounded. Coming from Jim Reynolds, this was completely unexpected. "How come you didn't call sooner?" Farley inquired, knowing full well what Beardsley had already told him.

"Well, I know you had a lot on your mind, and I wanted to allow you to feel settled."

Farley replied, "I'm glad you called because if you had allowed much more time to go by you would have missed me. Spencer called and announced that the troops are reorganizing in Rome again shortly. Clement moved the meeting ahead."

"I have to laugh, Harold, at Spencer calling you with messages from Clement. You know him better than Spencer."

Farley responded with, "You know the chain of command, Jim. We have to play the game."

As Farley unpacked his things, he made a conscious effort to avoid anger at the fact that he received the same room assignment as his first meeting in Rome. What he didn't know was that the other American prelates all received more posh accommodations, if one could, in fact, refer to any of the accommodations as posh.

While all five bishops were flying to Rome together, they had agreed to assemble before dinner together to draw up an agenda and format for their meetings and form a summarization to present to the world commission.

In the reception area prepared for all the prelates assigned to the commission, Cardinal Fred Josephson and Archbishop William Carson, the two liberal members of the American group were conversing with Archbishop McConnell of Ireland. Farley walked into the room and immediately directed himself to that trio. In just a few minutes, he was followed by Cardinal Brendan Feeney and Archbishop Frank Carnavale, the conservative members of the group. Farley wondered how anything would be accomplished if the conservative and liberal thinkers were going to stay within their own peer group instead of mixing with groups of differing opinions for a varied dialogue. Cordialities were exchanged and each received a drink. Canapés were also available and the reception gave all the appearance of a black tie affair.

Although the American prelates were part of a larger grouping which included, among others, Archbishop McConnell of Ireland, they decided to excuse themselves from McConnell and retreated to an unobtrusive position. Farley had started to fine-tune the agenda they had agreed about on the flight to Rome. They agreed with Farley's summation and returned to enjoy the rest of the reception. The next day would bring the opening session of the marriage commission, a project near to the heart of the Holy Father.

The dawn came too early for the members of the commission as they struggled to arise from their slumber and face another day, an important day. The American contingent concelebrated morning Mass in a small chapel. After a light breakfast, they journeyed the short distance to the Vatican complex. They were generating an enthusiasm among themselves that Farley was hoping they could generate to the entire commission. *What a breakthrough this could be if we were able to arrive at a solution*, he thought.

A total of thirty-seven prelates were participating as members of the commission. A very few prelates, who obviously could spare the time, were in Rome to attend the meetings as observers. The five from the United States mingled with the others prior to the formal announcement that would start the proceedings. The Dean of the College of Cardinals, Giaccomo Fiorvante, called the meeting to order. He also happened to be a member of the Curial group.

The room became quiet as all proceeded to their assigned seats. The group that included America had agreed that Cardinal Frederick Josephson would be their spokesman for the opening remarks. Although he was a liberal, he spoke briefly but eloquently on the goals of their group and how he saw them as fitting in with the views of the entire commission.

The thirty-seven at the meeting represented all continents and they were split into six groups. Each group would have its spokesman who would talk as Josephson did regarding their vision of the commission. For the next few days, the groups of prelates would break into smaller regional groups, and through the means of panels, questions, and answers, they would arrive at a group conclusion. The spokesman for the group would then present that conclusion to the entire body. The five Americans were grouped with Australia, Canada, England, Ireland, and Mexico. Throughout the intense meetings of the next two days, Farley was becoming better acquainted with influential members of the Roman Catholic hierarchy. Nary had a thought gone to Ann, excepting prayers for her and his other friends.

When the group had compiled its information through discussion, they again were asked to examine all discussion and make a decision prelate by prelate. Farley's group had twelve members—two from Australia, two from Canada, and one each from Ireland, England, and Mexico. Of course, there were five from the United States. The Americans were well aware that their decisions would heavily weight their group. Josephson and Carson argued persuasively for change with the usual good reasoning and some newer ideas gleaned from the panel discussions. Feeney and Carnavale were just as persuasive in their plea for status quo. There was no denying that Farley was in the driver's seat of the American prelates.

Farley began. "I am afraid, fellow priests , that we stand here with the power to destroy the family as we know it. This would, in turn, destroy the Christian family. Marriage is a sacrament. I have heard not one word, so far, about removing the sacramental connotations to marriage. As a sacrament, administered by two people to each other—just think about that, gentlemen; I mean its seriousness—these people have between each other a sacred bond with Christ. If we allow the divorced to remarry, I doubt that we can call the second marriage a sacrament. Don't you see how ridiculous we would make the sacrament appear if a person can enter into it with no commitment? In other words, a person could say if this doesn't work out, I'll leave this partner and find another. The bond with Christ becomes ludicrous, the commitment doesn't exist. When we receive Holy Orders, it is for life. If we choose to leave the priesthood, we cannot return to receive the sacrament again. Receiving any sacrament involves commitment. If we don't believe in Christ, we mock the sacrament of confirmation. If we don't believe in marriage, we mock the sacrament of matrimony. If we remove the sacramental and sacred aspects from marriage and allow people to pick partners at random and then break up and find another when the going gets rough, then that's exactly what they will do. How can a family structure exist in an atmosphere like that? It can't. We will have destroyed the family. If a marriage consecrated by the church causes a severe problem for one or both of the partners, the church allows a separation and recognizes a legal divorce. But the sacramental marriage continues, for better or worse, until death. The partners are simply not free to remarry another. Our good friends, Josephson and Carson, want to prepare a list of special reasons for annulling a marriage and allowing Catholics to remarry and stay within the church. I say it's impossible."

Feeney and Carnavale resisted the urge to applaud.

Josephson stood and praised Farley for his eloquence, but he began his oration on the liberal view. "Yes, Cardinal Farley, I agree that the family could be destroyed, but isn't that what's happening right now? People are getting out of bad marriages every day now with or without our so-called permission. Can we sit back and allow this to continue, or should we explore some means of reconciling these people and strive to keep the values of family and religion alive in their lives? The status quo is not, I repeat, not, working."

The arguments continued, but it was drawing near the time for the American prelates to meet again with their regional peers, take a vote, and elect a spokesman for their group at the main assembly.

After dinner, Farley contemplated on the last number of days in Rome and how immersed in his work he had become. This was important because he had noticed that his physical longing for Ann seemed to be on the wane. His resolve to go straight to the top and speak to Clement about his situation had simply vanished. He felt good about himself and he renewed his inner resolve to be a good priest and concentrate on his duties for the commission.

At breakfast the next morning, Farley sat with the Dean, Cardinal Fiorvante, who was also the head of the Curial delegation to the marriage commission. Their discussion was on world affairs and it remained as light as possible. Farley knew he was talking to the heir apparent to the papal throne, but only if

Fiorvante outlived Clement, which didn't seem likely. He had nearly ten years on Clement and Clement was a young man by virtue of the average age of the papacy. Although the Holy Father had absented himself from the commission hearings in order to take care of the day-to -day activities of the papacy, Farley did want to talk to him prior to his return to the United States.

All members serving on the commission received a notice from Clement that within the next few days they would meet in a general session to present their groups' preliminary findings. The commission would then recess until again convened at Clement's pleasure.

Farley's group spent the day in discussion. They agreed that Farley would be their spokesman in delivering their conclusions to the general assembly. They all voted and handed the task of preparing the summation to Farley. He would deliver that summation tomorrow. Josephson was the vote tabulator for the group and when all were counted the vote was seven to five in favor of the conservative posture. Canada was split; Australia's two votes were for liberalization as was England's vote, and Ireland and Mexico took a conservative stand. Americans were split: three conservative and two liberal. Farley still felt he was sitting on the fence since many of the liberal points that were presented seem to bear merit. Now the group put its thoughts together to give Farley an outline of his presentation to the general assembly. He wondered how the other groups were voting since at the first preliminary session, the stance of the commission was toward liberalization but then not all the prelates were in attendance.

The morning sun shone brightly and the air was slightly humid as Farley strode to the hall for the general session. He was amazed at how rapidly things were progressing. With him were Feeney and Archbishop McConnell of Ireland. Clement would be at today's session. He was as anxious as anyone to hear the results of the first general session.

After a call to order by Fiorvante, Farley was the first to be called. He stood up to address the session and looked intently at Clement. Whether or not Clement's presence made Farley nervous, Farley's appearance said he was. He cleared his throat and again looked at Clement, almost as if he needed Clement's approval, and began.

He summarized his regional group's findings and delivered an eloquent address with the pros and cons of each direction. He even listed some of Josephson's and Carson's reasons for annulment which he found so difficult to agree with. But at the finish of his address, it was clear that the findings of his regional group at the close of the first session were for status quo. The five prelates who voted for liberalization were disappointed. However, after all the voting was counted it was extremely close. Only one vote more for liberalization. The prelates who voted thus were pleased. But they did know this was only the first session and things could change at the next meeting. Farley put his head down and thought for a minute about how he, as an individual, was going to have to look at this matter with a more open mind to change. It still didn't square with his conscience. He said a short prayer in silence. *Holy Spirit, I know you are present in the workings of your church. Guide me!* His next thoughts quickly changed to a final meeting with his fellow American clergy and then arrangements to go home.

Upon finishing his evening prayers, he turned his attention to thoughts of Ann for the first time in days. It wasn't really that he hadn't thought of her at all, but it was the first time in days that he had thought about his love for her. *Here I am wrestling with marriage problems of lay people in the church, and I'm experiencing a problem with my priesthood and a married woman. While true she's not married now, my strong affection for her began while she was not free to be intimately involved with another man. Talk about hypocritical...* His resolve to continue to wrestle with this matter and come out as a victor was as strong as ever; victory, in this case, being the retention of his priesthood. Whether or not the struggle was outclassing him remained to be seen.

A concelebrated Mass at St. Peter's followed by a message from the Holy Father would formally complete the first session of the marriage commission. Clement had again requested to see Farley before the closing formalities.

In the now familiar to Farley broken English of the Pope, Clement greeted him with a jovial, "Good morning." They sat down to breakfast. Farley gave a quick thought to discussion of the possibility of a cardinal being relieved of his vows, but decided against it. Instead, they conversed about the commission.

The Holy Father began. "Harold, your remarks yesterday were brilliant. In my informal discussions with the Curia on this matter, there is a general trend for the status quo. Right now, the Curia is pleased with your stand as opposed to the stand of the entire commission."

Farley was a sincere man, and he was happy about the Curia's approval because that was good for his ego. But he disliked the inner feelings he had that he might be pushed into a direction by outside influences. He nodded to Clement with a smile.

With no mention of his personal problems, they concluded their amiable conversation and exchanged warmth and respect for each other.

During their conversation, Clement had asked Farley as well as Cardinal Fiorvante to be the chief concelebrants at the Mass even though all prelates in attendance would be considered concelebrants.

The Mass itself was like a scene from heaven with the beauty of the choir and the entire liturgical rite in its most splendiferous. Several cardinals, including Carnavale, cast asides to those near them regarding the "Blessed Trinity" standing at the altar—namely, Clement, Farley, and Fiorvante. Other remarks alluded to the idea of either Farley or Fiorvante as successor to the papacy.

Remarks by the Holy Father were gracious to the commission and even elicited a laugh as he referred to their plush accommodations. He obviously impressed the gathered prelates with his sincerity and graciousness. He was a well-loved man, another John XXIII.

All the prelates had made their reservations to return home, Farley included, and the dinner that evening was a repeat of the magnificent evening held for the attendees on their arrival. They would all be returning home the following day.

CHAPTER ELEVEN

Karen kissed Tom goodnight as he left her apartment. She felt uneasy about setting the date for the wedding. She and Tom had enjoyed a most pleasant evening together with dinner out and drinks at home. A gentle yet highly emotional lovemaking session on the couch only reinforced Karen's overwhelming interest in this previously married man.

The newspaper from the morning lay open on the cocktail table with the article on page three staring at them all the time. The headlines blurted something to the effect that the papal marriage commission had come to the conclusion at their first full session that there could be some changes forthcoming, but that the American group under Farley was for status quo.

She recalled how they had conversed at dinner about her conflicting thoughts concerning her religion and the fact that she was Cardinal Farley's secretary and that Tom had a previous marriage. She recalled Tom's assurances that his religion didn't mean anything less to him because he and his wife could no longer live together. She recalled Tom's words to the effect that he still loved the church, but it was the church, the organization, not God, that loved him a little less, sarcastically adding, "They call it excommunication." She recalled her emotions during lovemaking and how extremely beautiful it all felt and when she lay in Tom's arms, spent and exhausted, she thought, *How can this be wrong?* She recalled and she recalled, but her conscience continued to gnaw away at her.

Despite her conscience, the date was set for a wedding in three weeks. She would tell Farley tomorrow morning. Of course she knew he would ask her to resign, but she was prepared to pay the price. Looking for a new job was easy compared to what she was going through now. She cleaned up her apartment and thought before sleeping about how she would break the news of her marriage and resignation to Farley.

Karen awoke earlier than usual in the morning and prepared herself hurriedly yet carefully for the day ahead. She contemplated how she would break the news to Farley and also to Mary.

She mentally composed a letter of resignation over and over in her mind, but it just didn't seem right. All these years and now this. She thought fleetingly about just announcing her impending marriage and then waiting to see what Farley's reaction would be. She kept coming back to the answer of resignation. How could Farley keep her as a secretary if she were going to marry a divorced man? It relieved her to know that Farley would not be back at the residence until late in the afternoon, and so she had a good excuse to put off the announcement until maybe the following day. There was no question that she was agonizing over this decision. She decided she would talk to Mary first, then see how she took the news and figure a way to break it to Farley.

She arrived at Mary's apartment, and the nurse brought her to Mary. Karen stared in disbelief. Her first thought was that Mary wouldn't last the day. Mary looked up at her and smiled weakly.

Karen asked what she considered to be a useless question. "How are you, dear?"

The best Mary could muster was a "Not too good, considering…"

In the vain hope that Karen could improve her spirits by getting Mary's mind off herself, she asked her for advice.

"Mary, what would you think if I told you Tom and I were getting married, but Tom is a divorced man?"

Mary just stared, but Karen could tell she was in deep thought.

"Karen, do what you feel in your heart is the right thing for you. I've known for some time that Tom is a divorced man. I've agonized with you over our church's laws concerning divorce and I've prayed so hard that the commission that Cardinal Farley is serving on will come to a reasonable and just conclusion. I think Tom is a wonderful man." She paused and sighed, showing a sign of weakening. "But you must be able to square away your conscience with church law. I sympathize with you. You've been so good to me and you are a caring person. You deserve happiness, and if you're happy and convinced that God loves you and you love him then do what you think is right. By the news reports, I see that Cardinal Farley's commission has a long way to go to ease the situation but I pray...oh, how I pray for a change in the church's treatment of the Tom Kiely's of the world and the Karen's of the world. Whatever you do, I love you for being the caring person that you are. You and Tom deserve all the happiness you can find together."

Karen was at her desk when Farley arrived, and she greeted him as warmly as possible under the circumstances.

"I know you're busy, Eminence, what with your many days in Rome, but I must see you tomorrow."

"Why not today?" he quickly replied.

"I need some time, perhaps an hour or so."

"Fine, Karen, tomorrow morning will be fine."

"You're sure that you can spare the time, Eminence?"

"I told you before, Karen, I always can find time for you."

"Thank you. I'll be in shortly to update you on all that has transpired clerically. Bishop Reynolds will be in at five this afternoon to brief you on other diocesan business.

He walked away from Karen, knowing full well her romance with Tom Kiely was going strong. No doubt she was about to tell him of her impending marriage. There was no time for that right now, so he pushed it from his mind and got to his cluttered desk.

Reynolds arrived promptly at five and briefed Farley on the state of the diocese. After the briefing, Reynolds began to talk to Farley of the negative rumblings coming from the faithful on his minority housing report. While he agreed with Farley in theory, he was still staunchly conservative concerning the funding of such a project. At times, their exchange could be heard down the hall by Karen. She kept her mind on her work in an effort to complete her tasks and get home. It was well past five.

The following morning dawned beautifully, but it did nothing to calm Karen's anxiety about confronting Farley on the change her life was about to undergo. She prepared herself hastily and drank only a cup of coffee before heading to the cardinal's residence.

Upon arrival, she quickly looked through the paper and noticed on page two an article on the papal marriage commission. She was able to glean enough from the article to see that Farley and his group voted to leave the annulment process as is. They commented on the vote being very close, and Farley at that point was leaning conservatively. Needless to say, she was very disappointed.

She entered Farley's office, and he greeted her warmly. She handed him the paper which she had refolded very carefully so as not to alert him that she had already perused it. Farley knew what she was going to talk about, so he asked her to make herself comfortable and he would be a good listener.

"Eminence, I don't know how to tell you this but I'll try. Tom and I are getting married in two weeks and as much as I would like a Catholic ceremony, I know it is out of the question. So we will be married in a civil ceremony. I realize that this will mean that I must give up my position here with you, but I do what I must. I love God. I love my church. I have enjoyed working for you, and I love you. But my love of a particular man and my desire to spend the rest of my life with him is too great. I personally feel that he has played a great part in bringing me closer to God, and I can't believe that a loving God formed an authoritarian church that would not allow us to form a marriage union. Sometimes people cannot continue to live together. They are not permitted to get on with their lives and perhaps find a new better experience with another person. I find that hard to accept. My love for God is as strong as it's ever been and my love for my church will never die. However, I also love Tom Kiely and I see nothing wrong concerning a marriage to him." Karen stopped at this point as if to invite Farley's opinion. She got what she wanted.

Farley, not often lacking for words, fumbled for the right ones. He asked her, "Is your conscience truly at rest with this decision?"

"Yes," she blurted.

"Well then, while I cannot give you my blessing, I certainly wish you and Tom much happiness and success with your lives."

"I suppose you'll want my resignation, so I'll—"

Farley interrupted. "Hold on! No! I don't want your resignation." He did think though that it would be awkward to retain her.

Karen replied brusquely, "But I think my position here as a woman married to a divorced man would be tenuous and I insist on resigning."

In reality, Farley was relieved, but he still felt deeply for Karen. "If it will make you feel better then I will accept your resignation."

That remark opened the floodgates and Karen began to cry and vent her anger. "Why does the commission seem to be in favor of change and yet you and the American group maintain a conservative posture? You have so much influence."

Farley realized at that point that she must have looked at the paper. He hadn't opened it yet, and he quickly deduced that there must have been an article on the commission. Otherwise, how would she have this information?

Karen continued. "It seems to me that you have the power to ease the situation for the Tom Kiely's and Karen's of the world, yet you are remaining steadfast against the tide. I love a fellow human being enough to share the rest of my life with, and yet to do that, I must give up my church. My church is my liaison with God. I can no longer enjoy that relationship because a group of celibates made up some so called 'rules.'"

Farley struggled to remain calm. "We've been through this before Karen, and you're way off the mark. I told you before that the love of a man and woman is sacred and beautiful and should be preserved. It is not something to be turned on and off at a person's whim. Preservation of the sacredness of marriage is what's at stake—not rules, as you call them, made by celibate men."

Karen sensed that Farley was becoming upset, so she made an attempt to dial things down. "Eminence, don't you see what I'm going through and thousands of others just like me? If you do, why are you bucking the trend of the commission?"

"Karen, my dear, this commission isn't a contest to see who has the most influence. This is a forum of free ideas by the top thinkers of the church to arrive at a consensus of opinion, which, by the way, will be nonbinding. I am being open-minded but my decision will have to square with my conscience and my church. The decision you are looking for is a long way off."

Karen wept, and as she dabbed her eyes, she said, "Thank you, Eminence, for all you've done for me, and I don't mean that sarcastically. I will remain here if it pleases you until I can train a new secretary."

Farley figured it was best to leave it at that, and so he gently kissed Karen and said, "I'll be of whatever help I can be to you until you leave. I expect, however, to remain in contact with you. You're a good person, Karen, and you've been a superlative assistant to me. You always are and always will be in my prayers."

She returned to her office.

CHAPTER TWELVE

Doctor Meyner was up early because he was anxious about his extraordinary patient, Mary O'Leary. As he prepared himself for his day, the sun was just making its appearance on the eastern horizon. The sun's rays came trickling through the columns of the high-rise buildings in his neighborhood, thus giving little light to the interiors of his apartment. Mary's condition was declining far faster then he had originally thought. The past week had arrived quickly and had sped away just as rapidly. He would stop at Mary's apartment early to see how she was doing, knowing full well that her condition would be deteriorating. The nurse that Ann Lincroft had secured for her would update Meyner on his arrival.

His arrival at the apartment confirmed his analysis of Mary's condition. She only had hours left—much less time than he originally gave her on his first examination of her and her rapidly advancing cancer. She was tenacious and still a great inspiration to him. Her spirits seemed to be more up than her condition would lead one to believe.

Meyner did his best to comfort her and directed the nurse to call Cardinal Farley. Farley had not said Mass yet, but nevertheless, he gathered the anointing oils he would administer to Mary. He was quickly on his way.

Meyner gave some instructions to the nurse to make Mary's last hours as comfortable as possible. He then had to leave for the hospital for his morning appointments. He wrapped Mary's hand in his and told her he had to leave. In his own way, he was saying goodbye. He marveled at what a great person she was, and he felt a deep reluctance to leave her, but he had no choice. He knew Farley would be arriving shortly and would prepare her for her final journey.

Some minutes after Meyner exited the apartment, Farley arrived. Mary welcomed him and weakly asked him to hear her confession. The nurse immediately left the room. Farley walked over to her bedside and pulled up a chair right next to her bed. Mary could barely utter the words, "I'm sorry." Amazingly, after Farley administered absolution, Mary seemed to perk up.

In a much stronger voice but just barely a loud whisper, she looked at Farley and said, "I know my time is almost at an end, so I must tell you this. I have so much empathy for Karen. Oh how much I wanted a family of my own. I went out with a fine lad by the name of Jim McFarland. Long into the relationship, we discussed marriage. Then he shocked me. He told me he had been married before, but only briefly, as though it didn't count." She paused to take a breath.

Even though she seemed to be doing better, it was still a struggle to continue to talk. Farley continued to listen. "I knew that as long as he was married in the church, that his first marriage did count. My faith meant too much to me, so I broke off the relationship. I cried for weeks. I never developed a real interest in any other man. I never got the chance to attain what I really wanted in life, a husband and family. I never became bitter, but I was very disappointed." She paused again and managed a weak smile and stared at Farley. "Taking care of God's priests was apparently my task in life, but I never knew the joy of my own family. I went by the rules." She closed her eyes momentarily and took another deep breath.

Farley thought about the remarks he made to Ann about Mary's seemingly dull existence. She seemed to enjoy life so much when she participated. He simply had no idea of the magnitude of the sacrifice she made in her life. Farley brought out the oils and administered the sacrament of the sick to Mary. He anointed her with the oils and said the proper prayers. Mary, again weakly, was able to recite with Farley the Lord's Prayer. She then drifted off to sleep.

Farley looked down on her and pondered the so called "rules". This was the second time in the last few weeks that he had heard that term used. *She lived her entire life without the one thing she wanted most desperately, a family.* It had simply never occurred to him. *I should have gotten to know her better. What a life. To be able to make that sacrifice and to make it alone. I never knew, and apparently, no one else did except God. What an inspiration. She obeyed the "rules" and convinced herself that the church directed her to its priests. Inwardly, she was not happy, but she convinced others she was. So, in a sense the laws of our church forced her to live a long life and never achieve what could easily have been attained. She loved McFarland so much that there could not be another. But she loved her church even more and literally gave her life for that. Her reward in heaven will be great and she will have more happiness then she could ever have imagined. How many others suffer so much to stay in the graces of the church?*

He continued to gaze at Mary as her breathing became more difficult. He thought about the marriage commission and its possibility of making changes. His heart ached as he thought of the thousands of Mary O'Learys leaving this life without a taste of their human desires to be experienced. He thought about how he had an idea of being released from his vows, but yet was steadfast, so far, in objecting to any easement of the marriage vows.

He asked the nurse to attend to Mary as it appeared that her breathing was becoming more difficult. Her eyes were still closed, and Farley leaned over and kissed her. The nurse looked at Farley and whispered to him that the end was very near. He would wait. In a matter of minutes, Mary O'Leary breathed her last. The nurse adjusted the bedclothes and left the room. Farley thought of the O'Learys, the McFarlands, the Michaels, and the Kielys of the world and wept bitterly. He could not be consoled.

Upon returning to the residence, Farley stopped at Karen's office to tell her of Mary's death. Karen could tell he was distraught and offered him comfort. He hugged Karen and thought about Mary's last words. Since he considered them a matter of confession, Karen would never know how closely Mary's life paralleled hers.

Farley went to his office to contemplate Mary's eulogy. It was so soon after the death of his dear friend Charles Lincroft. It was difficult to concentrate since the marriage commission and its work loomed largely in front of him now.

It was a cloudy, cool morning as the casket carrying Mary O'Leary's body was brought into the cathedral and then carried down the aisle. Bishop Reynolds and Monsignor Beardsley were also on the altar alongside Farley. They proceeded from the altar and down the aisle to bless the casket. Farley quickly thought about these two people and their recent deaths. He was associated with popes, mayors, and various other elites, but Charles Lincroft and Mary O'Leary were people he dealt with on a human level. They were people he could be natural with and now they were gone.

As he led the casket down the aisle, he noticed very few people in the cathedral. He did see Karen, Tom, and, of course, Ann. He wanted this to be a beautiful special Mass. The Mass is always a magnificent offering to God, but this time it would also be a tribute to a woman who had labored, in sacrifice, to the priests at the cardinal's residence. It was a beautiful Mass. Farley's wish was fulfilled. He delivered a marvelous eulogy, and he hoped that the Mass was as pleasing to God as it was to those who participated.

It was a fitting farewell to a woman who had devoted her life to the church.

It was cool and slightly windy at the cemetery, but those in attendance placed their flowers on Mary's casket with the full realization that she had attained a fitting place in eternity with God. She was in happiness beyond compare.

Karen and Tom went their separate ways at the conclusion of the cemetery prayers as did Ann. Farley returned to the residence and sat in quiet contemplation about the events of the past weeks.

CHAPTER THIRTEEN

Pope Clement was so elated about the progress of the marriage commission that he mentally pushed other priorities aside and made the commission top priority. He wanted to call another meeting sooner rather than later while there was still momentum in the commission. He was hoping they could come to a conclusion much earlier then anticipated. Their conclusions would not become dogma, but they would provide an incentive so the church could look at the sacrament of matrimony and deal with the problems it presented in the present times. It appeared that Clement wanted to look at this whole issue very intensely.

Farley was still in a somber mood; thoughts of the recent deaths of the two persons close to him were still hanging over him. He was startled by the ringing of the phone. Ann was calling him to ask him to dinner. He immediately thought it would be a good thing considering how low Ann was feeling, but then he thought of temptation. He quickly dismissed the thoughts of temptation because he knew Charles's death was too recent and Ann was too vulnerable. He knew he possessed enough strength as a priest and as a man to avoid temptation with Ann. He respected his friend Charles too much, and more importantly, his resolve was strong since his last confession. He still valued his priesthood greatly.

He had barely replaced the phone on the receiver when it rang again. He was informed that Cardinal Spencer was on the phone. "Harold, you folks on the marriage commission are apparently doing a great job. The Holy Father has advised me to get you all together for the next meeting and possibly come up with conclusions. He's very pleased with the progress to date and doesn't want the momentum to lag. How about in the next two weeks?"

"Are you asking me?" Farley replied.

Spencer chuckled and said, "No, I guess I'm telling you. It doesn't appear that there is any room for objection. He makes it pretty clear that he will be ready in two weeks."

"Wow. I have to put the finishing touches on my final report to our city's housing authority and I have a number of other duties to attend to, but I'm sure I'll find the time."

After some small talk, the phone call ended and Farley felt suddenly overwhelmed. He paused in silence and whispered a prayer for strength. He thought his trips to Rome were becoming like a commute.

Karen walked into his office with some more paperwork for him. As she placed the papers on his desk, she notified him that she had met with several good candidates who she felt were qualified to take her position in the office. She asked if he would like to interview them. He told her to arrange it as soon as possible, but he would be relying heavily on her recommendations.

"I will truly miss you, Karen. Your dedication to the job and to me was truly outstanding. I cannot emphasize enough how I wish you all the best in your future life. You are a wonderful person."

All Karen could do was mutter, "Thank you." She paused and added, "I enjoyed working here very much and felt it was a privilege to be of service to you."

Farley looked at her and exclaimed, "Now don't forget we're all going out to dinner for your so-called retirement."

She managed a chuckle and said, "That would be great."

Farley joined Ann in a cocktail before supper at her home and their discussion was about a number of things—the brief, but meaningful, friendship between Ann and Mary and his secretary's leaving. Regarding his secretary, Farley said he would soon be interviewing for Karen's successor and how much he was relying on her input for filling that position.

Ann asked him why she was leaving. Farley replied, "It was her decision based on her upcoming marriage. She didn't want to give scandal. I offered that she could stay, but she insisted, and after some thought, I felt it was probably the best course of action."

Ann then asked how the new housekeeper was adjusting and Farley said, "Very well. I thought it would be tough replacing Mary, but so far, she's been doing quite well." Then he quickly changed the subject and told Ann about his upcoming return to Rome.

She commented, "My, your frequent flyer miles must surely be piling up. I guess Clement is very pleased with the work the commission has done so far. He's really accelerating the progress."

Farley replied, "I don't want to oversimplify our task, but I do hope we can wrap it up and that it leads to a solution for marriage woes for Catholics who are in bad positions in that regard. I'm just not sure, myself, if there's any way we can change things."

"Why do you say that?"

"Because I favor the conservative view that marriage is a sacrament and cannot be dissolved. But the liberals make their point about changing times and working on some way to reconcile with so many who find themselves in a bad situation in an existing marriage and proceed to find a more loving relationship with someone else. Poor Karen comes immediately to mind. She's getting married shortly in a civil ceremony and is distressed that she can't formally receive God's blessing through

His church. My heart aches for her, and I pray for a solution to this dilemma."

Ann then shocked him by saying, "What about us?"

"You mean as friends?"

"No. I mean as more than that."

Farley was dumbstruck. "Ann, you are a beautiful woman, and it takes all within me to resist loving you physically and intensely. But I love my priesthood and I have taken a vow of celibacy before God. I am truly tormented, but choosing to be released from my vows would be a monumental decision for me to make and would have grave implications for our church."

"I'll give you some breathing room and change the subject."

"I guess that's a good idea. But to let you know, I've given much consideration to asking Clement personally to release me from my vows and return me to the ranks of the laity."

"You would do that for me?" Ann gasped in reply. "Don't make any hasty decisions, Harold. I think I love you, but I'm still mourning Charles's death and I don't fully trust my emotions yet. But give me some time and you do likewise. This would be a major step for both of us."

They continued their meal and even discussed the life of Mary whom they both thought they had known too little of. They also talked of Karen and made small talk in an effort to keep their true feelings at low ebb.

After dinner, as the hour grew late, Farley kissed Ann gently and thanked her for a great evening, but they both knew that there was much on both of their minds.

A week went by and Farley was preparing to leave for Rome. He had worked diligently on the final and official conclusion of the clergy report to the city housing commission on the topic of housing for the minorities and the disadvantaged. He had no time for Ann or anyone else as he felt a compelling need to finish the report before he left. He did manage, however, to interview two candidates for Karen's replacement. He and Karen had agreed that the best qualified candidate was a young lady by the name of Jane Hernandez. She was about the same age as Karen and was currently employed at a law firm. She was managing to get acclimated to the cardinal's office by coming in prior to normal starting time so she could complete her days at the law firm before she started at the cardinal's office. Farley thanked both she and Karen for putting in the extra hours. He knew she was a good replacement just by the fact that she was giving her previous employer a proper amount of time before she left. She didn't just walk out on them.

Karen walked into his office and told Farley how pleased she was with Jane's enthusiasm and her grasp of the tasks she would be performing. She knew Farley was pressed for time, but she asked him if he would be able to attend her wedding and reception over the weekend. He regretted having to say no to Karen, but he thought it would be best not to attend. He did say, however, that he would be more than pleased to take Tom and her to dinner Friday night as a combination retirement and great start to the rest of her life. She was not surprised at his reluctance to attend her civil ceremony but was thankful of his offer of a farewell dinner.

Farley asked Karen if she thought that his going to Rome on Sunday and her being away for her honeymoon would be a trying situation for Jane. Karen didn't think so since she was pretty well acclimated and Bishop Reynolds would certainly be considerate toward her. Farley accepted the explanation but was not totally comfortable with the situation.

He quickly got back to his report for the housing commission. There would be no surprises. It was definitely geared toward spending more money to build more adequate housing for those of little means. He was undaunted concerning his individual opinions and those of his fellow clergymen. He was still aware, however, that it would reverberate among the conservative-minded people in his life. That was just something he had to accept.

Karen and Tom held each other's hands at the civil ceremony for their marriage. They each looked into the other's eyes full of love and vowed to honor and cherish each other. After their wedding kiss, they left the ceremony for a small reception with their immediate families. Cardinal Farley was conspicuous by his absence but they were comfortable and were thankful for the previous night's dinner with the cardinal. Karen still kept a thought on the back burner that perhaps Farley could wield enough influence on the marriage commission to change things about the church's stance on marriage.

Cardinal Harold Farley was putting the finishing touches together for his return to Rome to finalize the marriage commission's findings. He also had distracting thoughts about his relationship with Ann.

Should he go directly to his friend, Clement, and ask for release from his vows? If so, how would he fare in his life away from the priesthood? His love for Ann was intense, but his love of God and loyalty to his faith were equally intense, and he was tormented by having to make a choice.

He prayed to the Holy Spirit for guidance. He immediately received a calming thought that perhaps Ann's feelings for him were not genuine and possibly the result of her extreme sorrow over Charles's passing and her newfound loneliness. He comforted himself with that thought and continued to prepare for his trip to Rome. Perhaps immersing himself in the marriage commission's work would rid him of the thought that Ann really loved him. Perhaps his being away from her would allow her to think more clearly and realize that her affection for him was based on loneliness. She would appreciate the time apart to adjust to being alone and not be dependent on him. He continued praying to the Holy Spirit for guidance and help.

CHAPTER FOURTEEN

Farley began his day early, as usual, and knelt down before the altar in the Lady Chapel prior to beginning the celebration of the Mass. He offered prayers for a safe journey to Rome. He also offered prayers to the Holy Spirit to inspire all those charged with the task of reviewing the matrimonial laws of the church. He prayed for strength in his priesthood and a longing to lessen his intimate thoughts concerning his friend Ann. He loved her intensely and knew the difficulties that lay ahead in his ability to maintain the relationship as platonic.

After Mass, he returned to the kitchen where Marcia had his breakfast waiting along with the morning paper. He noticed nothing in the paper on the final report to the mayor regarding the minority and disadvantaged housing problem in the city. This affirmed his trust in the other members of the clergy concerning leaking any information to the press. The media would have to wait for the mayor to release the report. In any event, it was mostly a rehash of the preliminary report with a few minor changes. He breathed a sigh of relief that it was done. He was content with his contributions to the report. He hastily finished his breakfast and breezed through the remainder of the paper before heading to his office.

First to arrive in his office was Bishop Reynolds who discussed with Farley the administration of the diocese in Farley's absence. After that discussion, Reynolds wished him a safe journey and said he would pray for the Spirit to enlighten Farley and his efforts for the marriage commission. Farley explained to Reynolds that the commission's previous findings seemed to be leaning toward a more lenient annulment process. However, a very close percentage of commission members were still promulgating that the present annulment process was still viable. Farley told Reynolds that the issue was extremely contentious and that the commission was very closely divided on the issue. He then added, "You have no idea how important I think this issue is. I'm still totally tossed as to how to deal with it. Arguments for change are compelling, but I still feel strongly about the sacrament of matrimony and its dignity. I don't see how we can affect change in marriage because of its sacramental status. Then again, how should our church reach out to those in bad marriages?"

Reynolds replied, "I'm glad it's you that's dealing with the problem and not me. But if the mayor releases your minority housing report while you're gone, I'll have to run interference for you. Then I will have to deal with the problem."

Farley chuckled. "Just tell the folks that they'll have to await my return. I have confidence that you can handle it though."

"I'm in your corner on this issue mainly because I think it's the only position we can take. Even our conservative friends will have to come to that conclusion no matter the extra expense. I've sort of abandoned my conservative bent on this issue and opened my eyes to all sides of the problem. We just can't leave our poorer neighbors out in the streets and hopeless."

They continued to talk with Reynolds wrapping things up with, "I will steer the diocese to the best of my ability in the absence of the captain."

Farley shook his hand with a hearty, "Thanks, Jim."

In a short while, Monsignor Beardsley came into the office to see if Farley wanted to discuss anything with his spiritual advisor. An avalanche of thoughts concerning Ann and his relationship with her coursed through his head, but inwardly he felt the Holy Spirit was giving him strength, so he politely told Beardsley he had nothing earth-shattering to discuss. He definitely would not tell him at this time of even the fleeting thoughts he had of asking Clement to laicize him. He felt strong enough to conquer that inclination. He asked Beardsley for a blessing, and after that they engaged in small talk. Beardsley left his office, but he still wondered inwardly whether or not Farley was over his infatuation with Ann.

Jane came into Farley's office with his travel arrangements. Part of the arrangements was for a hired limousine to transport him to the airport. The diocese had long since dropped having a limo available for the cardinal's use in the interests of economy. But Farley always had a limo available to him through Charles Lincroft. Now that Charles was gone, he would have to make do. He would be traveling without the other clerics on the plane going over as they had all made different arrangements from their hometowns. He spent the rest of his day tying up the loose ends. He closed his office, said good-bye to Jane, and went over to the Cathedral to kneel before Our Lady's altar and pray. There was much on his mind.

Ann was in her apartment in the city looking through the stack of mail that lay in a pile in front of her. The Lincrofts had always had their business mail addressed to the city apartment, while personal mail was addressed to their home in Rosewood. She opened one of the envelopes bearing a law firm return address. It contained a letter to the effect that she was to be part of a class action suit being brought on behalf of the surviving families of those killed in the plane crash. They were seeking two million dollars per next of kin or closest survivor to those killed. The letter advised the concerned that the airline offer of one hundred thousand to the nearest survivor was totally inadequate. Ann was disgusted and put the letter down. She thought, *How crude this is—attempting to put a value on human life. Was Charles worth one*

hundred thousand or two million? I would pay ten times that amount to have him back." She picked up the letter again and looked at the myriad of forms that were enclosed—a tremendous amount of information to be perused and signed off on.

My God, she thought, *I'll need my attorney to interpret all this before I can sign anything.* She then sighed. *What's the use in all of this? It's not going to bring Charles back and I don't need the money. Charles certainly provided for me adequately. But maybe I can do some good with it in Charles's name.* She decided to bring it to her attorney. *He can help me with the paperwork. Besides, he was so helpful to me on the automobile incident, I'm sure this paperwork to him is small potatoes.*

She walked into the kitchen to pour herself a glass of water and sat down. Thoughts raced through her mind. She had loved Charles with her very being and she missed him terribly, but he was gone from her life forever. However, she still had to go on living. Could she love again like that? Did she want to? She still felt young enough to love again, but it wouldn't be the same as Charles.

Perhaps a new love would open an entirely new chapter in her life. She would never stop loving Charles, but he was no longer here and she had to continue to live. She felt she could love again and then the thought, *Could Harold Farley be that person? I'm relying on Harold because he can comfort me at this time, but I have to allow more time to find out whether or not I am allowing the comfort he gives me at a vulnerable time in my life to be interpreted as romantic love. I will give it some time but I will not deprive myself of Harold's companionship. I am glad, however, that he will be out of the country for a while because I think the time separated is a good time to think.*

Farley returned to Rome on a beautiful day. He thought, *Why am I surprised at the bright sunshine? Doesn't the sun always shine*

in Rome? He did not ask for but did receive the same room assignment. This time he greeted the room with an air of levity. He thought it would humble him and he could offer it in atonement for his sins. He unpacked and knelt at the prie-dieu. He offered a prayer of thanksgiving for his safe journey. He also offered a prayer to the Holy Spirit to guide him on the work of the marriage commission. He finally prayed to allow himself to be free from thoughts of Ann. He knew that if he could immerse himself in his work, his stay in Rome would be so much easier to bear.

At dinner that night, the entire cast was assembled. Farley sat with Josephson, while Carnavale, Feeney, and Carson sat at another table near them. Farley thought this was good since liberals and conservatives sitting together would surely result in great dialogue. He laughed to himself when he thought of how the Holy Spirit worked in strange ways. Josephson and Farley talked about the upcoming assembly and what would be decided in the ensuing days of this final assembly of the commission. If significant change was promulgated by the commission, it would be revolutionary toward the church's stance on the divorced and remarried.

Farley broke in with, "I'm still in so much doubt about how much latitude we have in making any changes. After all, matrimony is a sacrament. Can we tweak it?"

"Well let's keep in mind that while the pope is asking us to bring before him a conclusion, it will still be non-binding," Josephson replied.

Farley continued, "I realize that basically we're looking to ease the annulment procedure, but I still feel that if we ease it, the result is a lessening of the importance of marriage and consequent demeaning of the sacrament. I have to feel, however, that Clement is open concerning change, or he wouldn't have accelerated the work of the commission. I'm also reticent about change because I think of the spot we would put Clement in if our commission proposes radical change. Think back to the commission Pope Paul convened to look at birth control. Their conclusion was that birth control, in some instances, could be permitted as long as the couple kept an open mind about bearing a child if one was conceived. They sighted that the love of a man and woman in the marital act could be interpreted as a means to binding the union besides being a means of conception, and therefore, a very important part of the sexual union. In other words, they didn't think that conception always had to be the primary reason for a couple to engage in the sex act. They felt that the love of man and wife was equally important. The findings of that commission tormented Paul. The results of the commission that he formed caused him no end of anguish which, I personally believe, caused his health to fail. The issue consumed him because the bottom line was the commission opened up the idea that conception did not always have to be the prime reason for the sex act. The love of two people for each other was also extremely important. Paul did not accept the findings much to the chagrin of the commission and the world's Catholics. I hope we don't bring that anguish to Clement."

Josephson said, "I'm still sure that the commission will leave the whole marriage issue intact. I don't think there are enough of us on the commission that are leaning to any great change, but after the last meeting it's very close."

Farley interjected, "I still see a problem for Clement no matter how it comes down. He would have to deal with the Curia if there is a recommendation for significant change. On the other hand, if there is no movement for change, he's left to wrestle with the liberal faction. He's in a tough spot. Truthfully, I feel for him because I'm still sitting on the fence and it's tormenting me. Once our findings are given to him, I pass the torment to him."

Josephson looked at him and all he could reply was, "I guess he asked for the problem."

"Yes, he did. I truly hope he can work with it."

They hastily finished their meal and decided it best to work the room. Farley was well known to most of the prelates, some of them cardinals as he was. He engaged in small talk with those he met, but invariably, the subject changed to the marriage commission. He felt a little pressured when one of the Italian cardinals told him his opinion would be highly regarded. He said in broken English, "The other members of the Curia and the pope speak very highly of you." He then quipped, "You could be the first American pope." Farley accepted the praise and thanked the cardinal for his support. He continued to work the room.

Karen and Tom were enjoying their honeymoon and were presently at supper. Karen brought up Farley's marriage commission. She started to discuss it when Tom interrupted. "I'm good with our decision to marry. I love you and I wish you wouldn't fret."

"Oh, I'm good with it also, but I just wish the church would adopt a different stand and see if there can be some resolution to the plight of the divorced and remarried. I hope the commission can find some way to ease the annulment process."

"I don't think that will happen," Tom replied. "There's a lot more to it than just changing their minds. And there is an annulment process already in place, as inadequate as it sometimes is. My conscience is clear in that there was no hope for my first marriage. There was no way we could stay together. I don't feel that a loving God would ask me to lead a life of celibacy because our first fallible choices were wrong. Sometimes the human condition changes people and what starts out with hope and promise changes dramatically. After all, a religious can seek release from their vows, while a husband or wife, who is forced to separate, must never know the joy of another loving relationship unless they can secure an annulment which is difficult at best. As humans, we make mistakes. Why are we expected to be infallible in our choice of partners, especially if those problems develop after the marriage? I don't intend to drive myself crazy over the so-called rules. I love you and at this moment expect to spend the rest of my life with you. I know God loves me. I know he doesn't love me less because I had severe problems in my first marriage and chose to start a new relationship with someone I love and cherish. God sees all. He sees the disaster of my first marriage and has allowed me to find a new life. I am grateful. I don't intend to lose any sleep and I don't think you should either."

Karen immediately grabbed his hand, leaned over and kissed him. "I love you very much."

Before Farley retired for the evening, he gave some thought to the next day's meetings. He then thought about Mary O'Leary and her broken romance. She had lived her whole life in sacrifice because of the love of a person she was not free to marry in the eyes of her beloved church. He thought, *I don't condone making the annulment process any easier, but we've got to look at individual cases more closely and perhaps offer people some relief. Perhaps if Mary had been able to marry her suitor, her life would have had significantly more fulfillment.*

He grew tired and began his evening prayers. He prayed as usual for guidance, for Mary's soul, and of course, for Karen and Tom. He prayed obviously for Ann and at the same time prayed for relief from temptation. But still, he could not rid himself of thoughts concerning a meeting with Clement to discuss relief from his vows.

158

CHAPTER FIFTEEN

A n early sliver of sunlight squeezed through the tiny window in Farley's room or "cell" as he referred to it. It nudged his eyes open, and in a matter of seconds, he awoke with vigor and in good spirits to face the day ahead. This was going to be the week that he and his fellow clergy would be making some possibly major changes in the annulment process. Maybe they would come to the conclusion that things should not change at all.

Under any circumstance, it appeared to be the church's attempt at possibly modifying canon law by the opinion of a commission—a touch of democracy, as opposed to the authority of the pope and the Curia. Clement was a very well-loved pope and an action like this at his behest was just one indication that he was well loved. He seemed to be opening the doors to input from a wider area of church hierarchy. Farley knelt at the prie-dieu and said his morning prayers and then proceeded to the bathroom for a shower.

After his shower, he gathered himself together and finished his dressing with his cassock and red sash. He walked across the beautiful Vatican grounds to the building where Pope Clement would normally have his indoor audiences. They would be using this building to conduct the business of the marriage commission since Clement's audiences were outdoors at this time of year. He walked through the building on his way to the cafeteria to start his day with breakfast. He marveled at the efficiency of the Vatican in being able to set up a temporary but fully functional kitchen in a small area of the meeting hall. Surprisingly, everything looked good, but he decided to opt for a smaller meal and chose toasted muffins and coffee. It appeared that he was the first to arrive, but in a matter of seconds, the rest of the prelates started to trickle in. Farley chatted with his American friends but branched out to the Asian group with which he hadn't had much previous contact. The cardinal from India, Rene Singh, was the leader of the Asian delegation, and he greeted Farley warmly. From previous meetings, Farley was well aware that Singh himself was supportive of leaving the annulment process as is, thinking it to be adequate. He didn't want to change anything about the sacrament of matrimony.

Singh expressed his concern at the prior meeting's consensus in favor of change although it was an extremely narrow lead. He encouraged Farley to take a position of leadership and speak on behalf of not doing anything that would remotely lead to the destruction of the family. He urged Farley to become the spokesman for the conservative side and help preserve the sanctity of marriage. Farley replied that being the spokesman for either side would be the call of the commission members. Singh told him, "I would vote for you to be spokesman and I know most of the prelates on the conservative side would vote for you also. You are well thought of and your opinion has weight."

He carried on a small conversation with Singh and they parted ways to become engaged with others at the meeting. Farley briefly spoke to Cardinal Tessier of France. Tessier was the group leader for most of Europe including Russia. At the time, Tessier was standing with Cardinal Fiorvante who headed up the group of Curial members. Again, after exchanging small talk, a fleeting thought coursed through Farley's mind. *Those two gentlemen appear to have the inside track to succeed Clement. But Clement is younger then they are, so that doesn't seem like it will happen.* Farley also allowed the thought to cross his mind that he was not a real admirer of either of the two and Clement was certainly closer to him anyway. But he did give them credit for being good priests and always acting with the best of intentions.

Bishop Reynolds looked at the morning paper and the headlines blared the findings of the clergy commission on minority housing. The leading clergy of the city found that the city needed to find ways to increase revenue and fund housing for the poor with the daunting goal that no one should be homeless. He knew the phones would be ringing soon, and he probably would not be able to dodge the issue. He would have to organize his thoughts and comment on the report as best as he could in Farley's absence. He continued to read conservative columnist Henley's opinion on the report and, as expected, it was derogatory. "Why is the liberal answer to every problem of the poor to keep throwing money at it? When will they learn that the problems don't go away with a sudden infusion of the taxpayer's money? We need to examine the root causes of poverty and find ways to make the chronically unemployed employable, thus earning money and contributing to society. I agree we can't tolerate homeless people, but let's think outside the box. Let's just not agree to throw more money out to the poor and then wash our hands and go on with our lives thinking we have solved the problem."

Reynolds read that far and put the paper down. "Maybe Henley had a thought there. Now how do I deal with this?" He summed up Henley's article with the same conclusion Henley had concerning Farley's thoughts in the preliminary report. "Why does it seem that the church conservatives are so politically liberal?" Reynolds gathered his thoughts and would answer the media's questions on the issue, but he would make it perfectly clear to them that they were his thoughts and not Farley's. They would simply have to await Farley's return to hear his comments.

The clergy gathered in the cavernous auditorium and quickly took their places. Cardinal Fiorvante called the meeting to order with a prayer and followed that by reading a message from Clement asking the Holy Spirit to guide them in their deliberations.

Fiorvante then spelled out that the six main groups should get together within each separate group and spend the next few hours arriving at a summation to be submitted later that day. Noticeably missing from the meeting were the two prelates from South America. Because of political problems in their respective countries, they had both declined to serve on the commission. That explanation was accepted by Clement. The summations at the end of the day by those prelates who were present would provide a guide as to what determination would possibly be made by the group. This would provide a track for the commission to use in hopefully bringing this matter to a final vote by week's end. Fiorvante stressed again that the pope knew this was a monumental task for the commission, but he had every hope that they would come to a conclusion that would be taken into consideration for implementation. But, he emphasized strongly, any decisions by the commission would be non-binding. The clergy on the commission were well aware of that anyway and chuckled to themselves about Clement covering all his bases.

Ann called her lawyer and explained to him the letter she had received regarding the class action suit against the airline. Her attorney said he would examine the letter and explain to her what her options might be. He also advised her that this would most likely be a long, drawn-out process considering the amount of money involved and the number of people. He told her that she should examine her options carefully before signing on, but he would be happy to look it over. She told him the money was not important to her personally, but she thought that if the suit was successful, she could put the money to good use in Charles's name. She scheduled an appointment with him for the next day.

Farley and Archbishop McConnell of Ireland were engaged while other members of their local group were split into other groups. McConnell advised Farley that even though his country and the United Kingdom were in his local group, the remainder of the European countries and all of Russia were under Tessier of France. Tessier was extremely conservative, while McConnell felt that most of the European countries were for an easing of the annulment process. They then joined others of their group and continued deliberating and anxiously awaiting a break to enjoy a cup of coffee.

Just as luck would have it, Fiorvante called for a break, and they eagerly gravitated towards the nearest dispenser of coffee. While sipping a cup that was not very good, but tolerable, Farley got together with the other American prelates. Josephson took the opportunity to explain to Farley that he thought they had a golden opportunity to provide a less cluttered pathway for so many people to the full state of grace within the Mystical Body of Christ and they should take advantage of that opportunity. Farley countered with, "And just how do we accomplish that? Do we basically allow divorce and remarriage thus demeaning the sanctity of matrimony? Doesn't it say 'what God has joined together, let no man put asunder'?"

Josephson quickly retorted, "But we are acting with the guidance of the Holy Spirit and not as men."

"Be careful," Farley replied.

Carnavale came over to join the conversation and wanted to know if all of them would be able to come to some conclusion within the week that lay before them. He said that his friend,

Feeney, thought that their hands were tied. There was absolutely no way to go but to leave everything as it is.

Josephson replied, "I think we have a great opportunity to ease the annulment process, and we simply must find a means to make that happen. We would still examine each case carefully, but the ultimate goal would be to keep people firmly in the arms of Holy Mother church. That, of course, will take much work. Truly, the easier thing to do is nothing, but I think we should do the hard thing. Too many are falling by the wayside."

Farley could find no argument with that thought, and with that, he sat more firmly on the fence.

The afternoon was getting late, and it was time for the five national groups and curial group to summarize their discussions of the day. The first to be acknowledged was the European and Russian group under Tessier. It came as no surprise that Tessier would be their spokesman. While his group was a majority for change, it was no secret Tessier was not. Farley listened to Tessier's summation and was amazed at how forthcoming he was with options for the easement of the annulment process even when Tessier himself was not in favor of it. He injected some stimulating ideas, and Farley had to admire him for his open-mindedness.

Between Tessier and the next speaker (Singh, representing Asia), Farley gave a brief thought to Ann and thanked God that the meetings were consuming his thoughts for the most part, but he still had the gnawing sensation that he should talk to Clement about his dilemma. He agreed, however, to wait to the conclusion of the week of meetings and perhaps he would feel differently.

Cardinal Singh approached the microphone to speak for the Asian group. Although he spoke with a heavy Indian accent, it was only a minor struggle for Farley to hear his thoughts. He did not disappoint. While Farley knew which camp he was in, he spoke about listening to all aspects of the matter and praying for guidance. Farley admired him for that and was sincerely trying to latch on to some of the arguments for change. He laughed to himself that he would have to tell Singh that he was convincing him to go with the easement faction even though Singh was conservative. In an effort to be open-minded, Singh was convincing him, if not the others, to go against the very path Farley was treading. His Asian group, unlike Europe, was slightly in favor of not doing anything to change the existing process of annulment. They believed nothing can be done that would diminish the sacrament.

Cardinal Naguchi from Japan and also representing the Philippines was next to talk. A slight man, he looked older than his age as he was bent over slightly. Farley thought to himself he looked too old to be eligible to vote in a papal election, but he was at least five years under that age. Farley had to put on earphones for an English translation as Naguchi spoke only Japanese. *His meetings with Cardinal Gamallo of the Philippines must have been laborious with the language barrier*, Farley thought. As expected, the two votes in this group were in the camp of no change.

Naguchi addressed the group. "I know our good Holy Father is tormented by the plight of those in bad marriages who have legitimately contracted the sacrament of matrimony. I don't think we as a group have the power to change or amend the annulment procedure to make it easier to bring an end to a marriage. The present procedure is adequate and has served us well over these many years. I can't imagine the Holy Spirit would allow us to say, 'I made a mistake previously, so now I'm inspiring you to change things.' The present annulment process allows adequate means for a couple to separate. I realize that the determination of what constitutes the validity of the marriage is a bit strenuous and that possibly the Holy Father is asking us to simplify that part of the procedure. But, my colleagues, I fear that if we do that, we open the floodgates to abuse. We consequently belittle the sacrament of matrimony. No longer will a couple have to seriously look at their commitment to each other. To quote, 'well if it doesn't work out, we'll simply get an annulment.' The sacrament is very much demeaned. I implore you, my brother priests, to maintain the dignity of the sacrament of matrimony and all it implies."

Farley definitely agreed with him, but he thought again of the O'Learys and the Karens of the world and said to himself, *Is there truly anything I can do for these people? This is truly a dilemma.* It was getting late in the day, so prior to African Cardinal Obiajunwa presenting the summation of his group, Fiorvante called for the adjournment of that day's session and politely apologized to the African cardinal. He told him that obviously he would be first on the agenda the next morning.

Since it was so late in the day, a buffet supper was arranged for the group in the makeshift cafeteria set up for their use. They actually enjoyed the meal immensely, finding it hard to believe a catered meal would taste that good. After supper, Farley moved around the room and tried to engage as many of his fellow prelates as possible to extract from them a trend on their feelings. He kept coming to the conclusion that it was a very close decision and it reinforced his fence-sitting position.

The clergy started to slowly drift from the dining area and return to their rooms. After reaching his room, Farley quickly changed into his bedclothes and proceeded to kneel in prayer. As usual, he included in his evening prayers, a request to the Holy Spirit for guidance. Even though the day's activities carried out to a late hour, he managed to find the time to catch up on some reading before drifting off to sleep.

Another day quickly dawned, and all started arriving at the auditorium after taking care of their morning rituals. Fiorvante called the meeting to order with a much earlier start that morning in the hopes of closing out the meeting at a much earlier time.

As expected, Cardinal Obiajunwa was the first presenter of the day. He stepped up to the microphone and displayed a commanding presence. A tall, rather well-built man, he was very well thought of by the College of Cardinals. Obiajunwa had done much in Africa to evangelize the Catholic church and he was a deeply religious man. Four other African prelates were in his group, but none was a cardinal.

He began to speak. He spoke in English but with such a heavy accent that Farley was forced to use the earphones again. "My fellow clergymen, our group is split on this issue as it seems the other groups are. There is so much to be said about preserving the current annulment procedures and thus preserving the dignity of the marriage sacrament. But we are here to find a way, if possible, of finding an easier annulment process and still preserve the dignity of the marriage sacrament. Much needs to be said about the human condition and how the needs and wants of one person and those of another person either merge harmoniously in a marital relationship, or diverge, causing an intolerable situation. While I see the possibility of abuse here if we ease the annulment process, I also see the need for mercy and helpfulness in easing a major problem for those in a bad marriage. I think that we should be looking into a marriage preparation program that will have some teeth and hopefully prevent a couple from entering a potentially bad marriage. I know we already have the Cana program, but perhaps a more intense program would help where Cana seems to have failed. I hold the fifth and deciding vote in my group, and right now, I am not going to change the annulment procedure. However, I do agonize over all those who are caught in a bad marriage. I want our church to be loving and consoling, but I don't want it to lose its compass and its steadfastness. When we cast our votes and present our findings to His Holiness, let us do so with open-mindedness, but most assuredly under the advice of the Holy Spirit."

Farley thought it to be a very good presentation and a model of "almost" fence sitting. *To put it bluntly, do we want to change the annulment process and hold on to our Catholics? Does this demean the sacrament? Is that what we're actually doing? Do we vote for no change and continue to alienate so many of our faithful? If we vote for easement, will that necessarily open the floodgates of abuse?* He sipped some water as he prepared to deliver the summation for his group.

Just as Fiorvante was to call Farley up to the microphone, the assembly was startled by the arrival of Clement. He took a seat to the side of the room where, under normal circumstances, he would be front and center. The assembly acknowledged him with applause. He thanked them and urged them to continue. He put pressure on his friend Farley as he quipped, "I see I arrived just in time to see what my good friend, Cardinal Farley, is going to bring to this discussion."

Farley made a great effort to look at ease, but he was clearly uneasy as he delivered the group's summation. He had one eye on his report and one eye on his friend, Clement. He probably was looking for some sign from Clement of either approval or disapproval of what he was saying. Clement, however, remained stoic and did not tip his hand.

Farley began his summation by acknowledging that his group was currently split seven to five in favor of retaining all the means currently existing to incur an annulment of a marriage. But as he spoke, he thought to himself that he was doing exactly as Tessier and Singh. As they did, he spoke about all those in a bad marriage and how it would be possible to dissolve those marriages and allow those people to remain in full communion with the church if they should remarry. Farley even alluded to the fact that he had seen firsthand in people close to him the awful conflict that ensues if they can't receive an annulment and yet want to remarry. He explained the lack of joy in their lives because they are forced to make a choice of perhaps a new more loving relationship in the human realm or their ongoing love of their Catholic faith. "We, as a group, have been issued a major challenge by our Holy Father, and I pray the decision we make can bring peace to all and be blessed by our church."

While his summation was brief, the members of his group that were leaning to liberalization were well pleased with his presentation. But it brought Cardinal Feeney to re-examine his conservative stance. Farley's talk invited him to look at things differently, and while he wasn't sure he would change, he still felt that he needed to look closer to easing annulments.

Farley took his seat and again looked over at Clement but could detect nothing in his body language that would express to Farley how his talk went over.

Last to the microphone was the Curial group led by Fiorvante. It was generally assumed by all, that this group would undoubtedly be rigid in its stance. They believed that the annulment procedure, as it existed, was perfectly adequate for enabling a couple to separate and remarry. It puzzled Farley that they were so close to the pope, but that they would be thinking along those lines when clearly, it appeared that the pope was looking for some method to ease the current process. Fiorvante did not disappoint as he spoke firmly against not only "tweaking" the annulment process, but even if this group had the power to do anything of the sort. He remarked that Naguchi brought up a very important point when he spoke as to this group's power to make any changes at all. He did, however, express sorrow for the people in the dilemma about which their deliberations were now in progress. He emphasized his extreme sorrow regarding all in the position of having to make a decision of love of faith and love of another person. When Farley heard that he cringed knowing that he, as a priest, was in that same situation. Love of his priesthood and his faith or love of another person. Farley was really bothered by this thought for the first time in the midst of these meetings. He struggled to rid himself of the thoughts and concentrate on the task at hand. Fiorvante continued to talk and all listened intently. When he finished and returned to his seat as chairman of the assembly, he called for a short recess. After that recess, he would call for a straw vote to see in which direction the commission was heading.

After what many considered to be a very brief break, the assembly was recalled. Fiorvante asked that each group take a straw poll on how their thoughts were progressing. Later they would try to bring the day's proceedings to a conclusion. With an idea of which direction the commission was heading, the assembly's next days of meetings would be intense in coming up with a conclusion to draft and pass on to the Holy Father. Each group would get together for the next ten minutes to declare their straw votes and manufacture a guide for further deliberations.

After what seemed like a very brief ten minutes, Fiorvante again called everyone to order and asked for their votes. The European and Russian group, under Tessier, caused no surprise. Only two votes, one of them surely Tessier, for status quo. The remaining six votes were for exerting more effort in finding some way to ease the annulment process.

The African group, under Obiajunwa, was just as he had stated in his summation. The split was close with two votes to liberalize and three for no change.

Singh's Asian group was split evenly at three votes each. Naguchi and Gamallo were both in favor of no change.

Farley's group remained at seven for retaining the current annulment process and five for finding a way to ease the process.

Finally to everyone's surprise, the Curia had one vote to ease the process with the remaining three votes for retaining the current process.

What surprised Farley as he quickly totaled the results was that since their initial meetings, the tide had turned from liberal to conservative. It was still close, however, with a total of seventeen votes for change and twenty for status quo. He thought, *Some of my friends have changed their thinking to take the conservative side. This puzzles me because it appeared to me that most of the summations dwelled very carefully on both sides of the issue in spite of the spokesmen's beliefs.* But he thought it was still close and there really wasn't any consensus of opinion on one side. He thought that tonight he would have some fun trying to figure who had changed their minds and whether they would change them again before a final tally.

After a few brief remarks and a closing prayer by Fiorvante, the assembly adjourned for the day. It was not quite midafternoon, but after yesterday's lengthy session, this was a relief. Clement made no effort through the entire proceedings to show which side he was on, but he listened to all the small talks and remained stoic. After Clement left the auditorium after a brief conversation with Fiorvante, the remaining clergy took their leave. Fiorvante raised his voice and called to Farley just as he reached the doorway and said, "Clement has asked you, Tessier, and myself to join him for dinner this evening." Farley was surprised, but he knew that anything he would partake of with the pope would be better than the many small restaurants surrounding Vatican City. The unusually good buffet they enjoyed on the previous evening was not on tonight's agenda. Tonight was dinner on your own. Farley felt truly blessed to be asked by the pope to dine with him. He parted ways with Fiorvante and went looking for his American friends and a bite for late lunch.

Ann sat in her attorney's office and seemed to be very uneasy. She was his first client today at this early hour. Her attorney questioned her as to whether or not she was feeling well. She replied she was, but she just resented having to deal with this situation while Charles's death was still fresh on her mind. She knew it would never go away, but she wondered if perhaps she could put her ordeal off. But she also knew there was a deadline to meet, so she summoned all her fortitude and discussed the class action suit with her attorney. They decided she had nothing to lose, so he helped her fill out all the forms and assured her that this would be a long process. At this time, it would be a good thing for her since she definitely needed some downtime. He advised her that since the money was not an issue for her that this was the way to go. For others, though, filing with this class action suit would nullify the original payout from the airline, and if the class action suit was not successful, they would not get anything. At most, they would get very little but definitely less than what the airline originally offered. She reiterated that she was not the least bit interested in the money, but if she were to come into a large sum, she would spend it on charity in Charles's name. Returning home, she had a fleeting thought about Farley and how his marriage commission was proceeding. She had to admit she did miss him.

After a small lunch at a corner restaurant near the Vatican, Farley returned to his room to prepare for dinner with Clement. While at lunch, he spoke with not only the Americans in his group, but also with Cardinal Middleton of Australia and Ortiz of Mexico. Absent were the other cleric from Australia, Archbishop Jessup; Archbishop McConnell of Ireland; the two clerics from Canada; and Cardinal Ainsworth of England. All of them agreed that the commission was proceeding very well and were amazed at how evenly split the sentiments were. Farley read his office in his room. He managed to catch a nap, dozing off while thinking about his discussions with his luncheon group.

He awoke suddenly, realizing he had only been asleep a short while. He decided to get ready for dinner. He thought about arranging a private meeting with Clement to discuss release from his vows. If he further ingratiated himself with Clement tonight, he would find the right time to approach him about a private meeting certainly after the conclusion of the marriage commission. But then again he wasn't sure about Ann's feelings for him, so should he even bother the pope at this time? He was still strongly in love with his priesthood and his church, but he was in inner turmoil over how to proceed. *I know my feelings for Ann are strong and genuine, but I'm not so sure that Ann is just reacting to loneliness. Perhaps I should return home and see how things develop. I won't bother my good friend with this matter right now. I love my priesthood and everything about it but I love this woman too.* He sighed to himself. *Help.*

CHAPTER SIXTEEN

Karen and Tom arose early on this morning of their honeymoon and decided to start their day with a jog along one of the island roads that nestled along the seacoast. The scenery was beautiful and added a wonderful dimension to their exercise routine. After jogging a while, Tom breathlessly uttered, "I love you" to his new bride. She, also breathless, managed an "I love you" in return.

It was obvious that they were very much in love. Karen was gradually getting herself used to the idea that this was meant to be, and that there couldn't possibly be anything wrong with their relationship.

They found their way back to the hotel and returned to their room, obviously looking forward to a shower and then breakfast. Karen realized that they were still on their honeymoon, but she was confident that the euphoria she was experiencing now would last for her entire marriage. She had hardly given any further consideration to her former boss and the marriage commission he was serving on. She hadn't even picked up a newspaper to see if anything pertaining to the marriage commission was within the pages. Her only interest was Tom.

Farley was on his way to the papal apartment and caught up to Fiorvante as he was only steps ahead of him. Fiorvante turned quickly and greeted him. He expressed to Farley his enthusiasm concerning the work of the commission and the total involvement of all the prelates. He bragged that he had helped Clement with the selection process, and they were content that they had made the correct choices.

They arrived at the papal apartment and Tessier was already there. He was conversing with Clement while each of them held a glass of wine. Monsignor Bella was standing at the door to greet them. He remarked, "They have started dinner without you. Didn't even toast you." Everyone laughed and Farley at once felt relaxed. He thought about his uneasiness earlier in the day when he spoke at the assembly and not perceiving any reaction from his friend, Clement. Both he and Fiorvante were served a glass of the finest red wine, and all four took a seat at the table. Only the butler and the nun who did the serving were anywhere nearby. Bella himself even left the room.

Clement started the conversation by commenting on the work of the commission. "I'm extremely gratified to see you people working so well on this project that I set forth for you. I have no preconceived notion as to what direction this should take. I just felt very strongly about forming a group of thinkers in our church hierarchy to thoroughly examine the annulment process. Perhaps it's too difficult and needs to be revised or maybe, upon examination, we need to leave it as is or even make it more stringent. And how will what you do affect the sacrament of matrimony? I'm looking to you to somehow sort this entire thing out. From what I've heard so far, there have been great arguments placed out there on both sides of the issue."

Tessier then interjected a question that was probably on the minds of those at the table as well as all the others serving on the commission. "If the vote is for easing the process, Holy Father, would you implement the recommended changes?"

"I would look at the matter closely, but I'm sure if the commission provided valid arguments for changes, I would think seriously about enacting them."

Tessier then questioned him, "And what if the commission decides no change?"

"I would again accede to the commission's decision."

Fiorvante then jumped in with, "Would you be willing to say as to whether or not you are in favor of any particular conclusions?"

"I am totally open-minded, as I would like to see all of our faithful who have experienced a bad marriage be fortunate enough to find a new partner in a more loving relationship and be reconciled fully with the church. I also know that any change that could lead to abuse could be very dangerous. I guess I'm throwing the burden on you people."

Tessier and Fiorvante almost chimed in together, but Fiorvante dominated. "So you're making a decision by the democratic process?"

Farley just looked on and became a little uneasy as it appeared the other two were badgering Clement.

Clement replied, "Of course, you realize any decision you make will be non-binding and will be an advisement to me by a group of my most respected clergymen. I guess you could say that I'm asking you for your advice and will render a decision based on that advice. However, if after looking at everything in connection with your conclusions, I'm not happy about making any changes for whatever reason, I will simply take the matter under advisement." He then added humorously, "It's still a dictatorship, but a benevolent one and one that seeks advice from its top administrators."

Farley admired the way Clement handled himself.

Clement then proceeded to change the subject and spoke to them about opening up the Vatican grounds to the public for a few hours each day. He spoke about the crowds that streamed through the museum and Sistine Chapel each day, and he longed to make the gardens and other sites in Vatican City accessible to his beloved faithful.

He also spoke about the relaxation of the papal election procedures that he had implemented, adding to the easement of the process started by John Paul II. John Paul had no longer sequestered the cardinals in the Sistine Chapel, but he had erected a small hotel on the grounds for the comfort of the electoral body. They received the comfort of a bath and bed as opposed to the wash basin and cot set up in the Sistine Chapel.

Clement provided for the cardinals to be sequestered in the Chapel for voting between nine in the morning and seven at night. Facilities for hygiene and a kitchen for lunch were provided just off the Chapel but closed off to the outside. If the day's voting was inconclusive, the cardinals were to adjourn and notify the doorkeeper by signal that they were in adjournment, and he would unlock the door. The cardinals would then be escorted one by one from the Chapel to their rooms at the hotel where they could partake of their evening meal. Their escorts would be seminarians studying in Rome and some volunteer clergy. At no time was conversation to be exchanged either with the escorts or with each other. Only an emergency would constitute a reason for the cardinal to leave his hotel room. A Swiss guard was posted on each floor of the hotel. Clement then quipped, "I suppose it's still pretty strict, but you can just imagine how bad it must have been in previous papal elections before John Paul instituted the prior changes. You men were locked in that Chapel until a candidate was chosen pope. It is still a tremendously serious process, but certainly much easier to handle, and certainly more comfortable. Time at the hotel at night is for contemplation and inspiration by the Holy Spirit."

They all continued to enjoy the fine meal and the excellent wine selected by their host. Farley spoke to Tessier and Fiorvante about other church-related matters and seemed to impress them. He was beginning to lessen his dislike for these men. Perhaps he had been rash these past few years and had misjudged them. He then chastised himself for even judging them at all. He also gave some thought to having never addressed Clement as "Frank" for the course of the evening and knew it would be prudent to continue that train of thought. He assured himself that was only meant for their one-on-one encounters.

Fiorvante brought the conversation back to the commission. He looked at Clement and said, "Holy Father, of course you are aware that the Curia has looked and so far can't find any reason to ease the annulment process. While we have heard some valid points during our assemblies for liberalization, we are in agreement that people are speaking from their hearts and not their heads."

Clement interrupted with, "But don't we always speak from our hearts?"

Fiorvante was caught off guard and surprised. "Holy Father, we forgive sins from our hearts, but we don't condone them from our hearts. We love the sinner, but not the sin. We must use our head to rule our hearts in these matters."

Now it was Farley's turn to be caught off guard when Clement asked he and Tessier what their thoughts were. They agreed that Fiorvante made a strong argument, but they also thought that looking at this matter closely with a keen sense of compassion might bring about a solution that could speak from the heart and the head. They both, however, at this time, were more closely aligned with Fiorvante.

The nun who was tending the kitchen brought out an excellent cheesecake for dessert, and the men were very thankful to the middle-aged woman. Farley thought quickly to himself that she had quite some access to the doings of the church if she was this close to the pope and his guests. Nonetheless, she didn't appear to be interested at all in their conversation. They asked her if she made the cake as it was quite good and tasted homemade. She laughed and said she definitely did not make it. Nonetheless, it was excellent and went well with the wine they were sipping with the dessert.

Now that Ann was home, Marie brought her a light lunch. Marie told her she had errands to run but would be back shortly. Ann looked out the kitchen window and thought to herself, *I know it's*

way too early to think about remarriage, but I do have strong feelings for Harold. I also still have fond memories of a loving husband and a wonderful life with Charles. How long can I bear these conflicting thoughts? What would Charles think? I must consider the matter of Harold's priesthood and his place in the hierarchy. This would never be a marriage that would be easy to contract. I know Harold is devoted to his priesthood and I respect that, but what if these feelings for him are genuine love? How long will I be in this torment as I move forward with my life? Does my future include Harold as a husband or does he remain a friend? I must think of some way to rid myself of these distractions by finding interest in something else. I must allow myself a certain amount of time to pass before I can reasonably make a decision.

Clement, Farley, Tessier, and Fiorvante continued their discussion until Clement mentioned the late hour. They agreed to call it a day and looked forward to the next day of meetings. Each thanked Clement profusely for the wonderful dinner and the privilege of dining with him. They also assured him that their work on the commission would continue in earnest in hopes of arriving at a stance on annulment that would be a help to all the faithful and true to the tenets of the church. Clement, in turn, thanked them for all their efforts. As they proceeded out the door with Farley tailing, Clement grabbed his arm and whispered to him, "I'll find some time shortly to sit down with you alone and discuss the old days."

Farley grasped at the chance and whispered in reply, "That will be great. I will be available whenever." He now knew he was going to get an opportunity to be one-on-one with Clement. He would be able to discuss his dilemma with the supreme worldly authority of the church.

CHAPTER SEVENTEEN

F arley awoke to a rare cloudy day in Rome. That morning only a sliver of very dim light snuck through the small window in his room. He had arranged to say Mass this morning in the Irish chapel in the crypt area below St. Peter's. His aide, seminarian William Armstrong, would meet him there and assist at the Mass. He showered and dressed and then knelt in his room to thank God for another day and ask his help and guidance for the work of the marriage commission.

It was still early and there were no crowds as yet filling the cavernous basilica. Farley walked slowly through the church and became totally absorbed as never before in the sheer beauty of the place. He thought how appropriate this all was to honor a wonderful loving God. But then he quickly thought that even with all that grandeur, they could not approach "appropriate" for such a majestic God, who loves his children despite their insignificance. He passed to the side of the main altar, unceasingly amazed at its beauty, and entered the stairway to the crypt. In a short time, he was in the tiny Irish chapel. Armstrong was already there and had prepared for Mass.

As Farley reached the part of the Mass where the celebrant washes his hands, he thought about the times he had flirted with breaking his vow of chastity and sincerely uttered the words, "Lord, wash away my iniquities and cleanse me from my sins." Then in a few quick seconds, a myriad of thoughts distracted him. *How can it be sinful to love a woman as much as I love Ann?*

And yet I'm working on a commission trying to find a way for a man and a woman who are forced to end a bad marriage to be able to marry again; that is, if they are fortunate enough to find another, hopefully better, person with which to share a loving relationship. Both they and I are currently forbidden that chance lest we violate our vows. These thoughts coursed through his mind in a flash and he quickly turned his concentration back to offering a most sincere sacrifice of the Mass to the God he loved with more intensity then he loved Ann.

After Mass, Farley and Armstrong walked together to the makeshift cafeteria in the papal audience arena where they had breakfast. They were joined by Cardinal Middleton of Australia, Ainsworth of England, and Archbishop McConnell of Ireland. All Farley's American peers were at another table with Ortiz of Mexico and the two Canadian prelates. Armstrong was awed to be in such company, but he quickly excused himself so he could head to classes for the day. He was truly disappointed to be unable to stay and perhaps hear some firsthand discussion by the marriage commission members. Farley and the prelates at his table engaged in vigorous discussion and while doing so, the din of the room was broken by uproarious laughter from the table of his American counterparts. Farley thought, *Frank Carnavale and another joke.* He had to admit, though, that he was a delightful man with a keen sense of humor. It was no secret that he enjoyed life. Farley glanced over at the table and even saw the normally subdued Cardinal Feeney managing to enjoy a good laugh.

Shortly after finishing breakfast, they made the short walk to the assembly hall that been set up with chairs and tables so that each group could further engage with each other. All of them knew the pope was looking for a conclusion by the week's end. Most of the prelates were also getting anxious to return home to catch up on the work they left behind in their respective dioceses. It seemed as though it was paramount for all to bring the commission's work to a conclusion soon.

The morning was proceeding quickly, and Farley reminded himself that lunch today would be with Middleton and his American friends.

Reynolds arose early to take care of the diocesan business, but first and foremost to say Mass. He was not stationed at the cathedral so he offered early morning Mass at his own church and then drove the short distance to the cardinal's office.

He greeted Jane and she brought him up to date on matters of concern. He commented to Jane, "I can't wait until our friend Cardinal Harold Farley returns. I don't envy his position one bit."

Jane said, "Look at the letters to the editor in today's paper. I'd say it's split about half and half in supporting and opposing the minority housing report. But the letters against are really disturbing and most are lashing out at our dear friend, Cardinal Farley, even though he was only one member of the group."

Reynolds replied, "But he's the highest ranking member of that group, so he will bear the brunt of the criticism. I guess it goes with the territory. But what seems to be the main objection?"

Jane answered, "The fact that they want the taxpayers to fork up more money to put into a bottomless pit fairly well sums it up."

Reynolds responded that he would certainly be overjoyed if the marriage commission finished its work by week's end. "Then Farley can return and address the criticism himself." Reynolds then looked at the bright side of the criticism and dwelled on the fact that half of those writings were in favor of the report. He took some paperwork from Jane and began another day of being in the driver's seat of the diocese.

At the marriage commission meeting, a long morning of discussion had dragged on to early afternoon. A summation and a break for lunch were looming in the near future. Fiorvante thanked all for their participation and invited them to return in two hours for an afternoon of more work.

As agreed earlier, Farley was to lunch with the Americans and Cardinal Middleton of Australia. A small restaurant a few yards from Vatican City was their choice of venue amid some carping by Carnavale over, "Why are we spending money to go out to eat and passing up free lunch at the cafeteria?"

"It gives us a chance to have some uncensored conversation and a chance to come up with some ideas unfettered by the 'eyes of the Curia,'" was Carson's retort.

They arranged themselves around the table and settled in. A young waiter came to the table with water and asked them if they would care for a drink. All of them ordered wine except Josephson who requested a diet soda.

Middleton was first to blurt out that he has major problems with the whole concept of the marriage commission.

"How so?" Farley asked.

Middleton had command of the table and said, "All of us are celibate clergy. How do we know what a married man experiences in a bad marriage or even in a good marriage? Even more so, we are all men and so how do we have the temerity to think we know what a woman experiences?"

Feeney suggested a little lower tone to the effect that the walls had ears.

Farley swallowed hard and realized Middleton was raising a very valid point. He also knew that Middleton had no idea that he, Farley, probably did have some idea concerning the love of a man for a woman. He decided it best to withdraw somewhat from the conversation and just leave his ears open.

Josephson said, "We are only being charged with looking at the annulment process. We're not probing the inner workings of a man and a woman."

Middleton interrupted, "But that's my point. You're intimating that we don't have to be concerned about what is going on in the mind of a man or a woman in a bad marriage. But I maintain that in order to review the annulment process, it would be very important to know what motivates a couple to even seek an annulment. Add to that the human condition that moves them to look for a new relationship—a hopefully better one; and that through lack of an annulment, they are denied that basic human instinct. We have managed to sublimate those desires in adherence to our vows, some of us better than others. We have never, however, experienced a marriage and all that it implies, and even more so what a couple experiences in a breakup. And after the break up, there is the trauma their lives go through. Perhaps it takes years to get over the breakup and finally a glimmer of light appears at the end of the tunnel. It takes the form of a new relationship, but we snuff out the light, and force them to be celibate—unless they can get an annulment. My friends, we all know that to be a difficult task under the best of circumstances. We are engaged in a difficult situation here because, in my estimation, we are unqualified."

Feeney asked Middleton if he had spoken to the others in his local group about his feelings.

"No. I wanted to do it in this forum, informally, to see what your take is." He then laughed and said, "I go right to the top. You Yanks are informally in charge of our group, and of course, you, Harold Farley, are at the top of that pyramid. I mean no offense to my other American fellows, but I'm sure you are as aware as I am of Farley's prominence in the College of Cardinals."

Farley looked around the room for a place to hide. He thought, "If only he knew."

Carnavale then surprised Farley. "Why so quiet, Harold? We're not going to give you the check. Let's see, I think we'll give it to Carson."

All laughed and the waiter came out to take orders. Josephson asked for another diet soda. The rest were still nursing their wine.

After all placed their orders, Farley gathered himself. "I simply think we have been asked to serve the Holy Father on this commission, and we have to do the best that we can. Speculating on our qualifications will not solve any problems and will certainly impede our progress. We represent the authority of the church, and the annulment process is a church procedure to be investigated by a clerical body. Perhaps we can, however, take some advice from our friend, Cardinal Middleton. Let's try to put ourselves as best we can into imagining the torture of those who were involved in a bad marriage and who are surviving a break up and still hoping for a new life, only to be deprived because they are unsuccessful in obtaining an annulment. All we can do is our best."

Farley knew Middleton had hit a sore spot but he had to continue as though he had not. He immersed himself again in the lunchtime conversation and tried to steer his peers toward resolving to return to their discussions with renewed vigor and determination to come up with an easement or not by week's end. The waiter started to bring out their plates, and they navigated through the remainder of their lunch with mainly conversation concerning their individual dioceses. No one expanded on Middleton's observation.

In Rosewood, the clouds dominated the early morning sky. A short distance from Ann's home, her friend and neighbor, Carl Winstead, was sipping his first cup of coffee. Since his wife died five years ago, he had been seeing many different women. If there were an event to attend, he always managed to have a lady friend with him. Carl was a stockbroker, recently retired, who had managed well for himself. He was a tall man with distinguished white hair and was considered by many unattached women as a great "catch."

As he sipped his coffee, it came to him like a bolt from the blue. Although he had dated many women in the last few years, none seemed to have the magic that could have evolved into a loving relationship. The bolt that struck him was recently widowed Ann Lincroft.

Carl and his wife and Charles and Ann had been friends for many years and the Lincrofts were very supportive of Carl upon the death of his wife. *I've always thought Ann to be a lovely woman. I wonder what she would think if I asked her to have dinner with me?* He sipped his coffee again and bit into a piece of now cold toast and continued in thought. *Charlie's death is so recent, I wonder if I'd be pushing the envelope. But then again, how could a dinner together be any more then a sign of friendship. After all, she and Charlie were so good to me after my beloved Sarah's death? I'm sure she would be surprised since in the last few years, any time we've been at the same social occasion, I've always had a date. Damn, I'm going to call her if for no other reason than to offer her some comfort. I haven't been very good at returning all the kindnesses she and Charlie showed me in my grieving. I just hope that she doesn't resent my calling too soon or possibly think I'm pushing for more then a dinner...I'll have to take that chance.*

He cleaned up the small mess in the kitchen and made up his mind to give Ann a call that afternoon.

Karen and Tom were coming to the end of their honeymoon. Both remarked how fast the week was going and dreaded the thought of returning to reality. Tom's job was waiting for him; but Karen, by her choice, was unemployed. She would devote herself full time to job hunting upon their return. On this particular day, they had decided to stay close to the resort and relax on the beach. If the urge to make love came over them...well, that would be great. Of course they would have to return to the room since the beach was never deserted. Her thought quickly changed to Farley's marriage commission, but it was a thought that was then quickly dismissed. She would rather think about love. She was anxious to delve back into a book she was reading and at the same time absorb some of the sun's rays on the beautiful beach. Tom thought of the possibilities of kayaking and decided he'd save that for later in the day. Before they trekked down to the beach, they embraced, and for what seemed for the hundredth time that week , they professed their love for each other.

The afternoon session of the marriage commission got under way shortly after the small American group of prelates paraded into Vatican City from their lunch venue just a few blocks away. The sun had made its appearance during lunch, and it did so with a fury. It was bright and warm.

The Dean of the College of Cardinals, Fiorvante, called the afternoon session to order. The various groups got together and picked up where they left off earlier in the day. Farley addressed his group. "It appears at this time that our group consensus calls for no change, but this is by a very slim margin. I would like to ask my friends on the liberal side of the issue as to just how they would propose the implementation of easing the qualifications for an annulment."

"Good question," Feeney chimed in. "I have to admit I came to this commission pretty much convinced of no change. But I'm being flooded with opinions from the opposite side of the issue and most of them are making sense. Then I think to myself, 'Just how are changes to be implemented?' At present, a couple presents itself to the marriage tribunal and a trial is held. How do we effect changes in that procedure?"

Carson asked quizzically, "Is that also our job? Isn't our job just to call for an easement if that, in fact, is what we decide to do?"

Ortiz from Mexico replied, "I think if we decide for easement, we need to have some idea as to how that would be implemented."

Ainsworth interjected, "I agree. My thinking would provide the elimination of a trial and instead an appearance by the couple at a panel where a decision would be made to dissolve the marriage based on the ordinary criteria presently in use and any additional criteria which we would decide upon. The decision would then be rendered by the diocesan panel."

James and Proctor, the two prelates from Canada, tried to override each other, but James won out. "What if one of the married couples refuses to appear before the panel? Will the panel then be able to make a decision on input from only half the partnership? If they then can't render a decision without the appearance of both partners, how do we relieve the other partner?"

Feeney just sat back and, with a rather smug look, asked again, "So, gentlemen, how do we implement any changes?"

Carnavale was unusually quiet, but he did chime in with, "Remember, men, we have only to the weekend." McConnell alluded back to Carson's question in stating, "I don't think it's our job to get into the details of implementation but just to cite reasons for easing or not easing the process. The fine details of implementation will be hammered out by subsequent commissions if, in fact, we do decide to change the process. And then again, if we do decide to change, we must bear in mind that this decision is non-binding and it would be up to Clement to go with it and implement changes or take it under advisement."

Farley said, "Seems like a good idea to me to adhere to McConnell's thoughts. Let's just see where we stand on the primary issue of citing reasons to ease or reasons to continue the existing annulment process."

Middleton and Jessup agreed with Farley's conclusion and echoed his thoughts.

"I think by tomorrow Fiorvante is going to call for a final vote, so we should start collecting our thoughts and arriving at a conclusion by our group so we can be ready tomorrow," Farley declared.

Ortiz commented, "You heard the boss, so let's get to work!"

Carnavale, always in a good mood, chuckled and asked, "When did we make him boss?"

Carl Winstead laughingly thought of himself as a smooth operator, at least since his wife's death five years ago. He was hesitant, however, as he picked up the phone to call Ann Lincroft. He had the Lincroft number on his speed dial, so it was only seconds before he heard the voice of Marie, the housekeeper, on the other end. Her greeting seemed well rehearsed to him as her line was, "Lincroft residence, may I ask who's calling?"

"Hello, Marie, this is Carl Winstead. May I speak to Ann if she's not busy?" Cautiously, Marie replied, "I'll check with her."

In a matter of seconds, Ann was on the phone with a cheery greeting. Winstead first apologized to her for not keeping in touch with her on a regular basis. He then said that he would like to amend the situation and asked her if she would care to go out with him to dinner the following night. He had a quaint but pricey restaurant in Rosewood in the back of his mind.

Ann was at once startled at the request, and there just wasn't sufficient time to give the matter any detailed thought, so she replied positively. "Why Carl, how nice of you! I'd be delighted." They engaged in further conversation and then Carl finished the call by explaining the details of what time he would call for her.

She hung up the phone and her first thought was, *What have I done? I always liked Carl and Sarah. He wasn't one of the usual stodgy bank people that were kind of hangers-on to Charles. I just never thought of him as a companion on a date.* Ann then gave some thought to her seemingly growing love for Harold Farley and for her never-ending remembrances of her sweet Charles. *Maybe this will get my mind off Harold. Who knows? Carl has always been an interesting man, and perhaps this would be a good test as to whether or not my feelings for Harold are as genuine as I think. So I guess I'm comfortable with the fact that I made the right decision. Besides, Carl is probably only feeling that this is an obligation he has to console me. In any event, we'll see what happens.*

She moved to the kitchen and let Marie in on the fact that Carl had asked her out to dinner. Marie replied, "Far be it for me to comment on your private life, Ann."

Ann was very pleased at how loyal and unobtrusive Marie was after so many years. She had been faithful to the Lincrofts for so many years, and for a brief moment, Ann gave thought to comparing her to Mary O'Leary and Harold Farley. *Perhaps we take these loyal people for granted. Marie has devoted so many years to us in loyal service and devotion, and I need to think about doing something special for her. Harold was distraught over the little attention he gave to Mary until it was too late.* Then and there, Ann asked Marie to sit down with her for a while and take a break.

"All I'll say regarding Carl is that he always appeared to be a gentleman. I hope it turns out to be a great evening for you. Perhaps it will relieve your grieving."

They then broke into more casual conversation and Ann agreed this was long overdue. Marie even laughed at some of the comments Ann made regarding some of the bank people, who Marie knew only too well from the many functions that were held by Charles and Ann in which she played a vital role. Ann felt good about what she was doing and even felt more elated then she had been since Charles' death.

Later in the day, Fiorvante called all the representatives on the marriage commission into assembly and advised them that it was his desire to bring the matter to a formal vote the following day, if possible. If there was anyone present who didn't feel that they could come to a final conclusion by tomorrow, they should make themselves known. Not one person did so.

Farley thought, *Tomorrow is D-Day.*

Fiorvante urged them to pray and ask for the wisdom of the Holy Spirit to counsel them. After a few parting words, the commission adjourned for the day.

There was no dinner out that evening as everyone agreed that the matter was coming to a conclusion and that perhaps they all ought to stay close and enjoy dinner together in the makeshift cafeteria.

While Farley strolled to the cafeteria, Armstrong walked at a brisk pace behind him to catch up to him and advise him that Clement wanted to meet with him the next evening. Farley jumped at the chance and told Armstrong to inform Bella that he would be happy to meet with his friend, Clement.

As he continued to work his way to the serving area, he hoped for a successful conclusion to the marriage commission and looked forward to his meeting with Clement. He said a little prayer that the meeting would be just between him and Clement, and he made up his mind that if that was the case, he would talk to Clement about his dilemma.

As he proceeded to a table with his tray, he realized that at that time only three people knew anything about this problem—he, Ann, and his spiritual advisor, Beardsley. He thought to himself, *Not one of my fellow prelates has a clue.*

Ortiz and Jessup sat with him and they began to converse about the commission. Farley was appreciative of being able to switch gears.

CHAPTER EIGHTEEN

A nn rose early on a rainy morning in Rosewood and proceeded to the kitchen to make herself a cup of coffee. She still had a limp, but she was improving. It was Marie's day off. She pondered what she would wear tonight for the dinner date. She was also aware that she hadn't heard anything from Farley, but then she didn't expect to. She knew that calling him, unless it was an emergency, was not the thing to do. She did know, however, that her name was on the approved list of callers for Farley. She gave some thought to the fact that his commission was in full swing by now and wondered how many more sessions there would be.

She journeyed to the pantry with just a small amount of hassle but pondered whether or not she would ever walk normally again. Her hastily prepared table included cereal, coffee, and juice. She finished only half the cup of coffee and even passed up her usual second cup. She was still mildly depressed. After rinsing the few dishes she used, she placed them in the dishwasher and proceeded to the den. She compelled herself to open the mail that was delivered yesterday. For some reason or other, she didn't feel like going through it yesterday. Maybe it was because one of the envelopes was on American Bank stationery. *Now what could the bank possibly want at this juncture?* While Ann had very few shares of the bank stock, she was, in fact a very minor shareholder. She consequently had very little interest in the bank. Charles provided for her so that she would be well taken care of financially with little or no participation in the bank's affairs. She liked that. She opened the envelope and it revealed an invitation to attend the installation of John Martin as president of the bank. She liked John Martin and his wife, even though she admitted he was only a tad stodgy, unlike the other bank execs. She thought, *This will be something I have to attend as Charles' widow, but I wish I could avoid it. It's indeed a shame that we didn't have any children. Now a non-family member is in charge. But that was Charles's wish. Martin, however, was loyal to Charles and I think Charles would be satisfied with the choice of John Martin to take over.* The installation would be in the bank's conference room on a Wednesday evening in the next week. Refreshments would obviously be served, and Ann thought for sure that would include alcohol. *My better judgment tells me I should stay in the city that night. Oh! I really wish I didn't have to go, but I must.*

The only other piece of mail she wanted to open was from her attorney. She was advised that all the forms for the class action suit had been filed, but it would probably be a while before they heard anything on it. He did, however, advise her that if anything on the matter arose, he would inform her promptly.

She went to her bedroom to select her wardrobe for her date. She was determined to make the best of it.

It was now well past one in Rome, and yet another sunny day. Each subgroup of the marriage commission was at full speed to come to a summation and vote by day's end. Fiorvante announced earlier that at approximately three o'clock, he would call for a vote and have the prelate in charge of each group announce their votes and give a brief summation.

Farley was chairing his group's discussion and was content in knowing that they would meet a three o'clock deadline. The preliminary vote by his group was seven to five in favor of retaining the current annulment process. The total vote of the commission, which still surprised him, was twenty to seventeen in favor of no change. He wondered to himself that even though he was leaning to no changes and voted for no change in the preliminary vote, he did secretly wish that the commission would call for an easement in spite of his conservative stance. That, of course, would be hypocritical. He was bearing internal agony over that decision. He was also wrestling with his love of God and his priesthood being compromised by his love of a woman. In his mind, the right thing to do was to vote his conscience and it was telling him to not allow anything to possibly demean the sacrament of matrimony. But he thought of the Kiely's, the O'Leary's, and the Michaels of his life, and also of his own particular dilemma; and then he thought of the enormous pressure he was under to make a decision on what his vote would be. *This is a tremendous challenge.* As of now, his love of his church and all the sacraments, including matrimony, was winning out. The total vote was extremely close, and Farley knew his decision would be crucial.

Farley addressed his group and spoke about his pros and cons on the issue. "I really feel we could open the sacrament of matrimony to abuse depending on how much we ease this process, if that, in fact, is what we decide to do. With all my inner strength, I do not want to do anything to detract from the holiness of the marriage sacrament. If a couple feels that it's too easy to separate and thus makes only a halfhearted commitment to better or worse, I think it's a detraction from the sacrament. I think a lot of marriages would be approached with far less than a firm commitment. It, therefore, becomes less special. On the other hand, what do we do for someone who has tried everything and still can't hold the marriage together? They can get a legal divorce, but they can't remarry unless they go through a now difficult annulment process. If they don't succeed at that juncture, they are closed off to all possible future relationships of a loving nature that could lead to a possibly better life for them. Don't forget—we are all human and can make errors in judgment."

Farley continued and considered that if the others knew of his personal situation, he would definitely be dubbed a hypocrite. "Furthermore, my friends, we can be released from our vows, in some cases, and allowed to continue to partake of life. If a married couple is unable to obtain an annulment, we are saying there is no way we can release you from your vows. You must now remain celibate until either partner dies. We are, in precise terms, forcing them to a vow of celibacy which they didn't ask for. That's pretty tough on anyone. Yet, I have to say that while I am taking all of this into consideration, I am still going to vote to maintain the current annulment process. I'm just too afraid of abuse, and I'm going to err on the side of caution."

"That's interesting," Feeney said. "Because I've made up my mind to look at an easement. I will be changing my vote. Even what you just said, Harold, convinces me that we have to ease the process. Our church is slow to change and I think that's good, but in listening to all the preliminary summations and our present discussions, I think it's time to implement change. The Holy Father would not have called this session if he wasn't inspired to look toward change."

"That puts our group at six to six now. Are there any other changes of mind?" Farley asked.

There appearing to be no other changes of mind, Farley called the roll. Feeney was the only one to change his vote. Josephson, Carson, and now Feeney voted for change. Carnavale and Farley voted for retention.

Both Canadian prelates were still split.

Ortiz from Mexico, McConnell from Ireland, and Ainsworth from England all stayed with their original votes to maintain the current annulment procedures.

Finally, Middleton and Jessup of Australia still voted for an easement. That was no surprise to Farley.

As Farley tallied the six to six vote, he wondered if there were any radical changes coming from the other groups. This was at once becoming interesting. Farley looked inwardly at his vote and decided that his vote was becoming excruciatingly crucial. *It's possible this whole commission could hinge on my vote.* He quickly looked at his tally from the original vote taken by the entire commission. He saw that if nothing else changed, the vote was now nineteen to eighteen in favor of no change. He wasn't sure how he felt about that.

Farley then directed the group to assist in writing the summary that he would present later that day. That summary would include all their thoughts and the reasoning behind those thoughts.

The Curial group was at the same time in discussion with Fiorvante. He was content that his group was in line with him that the present annulment process should be retained. Cardinal D'Angelo, however, surprised him. He was now joining Archbishop La Viola in favor of change. According to Fiorvante's mental tally, that now split his group evenly at two to two. Fiorvante was disturbed since, unlike Farley who was fence sitting, he was vociferous in his support of no change. Now he saw the Curia itself looking at easement after he was so comfortable with his thinking that at least three of them were in his camp. He asked, "Is our vote at this time final?"

All answered, "Yes."

"Then let us prepare our statement. I must tell you, however, that I am disappointed. I went into this commission feeling for sure that the Curia would be unanimous in its support of the dignity of the marital sacrament. They would not even allow the slightest change to possibly besmirch the dignity of the sacrament."

La Viola replied, "We must look at change. Times change and we must adapt. I don't think that allowing for a marriage to be annulled more expeditiously than it is at the present is going to automatically result in abuse of the sacrament. Just look at the marriages that do break up and cannot gain the benefit of an annulment. Most people go ahead and remarry anyway and then give up on their faith. I think we should do what we can, without violating our moral authority, to see that these people stay among our faithful."

It was apparent to Fiorvante that this latest vote would remain the same. He was not happy with the vote change, but he deeply believed that the Holy Spirit was guiding their decision.

It was after three o'clock when Fiorvante called for everyone's attention and asked if the statements and final votes were ready. Only the African group asked for a few more minutes, and Fiorvante acquiesced and said he would call them last. He allowed everyone a few more moments and then totally surprised Farley by calling up his group first.

Farley stepped up to the dais to deliver his summation. He hoped he could incorporate a little campaigning for the conservative view in his summation. "My fellow prelates, our group is probably indicative of all of us in total. We are evenly split, six to six. I urge everyone to sincerely dwell on the importance of what we are doing here. Is there a possibility of abuse if we ease the annulment procedures? Will easing them really mean that fewer people will abandon our beloved faith? It is in our hands, so if any of you have not made a decision, I implore you to proceed with the utmost diligence." Farley moved to return to his seat when Archbishop La Viola, who was recording the votes, asked him to state the votes of his group again for the record. Farley replied, "Six votes for retention of current procedures and six votes for easement."

Fiorvante was writing this down as well. Right now he knew the Curial vote was split evenly, and the American vote was also an even split. He was becoming slightly agitated. Farley noticed Fiorvante scribbling on his notepad and was amused to see that he too was keeping a close tally. He was also looking forward to the remaining votes to see if there were any more changes from the first vote.

Fiorvante then stepped up to the microphone and announced that he would have normally called for the African delegation at this time, but since he consented to move them last, they would be hearing from his own Curial group now. "I too agree with my good friend, Cardinal Farley, that relief in the annulment process could lead to abuse and a lessening of the holiness of matrimony and the commitment it requires. The so-called changing times should not propel us into making decisions that could in any way demean what is, in our church, a sacrament. For me, I am personally saddened to see the Curial vote is now two for retention and two for easement." You could feel the emotion in the air. Everyone was totally surprised at the Curial vote.

Farley now noted that in total, the vote was evenly split at eight to eight. He even thought, *I guess Karen will be happy.* With that thought, he knew that he was still deeply wrestling with what to do not only for Karen, but for all others who were in her position but still wanted to remain faithful Catholics. He loved his church and didn't want to do the slightest to lessen the dignity of the marriage sacrament. That was foremost on his mind. However, he still felt for the O'Learys, the Kielys, and the Michaels. He also thought, *We could be making history here.*

The Japanese group was next and there was no surprise as Cardinal Naguchi announced their vote as two for retention and none for liberalization. He ended his summation with, "We should be looking for a means to solidify the marital relationship and not looking for a means to make it easier to separate."

Farley and Fiorvante both breathed a little easier since that now brought the total to ten votes for retention against eight votes for easement. Fiorvante was definitely delighted but Farley just added more turmoil to his decision. He wondered if it was possible for him to be a hypocrite. *Is it possible that I really want the commission to vote change, but allow myself to remain a conservative in the view of my fellow prelates? Is this becoming all about me and not what's good for our holy church? Am I being inspired to vote for change, but voting opposite to that inspiration? If so, for what reason? My own self-aggrandizement? In my own life, I have witnessed situations where easement would have made conditions so much better for people. I am, however, very much concerned about maintaining the dignity and solidity of marriage. I pray that my decision and those of the commission will be with the inspiration of the Holy Spirit. God give me the strength to do what is right.*

Fiorvante called for the European group and Tessier took the center of the dais. Farley was anxious to hear this group summation since it voted heavily in favor of liberalization on the first vote. He noticed that Tessier, who was one of two conservative votes for the group, had a livelier step and demeanor.

Tessier started. "My fellow priests, I agree so strongly with our conservative brothers that a change in the annulment process should be looked at with the intensity of a microscope. So intense, that in my opinion, it cannot be done. I feel extreme sorrow for those who leave the church over this issue, but perhaps we need to look more carefully at the start of the marriage. Better preparation is needed. That being said and after much discussion, I was only able to sway one vote in my group to the side of retention. That results in our vote being three for retention against five for liberalization."

Farley tallied quickly with Carnavale looking over his shoulder. Now the total stands at thirteen for retention and thirteen for easement. A dead heat. "It appears as though my vote will be crucial." More agony.

The Asian group, represented by Cardinal Singh, was next to take center stage. Their original vote was an even split at three to three, but it had now changed to two for retention against four for liberalization. Sikh presented a brief summation and prayed that all had made decisions according to their best judgment.

Farley's tally now climbed to fifteen for retention and seventeen for liberalization. This was swinging back and forth beyond anything that he could have imagined. But it came back to hanging in the middle.

The original African vote was three to two in favor of a conservative stance. If that didn't change, the final vote would be eighteen for the conservative view and nineteen for easement. Extremely close, one vote, and a vote by the commission to ease the annulment process in the Catholic Church. Everyone, especially Farley, waited with bated breath for the African summation.

Farley adjusted his earphones as Obiajunwa approached the podium.

Obiajunwa began. "Our group has most assuredly done due diligence in arriving at its final vote. We have changed one vote to conservative, and so our final vote is now four for retention of current procedures and only one vote for liberalization."

Farley didn't even listen to the rest of what Obiajunwa was saying but quickly noted the final tally at nineteen to eighteen in favor of retaining the present procedures for annulment. Fiorvante was delighted and Farley had mixed emotions. It was almost if he had secretly wished it had gone the other way. *Did I truly vote my conscience? I force myself to say yes but I still have gnawing doubts. Only one vote. If I had gone in the opposite direction, we would be looking at a new day for married couples who find themselves in the unfortunate position of a marriage gone bad.*

The afternoon labored on, and Fiorvante announced a short break before they would return to the auditorium for the closing session. Everyone breathed a sigh of relief.

While on break, Farley was interrupted in his conversation with McConnell by Armstrong. Armstrong handed him a tiny piece of paper on which was written a reminder of his dinner that night with Clement. Farley thanked Armstrong, and as Armstrong walked away, Farley folded the note. He sincerely hoped it would be just him and his friend, Frank. He laughed to himself at the fact that he really wasn't able to decline the invitation as Armstrong had walked away so fast. Then he laughed again as he thought that it was probably rare that the Holy Father got a refusal. Although he remembered that the South American prelates did refuse his invitation to serve on the marriage commission. McConnell, surmising the contents of the note, patted Farley on the shoulder and commented, "You didn't see anything on that note about my being invited to the papal apartment, did you?" Farley just chuckled with him.

After a short break, everyone returned to the audience hall. They were surprised to see Pope Clement already sitting in the vast room. Farley thought, *Why am I surprised? I should expect that Clement would be here for the closing session. Just how did he get here so quietly?* All the gathering prelates took their places, and Fiorvante called the session back to order.

"I personally thank all of you involved for the time and effort you exerted in this most important matter for Holy Mother church. I realize all of you wrestled with this subject and exchanged varied opinions before arriving at your decisions. The movement of the Holy Spirit through this assembly was palpable. Apparently, we are almost evenly split on our final decision which means this may not be the final effort in dealing with the subject. The church moves slowly, as you all know, but I have faith that the Holy Spirit has prevailed. I thank you all most sincerely. Before I call the proceedings of this commission to a close, I will inform you that I have officially recorded the final vote and presented it to our Holy Father. There were nineteen votes to keep intact the annulment procedures as they presently exist, and there were eighteen votes to adopt changes in order to ease the annulment process. It is my extreme pleasure to greet our Holy Father who will present to us some closing remarks."

Fiorvante remained standing and the rest of the prelates all rose in applause. As Clement took his place at the podium, the prelates all took their seats. Clement stood at the podium and looked out into the audience of some of his most eminent fellow priests and smiled gently.

"My good priests, I stand here assured that our Lord is pleased with all of you and the effort you made to study a process within our church that can dissolve a bad marriage and allow those involved to find happiness again in another marriage without having to abandon their faith. You dealt with this project over the past many weeks with loving respect for the sacrament of matrimony and the dignity of the human being. The fact that the final vote was so close is an indication that you looked at this from all possible facets. Half of you had exceptionally good reasons to urge for easement while the other half presented exceptionally strong arguments for leaving the process as is. The decision stands. The hierarchy of the church will do nothing to change the annulment process. Perhaps this subject will be looked at again at some future time, but as of now, the church accepts your recommendation of no change. I still want you to pray for all those who cannot obtain an annulment that in spite of their suffering, they will remain true to their faith and ask the Almighty God for the graces to help them through their difficult journey. My sincerest thank you again to all of you for your devotion to this commission and to our Holy church."

As everyone stood up to applaud, Farley swallowed hard. One vote was the difference. If he had voted the other way, there would be a new outlook on marriage and annulment in the church. He was not in favor of making it any easier to obtain an annulment in spite of the many people in his life who either had to deal with the problem or were currently dealing with the problem. He was going to ask for release from his priestly vows in exchange for a marriage vow, but there was no such chance for Karen Michaels or even Mary O'Leary. The men they were in love with were not able to break their marriage vows according to the church, and so the women had to leave the church in order to marry a man who was ineligible. Mary opted to stay with her faith. Karen, however, did opt for the marriage and thus made a decision to not partake fully of her church. As he watched the one reporter who was permitted access to their meetings dash out of the auditorium, he knew it wouldn't be long before Karen would read about this and realize that he possibly cast the deciding vote. His turmoil was ongoing.

Pope Clement acknowledged Farley as he left the auditorium. Since the meeting had adjourned so late, Farley hastened to the refreshment of a shower and some quiet time in contemplation of the monumental decision he was about to make.

CHAPTER NINETEEN

The evening in Rome was getting on, and it was nearing nine o'clock. Farley thought he would like more time to meditate, but he was asked to be at the pope's apartment by nine. He also knew he had to place a phone call to Reynolds. Then he decided on top of that to give Ann a call. He wanted to inform them that the commission had concluded, and he would be returning shortly.

His first call went to Reynolds.

"So great to hear from you, Harold. How's everything going?"

"I guess the primary purpose of my call was to ask you the same question," Farley replied.

"Of course you know by now that the public is evenly split over your report on the housing problem. It's just that the negatives are vicious. The press is constantly on me for my opinion. I'm holding them off until your return so that my opinion goes out only after you have had a chance to comment first. I told them that you would then state the reasoning behind your decision, as well as the decision of the entire clergy board. Everything else is fairly quiet although I'm getting some grief over the potential closing of St. Margaret's downtown. I guess that's to be expected from people who become so attached to their church. I will try to smooth things over by explaining the dire financial straits the church and the diocese are both in. Jane is doing very well keeping me abreast of the daily routine and Marcia is keeping the household intact."

"Thanks so much, my faithful auxiliary, for holding the fort. I'm on my way to dinner tonight with Clement, and the good news is that we wrapped things up today after a long day. I will be returning within the next couple of days. You'll see it in the papers shortly that the final conclusion of the marriage commission was to maintain the current annulment process. That decision was arrived at by one vote."

"Would that be your vote, Harold?"

"Could be," he replied humorously. He knew that there was no humor about it at all. He was not comfortable about being the deciding vote. "I'll give you all the details when I return, but in the meanwhile I thank you again."

Feeling content that the diocese was functioning well in his absence, he quickly picked up the phone again to dial Ann. Marie answered the phone and was surprised to hear Farley on the other end. She greeted him cordially and said she would get Ann to the phone right away.

Ann, surprised at the call, limped over to the phone and said, "Harold! How good to hear your voice."

She gave a fleeting thought to how she now casually addressed him as "Harold" and not "Father Harold." She lowered her voice on the next inquiry to hopefully keep Marie at a distance. "What possessed you to call me in the middle of your meetings?"

"We're finished. You'll probably see it in the paper tomorrow. By one vote, the annulment process is still in place."

"That's not a great consensus. I think you should go back to the meetings and hash it out some more. Only one vote. That's going to be agonizing for some people to read about. How did you vote, or are you allowed to let out that information?"

"I voted to keep with the present situation but I still have so much doubt. I'm just overwhelmed with the idea of not doing anything to make the sacrament of matrimony any less of a committed relationship consecrated by our church to last until death." He continued. "The real reason for the call is to let you know I'll be traveling home soon and I look forward to seeing you. So how are you doing?"

"I don't know how you will accept this news, but I'm dining out later this evening with Carl Winstead. He said he wants to make it up to me for his lack of attention to me at Charles's death. He said Charles and I were a huge comfort to him at the loss of his wife."

Farley kept his true feelings hidden and told Ann he was happy for her. He then informed her that he would be dining with Clement that night. She congratulated him and wished him well. Apparently both were trying to hide their true feelings for each other.

"I must be getting to this dinner as it's getting late, but I wanted to check in with you and see how you were getting along. Also to let you know that I'll be home soon." He thought it best to leave it at that.

After Ann told him that she was happy he called, she returned the phone to the receiver and went upstairs to prepare herself for her evening with Carl Winstead. As she climbed the steps, she went into deep thought. *I still have strong feelings for Harold, but I'm hoping this evening will bring me a conviction that these strong feelings for Harold are born out of loneliness. I might find that spending time with Carl could be very enjoyable. But if my feelings for Harold prove genuine, do I really want him to leave the priesthood? He is so well thought of in the hierarchy that I can't imagine the effect his leaving would have on the church. Besides that, I'd be directly involved and it wouldn't do my reputation a whole lot of good. I just don't know. So much confusion. I'm making up my mind to enjoy this evening.*

Farley made his way to the hallway leading to the papal apartments. He nodded at the Swiss guardsman outside the door and entered the apartment. Monsignor Bella greeted him and led him to the dining room where Clement sat waiting for him. Clement arose and greeted him warmly. Farley took his place and Bella left the room informing them that he would be returning to his own apartment. Only the kind nun remained in the kitchen. Clement advised Farley that sister would be placing dinner on the table and that desert was already prepared. She also would be placing two bottles of wine on the table and then she would be leaving them. Farley was elated as he would now be alone with Clement to ask about his release from vows.

Clement started the conversation with, "Let's not be formal tonight, Harold. Just call me Frank and enjoy the camaraderie for the evening. I do want to know your feelings concerning your vote on the commission, however and your insights as to the commission's findings."

Farley offered to pour a glass of wine for his friend and he graciously accepted. After a toast to their long-standing friendship, each took a sip. Farley nodded to Frank that it was great and desired to know the vintage. They both sipped again, and Frank remarked to Harold, "My 'wine steward,' Monsignor Bella picked it. I'm not a wine connoisseur, but I do agree with you that it's great. But now let's talk about the commission."

"Where would you like to start?"

"Nowhere in particular, but I'd like to talk to you of my inner desires and the results of your findings. The commission has spoken, but I don't know whether or not I am content with their decision. It was so close that it causes me to think that possibly the Spirit is prodding us to change. It's almost as if I wanted to see easement myself and rather than make a unilateral decision, I convened a commission to do it for me. But I still have that nagging doubt about the possibility of easement making the sacrament less holy. I just don't know."

"We think in the same manner, Frank, because those are my feelings exactly. And to add to my torment, the decision was made by just one vote. If I had voted the other way, you and I would be having an entirely different conversation now. Just recently, I have experienced two instances in lives of those close to me where perhaps an easier annulment procedure would have made such a huge difference in their lives. My own secretary is one case and my deceased housekeeper is another. Both of these people have made extreme sacrifices. One of them kept her faith and never married because the one she loved was not free to marry in the church. The other put her faith on the back burner to marry a man she loved who was also not free to marry in the church."

"Harold, perhaps at another time we can call a new commission and look the process over again, but the decision has been made. Even my Curial vote was split. What truly concerns me is why you voted conservatively and yet inwardly wanted change. Since I felt the same way, maybe your reasoning behind your decision will give me some insight as to why I feel the way I do."

"Perhaps I am afraid to make the decision for change and was hoping that the commission would do it for me. Then I would accept the changes, if they were enacted, knowing I didn't vote for them. I know that is totally deceitful, but I salve my conscience by saying to myself, 'Bottom line—no demeaning of the sacrament.' I just can't find my true position. I must force myself to contend with the fact that I made the right decision."

Frank laughed and said, "I did a number on you. Truly, what you just said may be the real reason I convened the commission. We joked the other night about the church becoming a democracy, but I torture myself with the same reasoning you just explained. Perhaps I wanted to see change also but just couldn't go the final mile and so asked others to make the decision for me. Because of the closeness of the vote, we may call another commission to restudy the issue at some point in the future. I am still concerned."

During the conversation, the nun had placed the meal on the table and then left the apartment. Farley joked, "Do we do the dishes?"

Frank replied, "We at least have to put them in the dishwasher. Then we'll have to get our own dessert. Due to the late hour, I wouldn't ask the poor sister to remain here. Maybe we'll get a few years off purgatory."

They enjoyed the meal immensely and conversed about the old days. They reminisced with great vigor, paying close attention to the more humorous events they were part of.

As the evening passed, Farley was trying to figure a way to spring on the pontiff the thought of his returning to the ranks of the laity. It was getting later, and he had to broach the subject soon. As they both arose from the table to place their dishes in the dishwasher, it occurred to Farley what a humorous situation it was. Would anybody believe this? He and the pope doing the dishes.

Frank intoned, "In spite of what you may think, I am familiar with the kitchen, sometimes to the annoyance of Sister." They picked up their dessert and returned to the dining room.

As they took their seats again, Frank startled Farley by saying, "I need to confide in you my good friend. The house physician has made a few visits to the papal apartment. It appears as though I'm dealing with some heart problems. Only Monsignor Bella knows and I've asked him not to reveal anything to anyone until we see how this plays out. I may have to have a bypass, but we are awaiting test results. Obviously, if it turns out that a bypass is necessary, everyone will be told, but I think it better that it stay under wraps for the time being."

Farley sat stunned. "Frank, you're the picture of health and you're still a young man. I can't believe it. When will you get your test results?" Now he thought about the timing of his bombshell to the Holy Father.

Frank answered the inquiry regarding the test results by explaining that he would know sometime early next week.

"My God, what a shock, Frank! You do, however, have the advantage of your age, so I'm sure you'll get through this."

"Keep me in your prayers."

For what seemed like an eternity, Farley debated the timing of his unusual request to his good friend. He simply had to get this over with. Realizing the awkwardness of the situation, he managed to stumble through. "I too Frank, have something to confide in you."

Groping for the correct words, he felt more emotion in his body than at any time in his life. "I am in love with a woman. She was just recently widowed. I'm not entirely sure if her love for me, which she professes, is genuine or is just a result of loneliness. I've known her and her husband since my early years in the priesthood. I am sure of my love for her. I also love my priesthood, and my life is filled with conflict. I am contemplating asking you to release me from my vows."

Frank looked at Farley in total disbelief. "Harold, your calling is with your church. You're a much respected member of the hierarchy. I can't imagine that you would even think for a minute that our church can do without you as a priest. Just how much thought have you given to this?"

"Frank, you can't imagine. I do love my priesthood and my service to the church. I haven't given much thought to what I would do as a layman. I have such deep affection for this woman, and I'm afraid that I can't overcome the temptation that arises when I'm in her company. I don't know how I can continue to be a good priest without removing this woman from my life, and that is not an option."

Frank, who was normally easygoing and always gracious to Harold Farley, seemed to become agitated and not sympathetic at all. "I don't believe I'm having this conversation, Harold. There's absolutely no question in my mind that, spiritually and intellectually, you are a most valuable asset to our church. Aside from the bad publicity the church would accrue from this action, I think it would damage you as a person. My first instinct is to say an emphatic no to any inclination you have to leave the priesthood. You must pray to overcome this temptation. You said you were still in love with your priesthood, so in heaven's name, say no to this temptation. I consider you a great friend. I appointed you to the College of Cardinals. I can not imagine myself ever allowing you to return to the ranks of the laity. Please give this so much more careful thought."

"Holy Father, I have agonized over this so much already. I am being turned inside out. I must make a decision."

Clement interrupted. "I'm just thinking here that you voted to keep the annulment process intact because you did not want to demean the sacrament of matrimony. You will not allow a couple to dissolve their marriage vows unless it is through the now difficult annulment process. Yet you sit here with me to ask for a release from your priestly vows just like that. Don't you think you're diminishing the sacrament of Holy Orders?"

Farley knew he made a point. He also knew that he had thought about that many times in the past number of weeks. He didn't have an answer.

Clement arose from the table, his desert half-eaten, and walked over to Farley. Standing next to him, he looked straight at him and said, "Harold, you cannot do this. The consequences for you personally and most certainly for the church would be disastrous. I absolutely refuse to make a decision now, and I implore you to wait a while longer before you make any further decisions. I can't tell you how much this upsets me."

Farley felt badly about seeing the evening take a bad turn, but he did feel a tinge of relief that he had finally brought this matter to the pope's attention. "Frank, I didn't mean to cause you any distress, but I had to unburden myself."

"Well unfortunately, it's very distressing. One of the preeminent clergymen in the College of Cardinals is asking to be released from his clerical duties. How many others are aware of this problem?"

"Just Ann; my spiritual advisor, Monsignor Beardsley; and now you. Of course, me too."

"Thank God for that. It's just so out of the question. Of course, you know if I absolutely had to release you from your vows, I would, but I most assuredly do not want to do that. I invited you here tonight to talk about the commission and go over old times, and it's as though I've been betrayed. This is not a good night."

The pope walked back to his place and picked up his half-eaten desert to take it to the kitchen. Farley arose and followed him to the kitchen. "I apologize to you, Frank, with all my heart. I had to tell you."

Frank turned around, faced him, and calmly spoke to him. "You must take more time to think this over. Pray with all your heart and soul that God's will be done. I can't imagine that His will would be to release you from the priesthood with all the good you have accomplished for His church. Promise me that you will pray over this matter for the next few weeks and please don't say anything to anyone else. I'm deeply distressed."

Farley was also distressed at this turn of events, but he was also aware that this news would not sit well with Clement. He hugged the Holy Father and apologized again. Farley returned to the dining room, picked up his unfinished desert, and brought it to the kitchen. Suddenly, there was no humor anymore in seeing the Holy Father doing the dishes. He thought to himself about the Holy Father presenting the news of his heart problems and then his trumping of that news with his "special request." He again hugged Clement, and they both parted on a physical and mental low.

Clement actually tidied up the kitchen a little to see if he could ease his anger and his tension. Upon completing that minor task, he adjourned to his bedroom and began to pray earnestly.

Farley returned to his room with his inner turmoil boiling over. *Where am I going?* Before he drifted off to sleep; his thoughts were not only of his inner turmoil, but also the problem he had inflicted on his good friend.

Karen and Tom embraced and complimented each other on how nice they looked. They walked from the cabana and up the steep steps to the main lodge for cocktails. As the sun set over the open sea on that clear and just slightly humid night, they marveled at its beauty and lamented the fact that they would be returning home the next day. They walked into the lodge and sat at a small table with another honeymooning couple and proceeded to have a great conversation. When their drinks were finally placed at their table, they toasted each other in lament over their last night in "paradise." The other couple informed them that they would be leaving for Boston the next afternoon. Karen replied that their plane was scheduled for early evening so they would be able to spend a few more hours on the isle. She then said, "I guess we'll just be postponing the inevitable." She sipped her drink and thought that this had been the start of a perfect relationship. She did allow, however, for the first time this past week, a pang of regret about not being in a sanctified marriage. She quickly dismissed the thought and promised herself to enjoy the last few hours of her honeymoon.

Ann was dressed smartly in a neat suit which, although very businesslike, would be suitable for the restaurant to which Carl was taking her. She looked in the mirror once more and primped just a little. She reveled in the thought of how good she felt. Harold would be returning soon, but she was determined to enjoy her evening with Carl. Maybe this could be a help to her in determining her course for the future. If she enjoyed the evening with Carl, she might realize that her "love" for Harold was merely "infatuation." On the other hand, her relationship with Harold could become more intense if spending time with another gentleman didn't particularly set her "aglow." Also, above all else, she was still mourning Charles. She chose to remain open-minded. *I really have no pressure on me to make any important decisions about my future. No one is rushing me so I'll just take each day as it comes.*

While in deep thought, the doorbell rang and startled her. When she opened the door, she became slightly disconcerted. Carl looked very handsome in a well-fitted sport jacket. And that was the problem. He appeared so different from the other occasions when he had visited their home as a friend or when they had traveled together as couples. She greeted him with a peck on the cheek and complimented him not only on his jacket but also the fashionable tie he was wearing. He also complimented her on how lovely she looked and immediately apologized to her for not being more supportive of her after Charles's death.

After the short ride to the restaurant, they settled in at a corner table. The place was not particularly crowded, so they had much privacy. Carl opened with small talk as to how she was doing. She replied by talking about the class action suit against the airline. She talked about the slow but steady progress of her leg since the accident. She talked about the settlement from the driver's insurance company and his sentence for careless driving.

"Were you satisfied that justice was done?" Carl asked.

"You know, Carl, I was totally ambivalent. I kind of felt for the guy. He had a small family and all, but I knew in my heart that he had to be held responsible for his actions. I was just grateful to be alive. So, in essence, yes. I am satisfied that justice was served."

As the evening progressed, they enjoyed cocktails, appetizers, and entrees. Ann enjoyed roast duckling while Carl reveled in prime rib. Ann gave some thought to asking Carl to attend Martin's installation at the bank, but she quickly dismissed it. *I don't want those folks at the bank to see me dating anyone so soon after Charles' death.* Then another thought came to her. She was actually enjoying her evening with Carl. He was inquisitive about her relationship with Farley to prod her for any information she might have about the progress of the marriage commission Farley was serving on. He was well aware of the Lincroft's friendship with Farley and had spoken with him on many occasions at the Lincroft home. He did not, however, have any awareness of a romantic interest between Farley and Ann. She didn't want to let on to him that Farley had called earlier that evening and that she already knew the findings of the marriage commission. "I think we'll just have to wait and read about it in the paper," was her curt reply. She hoped she could dodge the issue and talk less about Farley.

To change the subject, she asked Carl how he got along with the household chores. He replied that he still had Ella working for him and she kept his home in order. "I guess I get under her skin once in a while if I'm home and not out on the golf course. Sometimes she's like an army general." He laughed.

They ordered after-dinner cordials and reminisced about the many trips the Winsteads and Lincrofts had taken together.

Not wanting to push things but thoroughly enjoying the evening, Carl decided he would take Ann home directly after their dinner.

Upon finishing the cordials and the ritual of paying the check, they walked arm in arm from the restaurant. He told Ann to wait at the door and he would get the car. In a short time he was at the door to carefully help Ann into the car. He was mindful that her leg was not yet completely healed, and it was a bit of a struggle to get in and out of the car. On the way home, Carl expressed the fact that he had enjoyed the evening immensely and once again apologized to Ann for not being more attentive in the last few weeks. She told him she also enjoyed the evening. However, she decided at the back of her mind that she didn't want to give him any encouragement until she could wrap her mind around the direction her life was taking.

Carl walked her to the door of her house, kissed her on the cheek, and thanked her for a lovely evening. He asked her to wait at the door while he went in first to turn on the lights and check the house. He then saw her inside and returned to his car. He drove away with a new interest in Ann. *She always was and is a delightful woman*, he thought.

Ann turned out the lights and slipped into bed. She saw Carl in a new light. *He's a very interesting man. This makes my situation ever so much more challenging.* She did enjoy the evening.

Reynolds went to sleep that night greatly relieved that Farley was returning. His work load would be decreasing. Also, he could finally satisfy the media by retreating from them and handing them over to Farley. He prayed for Farley's safe return and thanked the Holy Spirit for guiding him and helping him with the duties of the diocese.

CHAPTER TWENTY

Farley was startled out of his sleep by a sharp rap on the door to his room. He was still fuzzy, but he looked at his clock and saw that it was five forty-five in the morning. The sliver of sun that came into his room at his usual waking hour had not yet made its appearance. Another knock on his door and he arose from the bed and put on his robe. He went to the door and before opening inquired as to who was knocking.

"It is I, Bill Armstrong."

Farley quickly opened the door and was faced with a frightened-looking Bill Armstrong.

"I have terrible news, Eminence. The Holy Father is dead. Monsignor Rinaldi asked me to arise and notify you immediately. He told me to tell you that Fiorvante and Bella are at the papal apartment now and have asked you to join them there."

"Give me a minute to get dressed and I'll be right there." Farley wondered if he was dreaming. His friend, Pope Clement XV, couldn't possibly be dead. Their last moments together were strained and if his death is certain, he would surely agonize over their last moments together. *Do they really know at this time that he is dead?* He quickly got dressed and made his way over to the papal apartment. Armstrong had given him a flashlight to better navigate the streets and find his way to the papal apartment in the predawn darkness.

He arrived at the apartment just behind the pope's physician. The nun who cared for the papal apartment was standing near the door, obviously in a state of agitation. Alongside her were Fiorvante, clad only in pants, T-shirt, and slippers; and Bella, clad in pajamas and a robe. Bella and Farley peered into the bedroom where they saw the pope's physician examining the body of Francone as he lay on his bed. He was feverishly looking for a pulse, but Farley could see that there was no life just by the telltale sign of the pope's mouth being agape. Farley and Bella returned to the reception room with Fiorvante and the nun still standing there. All were quiet. No one knew what to say. Farley dwelled on the fact that no one knew of the pope's heart problem, but he and Monsignor Bella. He didn't know for sure how much Bella knew, but he must have known something seeing the comings and goings of the papal physician in recent days. The physician came out of the bedroom and confirmed what they already knew. The life of Clement XV was over. No one moved. It appeared to Farley that the world stood still for an enormous amount of time that probably totaled less then thirty seconds.

Bella knew that he had to hurry and get dressed and work with Fiorvante to go through all the rituals involved with the death of a pope. Then they would have to release the news to the world. Finally, Bella would have a most unpleasant duty to perform. As prefect of the papal household, he would have to clear the bed linens and arrange to gather the pope's possessions. They would be placed in temporary storage. He would then seal the apartment until it was reopened for Clement's successor.

As Bella hurried out of the room, the nun who had faithfully served Clement for his years as pope broke down in sobs. She also left the room and went to the nearby chapel to pray.

Fiorvante and Farley stood alone in the reception room after the physician went to a nearby office to fill out all the necessary forms and documents to certify the death. Fiorvante wore a puzzled look. Apparently, he wasn't sure if this was really happening. "We must prepare for the funeral and beyond that a conclave. However, I must calm myself and take one step at a time. I will first contact the embalmer and prepare our good friend to lie in state and subsequently to be entombed."

Farley wondered why he was asked to the apartment since he was not on the pope's staff nor was he an advisor to the pope. He was not involved in any of the rituals of the death pronouncement such as the removing of the papal ring and the symbolic tapping of the hammer. Those tasks belonged to Bella and Fiorvante and they would be performed upon Bella's return. Farley asked in a low voice, "Cardinal Fiorvante, Clement was a good friend of mine on a personal level. Whatever I can do to help, I will do. I would deem it a special honor to be a presider at his funeral Mass." He then quickly gave thought as to whether or not anyone else except he, Bella, and the doctor knew that the pope had heart problems.

Fiorvante then scowled at Farley and in a tone that bordered on anger blurted out, "You were the last one to be seen with him. Was he ill? What happened?"

So that was it. That was why he was called here. Farley became agitated. "You're not accusing me of killing my friend, I hope."

"God bless us Farley, you're really stretching with that remark. I just simply want to know if you caused him any stress."

Farley, who never cared much for Fiorvante but had accepted him more graciously during the deliberations of the marriage commission, now returned to the dislike mode. *What made him think I caused my friend any great stress?*

A short moment of silence ensued and Fiorvante became more somber. "I apologize," he said, which totally surprised Farley.

"Apology accepted," he replied.

"Possibly you had a difference of opinion on the results of the marriage commission."

Farley had to expend great effort on not becoming angry, especially when he knew that Clement and he were in agreement on their personal feelings about the commission. He now added to his inner turmoil by knowing something about Clement that most assuredly was responsible for his death. Yet he was not able to divulge that information. To add even further to his woes, according to papal protocol, there would be no autopsy. The cause of death would probably be listed as a heart attack. He had to live with the fact that he knew the pope's heart was not good. But he also assumed the guilt of possibly putting his friend over the edge. However, a glimmer of hope made its appearance. The results of the pope's tests would be known in about a week. Hopefully, that would reveal to all what Farley already knew. Spiritually, Clement's heart was in great shape, but not physically.

Farley looked at Fiorvante and, thinking of his own guilty feelings, thought of himself being tried, judged, and sentenced at the same time. Trying to regain his composure, he again eyed Fiorvante and calmly replied, "He didn't appear ill to me." Farley was telling the truth since Clement certainly did not appear to be ill. He also knew that Clement's conversation about his heart problems was meant for Farley's ears alone.

"I can't believe this," Fiorvante muttered. "Yes, of course, you will be a concelebrant at the funeral Mass. As a matter of fact, even though your work on the marriage commission has concluded, you and all the cardinals will remain here for the funeral and conclave. I will have to wire those cardinals not present to come to Rome for the funeral and subsequently stay for the conclave."

Both Farley and Fiorvante had been insulated by shock but that was wearing off and they were now plunging into reality. "I just cannot believe this," Fiorvante muttered again.

With terrible guilty feelings taking hold of Farley as the reality of what had happened was becoming clearer to him, he stammered, "I must talk to you now in the solitude of the penitential sacrament."

Fiorvante's mood changed. He looked at Farley with great suspicion and asked, "Right now? Be aware that Monsignor Bella will be returning shortly."

Farley said, "I'll take the chance that if he returns, we can somehow wave him off until I've made my confession." He then explained to Fiorvante his previous evening's confrontation with Clement.

After Fiorvante listened to what Farley told him, he stared at Farley for what seemed to be an inordinate length of time. "You what! You asked for dispensation from your vows to marry! You—a possible successor to the throne of Peter! No wonder Clement was aggravated. I have to think you don't realize how serious this matter is. My God, Harold, in the next few weeks we go into a conclave and you are a leading candidate. The Holy Spirit guides the church and if you are serious, you must leave the priesthood immediately. We certainly cannot elect a priest who is having an affair with a woman to become the pope."

Farley interrupted. "I'm not having an affair with her. I love the woman and wish to be with her, but I respect her especially since she is recently widowed. There has been nothing of a sexual relationship with this woman, but my attraction to her is very strong."

Fiorvante said, "If you are serious about this, since I am technically in charge until a new pope is elected, I will arrange it for you as speedily as possible. However, and I say this with all sincerity, think about what you are doing and what your leaving will mean to God's church and to his people. I even wonder if the conclave wouldn't be severely hurt by an announcement that a cardinal could not participate because he is being released from his vows to marry. On top of that, think of the shock it would create when that cardinal happens to be the first American with the possibility of ascending to the throne of Peter. Also, think about the notoriety received from serving on the marriage commission and what the subsequent public reaction would be in relation to that service you performed for the church. In the name of all that is good and holy, please don't do this. And allow me to add that it is with certainty that I can assume that this revelation to Clement was very emotionally disturbing to His Holiness."

Farley asked for forgiveness within the penitential sacrament for any distress he caused his good friend, who just happened to be the Holy Father. Fiorvante felt he had made his position clear and offered Farley the forgiveness he sought. He asked Farley to pray the rosary and to contemplate on his priesthood and devoting the remainder of his life to that calling as he had promised on his ordination day. Fiorvante urged him to resist worldly temptation. Farley made a sincere Act of Contrition and put his ever increasing inner turmoil on hold. What mattered most at this time was dealing with the untimely death of the pope.

Fiorvante then explained to him that he would be preparing for the funeral rituals and restated his earlier commitment to Farley about concelebrating the funeral Mass. "Of course, he was a personal friend to you, so you will definitely be on the altar with the other concelebrating prelates." Farley felt humbled and thanked Fiorvante. He then summarily dismissed Farley as Monsignor Bella returned fully vested to perform the necessary rituals. As Farley left the papal apartment, he saw Bella conversing with Fiorvante. Fiorvante then left the apartment to vest himself and return to assist Monsignor Bella. Farley knew that shortly the apartment would be sealed and he glanced back once more, still amazed at how surreal all of it seemed.

Farley returned to his room, walking at a slow pace through the streets of Rome. He was still in a state of shock, but this didn't prevent him from shedding a tear. *I pray with all my soul that our confrontation wasn't responsible for his death. Can I forgive myself? Almighty God, please have mercy on his soul and grant me strength to deal with this. I have never so desperately needed your help.*

When he returned to his room, he sat in the lone chair and again wept over another death in the past months. He hoped that Bella knew something of the pope's condition and perhaps would release that information when the test results were known.

In a moment that appeared to him as though the Holy Spirit was intervening to provide him a smidgen of relief, he thought about the headlines in the morning papers back home and the media throughout the world announcing the death of Clement. He thought this would definitely trump any coverage of the marriage commission. The sun had broken through the narrow window in his room and cast its characteristic sliver of light across the room. He continued in contemplation.

Fiorvante was now temporary head of the church, and he and Bella were properly vested and performed all the rituals required upon the death of a pontiff. The door was ceremoniously sealed and a Swiss guardsman stationed at the door. The era of Pope Clement XV was at an end.

Fiorvante called the Vatican Daily to inform them of a news conference at nine in the morning. They in turn would notify other members of the media. The conference would take place in the same auditorium that, just yesterday, heralded the conclusion of the marriage commission. Obviously the word had spread very quickly as the sun began to fill the sky. One by one, the prelates, especially the cardinals, reported to Fiorvante to express their sorrow. It would turn out that he would ask Tessier and Obiajunwa to also be concelebrants with him and Farley. The Vatican would continue to provide accommodations for all the prelates that were already there for the marriage commission meetings. All the cardinals not serving on the marriage commission would be notified to arrive in Rome within the next few days. Their accommodations would be in the new hotel erected for the purpose of housing the cardinals during the conclave. They would join those cardinals already in Rome serving on the marriage commission who would be changing their accommodations to that of the hotel. Fiorvante was only allowing a small window of time between the completion of the funeral rites for Clement and the start of the conclave, just enough time to allow workers to install the necessary furniture in the Sistine Chapel to accommodate the electors. The time would be so brief that most would opt to stay through the conclave.

In spite of all this, he was still angered at Farley for what he considered to be a totally frivolous dilemma into which he brought the Holy Father. Since it was a matter of confession, Fiorvante had to keep the matter to himself. *I can just imagine how stressed the Holy Father must have been with Farley. They were best friends and both church leaders.* He then asked the Almighty God to remove bitterness from his heart and allow him to prepare for the burial of the Holy Father with all the dignity that it deserved. He left his office to offer Mass and pray for the repose of Clement's soul.

Farley got up from his chair and went to the shower. He dressed quickly and searched for an empty chapel in which to offer Mass. Bill Armstrong just happened to be walking down the hall and offered to assist Farley in locating a chapel. He also offered to serve Mass for Farley. Farley welcomed him, and no more words needed to be exchanged. Both were in extreme sorrow.

At nine in the morning, Fiorvante reported to the reception area for the news conference. He wondered how so many already knew about the death. Then again, in these days of modern communication, he wasn't so surprised after all. In just a few hours, all the media in America would blare the news. The results of the marriage commission would be relegated to page three or not mentioned at all.

Fiorvante spoke in Italian to the gathered media and sadly announced the death of the pontiff. He explained that there was no response to the morning knock on his door by the housekeeper. She then summoned the Prefect of the Papal Household,

Monsignor Bella. He had entered the pope's bedroom and tried to elicit a response from the Holy Father but was unable to do so. He then summoned the pope's physician, who after a brief but thorough examination for life signs, officially pronounced the Holy Father dead. His physician estimated the time of death was approximately three fifteen in the morning.

Fiorvante then added that by regulation, he was the temporary head of the church. He also announced that he would be arranging the funeral liturgies and once they were completed, he would announce preparations for the conclave.

Farley was at the media conference but was only able to pick up small bits of Fiorvante's explanation. He was familiar with some Italian, but not all of what Fiorvante was saying was intelligible. Cardinals Josephson and Feeney were also at the conference and when they saw Farley, they went to him and consoled him on the loss of his friend and their shepherd.

"Didn't you have dinner with him last night?" Josephson asked

Farley answered that he did but very little of what they had discussed could be revealed. They repeated what Fiorvante had already asked him, "Did he seem at all out of sorts?"

Again Farley bent the truth and replied, "He seemed fine, health-wise."

"We will have to get in touch with our people back home to tell them we will not be going home right away," Feeney said. "We'll probably stay right through the conclave since the small amount of time between the funeral and the conclave would preclude us from going home and then coming right back."

Farley knew Feeney was right because he recalled Fiorvante telling him that he would be wiring all the cardinals not already in Rome and summon them to be here for the funeral and remain for the conclave. He got the impression that the expanse of time from the completion of the funeral rites and the start of the conclave would be very brief. *Perhaps he's afraid of being the head of the church, and he being a possible successor!* Farley thought.

"And you didn't see any problems with your friend last night?" Josephson then reiterated quizzically.

Farley again replied, "No." He then added, "We spoke about the marriage commission results and he gave me his opinions, but I feel those should be confidential. Suffice it to say that he felt the commission did a yeoman job and he was gratified. He also said that maybe the same subject can be broached at a future time. Other than that, we talked about our personal lives and I left his apartment shortly after eleven."

Farley then thought about the humorous aspect of the evening and passed that on to Josephson and Feeney. "I thought it so out of context that the Holy Father actually cleaned up the kitchen. He let his housekeeper, who arose early in the morning, to return to her room at a decent hour. That gave me great insight into his kindness."

In the background, Fiorvante was answering the last of the questions and anxiously closing out the conference. His information at the present time was limited. The three of them walked toward the entrance to the auditorium.

Feeney looked at his friends and repeated what came across Farley's mind earlier that morning. "Our marriage commission results will certainly take a back seat to this event." All were in agreement.

The three of them parted to return to their rooms and agreed to meet for lunch. It was only five in the morning back home, and they knew that most of the sheep of their flocks had not been startled by the news yet.

Farley spent the remaining morning hour or so in his room. He would call Ann after lunch and tell her of his extended stay in Rome even though she would be fully aware of that when she heard the news. More importantly he would call Reynolds with a plea to continue at the helm of the diocese in his absence. He knew this plea would be greeted by Reynolds with not a minimum amount of trepidation. He then prayed for guidance.

He also prayed for strength to concentrate on the matters at hand and tried to reflect on his situation. He felt uneasiness at having trivialized his desire to leave the priesthood. He felt that the Holy Spirit was possibly pushing him to involve himself more with his priesthood. He was actually thinking more of his love for Ann as being a passing infatuation due to her vulnerability and their friendship. He continued to sublimate his thoughts of Ann and vowed to do so through the conclave. He prayed in earnest to be a good priest, especially at that crucial moment in church history. He vowed to concentrate on his proper priestly role in the funeral of another of his friends and in the election of a new pope, *Probably Fiorvante*, he thought. He would concentrate on his priesthood, which he still knew he loved, and that gave him some peace. He prepared to go to lunch.

Archbishops Carson and Carnavale and McConnell from Ireland joined Feeney, Josephson, and Farley for lunch. They noticed Cardinal Naguchi and Cardinal Gamallo having lunch at a table nearby and all nodded a somber hello. It was indeed a somber atmosphere. Carnavale, as usual, tried to lighten the atmosphere by announcing that at least he could head home after the funeral. He would be glad to do so, since his diocese was in the hands of his auxiliary in whom he didn't have much faith. He emphasized that he had no idea what shape the diocese would be in. "You, cardinals, will remain here for the conclave. And don't remind me. I know I can't discuss the conclave with you, but, just as a note, I'm betting on Fiorvante."

Farley interjected, "By the way, Fiorvante has asked me to be on the altar with him, Tessier, and Obiajunwa. Even though all of us will be officially concelebrants, I was deeply moved by that request. He was aware of my friendship with Francone."

"You'll be right up there with the papabili," McConnell said.

"Remember, he who goes in as a pope, comes out a cardinal," Farley replied. "However, that being said, I think Fiorvante is a strong contender." Farley then gave some thought to his on-again, off-again feelings toward the man who could be pope. Then he thought to himself, *If only they knew what was going on in my life—the fact that Fiorvante is aware of my confession and the undue stress I may have caused Clement.* He strove to change the subject and tried to steer things to the marriage commission.

Feeney would not allow a change of subject because at that moment he again inquired about the pope's death and how mysterious it was, and how similar to the death of John Paul I. "No previous signs of illness and just to die in his sleep. Very mysterious indeed."

Then, looking at Farley, he said, "And you saw no signs of problems? Harold, you were the last person to see him alive. You told us the housekeeper was dismissed, so no one was with him but you. When you left the apartment, the pope retired and never woke up."

Farley became somewhat disgruntled and replied, "So you are insinuating what?" He gave thought as to how much longer he would be able to contain the pope's secret heart problem.

"My God, Harold! I'm not accusing you of anything. I'm just dumbfounded that you saw nothing unusual about your friend. You left him at eleven last night, and by three in the morning, he was dead. It's just so mysterious."

Not willing to tip his hand, Farley replied, "Perhaps he had a problem and no one knew about it. Maybe his physician will release that information shortly."

"I think if the doctor knows something, he should say so now and relieve inquisitive minds like mine."

Archbishop McConnell then joined the conversation. "I hope I'm not divulging something I shouldn't be, but I saw Fiorvante conversing with the physician and another prelate, who shall remain nameless. I overheard something. The physician had information concerning the pope's health, but the Holy Father had asked him to keep it under wraps until the test results were in. The physician felt duty-bound by the pontiff's request until all the test results were in. He said only he and Monsignor Bella were aware of a problem. So apparently some testing was done, relating to what I don't know, and the results are simply not available yet. Fiorvante will be notifying the media either later today or tomorrow. I don't want to spread false rumors so I would keep this among us and wait until Fiorvante makes it official."

Farley sensed a great relief and hoped this was not a rumor but a fact. It would certainly put him at some ease. However, he knew that even if the test results showed a pre-existing condition, he was the last one with him, and he was aware of the stress he had caused his good friend.

They continued their lunch and shortly they would return to the Vatican to hear news of the funeral arrangements, and hopefully for Farley, news of the pope's pre-existing condition.

Reynolds awoke early and was understandably shocked by the news of the pontiff's death. *Well, Harold will have to break his promise to me of coming home. Maybe there will be some time between the funeral and conclave for him to come home and be updated. But I should not be concerned about my well-being at this time. I should be concerned about the repose of the soul of our Supreme Shepherd. A good man who was intensely interested in the well being of his flock. He will be missed.*

He strove to drive away selfish thoughts about keeping the ever intrusive press at a distance, not only concerning Farley's report on the minority housing issue, but also concerning the results of the marriage commission. But then he thought those issues would certainly be subordinate to this shocking development. He knelt at the foot of his bed and prayed earnestly for guidance during the day and for the repose of the soul of Clement, his bishop. After prayer, he showered and prepared for his day which he knew would be very busy. He also hoped that Farley would communicate with him as soon as possible and advise him of his plans for the next few days.

Ann was used to rising every day at the same time, but she continued to set her clock radio each night. As she lay in bed removing the early morning cobwebs, she was startled by the news on the radio of the pope's death. *My God!* she thought. *Harold just told me yesterday he was having dinner with the pope. What happened?* Her mind rambled in all directions. *I wonder how Harold is. Was he with Clement when he died? Will he be able to call me? This is overwhelming. Of course, he won't be coming home as promised. In fact, he will have to stay for the papal election. Did he say anything to his friend, Clement, about our relationship?* She quickly arose from the bed to get ready for the day. Her previous evening with Carl seemed to fade to the background.

When she finally went downstairs to partake of breakfast, she sighed. *I don't believe this. It's like the perfect storm.* The phone rang, startling her at that early hour. Marie still had not yet arrived, so she allowed the answering machine to announce her unavailability to answer the phone. *Oh, God! I should have picked up, that could be Harold.* She raced to the phone but arrived too late. The message being recorded was not from Farley but from Carl Winstead.

"Ann, sorry to call you this early, but I wanted to know if you heard the news. I'll try you later. Hope all is well."

Ann returned to the kitchen to finish her light breakfast. She planned to return the call at a later hour.

Reynolds arrived at the diocesan office early that morning, and there were already numerous messages left on the phone by the press. Jane wouldn't be arriving for another hour or so, but when she did arrive, he knew he would have to arrange some sort of media conference.

They would want to know all about the facts regarding the pontiff's death. At this early hour, he had very little information. *I wish Harold would call so I can be better informed. He dined with Clement last evening. He must be in a state of shock.* It was almost miraculous that the phone rang on the private line, so Reynolds knew that had to be Farley. His relief was confirmed when he picked up the phone and heard Farley's voice on the line.

"Jim, we're all dumbfounded here. I must advise you and I'm sure you're already aware of the fact that the diocese will be in your hands for another few weeks. There won't be enough time for me to come home between the funeral and the conclave, so I'll be staying here. There is supposedly going to be another media conference on Clements's death. Fiorvante may have more information from the pope's physician."

When Farley mentioned this to Reynolds, he hoped with all his might that that would be the case. "I wouldn't mention that to the local press just yet. Just tell them that your understanding is that more information will be released at a later time, and you will update them when you have that information."

"And you just dined with him, Harold. Did you notice anything?"

Here we go again, Farley thought. "Not a thing, Jim. You can imagine my shock early this morning when I heard the news. We had dinner and conversation until late last night, and I still can't absorb it. By the way, I'm sure the press, through the wire services, has been informed of the determination of the marriage commission. There probably shouldn't be any further questions on that. The Vatican press attended the final meeting so that information should be readily available. I'm betting though that any more news on that is certainly on the back burner today. It's my belief that Fiorvante has called another news conference for tomorrow. Hopefully there will be more information forthcoming as well as the details of the funeral rites. By the way, Jim, pray for me and pass the word to Beardsley, too. This is quite a conglomeration of events and has sort of turned all our lives upside down. I'll call you again as soon as I have any new information and thanks, Jim, for your help which is certainly now above and beyond the call of duty. Talk to you later."

Farley disconnected, and Reynolds gave quick thought to doing battle with the press, which he certainly did not enjoy. He thought to himself, *They still haven't heard from Farley on his report to the city on housing for minorities.* Reynolds replaced the phone and went to get a cup of coffee that would start his day, which would be busy. It would also be a turnaround from his feeling of relief in knowing that Farley would soon be home.

Farley returned to his room for contemplation. Upon his return, he found a note from Bill Armstrong concerning a special Mass that evening. Fiorvante had invited all the prelates who were presently at the Vatican for a concelebration of a Mass for the happy repose of their late bishop's soul. Many of the world's bishops and cardinals would be arriving tomorrow or soon thereafter, and so Farley surmised that the funeral rites would probably be underway the next evening. He also surmised that Fiorvante would announce further plans at that evening's Mass. Upon continuing the note, he noticed that his room assignment had been changed to the reasonably new hotel facility, the Domus Santa Marta, which was erected at the Vatican to house the cardinals in conclave. He decided to put his meager belongings together. He also decided to ask Armstrong to take his laundry and have it returned to him at his new location. Before continuing his transfer movements, however, he sat on his uncomfortable chair and decided to take a break for meditation.

Karen and Tom awoke early and didn't know why. Tom still had another day of vacation left and they were both exhausted from the long trip home last night. Tom went to the kitchen to prepare the first of his many cups of coffee for the day. Karen headed to the bathroom and a wake-up shower. Tom turned on the television and gasped when he saw the news of the pope's death being flashed across the screen. He ran to the bathroom and knocked on the door. Karen, in the midst of her shower, barely heard the knock, but she yelled out to him, "What's up?"

"Pope Clement died last night. Not many details yet."

"My God!" was all Karen could muster. "I'll be right out."

Tom returned to the kitchen and stared at the screen while anxiously awaiting his first sip of coffee. In a few minutes, he was joined by his new wife. Her hair was still dripping and she was clad only in her terry cloth robe. She took a cup from the cabinet, and as the coffee was now ready, she poured herself a cup. She looked at the television in disbelief. Neither of them gave any thought to the marriage commission.

The late afternoon sun shone on the Vatican, but the mood that permeated was somber. Farley hurried through the streets to Vatican City and went to the hotel. At the desk, he received a key to room 208. He took the elevator to the second floor. He emerged from the elevator. It was only a brief walk to his room. He noticed a Swiss guardsman at the end of the hall. He thought, *The conclave doesn't begin until after we bury the Holy Father. What's he doing here now?* He walked up to the guardsman and asked him why he was there. The guardsman related to him that he was stationed there on Fiorvante's orders. He told him that beginning tonight, all the cardinals arriving there would be told that "silencia" would be the rule while they were in the premises. He also stated that they would all be assigned to that hotel throughout the pope's funeral rites and up to the conclave. Prior to the conclave, conversation would be permitted among the cardinals at any time with the exception of the hotel. When the conclave began, they would be totally sequestered and alone between there and the Sistine Chapel. Farley thanked the man for the information and mused that it seemed a little like overkill. *There's at least ten days until the conclave under the normal period of mourning following the pontiff's death.* Of course, he also knew that under the new procedures, Fiorvante could shorten that period. *Still,* he thought, *we will have plenty of time to communicate among ourselves while not here at the hotel. So why the security now?* He brought into question Fiorvante's motives, but he thought it best to let it be. There was already way too much on his mind. He also thought that while he had no great love for Fiorvante, he was probably the best man for the papacy. In any event, since Ann was still a major part of his life, he would have to deal with Fiorvante on that matter. Since he was aware of Fiorvante's feelings on his predicament, he knew he was going to have to ingratiate himself to the pope elect. *I better develop a liking for this man if the Holy Spirit is calling me to elect him.*

He turned around and walked toward the door to room 208. He used the magnetic key card to open the door and gazed upon a comfortable room for the first time since he arrived in Rome. The room wasn't as large as he thought, but it was one thousand percent more inviting then his room at the college. The floor was carpeted and he had a private bath. There was a desk and a comfortable easy chair. *Well this will be my home for the next few weeks.* He spent some time in prayer and contemplation to allow the Spirit to enter him and prepare him for that evening's Mass.

Ann returned a call to Carl late in the morning. Carl looked at his caller identification when the phone rang and picked it up instantly. "What a shock, Ann! Do you believe it?"

"I'm totally flustered," Ann replied. "Such an unexpected event."

Carl knew that the Lincrofts were friendly with Farley since he had been at the Lincroft home on many occasions and had shared many conversations with Carl. His next question then was not unexpected by Ann. "Has the Cardinal tried to reach you at all?"

"As a matter of fact, he called me yesterday afternoon and told me he was dining with the pope. I don't expect to hear from him any time soon again. I'm sure his schedule will be very crowded with all the rituals and ceremonies that will be taking place within the next few days. Also don't forget the conclave that follows. He will be totally isolated."

Ann made an effort to sound very nonchalant in making her remarks. She wasn't going to make it sound at all like her relationship with Farley was serious. She was hardly ready for that concept, and she definitely didn't think the rest of the world was ready.

While conversing with Ann, thoughts were racing through Carl's mind. He knew that Farley was very close to the Lincrofts, but he was still surprised that Farley would call Ann all the way from Rome. He had asked the question more in jest, so he was very surprised to learn that Farley had called. Turning back to reality and not wanting to push the envelope, he remarked again to Ann that he had enjoyed their date immensely and if perhaps they could get together again.

Ann, keeping an open mind but not wanting to encourage him, replied, "I enjoyed the evening also. I would say that getting together again is well within the realm of possibility, but I will be busy the next few evenings. You know…bank business."

Carl replied. "If there is anything I can do, please feel free to avail yourself of my services."

Ann thanked him, but she knew it was best to attend the bank installation affair on her own. She laughed when she realized that she had told Carl she was engaged in bank business. As of now, he had no idea that Charles had left her well off without the worries of the bank. But after all, the installation party was bank business.

Reynolds called Jane into his office to have her prepare some written remarks to present to the media. "Good morning, Jane."

"Good morning," she replied. "Although it seems improper to bring this matter up, which appears to be trivial in light of the fact that the Holy Father has passed away, but just who do I work for?" She continued in a light and humorous vein, "It seems I was hired by Cardinal Farley and worked for him very briefly. My good Bishop Reynolds, have you hired me away from him?" She then laughed heartily and Reynolds, who was a good-natured man, laughed with her.

"It sure looks that way, doesn't it? And now with the news of the pontiff's death, it looks like you and I will be partners for a few more weeks. But think of my secretary who is taking care of my parish duties while I'm over here. In addition to all she is doing in managing the parish, she also takes time to keep me informed. But I have faith in God that all this will sort out in the next few weeks."

Reynolds handed Jane some notes he had made regarding the death of Clement, and she took them to her office to make them ready for distribution to the media.

The evening Mass was about to commence. While all were vesting, Fiorvante told them that there would be a news conference the next morning with the pope's physician present. The pope's body would be placed in front of the main altar at St. Peter's in the afternoon. The Basilica would then be open to the public so that they would be able to pay their respects to their beloved Pope Clement. There would be a memorial liturgical service in the evening to which prelates of other faith communities would be invited to attend. The solemn funeral Mass would be the following day at three in the afternoon followed by entombment in the grotto of the Basilica.

All the prelates were now vested, and they stood in line for the procession to the main altar at St. Peter's. The Basilica and the plaza outside were filled. It was a formidable tribute to the love of Clement by the sheep of his flock. When the choir began to sing and the cardinals, bishops, and priests processed down the main aisle, Farley struggled to keep his emotions intact. The shock was wearing off and reality was increasing its grip. He thought about how kind and loving this friend of his was. He tried not to dwell on the aggravation he had caused his friend. He concentrated instead on offering the Mass with the utmost sincerity he could muster so that it would be a worthy tribute to his friend. How moving this tribute was and it made him feel so close to his beloved church and to his priesthood. It was truly an honor for him to be in this procession and to partake of the beautiful celebration of the life of the Shepherd of the Roman Catholic church.

Fiorvante delivered a moving eulogy that brought many to tears. Farley again thought about his dinner with the pope and begged God to rid him of thoughts that he was, in any way, responsible for the death of the pontiff. He hoped that the pope's physician would shed new light on Clement's death and perhaps alleviate his guilty feelings. He was asked to participate in the reading of the Eucharistic Prayer in Latin, of course. It didn't matter that it was in Latin since Farley knew the Prayer by heart. He was filled with emotion as he did so.

At the conclusion of the Mass, everyone in attendance maintained their somber air, and very little conversation took place. The quarters were also quite crowded with the number of prelates in attendance. One had to wonder how all the priests that would be arriving tomorrow would be able to vest properly for the various ceremonies. As Farley walked to the door, Fiorvante approached him. He looked at Farley as though he could look right through him and said, "I would like for you to address the eulogy at the funeral Mass. You were close to him, and I think the eulogy would be a fitting tribute to him coming from you."

Farley was totally awestruck and deeply moved. "I would deem it the highest honor of my life. Thank you most sincerely," was all he could think of to say. He knew now that he would have to sit down and compose a eulogy that would embody the life of not only a good friend to him, but a loving person to the entire world. He wanted to do his best for this person who was so worthy of admiration. He thanked Fiorvante profusely and again thought about the fact that he just couldn't figure this man out. Sometimes he could appear so uncaring, and sometimes he appeared so loving, but the man was staunch in his beliefs, and you could not take that from him. More and more, Farley felt he would be the future pastor of the church.

After leaving the Basilica, Farley and the rest of the clergy returned to their respective quarters to dwell on the monumental events that had just taken place.

CHAPTER TWENTY-ONE

As Farley arose to the break of another day, he went to the large window and opened the drapes. The sunlight was dazzling. He thanked God for another day and contemplated on the extraordinary series of events that had taken place in the last few days. He proceeded to his chair for his morning prayers. Armstrong would be arriving within the next half hour hopefully with his laundry and dry cleaning. After prayers he moved to the luxury of a private shower. He gave some thought to the upcoming press conference. He hoped that it would fully explain the late pontiff's health problems. He still wrestled with the annoying thought, however, that his conversation with Clement concerning his love for Ann was the cause of major distress for his friend. He had to accept the fact that he just didn't know how seriously ill the pope was and how closely he, Farley, was regarded as a priest by his friend. He simply didn't think that this would cause more than a mild distraction for the pope. Even though they were friends, he had no idea of the esteem in which the pope held him. He himself had to come to grips with how serious his priesthood meant both to his peers and himself, and more importantly, to God and his church. Emerging from the shower, he wrapped his robe around him and then heard a knock on the door. When he opened the door, Armstrong stood there with an armful of Farley's newly laundered and pressed clothes. Farley thanked Armstrong and said he would be concelebrating Mass that morning with Cardinals Josephson and Feeney, who were lodged on the fourth floor. Armstrong volunteered to serve at the Mass. Farley told Armstrong that he would meet him at the chapel. As Armstrong walked down the hall, he eyed the Swiss guardsman who said nothing to him even though he had broken the rule of "silencia." Farley closed the door and proceeded to finish dressing. He thought about two of his fellow American prelates on the marriage commission, namely Carson and Carnavale, and wondered how they were holding up in their meager accommodations back at the College.

After Mass, the three celebrants and Armstrong went to the dining room at the hotel for breakfast. The dining room was furnished rather simply, apparently in an effort to maintain austerity. Despite the rule of silence, they conversed with each other. There was no sign of security at that time in the room. Feeney and Josephson questioned Farley asking him if he had changed his mind about trying to get back to his diocese before the conclave. They were aware that the time would be brief. He explained that he had already informed his auxiliary that he would not be coming home until after the conclave. "Not enough time," he said." "Fiorvante must be inpatient about assuming the papacy since he's calling for a conclave so quickly following the entombment of Clement." They all laughed.

"In the few conversations with fellow electors serving with us on the commission," Feeney said, "I'm not so sure that Fiorvante has a lock on the papacy. His staunchest support is with the Curia, and he was unable to get a unanimous vote from those people siding with his views toward annulment. There's a lot of support for Tessier and Obiajunwa and even you, Harold."

Farley quickly dismissed that thought and put a damper on the conversation by reminding them that "campaigning" or even discussing the conclave was frowned upon greatly. "We must contemplate inwardly and allow the Holy Spirit to enter and guide us."

Josephson interjected, "You're right, Harold, and besides we definitely should be devoting our time to the repose of the soul of our shepherd. In any event, I'm looking forward to the press conference that will hopefully shed light on the pope's untimely passing."

Farley echoed Josephson's sentiments for obvious reasons. He then added, "Oh! By the way Fiorvante asked me to do the eulogy at Clement's funeral. I have to tell you, I feel so humbled."

"Well, after all, you were close friends for many years, so I think that it was an appropriate gesture," Feeney interrupted.

Farley replied, "Thank you and I hope I can deliver a eulogy that is worthy of Francone's life and his legacy to the church. In fact, prior to the press conference, I'm going to my room to begin preparations. Also I have no idea who will be doing the homily at our service this afternoon. It would be useful to know, since I don't want my eulogy to be repetitive."

They all pushed away from the table and went their separate ways. Upon returning to his room, Farley suddenly remembered that he never called Ann to let her know he would be staying through the conclave. He thought, *Maybe my love for Ann is truly just infatuation. I do love my priesthood and in these past few weeks my priestly obligations have consumed me. I have become so involved in such an extraordinary series of events that I have truly given little time to Ann. That doesn't speak well of my "interest" in her. But I will call her after lunch.*

He sat down and began to prepare the eulogy he would deliver at the pope's funeral Mass that would be celebrated the next day. He said a short prayer for guidance as he put pen to paper. He wanted it to be the greatest possible tribute to the deceased Shepherd who was a great, humble man. He could do no less. He had ample time to gather his thoughts since the press conference was still an hour away.

After noting a lengthy outline, he was pleased with what he had put together so far. He gave some thought to the fact that he should be an expert at that. In the last few weeks, he had delivered eulogies for a good friend and also for his housekeeper. He freshened up after approximately an hour's worth of thought-gathering and prepared to walk over to the press conference. He closed the door to his room behind him, and to his amazement, both Cardinals Mayfield and Spencer were walking down the hall. Only appearing somewhat haggard from their overnight flights, they all greeted each other warmly.

Mayfield was first to address Farley. "I see you're in room 208. I'm in 212 and my pal, John here, is 216."

Farley chuckled and replied, "Josephson and Feeney are on the fourth floor." Spencer chimed in, "What's with the Vatican police up here?"

"Oh! Fiorvante has them practicing for their security detail during the conclave. We are to have limited contact with each other up to and certainly including the conclave."

With that, the guard politely rebuked them, "Please, Fathers, with all due respect I have a job to do. No conferencing in this building."

They motioned to each other that they would meet at the press conference, and so Mayfield and Spencer went to their rooms and Farley boarded the elevator.

Upon alighting from the elevator in the lobby, he decided to take the long way to the auditorium through St. Peter's Square. He was totally awestruck by so many of the faithful already in the plaza and on line to view the body of Clement. The Basilica would not be open to the public for three hours. It amazed him to see those people standing there in the relentless sun, awaiting a chance to pay their respects to their beloved pontiff. The Basilica was presently closed to allow the embalmers to prepare the pope's body for viewing. Arriving at the auditorium, Farley was dressed in cassock and red sash while many of the other prelates were simply attired in their standard black suit and roman collar. The auditorium was crowded, and Fiorvante strutted up and down on the raised platform, still there from the marriage commission deliberations. The pope's physician was on the platform with him but was conversing with Monsignor Bella.

At exactly nine, Fiorvante asked for the attention of everyone in the room. He started his announcements with the plans for the liturgical rites within the next two days. The pope's body would lie in state at the main altar in St. Peter's beginning at noon. At five that afternoon, there would be a liturgical service. After the service, the pope's body would remain in state until nine in the evening to allow the faithful to pay their respects. At three the next day, the funeral Mass for the late pontiff would be held and Cardinal Harold Farley of the United States would eulogize the late Clement. After the Mass, Clement's body would be entombed in the crypt at St. Peter's with so many of the church's past shepherds. The funeral Mass would be held indoors, but large screen televisions were also being installed to convey the proceedings to the throng on the plaza. After explaining more of the details of the next few days' events, he then asked the pope's physician, Doctor Antonio Bellini, to clarify, as best as possible, the details concerning the pope's sudden death.

Speaking in Italian, the doctor said, "My dear prelates and faithful of our Roman Catholic church, it is with much emotion that I grieve with you the loss of our beloved Pope Clement. His wish was to cause no unhappiness to anyone while he was pontiff. In that vein, he asked me to keep any of his health problems to myself until it was definitely proven that he, in fact, had any problems. In the past month, he asked me to check him for problems he was having with shortness of breath and occasional minor pain in his chest. I was concerned enough to order some tests. The results of those tests were speeded up and I received them yesterday. I can report to you that our beloved pope had heart problems that were much more serious then he thought or that I suspected. There was a serious malfunction in one of the upper heart chambers. I must confess that in my preliminary examinations of our pope, I didn't detect anything quite so serious. He was apparently experiencing more pain and discomfort than he conveyed to me. Sad to say, the test results indicated that his condition was deteriorating so much so that the chance of adequate treatment was very remote. Death was imminent. Clement's death was caused by myocardial infarction or heart attack. I pray that since he died in his sleep, there was no pain and that he slipped the bonds of earth in peace. He deserved that." Doctor Bellini stepped away from the microphone and, almost in tears, returned to his seat.

Fiorvante then directed to the press that there would be no questions taken concerning the death of the pontiff. Doctor Bellini's explanation was adequate. He would entertain questions on the upcoming funeral rituals for the pope, but there would be no questions concerning the upcoming conclave. There were only a few questions asked concerning the rituals of the next two days involving the final ceremonies honoring Pope Clement. The conference ended, but it brought many solace in allaying any suspicion about the pope's demise.

Farley breathed an enormous sigh of relief. It eased so much suspicion about him and his last moments together with his friend. But he was also aware that Fiorvante and he knew all about those final hours. As much as Farley felt relieved, there was still a tinge of guilt about his last hours with his friend. *Did I push him over the edge? Bellini said death was imminent. The matter we discussed now seems so trivial. I still love Ann, but is it true lasting love, or is it possibly lust? It can't be lust; I love her and respect her too much. I have to make some decisions here. I must admit that the events of the past few weeks have totally wrapped me in my priesthood. Am I willing to give this up to marry a woman I love? It's probably only been easier to suppress thoughts of Ann because she isn't around.* He then went into prayer and again asked the Holy Spirit to guide him and be with him not only for the next few days but also through the conclave. *After the conclave, I can hit this matter square on with Fiorvante. I will call Ann later today. I'm not sure that's a wise decision, but I must call her. Please help me!*

Emerging from thought, he wheeled around and caught sight of so many of the prelates who were on the marriage commission with him. He also noticed many of the newly arrived prelates. He walked over to greet Tessier, Obiajunwa, and Singh. All were gracious and expressed their sorrow to each other about the loss of Clement. All of them also gave four stars to their new "luxurious" accommodations. Cardinal Middleton from Australia joined them and explained to them his feelings of being overwhelmed by the series of events in just the past few days. "How quickly life can change. All of us being immersed in the marriage commission, and then, in a flash, all that work and effort becomes secondary to a more extraordinary event. The changing of gears is quite dramatic."

Spencer and Mayfield were conversing as best they could with Cardinal Naguchi of Japan. He had the luxury of a young seminarian to assist him with translations. Farley walked over to them. Mayfield said he noticed Farley with Tessier and Singh and mentioned that while he had an occasional conversation with them on the phone, he had never formally met them. He said that he had met Obiajunwa and was very impressed by his spiritual demeanor. Spencer, of course, as delegate to the United States, had met all of them on various occasions. Obviously, however, he knew some better than others. While all the cardinals and bishops roamed the auditorium and carried on conversations with their peers, one could not help but notice that with the upcoming conclave, this could give the appearance of "politicking." However, the chief candidate, Fiorvante, was still conversing with the press and was not out in the body of the auditorium. All of them were careful to avoid any conversation regarding the conclave. In spite of this, Farley gave thought to Fiorvante's not mingling with the group. *I have no idea why he is so busy with the press. He assured them that there would be limited information to them subsequent to what he and Doctor Bellini had spoken to them about. I'm also sure that he's so confident in his election, that he feels no need to make contact with the other electors.* Then Farley asked God to rid him of such petty criticism and concentrate on the moment at hand—preparing the eulogy that he would give at the pope's funeral and saying farewell to a friend who also happened to be his Shepherd. Prior to returning to the solitude of his room, he agreed to meet with Cardinal Spencer and Archbishop Carnavale at lunch time. Farley returned to his room and solitude.

He put pen to paper in his room and began a brief outline of the eulogy he would deliver at the funeral Mass. He knew it had to be perfect because it was going out to a worldwide audience. Ridding himself of thoughts of the awful events surrounding his last conversation with the pope, it became easier to remember all the aspects of the good relationship they had always had. Again he was especially impressed with the pope's kindness. That would be the overwhelming theme of his tribute to Clement. It seemed that suddenly good thoughts were bombarding him, and he found it a joy to express them on behalf of his friend, Frank.

In what seemed like no time at all, he eyed the clock in his room and it was near twelve thirty. He would be meeting Spencer and Carnavale within the next half hour. They would meet at the Vatican Visitor's Center due to the tight security at the hotel.

Farley was now quite familiar with the area and knew of a satisfactory restaurant nearby, so after meeting with Spencer and Carnavale, they walked to Victorio's. While walking, Spencer nudged Farley and quipped, "So what ever happened to the marriage commission?"

"Very close vote! By just one vote we arrived at a decision of no change," Farley replied. Carnavale piped in, "Surprised me. Even though I'm happy with the decision, I actually thought that during the meetings, the consensus was to alleviate substantially the stumbling blocks of annulment. But after the debates and discussions, some of the early votes changed. While some conservatives changed to liberal, obviously more liberals went to conservative; but, as I said, I'm happy with the conclusion."

Spencer said he was happy too, but he wondered if the faithful would ever be aware of the outcome in light of the events of the past day.

The day was sunny but just slightly cooler and very comfortable as they made their way to Victorio's. Apparently it was the place to be as so many of the other prelates were there for lunch.

Reynolds picked up the paper and read all that appeared in the paper concerning the death of Clement. The television was already reporting the more detailed account of the pope's demise that was delivered by his physician. This was in contrast to the paper's report which was filled with speculation, since the paper was printed prior to the information from the news conference reaching the United States. He noticed in the paper, however, that there happened to be a sidebar within the report of Clement's death that referred to the marriage commission. The sidebar referred the reader to another page to which Reynolds immediately turned. The paper repeated what he already knew, that the marriage commission's decision was to retain the annulment process as is. It reported also that the decision was reached by one vote. There were very few details given except to highlight some of the remarks made by some of the individuals serving on the commission. Farley was quoted as was Fiorvante, and even Archbishop Gamallo of the Philippines, and Cardinal Naguchi of Japan. The press seemed to be very impressed with Cardinal Obiajunwa from Africa. Of course, the reporters in the United States were dissecting the remarks as liberal or conservative and trying to interpret those leanings as to how they would play out in the upcoming conclave. Reynolds said to himself, "It's really something how the reporters take what was said at the marriage commission meetings and make a deduction from that as to how the papal election will be decided. First of all, not all the prelates quoted were cardinals, so they're really reaching when they try to tie the remarks of a committee to the election of a new pope." He turned his attention back to the television to get more details on the pope's untimely death. He then went to the kitchen for coffee and returned to Farley's office which he now considered his by acclamation. He began the day's work.

Karen and Tom enjoyed breakfast together but bemoaned the fact that their honeymoon was over. Tom would be on his way back to work and Karen would be alone. She hoped, however, that the honeymoon really wasn't over but just beginning. Then she said, "I better hit the pavement and start looking for gainful employment."

Tom replied, "Enjoy your newfound freedom for awhile. We're going to be all right. Don't stress yourself about a job right away. We've got the rest of our lives."

Karen kissed him and said she loved him. She pondered how she would do without him until he returned in the evening.

When Tom finally left for work, she perused the morning paper and read what she could concerning Clement's death. While reading that article; she was drawn to the sidebar concerning the marriage commission. It was probably Tom's absence that suddenly spurred a renewed interest in the commission's findings. She was amazed to see that a decision was reached by only one vote. She continued to read the article and was not surprised that Farley voted the way he did but had to admit she was disappointed. She put the paper down and turned on the television. She started to become engrossed in the coverage of Clement's death. She listened intently to the newly released findings surrounding that event. Then she decided she would call Farley's office. She thought that her replacement, Jane, was probably overwhelmed at the office with all the events that

Bishop Reynolds was contending with. *Both of them are virtually "new" at the job and with all that's taking place, perhaps I can help in some way.* She felt that it would be the right thing to do. Her job search could wait until another day.

Farley, Spencer, and Carnavale took one of the few available tables. They quickly noticed Tessier and Obiajunwa at another table with McConnell and Middleton. Carnavale passed a remark as to how Tessier and Obiajunwa were communicating with Obiajunwa's hardly understandable English and Tessier's heavy accent. He remarked, "The Holy Spirit is working overtime at that table." Just as they got seated, Cardinal Ortiz of Mexico asked if he could join their company. "Grab that extra seat," quipped Carnavale. Ortiz was fluent in English, but as expected, he had a heavy Latin accent. All of them passed on a drink. They would all be celebrating the liturgy for the pope later this afternoon. They briefly reviewed the menu and placed their orders as soon as the waiter arrived at their table.

Farley had worked with Ortiz as part of his group on the marriage commission. He found him to be a very holy man. He also had the reputation for being a good business man. *That was a quality often lacking in priests*, thought Farley and he included himself in that group. *That would be a great qualification for the papacy*, he thought. They all continued to converse about the events of the past few days, and during the conversation, Farley drifted off in thought again. *I'm not comfortable with voting for Fiorvante, and I presently am leaning toward Obiajunwa. But I just don't know enough about him. Maybe Ortiz would be the choice.*

As usual, Camavale was the first to nudge Farley away from his daydreaming. "Stay with us, Harold."

He quickly responded, "I was just contemplating on the last few days and even the upcoming days. I'm sorry but I guess I'm still in shock over the death…trying to think if I'm anywhere near fully aware."

As they continued talking, their meals arrived. When all were served, Spencer said a blessing and all began to eat. They thanked Farley for the recommendation and agreed the meal was exceptional. While Ortiz was not normally as free-spirited and outgoing as Carnavale, he took the opportunity to nudge Spencer about his status as Apostolic Delegate to the United States.

Spencer intoned, "I'm hoping for a reappointment by our newly elected Shepherd, but I stand ready to do whatever is asked. To be truthful, I haven't given it a lot of thought." He then looked at Ortiz, who was smiling, and asked, "Why? Are you looking for that position?"

Ortiz laughed heartily and replied, "No. Actually I'm looking for the position of the one who would make the appointment—the top."

As everyone laughed, Carnavale chided, "Be careful, men. No campaigning."

Farley intoned that perhaps they should maintain a more somber demeanor as the prelates at the other tables glanced toward them. "Let's keep the tenor of the day in mind," he advised.

They continued to converse as the lunch hour moved on. They all agreed to skip dessert, and they asked for the check. While waiting, Obiajunwa and Tessier came over to the table to greet them. Everyone gave thought to the fact that both of these men were *papabili*. Obiajunwa had a definite edge on holiness. It wasn't that Tessier was not a sincere man; it was just that he was so much more of a politician. Obiajunwa projected an image of an inwardly spiritual man and spoke very softly. His heavy accent was, at times, an obstacle in understanding his often profound words. Brief greetings were exchanged and everyone knew they would be together that afternoon at the service. Obiajunwa said that he would be delivering the homily or remembrances of the pope's life at the service. Farley told Obiajunwa that he would be delivering the eulogy at the pope's funeral Mass and expressed his desire to be as articulate as he knew Obiajunwa would be that afternoon. Right after Obiajunwa and Tessier left the restaurant, the check arrived and Spencer announced it was on him. They all got up from the table to return to the Vatican.

Back at his room, Farley continued to work on the eulogy. He was only somewhat relieved to know who would be doing the homily today. He knew his work was cut out for him, for he was aware of Obiajunwa's mastery of an excellent homily. He truly meant it when he told Obiajunwa at the restaurant that it would be difficult to be as articulate as he would be.

He suddenly remembered that he had to call Ann. Just how to do it was the question. The cell phone was not an option and he had to leave his semisequestered room to use a landline. He remembered that while he was serving on the commission, Rinaldi was somewhat his mentor through Armstrong, so perhaps he could ask Rinaldi for the use of his office phone. He jotted a few more notes on his eulogy preparation. He then got his vestments together for the liturgical service that afternoon and placed them in a small carrier. He would go to Rinaldi's office and proceed from there to the Basilica to get vested.

He hastened to Rinaldi's office and luckily enough found Monsignor at his desk. "Greetings, Cardinal Farley! How can I help you?"

"Would it be possible to use your phone for a quick call to the USA? I'm sure you're aware of the strict security at the hotel."

"Armstrong informed me of that. Sure, it's okay. I'll send the bill to your diocese. Shortly, however, I'm headed to the Basilica for the service."

"I won't be long," Farley assured.

With that, Rinaldi left the office to allow the cardinal privacy.

cᐧ𝒷o

Ann picked up the phone while still clad in nightgown and robe. She was surprised to hear Farley's voice on the phone. "How great of you to call amidst all the activity over there, but I'm glad you did because I longed for the sound of your voice."

"You aren't kidding about all the activity here so you're probably aware that I don't have much time. I do want to tell you though that I miss you and I love you."

"Oh God, Harold! I love you too, but can this relationship continue? I've been agonizing over all the problems that would be inherent in this relationship. Just how could this survive a marriage? You would be giving up so much. Don't forget the bad sentiment that would fester toward me if I were to coax you from the priesthood. I probably wouldn't be too welcome at my church in Rosewood. Both of us would have to deal with so much more than we can imagine. I know true love conquers all, but are we both ready to deal with so many problems? Of course, it's easy for me to say this when you are so far away, but I'm just not sure we're looking at all the issues this would create."

Farley interjected, "I'm sure Fiorvante will be elected, and I will have to deal with him, but I must tell you he is fully aware of the situation. He's not happy to release me, but I'm sure he would if he had to."

"Harold, dear, let's wait until you return. Let's really continue to give this the most diligent thought. I'm sure I would be happy with you, but I'm so afraid of the fallout. You would have to find another situation at this stage of your life. People would look at me as a woman who destroyed a good priest. I propose that we wait until you return and we can spend some time together and give it all due consideration. I do love you, Harold."

"Perhaps you're right, Ann. These past few days have had everyone in high gear. Sometimes I wonder if I'm thinking with a clear head. After I return, we will discuss it at length. I do love you, however, and I have so much respect for you. Inwardly and outwardly, you are a beautiful woman and Charles was a much enriched man with you as his spouse." After a pause, he added, "I must leave, Ann, and I probably won't be in touch with you until I return."

Before she would let him go, she told him she would be attending the installation of John Martin at the bank that evening and she would be staying in the city. She also stated that she would be attending the installation alone out of respect for Charles.

He told her to be careful while in the city and to enjoy the installation festivities. "I love you, Harold," she said.

"God bless you, Ann. I love you, too."

He replaced the phone and exited Rinaldi's office. Rinaldi was standing outside the door talking to Armstrong. Farley thanked him profusely, and they all agreed it was time to get set for the afternoon's service.

Mobs of people were still lined up throughout St. Peter's Square and into the Basilica. They were about to be cut off as preparations for the liturgical service were coming to fruition. Many of the faithful would wait on line until after the service for a chance to glimpse the body of their beloved Clement. As Farley traversed the square, he noticed how pleasant the day was; however, if you were standing in the direct sunlight, it could become trying. *What a tribute to Frank*, Farley commented to himself. He saw so many of his fellow prelates on their way to the Basilica for the tribute to the late Pope. He also wondered to himself if the passing limousines out beyond the square belonged to some famous heads of state.

Clearing the throngs from the Basilica took more time than anticipated, but after a while, the afternoon's liturgical ceremony finally got underway. A massive procession of cardinals, bishops, and priests filled the center aisle on their way to the altar, in front of which lay the body of their Shepherd. As was appropriate, he was attired in his vestments. As Farley passed the bier, a wave of emotion coursed through him and a tear trickled down his cheek. He said a quick prayer in the hopes that their discussion in the pope's last hours did not cause his demise. *Help me to concentrate on a perfect offering of this liturgical service in memory of my good friend and what I feel certain about—the happy repose of his soul.* Now he became fully immersed in his priesthood and the privilege of being able to participate in the celebration of the life of a great church leader and a gentle loving man. He stood up at the altar with so many of his friends in the clergy. He saw so many others of his friends taking seats out in the church and up as close to the front as they could get. He was also aware that some of the prelates he knew had not arrived yet. This caused him to again drift to thoughts of why all these ceremonies were being rushed. Coming back to reality, he pondered, *I will drive these useless thoughts from my mind and dwell only on tribute to my friend.* The time for the eulogy by Obiajunwa was at hand. The church was unusually silent for such a vast throng. Farley gave some thought to the amount of people who were outside on the plaza and who were watching on television and of course, all those around the world watching on television. Unfortunately, Obiajunwa was difficult to understand even though he was delivering the eulogy in English. Farley was grasping at what he said and was pleased with the fact that Obiajunwa was keying in on Clement's humility. He even mentioned the marriage commission as a chance for Clement to reach out to those who felt disenfranchised by their church. Clement wanted to embrace all in the love of God. The eulogy was concise but meaningful. Obiajunwa concluded by words which were prayer-like, profound, and beautiful. "Our good shepherd has boarded the white vessel voyaging across what we perceive to be a vast ocean but is, in fact, a narrow river. Even though we cannot see the other side, it is there. He has left the port here on this side of the river. With tears in our eyes, we wish this holy and loving leader of Christ's church on earth, farewell. We will miss him. But when he arrives at the dock on the other side and disembarks the white vessel, oh what joy. He disembarks in all his holiness and purity to be greeted by the angels, saints, martyrs, and citizens of heaven. They will greet him warmly. He will look at the face of Jesus standing there, and Jesus will embrace him and say, 'Well done good and faithful servant. We welcome you to the glory of heaven and eternal happiness.' Knowing this we are happy for you, Giuseppe Francone. We thank you for your leadership, your inspiration, and your holiness. You have left us a beautiful legacy and we are so grateful."

Everyone in the Basilica sat in silence as Obiajunwa took his seat. Farley hoped he could be as profound and moving as Obiajunwa when he delivered his eulogy tomorrow. Farley was becoming increasingly enamored of the man.

The service continued as the prayers of petition were read. One of those petitions was for the guidance of the Holy Spirit in the upcoming conclave. Farley's thoughts were far away from that now. He just dwelt on the solemnity of the moment.

At the conclusion of the ceremony, all were again crowded into the robing rooms, which were way too small to handle the numbers of clergy. While there was much conversation, that conversation was very somber. Farley agreed to have dinner that night with Tessier and Obiajunwa. It probably didn't matter much as to who he had dinner with, since most of the prelates seemed to gravitate to the same restaurants. Everyone seemed to stay in touch each day. As Farley emerged from the Basilica, he was again struck by the multitudes waiting in the square to enter the Basilica and pay their respects to Clement. He had about an hour to spare before dinner, and so he returned to his room to spend more time in preparing his eulogy for the funeral Mass the next day. He was aware that Obiajunwa had presented him with a significant challenge.

After spending time on the eulogy, Farley later met up with Tessier and Obiajunwa, and they made their way through the throngs of people in and around St. Peter's Square. They were headed to the restaurant. Through the dinner meal, the conversation was somber. Farley was becoming more enamored of Obiajunwa. He was also impressed with Tessier. The Holy Spirit was surely working overtime on inspiring him as to who would be Clement's successor. In just a brief period of time, he had given consideration to Fiorvante, Obiajunwa, Ortiz, and now, Tessier. Farley was seriously considering all these men. This was probably on all their minds, but they all strictly adhered to the rule of "no campaigning." At the conclusion of a wonderful meal and time together, they all returned to their rooms. The next day would bring the solemn funeral rites for their late pope.

Ann boarded the train into the city for that night's installation of John Martin to replace her husband as head of the bank. As she sat on the train gazing out at the trees and countryside passing rapidly across the window, she suddenly became aware of her loneliness. Charlie was gone and she was sitting there by herself. No limousine to the city, and no one with her at the apartment in the city. She never fully realized how much she depended on Charles, or Charlie as she sometimes called him. She truly did love him. The thought coursing through her mind was could she love like that again. *I feel an intense closeness to Harold, but I also feel I still need to give it more time. Just how much time is the question. He truly loves me. Can I keep holding him off? Do I want to hold him off?* She continued to look out the window and noticed that the houses were passing by her window more swiftly. The train was entering the more crowded suburbs. In just about twenty minutes, she would be in the city. *I must do exactly as I told Harold to do and that is to give this more time. I have no choice now except to await his return. When he does return, we can delve into this*

relationship and all its ramifications. She then contented herself to try and put the Farley romance on the back burner. *I must make an effort to take care of the matters at hand. I will be very gracious to the Martins and to all at the bank this evening. So make up your mind, Ann, to enjoy the celebration.*

Carl Winstead dialed Ann's number but received only a message on her answering machine. He thought he should keep in touch with her because he enjoyed his evening with her so much. He wanted to cultivate a relationship with her. He left a brief message asking how she was doing and said he would call her later. He thought, *I have to be careful. I don't want to look like I'm pushing things.* He sat down in his favorite chair and picked up the local paper. He too had thoughts of being alone. He wasn't enjoying those thoughts.

Karen returned home to prepare supper for Tom. She had managed to help Jane very little since Jane, Bishop Reynolds, and she were glued to the television watching the special liturgy for Pope Clement. Although the proceedings on the television were very somber, she returned home in a joyful mood. She was happy at preparing the evening meal for her husband. She poured a glass of white wine for herself and went about her new role of chef. She paid no attention to the time, but it seemed only minutes before Tom walked in the door. She quickly turned around and Tom embraced her and kissed her. She asked how his day went.

"Not bad. I actually got right into it only a few moments after I arrived reporting for duty."

"You mean you forgot about me that fast?"

"Oh, no. I never lose thought of my wonderful wife!"

"I know that. I'm just kidding. Care for a glass of wine?"

"That sounds great."

She went to the kitchen to open a bottle of a special new red she wanted Tom to try. "Did you manage to see any of the rituals in Rome today?"

He paused and sighed. "Truthfully, Karen, there's so much going on at work that I didn't give it too much thought. Anyway, there's no way we have television in our work place and even if we did, there wouldn't be a pause for everyone to zone in on the papal funeral. You also know that I'm outnumbered at work. A few Jews, and a lot of Protestants, and even one Muslim. They are somewhat interested in what's going on, but certainly not near the interest of the Catholic constituency."

She raised her voice slightly from the kitchen as she struggled with the cork. "It was beautiful. I even saw Cardinal Farley on the altar. Strange as this might seem, Tom, I almost laughed at the fact that the marriage commission had so much diminished in priority."

"Karen, are you still concerned about the marriage commission? Sometimes I wonder about your commitment to me."

She rushed out of the kitchen with his glass of wine, handed it to him, and kissed him. "Have no fear, my love. I am deeply in love with you. But, and I emphasize the word but, I am in love with my being a Catholic."

"It was only one vote, sweetheart. That could have been Farley's vote. Did he give you a thought?"

"You know, Tom, that I love you with all my heart. I would so love to be in compatibility with my church, or should I say our church. Let's not forget that I worked for the cardinal for a few years. I can't just throw my faith to the winds. And to answer your previous question, yes, I do think he might have been the deciding vote and that truly disappoints me."

With that Tom embraced Karen and said, "I love you dear. Do you think God is angry with two people in love?"

"I'm sorry, Tom. I have to be truthful. I want so much for our marriage to be blessed by the church. Please bear with me and accept the fact that that is what I wish."

"Fine, Karen. Just don't obsess over it. Let's not allow anything to interfere with our love for each other. Someday in the future, perhaps our marriage will be correct in the church. The fact that the marriage commission was convened means that the church is looking at the situation. Have hope. You know sin involves an evil act to another person or to one's self. We are in love, which is not evil, and expressing that love for each other. My first marriage was irreconcilable. I am fine with our relationship, and it troubles me to think that you are not."

"Oh, Tom, I'm good with it too. It's so wonderful to be in love. It just would make me feel a little better to think that my Catholic church was also accepting of our unity."

"I cannot obtain an annulment under the present conditions. The church just ruled, by one vote, that they would not ease the annulment procedure. Just to make things interesting, it's possible that particular vote could have been Farley's. He had firsthand knowledge of your situation. Please, Karen, let's drop the subject and enjoy life together."

Karen sighed and knew that Tom was right. "I love you, Tom," she simply said.

Bishop Reynolds returned to his parish rectory after spending a not-too-fruitful day at Farley's office. He and Jane and Karen and even Marcia spent a few hours of the day glued to the television and viewing the liturgical services from the Vatican. He proceeded immediately to take a shower and prepared to go out to eat with Monsignor Beardsley. His housekeeper was off for the day. Emerging from the shower and clad only in a robe, he was startled by the phone. With no one in the office or in the rectory but him, he went over to the phone in his bedroom.

The mayor, himself, was on the phone. "Sorry to call you at this time, bishop, but I have a problem. Can you spare me just a minute?"

Reynolds sighed, and slightly annoyed, replied "Sure! Certainly."

"I know this is not number one on your agenda at this time, but I'm getting hammered by the media for a conference regarding the minority housing report submitted by Cardinal Farley and the clergy. I'm well aware that Farley will not be returning until after the papal election. Therefore, I'm going to ask Father Collins, the rector of Christ Episcopal Church and vice-chairman of the clergy group to stand with me if I give the press their conference. My question is, do you think the cardinal will object?'"

"I seriously doubt that, your honor."

"Is there anything you know of concerning the report that might have been special to the cardinal and that we might not be aware of?"

"You have the written report, and I'm sure if there was anything special to the cardinal, it is included in the report. I'm not aware of anything he would withhold; that would not be his style. If the entire group was in agreement and the cardinal summarized all the thoughts of the group, I don't see anything that should be added."

The mayor again questioned Reynolds as he stood next to the phone clad only in his robe and not completely dry. "Do you have or did you have any input on the report?"

"Absolutely not. I had various discussions with the cardinal, but nothing I said was ever injected into the report. I'm sure Collins has all the information you need. If I may ask, why are you rushing this conference? Farley should be returning within the next few weeks. Can it wait until he returns?"

"The press is relentless. They want to know how the findings of the committee will be implemented and they don't want to wait until the cardinal returns." Then the mayor chuckled. "It's the political thing, you know. I just wanted a heads-up on anything you might know about the report so that there is no conflict. I fully understand the cardinal's absence, but I can no longer hold off the press."

Reynolds said, "If I knew anything that would be controversial, I would definitely defend Cardinal Farley. I just wish you could make some kind of statement and hold them off. They're certainly aware of the circumstances. With that being said, I'm sure Collins will be extremely diplomatic."

Now it was the mayor's turn to sigh, "Sometimes it's very difficult to be a politician. You're so afraid to offend someone, not the least of which is the press. You always want to be positive. You never want to say no. But that again is my problem. Please wish Cardinal Farley my best if you're in touch with him and thank you so much, Bishop Reynolds for your time."

Reynolds hung up the phone and continued dressing. He was looking forward to his evening meal with Monsignor Beardsley. He chuckled at the mayor's "predicament" and said to himself, *You worked very hard to attain your position, Your Honor, so don't complain to me.*

Ann arrived at the bank conference room fashionably late. All the execs were there with their spouses or friends, whatever the individual case might be. Prior to her arrival, she had freshened up at her apartment and changed. She was attired in a well-tailored suit, and she looked impeccable as always. A table was set up at the far end of the room with enough liquor on it to make any restaurant or tavern envious. The choices were many. Ann walked toward the bar but stopped to greet the Costmans. John, and his wife, Isabelle, commented on how lovely Ann looked. Isabelle lowered her eyes and politely asked Ann how she was getting along. She remarked how painful it must be for Ann to be here and how she admired Ann for just getting herself to this joyous occasion for the Martins. They exchanged pleasantries for a while, and Ann excused herself and walked over to John Martin and his wife, Catherine. She extended her hand with confidence and offered her congratulations to John. "I wish you much success." Then she looked at Catherine and humorously suggested, "And I wish you much success, Cate, in putting up with him as he takes on the added responsibilities."

"I take that in all its importance, Ann, since you are the voice of experience." They all laughed.

John looked at Ann, and in a more somber tone, said, "Thank you so much Ann. I know this occasion must be painful for you. Please be assured that Cate and I are so glad you came to support us. Your confidence in me overwhelms me. Charles's shoes will be hard to fill, but I will do all in my power to preserve the legacy he so superbly bequeathed to this bank."

Catherine interrupted and said, "Anything we can do for you, either through the bank or privately, just feel free to ask."

John asked Ann if she would care for a drink. She replied that a glass of whiskey on the rocks would fit the bill. John hastened to the bar to get her a drink.

Turner Atkinson, one of the board members, walked over to the bar when he saw John standing there waiting for a drink. "What are you drinking, John?"

"Oh, Turner. Good to see you. I'm taken care of. I'm getting something for Ann Lincroft."

Atkinson raised his eyebrows and advised John that in a few minutes he would like to propose a toast. He also wanted to say a few words regarding Charles and his great work for the bank. John said that as soon as he brought the drink to Ann, he would give the floor to him.

John Martin did exactly as promised. First he brought Ann her drink and then picked up a small cracker and lathered it with caviar. He cleared his throat after swallowing and announced loudly for all to quiet down and direct their attention to him.

In just a few moments, the room quieted down and Martin began a short speech he had prepared. He made references to Charles being his mentor and how grateful he was for that. He concluded with, "It is my firm desire to bring to this bank the great dedication that Charles Lincroft brought to it. I hope I will have the ability to continue his family's great administration of this fine institution. I ask your help."

The small gathering applauded. He walked over to Ann and gave her a kiss. Then he went to his wife's side, gave her a kiss, and grabbed her hand.

Turner Atkinson then called for the attention of those in the room. He proceeded to say some things on behalf of the board. He lauded Charles and expressed his assurance that John Martin would be most capable of continuing the great success of the bank. "We of the board are extremely confident in John, and we wish him great success."

Again, everyone applauded and John urged them all to continue to enjoy the evening.

Ann went around the room conversing with the various executives at the bank and the members of the board. They all respected her as a great woman. They were also aware that Charles had left her only a tiny interest in the bank, but her appearance at the occasion reinforced their thoughts about just how great a woman she was. She, however, still thought many of them to be stodgy.

She returned to John Martin. He said, "By the way, Ann, what have you heard from our good friend, the cardinal? I caught a fleeting glimpse of him on the television."

Not wishing to get into a dialog with John about Farley, she skirted the issue. "Not much. He's been away for quite a while now. He'll be away for still longer now."

John interrupted, "Yes, that's right. The conclave is coming up soon after the pope is put to rest. Tomorrow is the funeral Mass, and I suspect we'll see him on television again. I have to tell you,

Ann, that I feel privileged to know him. He's a good priest and a gentleman. I'm anxious to get his input on the decision of the marriage commission. It was very close, and I wonder how much of their deliberations will be made public, or if he will even be able to talk about. It will be interesting."

Ann continued to work the room.

Catherine Martin glanced at Ann and remarked to Isabelle Costman, "What a lovely woman. I know it's premature, but I do hope she can find someone to share her life with. I know she's still grieving the loss of Charles, as well she should. But what a tragedy…such an untimely death. John certainly thought a great deal of both Charles and Ann and I have to say that I did too. I don't see a woman like her staying single for too long."

"I couldn't agree with you more," Isabelle replied. "She's an attractive woman and a pleasant person and I wish her all the best. If that includes a new husband, I would be very happy for her. Tell me, Catherine, is she a director of the bank?"

"No. A stockholder but not anywhere near a majority. Charles set her up very well financially but separately from the bank. He never wanted her to have any 'worries' of the bank."

"So then she is not involved in any management position?"

"No. John wanted her here tonight as a courtesy and I agree that was the thing to do."

"I agree definitely. My John always had the highest respect for Charles and Ann and also for you and your John. We've enjoyed so many social occasions with them and also with you. I hope our relationship will continue."

"I see no reason why it shouldn't."

The time literally flew and some people started to leave. Ann walked up to the Martins, bid them good night, and again expressed her congratulations. Martin assured her he would keep in touch with her as much as she wanted and again expressed his condolences to her. He then asked her if she was returning to Rosewood that night. She replied that she was ensconced in the city that night. He smiled and said, "That's probably the best thing to do. Always remember Ann, I'm just a phone call away. Can I get you a ride to the apartment?"

"That would be nice, John."

He moved toward the door, found his chauffer, and directed him to return Ann to her apartment. When Ann got back to the apartment, she undressed quickly and put on her nightgown and robe. She sat in the lounge chair of her bedroom and turned on the television. After reviewing many channels, she found them devoid of anything entertaining. She passed up the channels showing repeats of the services for the pope earlier that day. She had already seen parts of it. She turned off the television and went into thought. It was so quiet that a myriad of thoughts began to race through her mind. She still missed Charles greatly, but she also missed Harold. She was thankful for friends like the Martins, and she even gave some thought to Carl Winstead. She fell into sleep right there on the chair. It was a deep sleep.

Carl Winstead called Ann twice that night. After his second attempt to reach Ann, he hung up rather than leave another message on her voice mail. He certainly didn't want to pester her. *I wonder where she could be?*, he mused to himself. He would call again in the morning in the hopes that Marie would be there and she could minimize his curiosity as to where Ann was. Although he was concerned, he realized he would be out of line to continue to try and reach her. He didn't want anything to negate the wonderful start he perceived of their relationship. He spent the evening watching an old movie on the movie channel. It was *Casablanca,* and although he had seen the movie numerous times, he was drawn to watch it again. Unfortunately, though, he fell asleep just as Rick was reminiscing about his time with Ilsa in Paris. When he awoke later, the movie channel was showing a documentary on wide-screen format movies. He was not interested. He groaned a little that he had missed much of the movie, but since he had seen it so many times before, the displeasure was short-lived. He turned out the lights and adjourned to his bedroom.

CHAPTER TWENTY-TWO

The morning sun broke through the windows and brightened the drapes in Farley's room. He slept well in spite of the fact that he was still anxious about completing a fitting eulogy for the Holy Father. He arose, showered quickly, and dressed to begin the somber day. He took the elevator down to the dining room where a small continental breakfast was spread out on a buffet table. He entered the room and saw Cardinal Naguchi conversing with Cardinal Singh. He nodded to them and proceeded to the buffet table. He surmised that Singh understood Japanese since Naguchi spoke very little English. He picked up a bagel and spread cream cheese on it and then went to the coffee urn. He walked over to the table where Naguchi and Singh were sitting and asked them if they were saving seats for anyone. They replied in the negative and Singh said they would be delighted for him to join them. They had all forgotten about the rule of silence in the hotel. The Swiss guard in the room uttered in a very subdued tone, "Silencia." They took the hint.

Before Farley actually took a seat, he returned to the buffet table for a glass of juice. He returned to his table and removed two pills from his pocket. He took these every morning; one for blood pressure and one for cholesterol. The three cardinals sat at the table and dined quietly. Farley gave some thought to how the Trappist monks were able to live their entire lives without conversation. *I guess this would appear normal to them*, he thought. Singh slipped a note to him that he and Naguchi would like to see him outside after the meal. Farley nodded approvingly. They all continued to eat their breakfast in silence. Upon completion of their meal, Naguchi and Singh arose from the table and pointed to the door. Farley conveyed to them that he would be outside shortly. They walked out to the lobby and out the front door as Farley was sipping the last of his coffee.

At that point, Cardinals Feeney and Josephson with Mayfield and Spencer entered the room together. Mayfield said a loud "Good morning" to Farley, who was now sitting alone at his table. The Swiss guard in the room again subtly whispered, "Silencia." Mayfield had forgotten the rule of silence and thought it was a little over the top. But he also knew that Fiorvante was the boss. Farley looked at all of them and wondered how they all managed to get together without him. Thoughts went through his mind concerning the possibility that they somehow communicated in violation of the silence and that he was not in the loop. Farley got up from the table and nodded to all of them and proceeded to the front door.

Singh and Naguchi were waiting for him. Singh said in his clipped English, "This silence rule in the hotel is a little much." All three agreed.

Farley interjected, "Wait until the conclave when we will be held to silence throughout the entire process. We will even be given escorts to make sure we don't communicate with each other."

Naguchi commented as best he could with his poor command of English. "Well that I can understand but not at this time prior to the conclave."

Singh took over and said both he and Naguchi applauded the role Farley had taken at the marriage commission meetings. They were very supportive of his vote and assured him that he voted correctly. Singh said he had prayed to the Holy Spirit that the commission would render the correct decision, and he felt sincerely that the Holy Spirit had spoken. They praised Farley for his eloquence at the meetings and felt that he was a strong leader.

Farley lapsed into quick thought. *If they only knew how conflicted my decision was. And not only that, but how conflicted Clements's thoughts were.* He looked at them and thanked them for their support. He likewise complimented them on the good work they had done. They continued to converse for a while, and then Farley begged their pardon so he could return to his room and complete his preparation of the eulogy. They walked toward the Basilica. Farley turned around and went back through the door into the hotel lobby. On his way to the elevator, he passed the dining room and saw the four American cardinals sitting at their table in total silence. He laughed to himself on how childlike they looked, almost like a group of school children being punished. He took the elevator to the second floor and went directly to his room. The Swiss guard at the end of the hall seemed bored with it all and managed a big yawn. He entered his room and sat at the desk to fine-tune the eulogy he was preparing.

Crowds of people maintained their vigilance in St. Peter's Square. Again the sun was bright and strong, but the temperature was moderate. However, standing out in the direct sun was a trying experience. But the pilgrims who flooded the square didn't seem to object. They were persistent in their remembrance of Clement.

The solemn funeral Mass would begin at three. Prior to the Mass, the body of Clement would be placed on a wheeled platform and processed through St. Peter's Square before being returned to the Basilica for the Mass. An honor guard of Swiss guardsmen would surround the body.

Cardinals D'Angelo and Fiorvante were meeting in Fiorvante's office and discussing the logistics of the funeral Mass. They also spent time discussing the preparations for the upcoming conclave. D'Angelo was the proto deacon of the College of Cardinals and would fall in line behind Fiorvante during the interregnum. Since Pope John Paul II had erected the Domus Santa Marta, the hotel housing the Cardinals, and had also made some changes in procedures for the conclave, nothing had been done to change those procedures for many years. Then Pope Matthew and Pope Clement made minor changes. In Clement's case, he was always pursuing means to bring the church closer to the people and make the Vatican, the home of their church, more open and visible to the faithful. In deference to travel arrangements and the schedules of the cardinals, many of whom were bishops of a diocese, Clement had modified the nine days of mourning for the pope after his burial. While his wish was to continue that tradition, he allowed the Carmelengo to adjust the period of mourning at his discretion to no less than five days.

Since most of the cardinals were already gathered for the funeral, Fiorvante exercised his option and reduced the mourning period to five days. He didn't feel it was a good thing for the bishops to be away from their respective dioceses for such an extended period. Many of them, including Farley, had already been there for an extended length of time serving on the marriage commission. Thus, he justified his position on reducing the mourning period prior to the conclave. In observance of the days of mourning, however, the cardinals would be sequestered at the hotel. They would remain sequestered until the election of a new pope. Fiorvante and D'Angelo were also dealing with the work crews in preparing the Sistine Chapel for the conclave.

Farley was putting the finishing touches on his eulogy. He hoped it would be as moving as the eulogy delivered by Obiajunwa. He owed that to his friend Frank. He put the pen down, spent time reviewing his words, and went deep into thought about Clement. *He was a good man and a holy man. I can't possibly do justice to his commendable life, but I will try.* While in thought, the phone in his room rang and startled him. *Can I answer that? Why is my phone ringing when we're supposed to be in strict silence in here? We are permitted emergency phone calls. I sincerely hope this is not another emergency. I better answer.*

He picked up the phone and heard the familiar voice of Fiorvante on the other end. "Good morning, Cardinal Farley.

You must excuse me for breaking the rule of silence within the hotel, but I would like to see you at my office in about an hour. Can you spare me some time?"

Farley was bewildered but didn't think it would be appropriate to refuse. "Of course, Eminence. I'm just finishing my preparation of the eulogy, and I will be in your office in about an hour."

"Thank you, Cardinal Farley."

Farley hung up the phone, wondering what it could be about. It was late in the morning, and before the Mass that afternoon, he wanted some quiet time. He hoped their impromptu meeting would be brief. He also knew though that it had to be important, or Fiorvante would not have called him and broken his own rule of silence within the walls of the hotel.

The hour passed quickly, and Farley was on his way to Fiorvante's office. He emerged from the hotel and made his way over to the Vatican offices. He laughed to himself that he felt like a schoolchild being summoned to the principal's office and wondered what it could possibly be about. While he couldn't see the crowded St. Peter's Square, he could still hear the crowd of people there. It was a very subdued noise. He entered the office complex, decided to skip the elevator, and walked up the single flight of stairs to the second floor, where Fiorvante's office was. A Swiss guard announced his arrival to Fiorvante. The guard opened the already slightly ajar door more widely and beckoned to Farley to enter.

Farley walked into the office and found Fiorvante alone in the office sitting behind a somewhat opulent desk, but not at all like the desk he had pictured. He was surprised at his being alone since almost always Fiorvante had an assistant trailing him. The guard closed the door behind Farley, and he walked toward the desk and gave Fiorvante a hearty hand shake.

"Sit down, Harold," Fiorvante directed.

Farley took a seat in a comfortable chair facing Fiorvante's desk. Fiorvante arose, however, and took a seat in the chair next to Farley.

Fiorvante began, "I know once a penance has been given to a penitent as atonement for his sins, the confessor wipes it from his mind. It is done. The sin is forgiven. But Harold, I am troubled by what you told me the other day. Are you still serious about possibly giving up your priesthood?"

"To be truthful, Eminence, I haven't been dwelling on it at all. So much has happened here in the last few weeks."

"Well there, you see. This just might not be as serious a dilemma as you might think. I have to tell you that your reputation as a priest and leader is formidable. Your leaving the priesthood would leave a huge empty spot in our church hierarchy. But, and I say this in all importance, if you still feel a strong affection for a woman that you don't feel you can overcome, I will arrange to release you from your vows prior to the conclave. I know also that if you leave the priesthood, the world media will create a monumental negative issue for our church. By the way, Harold, don't chastise me for skirting the rules. I'm aware that I'm bringing up a situation that was a matter of confession, but the only two people here are the confessor and penitent." Then he added in a humorous tone, which was out of character for him. "By the way, I'm also aware that I broke the rule of silence at the hotel. But let's return to the point at hand. If you don't wish to discuss this issue with me, that is your prerogative, and I will abide with that decision."

"I just haven't given it the proper thought," Farley stammered. "I'm not prepared to give up the priesthood. In the little thought I have given to this matter, my thinking was to discuss this matter with my spiritual advisor when I returned home after the conclave."

Fiorvante interrupted him. "You know, of course, that you are papabili. You are possibly the first American to become the head of Christ's church on earth. What would happen then?"

Farley smiled and looked at Fiorvante. Knowing that Fiorvante was probably going to be elected the next pope, he replied, "I don't think that's a realistic worry. There are many candidates worthier than me." He meant that sincerely.

"Nevertheless, do you feel strong enough about your priesthood to go into conclave and not be distracted by thoughts of a woman?"

"My answer is yes, Eminence. I love my priesthood very much, and I want to pay proper respect to my departed friend as well as my God. I will continue to pray for help and guidance, and I will push myself to make a decision on this matter within a few months of my return after the conclave. I am so torn between the love of my God and my service to His church and the love of this woman, that it causes me great torment when I dwell on it. I fight constantly to do what I must do as a priest and that helps me to keep my mind away from thoughts of being in love with a woman. Right now all my thoughts are directed toward paying the proper respects to our departed Shepherd and then electing a new leader for the church. I so much want to be a part of electing a new leader, and I want to continue in God's service. When I'm near the woman I love, I justify to myself that loving another human intensely isn't an evil thing. God commands us to love all our brothers and sisters."

Fiorvante interrupted. "But not sexual love."

Farley quickly retorted, "Hence my problem. I yearn for that beautiful sexual fulfillment that is a true expression of real intense love. I realize, of course, that it would be a violation of my vow of chastity, and so far I have been able to avoid that situation. I ask you, Eminence, to give me time after the conclave to discuss this with my spiritual advisor and certainly with Ann. I must come to a decision, but I cannot be forced to make that decision right now."

Fiorvante sighed and arose from his chair. Farley did likewise. "So be it, Harold. I'm praying for you and I'm sure the Almighty God will inspire you to make the right decision."

They shook hands and Farley said, "Thank you, Eminence." He then added, "Thank you also for the privilege of being able to give the eulogy for my good friend. I promise to honor him. I do love my priesthood, and perhaps I will pray to my friend to guide me."

"I will see you this afternoon, Harold, and God bless you."

Farley exited the office and proceeded back to the Domus Santa Marta. He would partake of a small lunch in the dining room and then spend some time in prayer. He was concentrating on the life of his friend, Giuseppe "Frank" Francone.

Karen awoke to the noise of the shower running in the bathroom which signaled to her that Tom was getting ready to start a new day. She parted the drapes in the bedroom to reveal a dark and dreary sky. She went to the kitchen to prepare breakfast. First duty, obviously, was coffee. She started with that. Tom had purchased some bagels on his way home from work last night. Karen began the process of heating the bagels. Just when they reached the right temperature and just as the coffee was ready, Tom walked into the room. He embraced Karen and kissed her. "Good morning, lovely wife." Karen thanked him profusely considering how she looked in her robe and slippers, with her face devoid of make up. Tom asked her what she had in mind for the day.

"I'm going to watch the pope's funeral on television this morning. Maybe I'll spot my former boss. I guess I'm tuned in to this whole turn of events since Cardinal Farley is so involved. Maybe later on I'll write out the few thank-you notes we need to do for those who gifted us at our wedding. Which reminds me,

I wonder how Ann Lincroft is doing? Anyway, I promise to look for work as soon as all of this is over."

"I've repeatedly told you, Karen, that being my wife and the caring person that you are is truly satisfactory to my life. We can get along, so don't feel pressured to look for a job."

"Thank you so much, Tom. I do think, however, that I'd like to be busy and be a wage earner and contribute to our support." She poured another cup of coffee for Tom and herself, and despite the dreary day outside, it was bright in the kitchen. The light of love was extremely bright.

Carl Winstead looked at his clock and saw that it was near eight thirty. He wanted to call Ann. He dialed her number, and Marie answered the phone.

"Good morning Marie. May I speak to Ann. This is Carl."

"Ann is in the city, Carl. In fact, I'm leaving shortly to go to her apartment. She may be there for the next few days. Can I give her a message?"

"No. I was just checking on her well-being. I didn't know she was in the city as I called several times last night only to get her answering machine. So I can presume everything is all right."

"Everything is fine, and I will tell her you called."

"Thank you, Marie."

Carl hung up the phone and pondered why Ann went into the city. He kept in mind, however, that going into the city for an evening and remaining there for a few extra days to take care of some personal problems was certainly within her rights. She owed him no explanations. He sat down in the kitchen and started to read the morning paper. He passed on another cup of coffee. *I did so much enjoy her company, and I feel as though we've known each other for so long. Lord knows since the death of my dear wife, I've dated enough women to know a great one. So just how do I approach this matter? I certainly don't want to appear pushy, but I also don't want to lose the possibility of a relationship with her. How to proceed—that is the question.*

Ann was not expecting Marie to arrive at the apartment until about noon. She would get a late morning train and a cab to the apartment. Ann would reimburse her as usual. Ann had a morning appointment with Doctor Lang, so she hurried her dressing ritual and breakfast to get there early. Sometimes he had a habit of delaying his patients, and she didn't feel like sitting in his office for any extended time. After a brief taxi ride, she entered the doctor's office, and to her surprise found only one other person in the waiting room. *Well, this is unexpected, but certainly welcome*, she thought. She picked up a magazine and thumbed through it as the other waiting patient was called into the office. In less than ten minutes, it was Ann's turn.

After cordialities were exchanged, the doctor examined her leg and said, "It's coming along nicely, Ann, but a little slower than expected. I'm recommending that you see a therapist that has a practice in Rosewood. He can do wonders in eliminating the limp that you still have. I would think that with three or four visits, you could expect complete healing."

Ann was given the name of the therapist, and Doctor Lang urged her to make an appointment with him as soon as possible. The sooner she did that, the sooner she would be walking normally again. She put the information on her note pad and pushed it into her purse. She assured Doctor Lang she would do as he prescribed.

She emerged from the doctor's office and went straight to her attorney, who was conveniently nearby. Since he was part of a three-partner office, there were a number of people in the waiting room when she arrived. Fortunately her attorney was available, so her wait was short. She was swiftly ushered into his office.

Cardinal Farley was once again in the crowded robing rooms at St. Peter's Basilica. The flowers arranged in the Basilica were breathtaking. The pope's body was currently being moved to the rolling platform, which would process through the throngs gathered in St. Peter's Square. In the meantime, the gathered prelates would walk down the main aisle to the altar to await the body of Clement after making its rounds through the square. Thankful prayers were uttered by all for the beautiful day. If it had rained, a canopy had been prepared to cover the moving platform. The clergy watched as the platform made its way out of St. Peter's. They were hard-pressed to retain their tears.

After the platform left the Basilica, the procession of clergy began. Farley thought to himself that this was a magnificent church and a magnificent faith that he was part of. He was proud to be a leading prelate and contemplated on the wonderful gift of his priesthood. The emotion that permeated the Basilica and the crowds outside was extraordinary. The presence of God was all around, and Farley knew that there was joy in heaven at Clement's arrival. For a split second, the overwhelming thought that he was the last person to speak to Clement made itself known. He was happy that he was able to spend some time with him. Now, however, he was in the grip of grief about his death. The procession made its way to the altar sitting majestically beneath the Bernini columns. There were many priests actually up at the altar, but Farley was overwhelmed at being one of the chief concelebrants and also the eulogist. Clergy of all ranks were still processing down the center of the Basilica and were finding seats around the altar. In a few moments, the body of Clement would be returned to the Basilica and carried down the center to an honored place at the foot of the altar.

While the choir sang several beautiful chants, the body of Clement was slowly returned to the Basilica. The cart was wheeled down the center aisle to its place of honor. His body was gracefully and ceremoniously removed from the platform and placed on the catafalque by the honor guard of the Swiss Guard. Farley thought how fitting it was for the guard to carry their commander-in-chief. After the placement of the body, the choir sang "How Great Thou Art," in Latin, of course. It was one of Clements's favorite hymns. Farley started to shed a tear, so he tried hard to hold himself together for the eulogy.

Ann had some financial issues to go over with her lawyer and she also inquired about the class action suit. He advised her that the settlement of that suit was a long way off. He told her that on occasion, he would check on the status of the suit, but the final disposition was possibly a year away. He went into detail on her financial concerns, but her mind was drifting off. She wanted to get back to the apartment and view as much as she could of the funeral Mass for the pope. Possibly she would see Harold. In just about twenty minutes, her attorney had put her mind at rest regarding her financial concerns. Finances were never Ann's strong suit, and that was the primary reason Charles had set up special accounts and annuities to provide her with income. He didn't want any of the bank burdens to rest on her shoulders, and to that end, he left her with a minimal amount of bank stock. His shares were to be sold back to the bank at his death, and the proceeds used to establish the annuities. All of this was boring to Ann. *How I miss him*, she thought. *He took care of everything.*

She quickly returned to the apartment and turned on the television to watch the funeral Mass for Clement, which was already in progress. She caught a glimpse of Harold every so often. He was seated next to Fiorvante on the altar as the first reading was being proclaimed. Since the Mass was in Latin, it was difficult for her to become immersed in the service. The Mass throughout her life was always in the vernacular. Besides that, however, she thought the chants of the choir at the conclusion of the reading were beautiful. She continued to watch through the second reading and Tessier's proclamation of the gospel. The time for the eulogy by Farley was approaching.

Ann heard the door to her apartment open, and she knew Marie had arrived an hour earlier than Ann had anticipated. She announced her arrival to Ann, who asked her how her trip to the city had been. She replied that it was very uneventful. She asked Ann if there was anything she could get for her.

"Yes, as a matter of fact, a cup of coffee would be pleasing right now."

Marie walked into the kitchen and proceeded to make Ann's coffee. Ann spoke up so Marie could hear her in the kitchen. She was telling her that Cardinal Farley was about to give the eulogy. Marie brewed the coffee as quickly as she could and brought it into the den. It was certainly awesome to see Farley on television in the beautiful setting of St. Peter's. As Marie laid the cup down on the table next to Ann, she said, "I know this has nothing to do with what we're watching on television, but I'm afraid I'll forget. Carl Winstead called you and told me to let you know that he called. It was nothing important. He just wanted to know how you were doing."

"Thank you, Marie," Ann replied as she picked up the cup from the table. As she watched Harold stand and approach the pulpit, Carl was a long way from her mind. She did think he was a gentleman and knew he was concerned about her. She would call him upon her return to Rosewood. She returned her gaze to the television, and as Harold completed his short walk to the pulpit, she became engrossed. *What a privilege to know this man. Do I love him enough to let him go so he can continue his life in the priesthood?*

Tessier had read the gospel, and Farley was at the pulpit. He composed himself. He spoke in English and began the eulogy with stories of their mutual friendship. As he intended to do, he emphasized Clement's kindness, but he also spoke of his holiness. He concluded with, "His leadership of Christ's church on earth has indeed left us with a great legacy. I know he is looking at the face of God. I know God is saying to him, 'I entrusted my church to your care for many years, and I thank you for being a good steward and a good shepherd in feeding my lambs.' We can only imagine the awesomeness in receiving a 'thank you' from God. But I am certain God is pleased. Sadly, Clement's physical heart was not good, but his spiritual and emotional heart was beyond compare. His earthly life is over and Jesus is embracing him now and is saying to him, 'Well done, good and faithful servant. Welcome to the glory of heaven.' We can now put Clement's body to rest knowing that the angels and martyrs have given him a grand welcome into the eternal Jerusalem. Farewell, my friend, on behalf of your entire church. Enjoy now the happiness promised to us by Christ's death and resurrection and so richly deserved by you. As Paul said and we so knowingly apply to you 'I have fought the good fight, I have finished the race. I have kept the faith. From now on a merited crown awaits me and all who have looked for His appearing with eager longing.' You were a kind man and a spiritual priest. This is not good-bye my friend, for I know you are with us in spirit. We say instead 'farewell,' since that means only a temporary parting. We will see you again. Thank you for the gift of your life to us and your dedication to God's church." Farley walked back to his seat on the main altar. Try as he might, he could not control his tears. The whole church seemed to be moved by the eulogy, and, for a brief moment, not a sound made itself present in the vast Basilica.

After a few moments of silence, Fiorvante arose from his seat and continued the celebration of the Mass.

Ann thought the eulogy was magnificent, and it reassured her as to just how great a man Harold was. It also reassured her that he was a good priest. Did she really want him to give that up? How could he possibly remove himself from the priesthood? It was the life he was made for, the life he was called to. *I couldn't possibly imagine him doing anything else,* she thought. *How could he possibly be happy just loving me and not being involved in the life of our church?* She continued to watch the pageantry associated even with death. But she thought that Clement was a good pope and deserved the most magnificent tribute that could be mustered. Her emotions were riding a roller coaster. Harold Farley was a good man and she would be happy with him, but as she watched his participation in this beautiful ritual as a priest, she couldn't fathom his ever leaving the priesthood.

Karen watched Farley preach the eulogy and was very proud of him. She felt joy in knowing she had worked for him. She was not happy about his decision on the marriage commission, but she did think he was a good, sincere man. She was aware that many people said he was aloof, but she knew better. She so loved her Catholic faith, including all its pageantry and pomp at moments like these. She continued to agonize over her marital status, but she dared not show that to Tom.

Reynolds thought that the eulogy was magnificent and fitting. He sat and contemplated the recent events taking place in his church.

He glanced at the paper on his desk and was quick to notice an article concerning Farley's minority housing report. He wanted to continue to watch the funeral, but he was distracted by the article. He picked up the paper and read the article as quickly as he could. He didn't want to miss any part of the funeral. It seems the mayor had declared a news conference for the next morning. *I guess he just couldn't wait. The perils of a politician,* Reynolds thought. He turned his attention back to the Mass. *Clement was a good man. May God welcome him to heaven. I also pray for his successor, that he will continue to carry on Clements's legacy.*

The Mass was coming to its conclusion. Fiorvante walked around the catafalque and incensed the body of Clement. The sound of the choir was as a chorus of angels. They sang in Latin, but Farley knew the words by heart. "May the angels welcome you and may the martyrs escort you to the new Jerusalem." Farley had recited these words too many times in the past number of weeks. He still became emotional when he heard them, especially when they were sung so beautifully by the choir.

The time had come for the body of Pope Clement XV to be brought down to the grotto of St. Peter's and there to be entombed. The plain wooden casket waited for his body at the place of entombment. His body was ceremoniously lifted off the catafalque and placed upon a flat stretcher made of wicker. The elegantly clothed Swiss guard then marched in precision with his body from the main altar and over to the entrance to the grotto. Only those clergy that were actually on the altar followed slowly behind. The remainder of the clergy and public, both in the Basilica and outside on the square, watched on huge television screens. They arrived at the tomb which happened to be very close to that of the late beloved John Paul II. It took more time than Farley thought it would, but the pace was appropriately solemn and dignified. At the tomb, the guard carefully and with great dignity removed Clement's body from the stretcher and placed it in the simple casket. The casket was then closed. Fiorvante pronounced the committal prayers and ended with the prayer of the faithful departed. A moment of silence was next, and the guards then grouped together and slowly saluted the casket. They then marched out of the grotto. Each clergyman who had accompanied the body to the grotto then walked up to the casket and blessed it. They then proceeded up from the grotto to return to the altar. After all had left the grotto, the attendants extended their efforts at placing the casket in the tomb and sealing the tomb.

When all the prelates had returned to the altar, Fiorvante gave a final blessing and farewell and everyone on the altar began the recessional. The choir again provided a beautiful sound as everyone walked down from the altar. The crowd in the square applauded as an act of reverence for and appreciation of Clement's life.

While in the robing room, the word was passed that a repast was prepared in the auditorium. Fiorvante urged everyone to attend and to celebrate the life of Clement.

The realization of Clements's death was becoming more and more apparent to Farley. The shock was gradually wearing off. He considered the state of shock to be a gift as it permitted him to dwell on a proper tribute to his friend. The beautiful Mass, just completed, brought him back to reality. He started to cry, but he composed himself enough to think it would be better to communicate with his fellow clergy and not allow his grieving to dominate him. He spoke briefly to Tessier, and then he caught sight of Middleton. He became more relaxed and thanked God.

He walked over to the auditorium with Middleton and they conversed on their way there. Obviously, it was slowgoing due to the multitude of clergy that were traveling to the same destination. Finally they arrived at the auditorium, where two large buffet tables were set in place. It was not extravagant, but there was certainly enough to feed all. Middleton made a remark that they would certainly not have to pray for another loaves and fishes miracle. Middleton talked to Farley about his admiration of the people out on the square. He commented that even though the liturgy was concluded and Clement had been put to rest, many of them were still out there in prayer. Some small groups were praying the rosary together. "What a compliment to our church. I'm still amazed at how in the last few weeks, so much has transpired here at the Vatican. After tonight, we go into our period of mourning and then we go into the conclave."

Farley replied, "That period of mourning is going to be very much like a silent retreat. We will be confined to the hotel and our rooms. We will only see each other at meals and then in silence. And don't forget, during the conclave, our meals will be brought to our rooms. During the period of mourning, we will be allowed to say Mass in the Basilica, but we will be escorted there and back. Our endurance will surely be tested."

Middleton agreed that it would be trying, but he tried to look at the positive aspects. "It will surely give us a most welcome downtime from the events of the past few days. I guess I'm looking forward to it."

They claimed two vacant seats at one of the tables, and Farley suggested they head to the buffet table. Middleton agreed that that was a good idea and joined him. They stopped at one table where Archbishop Carnavale and Cardinals Spencer and Mayfield were sitting and began to exchange some conversation. After just acknowledging his American colleagues, Middleton excused himself and continued to the buffet table. He informed Farley that he would save his place at their table. Carnavale looked at Farley and said, "This has been quite a monumental few weeks. Again I'm glad to tell you that I will be leaving on the day after tomorrow. I can only imagine what awaits me on my return. If I don't get a chance to see you before I leave, and I doubt that I will, I'll be praying for you and the conclave. And it was a pleasure working with you on the marriage commission."

"Thanks, Frank. You were most certainly an asset to the group, and I appreciated your input. God bless you and have a safe journey home." Then he looked at Spencer and Mayfield and laughed, "I guess we'll be seeing a lot of each other in the next week."

Mayfield replied, "Only at mealtime. Remember not only silencia but also sequester. But you know, I'm already thanking God that I will be serving his church in helping to select a successor to Peter. It is truly awesome to be able to participate in that process."

Farley placed his hand on Mayfield's shoulder and said, "You are right. We are truly blessed. We have the next five days to not only step back a bit but also allow the Spirit to talk to us. We have a daunting task before us. Let's not forget the marriage commission, which is why some of us were here in the first place. When that returns to the forefront, those of us on the commission will have to explain our positions. Indeed, the road ahead looks challenging."

Farley left their table and finally arrived at the buffet table. As he spooned his salad onto a small plate, Cardinals Josephson and Feeney lined up behind him. Feeney joked, "I never like to be first on line, but I sure don't want to approach the table so late that the bounty is gone."

Josephson mused, "As I look around the room, it doesn't appear that too many of us have missed much of the bounty."

In overhearing them, Farley laughed. They briefly spoke to Farley regarding their accommodations and again expressed their pleasure. Feeney said, "I can hardly call it a sacrifice being sequestered in the new rooms. Compared to what we've been subject to since the start of the commission, these are luxurious."

Farley agreed with them and continued to fill his plate. Everything appeared delicious. When he could put no more on his plate, he returned to his table. Middleton had already started to enjoy his selections. Farley sat down, took a sip of water, and looked around the room. He spotted Fiorvante seated with Tessier and D'Angelo. He was tempted to call them the Holy Trinity. At another table, Ortiz was seated with Naguchi and

Singh. He was curious about how much knowledge Singh had of the Japanese language since he seemed to be able to converse with Naguchi so readily. He also had to translate for Ortiz. Farley commented to Middleton, "In the next few days, all the cardinals here will be on a silent retreat for five days. We will then be in a conclave together and will continue in our silence until a new pope is elected. I guess we need to converse with each other as much as possible before we return to our rooms tonight."

Middleton put his fork down and said to Farley, "I know I keep saying it, but how awesome is all of this? To be able to have a say in who will lead our church. Someone in this room within the next few days or weeks, however long it takes, will be sitting in the chair of Peter."

Farley acknowledged him and agreed with him wholeheartedly. It was truly an awesome time. They proceeded to finish their meals and many, though not all, made their way to the dessert table. Farley noticed a microphone and podium at one end of the vast space and saw Fiorvante making his way toward that spot.

As Farley selected a piece of cake, Fiorvante arrived at the microphone. He spoke briefly in Italian and then in English followed by other different languages. He was asking for the attention of the room. He then began his talk again in Italian and Farley assumed he would repeat his oration in the other languages. Farley remained standing while Fiorvante spoke.

He poked Middleton standing next to him and in an aside muttered, "He doesn't have the gift of tongues." Middleton snickered.

Fiorvante then began in English. "My fellow priests, I thank you so much for participating in the funeral rites for our beloved Clement. I believe it was a fitting tribute to a priest who deserved no less. For those of you who will be leaving, I wish you a safe trip home and I ask you to keep one another in your prayers. For those of you cardinals who will be participating in the conclave, I beseech you to use the next five days to communicate with the

Holy Spirit so you will be enlightened when you proceed to the Sistine Chapel five days hence. I ask God's blessing on all of you and may you continue to be good priests for our Holy Catholic church." In respect for Fiorvante's talk, Middleton and Farley remained standing at the dessert table until he spoke to all the different languages. When he had concluded with his blessing to all, the conversation began once again in the auditorium.

Farley and Middleton returned to their table to enjoy the black forest cake that they had both selected. Carson and Carnavale walked to Farley's table to say good-bye. Carson said, "We still have another night in those tiny rooms. I understand your new assignment at the hotel is a major improvement."

Farley laughed and said, "But you have only one more night. We have five days until the conclave, and then however long the conclave takes to spend alone on our new plush accommodations. I have a feeling that the new luxury rooms might prove to wear thin. In any event, have a safe trip home and thanks for your help on the commission. I'm sure when all of us return to our dioceses, we will have to deal with the results of that commission. God bless you, gentlemen."

Ann watched the funeral rites on television and listened to the commentary. She was still very impressed with Harold's eulogy, but above and beyond that, the grandeur of the ceremony seemed very much to her a fitting tribute to the pope. Marie fixed her a late quick lunch and continued in her other tasks at the apartment. Ann remarked to her that they would return to Rosewood the following day. After nibbling at a small sandwich and sipping a sparkling water, she went back into the den and turned off the television. She decided to go through the mail, but most of it looked like junk mail. Absolutely none of it had any importance to her, so she placed the unopened envelopes back on the desk. She gave some thought to calling Carl Winstead when she returned home. *"I think I truly love Harold Farley, but his entire personality is the priesthood. Since I'm still dealing with roller-coaster emotions, is it possible that Harold is just not right for me? Do I want to foster another relationship at this critical time in my life? Carl is certainly a good man too, but I'm too confused. I'm still mourning the loss of a dear husband. I know I'll never get over Charles's death and it's way too soon to even try. I simply don't want to."*

She awoke from her daydreaming and primped to go out. She wanted to pick up some things for herself at Greyson's. She quickly got ready and told Marie that she would be back in about an hour. She closed the door behind her and made her way to the elevator. In a few short minutes, she was on her way to Greyson's.

Karen was going to make something special for Tom that night, so she went into the kitchen to begin to prepare. She was proud of herself and how well she was adapting to being a good wife. *I'm really enjoying this role and I'm very happy.* Two thoughts quickly came to mind. First was that she needed to go out and see what was available on the job market. She was enjoying the role of housewife too much to give job hunting its proper consideration. She vowed she would do that as soon as possible. Secondly, she thought about how awe-inspiring the final rites for the pope were. She was reveling in how beautiful her church was portrayed in all the grandeur of the celebration of life. She was awed at the great part that her former boss played in that ritual. She was still uncomfortable about her new relationship to the Catholic church as she continued to gather the ingredients together for Tom's surprise supper.

It was still early enough for Reynolds to get some major work done. He had simply been too engrossed in the television for the past few days. He was looking at a fair amount of catching up. He was going over to St. Margaret's the following night to try and justify the closing of the church and the merger with Holy Spirit Parish. Jane was busy in her office fine-tuning his presentation. Her job was difficult because his notes were put together piecemeal. He had one eye on the television and the other eye on the preparation of his talk to the parishioners of St. Margaret's. He also gave very little thought to the next day's press conference concerning the minority housing report. Although he wasn't a part of it, he was still interested in how the report would be accepted. He was anxious to see how Father Collins as well as the mayor would handle it. It was not going to be televised, so he was thankful that it wouldn't be a distraction for him. He also had too much work to bring up to date, so he had no intention of attending it at the city hall. It was strictly Farley's baby.

Upon finishing their meals, Farley and his fellow prelates made their way out of the auditorium. He walked this time with Cardinal Ainsworth. They quipped to each other as to how that walk would be their last look at the outside world for the next week at least and possibly beyond. The evening air was refreshing as they continued toward the hotel. Farley said, "Middleton reminded me that with all the events of the past week or so, this could be viewed as most welcome downtime."

Ainsworth replied, "That's so true. Maybe we should be looking forward to it, but after a number of days, it could grate on us."

Farley agreed and they continued their walk to the hotel. Ainsworth walked into the lobby, shook Farley's hand, and said, "Now it begins. Silencia!"

Farley quickly interrupted, "You know what? I'm going to take a stroll through the gardens before I adjourn to my room and 'silencia.'"

"Great idea. I'll join you."

They walked the short distance to the gardens and continued their conversation. In about a half hour, they made their way back to the hotel. They again wished each other well and made their way to their respective rooms. Farley made himself comfortable and began his daily readings. He also prayed that the next five days would be fruitful in both mourning for his friend Clement, and receiving inspiration as to who would be best to succeed him. He prayed for all his fellow electors that they would be enlightened. In five days, the conclave would begin.

CHAPTER TWENTY-THREE

F arley arose early as was his custom, sat in the comfortable chair in his room, and said his morning prayers. Before indulging in a welcome shower, he thought, *Nothing to do today except find a place to celebrate Mass and then spend the rest of the day in meditation. In fact, that's the agenda for the following four days. I pray that in all this alone time, I won't be distracted by thoughts of Ann. But I love her and she penetrates my thoughts frequently. I am totally in awe of both her inner and outer beauty. She is a remarkable woman. Am I really prepared though to discard my priesthood and begin life anew as a married man? My priesthood is all I know, and I'm in love with that also. I am being tested ever so greatly. My God, I ask for your help.* He then, humorously, gave some thought to making the shower a cold one.

After showering, he returned to the bedroom and got dressed. While in the final tasks of buttoning his cassock and wrapping the sash around his waist, there was a knock on his door. Upon opening the door, there stood a Swiss guard. He saluted him but kept silent. He handed Farley a note. Farley nodded thank you and closed the door. The note simply said he was assigned to the Lithuanian Chapel in the grotto of St. Peter's for early morning Mass. He would have use of that chapel for the next four days of the interregnum. The note further stated that two other cardinals were assigned that chapel at the same time and he would be concelebrating with them. All three would be escorted to the Basilica and back again at the completion of the liturgy.

His escort would meet him in the lobby of the hotel at eight in the morning. It was now only six thirty, so Farley had some time before he would meet Armstrong in the lobby. He went back to his chair and opened his prayer book.

The time moved swiftly. Farley left his room and proceeded to the elevator and then to the lobby. Armstrong was waiting for him, and they nodded to each other. He also noticed Ortiz and Gamallo with their escorts. He concluded that they were his concelebrants. They all walked over to the Basilica and stepped down into the grotto.

Upon the conclusion of the Mass, they were escorted back to the hotel and they all went to the dining room. Their escorts ate with them. They were already sensing how austere the process was. They knew that when the conclave started, they wouldn't be eating in the dining room. All meals would be brought to their rooms. Farley again gave thought to the Trappist monks and their lifestyle, and he gained a great deal of respect for their life of sacrifice. Not being able to speak and converse with each other was much more of a problem than he originally thought. He noticed the other prelates gradually arriving in the dining room with their escorts. Many of them were celebrating Mass on the many side altars in the Basilica. All the grotto chapels were also being utilized. He sat in quiet at the table with Ortiz and Gamallo. Josephson took a place at the table and joined them in silence. He was followed by Middleton. As everyone sat in silence and ate their breakfast, Farley knew it would be a long five days.

With Farley out of communication for the next five days, life continued in his diocese. Reynolds came to work and was happy for the opportunity to be able to catch up. He was still laboring over his presentation to the parishioners of St. Margaret's. The closing of that church was a done deal and his task was to make that acceptable by the angry parishioners. It was a daunting task and not something he was looking forward to. He had all day to prepare.

Karen saw Tom off to work and decided to start that very day to knock on some doors and present her résumé. Not having the distraction of television, she was prepared to pound the pavement. She quickly got dressed, straightened the apartment, and started her quest. Her first stop was a prestigious architectural firm very near her apartment. As it turned out, they were looking for some help. She pondered whether her experience in the cardinal's office would be fruitful for her in that endeavor. She had to try though. Being so close to home, it would be an ideal arrangement. She gave her resume to the receptionist, and the young lady at the desk told her she would be contacted. Karen left her home phone number and cell number at the desk. She left the office to continue her quest and kept in mind that striking pay dirt on the first visit is so rare as to be close to non-existent, but she could hope. She walked a few more blocks and found an attorney's office. She entered the reception room and spoke to the woman at the desk. Unlike the receptionist at the architect's office, the receptionist here was not young. Karen thought that perhaps she should have been retired by now. The woman took her resume and said they really weren't looking for anyone, but they would call her for an interview if they decided differently. She left and after a few more blocks, she walked into a construction company. This was a high-end company so the office was quite different than she would have pictured for a business of that type. Again a receptionist took her resume and said they, in fact, had an opening at one of their sites, but it would only be while the job lasted. There was, however, always the possibility that she would be retained. The job site was a bus ride away, but Karen left her resume anyway and kept her fingers crossed that the job opening at the architectural firm would work out. If it didn't, she would have to take what she could get. The job market was not that great and she was thankful that two places she called on happened to have openings. She dispersed her résumé to two more offices. One was a manufacturing company with a dreary office, and the other was at the city transit authority. Neither had openings but told her they would keep her résumé on file. She felt she had accomplished much on her first sojourn into the world of job seeking and decided to spend the rest of the day window shopping. It was a beautiful day.

At ten in the morning, the mayor's news conference began. All the clergy members that served on the minority housing committee were present on the dais with the mayor, except of course, the chairman, Cardinal Harold Farley. Father Collins, who was vice-chairman, stood next to the mayor. The mayor laid out the basics of the report and then said he and Father Collins would entertain questions. Of course, the first question came from Henley, the opponent of the committee's study.

"How do you propose to fund the implementation of this report, Mr. Mayor?"

"At this time, this is just a report. When we decide to implement all the recommended stages of this plan, which, by the way, we are going to do, we will have our city council work on the sources of revenue for this project."

This was the answer Henley was hoping for. It just added to his criticism of the report. He furiously made notes in his notebook. He left his recorder running but wrote thoughts in the notebook. "Once again the bottom line is throwing money at a project and then magically it will disappear. No one has taken time to look at the track record. Suddenly adequate housing for disadvantaged and homeless will appear with an infusion of taxpayer dollars. Once the housing is occupied, the residents will still be jobless and poor. Let's not investigate the possibilities of putting money toward developing skills so the chronically unemployed or poor or homeless will have jobs and thus be helping society to prosper." Henley had already written half his column with one ear still tuned to the conference.

Lovett, the liberal columnist, had nothing but praise for the report and complimented Father Collins and the clergy who had served on the committee for a job well done and well thought out. He thanked them for their efforts.

The conference continued for thirty minutes with various clergy on the committee answering questions directed at their area of expertise. The reporters were obviously aware that Farley was in Rome, so they directed questions that would have been to him instead to Father Collins. He was very adroit in handling those questions.

At the conclusion of the conference, the reporters raced out to their various papers and media outlets.

Ann and Marie were preparing to leave the apartment and return to Rosewood. Marie completed the task of cleaning all the glassware and felt proud of her accomplishment. True, she was getting paid, but it was a formidable task nonetheless. Ann went through the apartment turning off all the lights and closing the doors. Soon they were on their way downstairs and out the door to hail a taxi to the train station.

Upon returning to the Rosewood home, Marie went to the kitchen to prepare lunch. Ann went to the den and checked the answering machine for messages. She laughed to herself when she thought of Charles's constant carping on her non-acceptance of a cell phone. She listened to all the messages. There were none from Harold, but she understood that. When she heard one of the messages from Carl, she knew she had to call him. After listening to all the messages, she realized that none of them, except the ones from Carl, were important.

She joined Marie in the kitchen and decided she would call John Martin first and thank him for the evening at the bank reception. She didn't think that the evening was as bad as she originally thought it would be. It did, however, bring back memories of Charles, but she was proud of the way she handled herself. The second call would be to Carl. This was becoming another dilemma. She did enjoy his company, but her feelings for Harold were much stronger. As always her thoughts would ultimately turn to the tiebreaker. She still loved Charles. But she knew that he was gone and life had to continue. Would Harold ultimately leave the priesthood? Should she try to develop a deeper relationship with Carl? Did she have to do either? The answer was apparently "no." She decided she would continue to see Carl, but she awaited Harold's return. Upon his return, she and Harold would discuss their future together. She was beginning to drift to the fact that a union with Harold was just too fraught with calamity.

Marie prepared lunch quickly, and she and Ann ate together. Marie casually asked, "Do you intend to keep the apartment in the city?"

Ann was astonished at the question because it was a good one. She awoke to the fact that she had not given a thought to that prospect. Indeed, did she need to keep the apartment? She replied, "You have just given me another task that needs to be looked at. I actually don't need it, and if I sold it, it would go for a good price. I'm just not good in thinking about these things. Charles always took care of these matters. I guess it's something else that now falls on my plate."

Marie countered, "I didn't mean to upset you."

Ann consoled her, "You didn't upset me. It just brought to the surface another matter that needs my careful attention." She didn't think Marie had any idea about her relationship with the cardinal. She surmised that she only knew they were good friends based on his frequent visits. But it was the romantic aspects of her relationship that were occupying her mind and giving the impression that she was becoming absentminded as to certain challenges that she would be facing as a result of Charles's death.

"Don't fret, Marie. You are right. I have to deal with the apartment. At the present, I see no reason to keep the apartment."

Marie chuckled. "And I just cleaned all the glassware."

"That's all right, Marie, because I'm sure as heck taking that back here. That will definitely not be sold with the apartment, if I decide to sell it."

After finishing lunch, Ann went to the den and called Carl. He picked up his phone on the third ring. Ann greeted him and said, "I heard you called to check on me. That was sweet of you, Carl."

"Just wanted to make sure everything was all right." He quickly thought about pushing the envelope but decided anyway to ask Ann out again. "I certainly don't want to be pushy and feel free to tell me if you think I am, but I'd love to take you to dinner tomorrow night."

"I would enjoy that."

"The little seafood place on Main Street is very good. We'll go casual and local."

"Thank you, Carl."

"I'll pick you up at about six thirty."

"That will be great. So by the way, how are you doing?" He felt it was too good to be true. She certainly didn't seem to be holding him off. He basked in the good feeling and they continued their conversation.

When she finished the phone call with Carl, she suddenly became aware of her increasing interest in him. When she had left the kitchen, she had every intention of calling John Martin first, but her mind again became so preoccupied that she totally forgot. She decided to call Martin right then.

John expressed his thankfulness that she would take the time to call him and reiterated his desire to help her in any way. "I'm just a phone call away." After a brief conversation, she concluded the phone call. She now knew that she had to call her attorney regarding selling the apartment. *"I don't want to do that today, but will I forget?"* She decided to give her thinking mode one more chance and agreed to put off that phone call to some point in the future.

Farley spent the evening in his room with his prayer book and his thoughts. Instead of dwelling on the conclave, he decided to devote his thoughts to his good friend Frank. He knew there was plenty of time left in the next few days to think about his preferences as to who would be the next leader of the church. Besides, this was a period of mourning and he decided that would be the right thing to do. He did slip into thoughts of Ann and anxiously awaited his return to her. He not only wanted to see her again, but he wanted to discuss their future together. He wanted to think of methods to allay her fears about marrying an ex-priest.

All the cardinals were in their rooms and they all adapted to the silence and the meditative atmosphere. They were all so close together, but at the same time so totally isolated from the world and from each other. The conclave would provide no relief since their lives would then be confined to their rooms and the Sistine Chapel. Most of the cardinals that Farley was acquainted with were sincere men, and he knew they were accepting this sacrifice in stride. At the end of it all, the church would have a new leader.

Karen greeted Tom when he arrived home for supper. She kissed him and informed him immediately about her successful quest for employment. Well, it was not actually successful, but it was extremely promising for just the first day.

"That quick?" he asked.

"Can you believe it? I'm hoping to get an interview with an architectural firm only a few blocks from here. I just don't know about my experience, but it would be great to work so close to home."

"As I've said to you before, my dear, take your time to find something you'll enjoy doing in a friendly and warm environment. There's no need to rush."

She kissed him and said, "You're wonderful. I love you so much." She poured a glass of wine and they toasted.

Reynolds now came to the realization that being a bishop could sometimes cause great anguish. He addressed the people of St. Margaret's in an eloquent manner, but they weren't going to listen. They were rebelling. He even received a few jeers as he spoke. He tried to sympathize with them, but they weren't having it. He stressed that he didn't want to see any church closed, but there were simply no alternatives. Financially, it was just not feasible. He went back and forth with the audience and made no progress. He tried to inform them of all the good things that would result from the merger, but nothing would salve them. Finally, a few of the parishioners urged respect for their bishop and exerted some effort at trying to convince the majority to look at the situation through the eyes of the diocese. The crowd eventually calmed down, but when the night was over, Reynolds was a wounded man. It seemed that a few parishioners, who wielded considerable influence in the parish, were able to influence the majority to accept the closure as inevitable. He did enjoy a humorous thought, *The mayor has his problems and I have mine. That's the human condition.*

The next day was a little cloudy, unlike the previous near-perfect day. Reynolds said Mass at his parish and rushed off to the diocesan offices adjacent to the cardinal's residence. On the way, he mused over last night's awful meeting. He knew people became attached to their parishes, but they, and he too, had to face the reality of the situation. He prayed that the parishioners of St. Margaret's would, over time, feel a lessening of their pain. He arrived at the office and dropped his briefcase by the desk. He walked over to the residence and toward the kitchen. He greeted Marcia. She had been steadfast in her duties replacing Mary O'Leary, but like Jane, she hadn't seen much of the boss, Cardinal Harold Farley. She did, however, bask in the knowledge that she wasn't doing the supper routine. Reynolds either returned to his own residence or went out. He was close to Beardsley, and they frequently dined together. Marcia had a cup of coffee and an English muffin ready for him. He took them into the office and opened up the paper to read about the minority housing report. He saw no surprises in the article. It read just as if he had written the script. *I'm just glad I didn't have to deal with that. I feel sorry for Harold. After the stress of the last few weeks in Rome and the conclave, he has to return to the diocese and deal with this report and the marriage commission findings.* His relief didn't last long as on page three, there was the report of his meeting last night with the members of the St. Margaret's parish. Interestingly enough, the article was very accurate, and it helped him to relive that awful meeting once again.

He went into Jane's office, and they went over the business of the day and their methods of attacking the problems. That would be their routine for the foreseeable future until Farley returned.

Karen received a call from the architectural office to come in for an interview. She was ecstatic. Of course, she knew it didn't mean she was getting the job, but it was a big step closer. She agreed to meet with them that afternoon and thanked God for the opportunity. *This would be so close to home and it's the first door I opened. I sincerely hope this works out.* She cleaned up the kitchen and went to the closet to figure what would be most appropriate to wear to the interview. She obviously wanted to look her best.

The day remained cloudy throughout, and as evening drew near, Ann began preparing herself for the dinner with Carl. *He did say casual, so that's exactly how I will dress.* Ann's wardrobe was extensive, so she didn't take long to make a choice.

When Carl called on her, he appeared at the door smartly dressed, but casual. She thought he looked very handsome. She greeted him warmly and asked him in.

"You look very charming, Ann. I hope you will enjoy the evening. Have you been to this place before?"

Ann looked at him and replied, "Believe it or not, with all these years in Rosewood, I've never been there."

"I trust you will like it."

"Charles and I often ate out at the marina or in the city. It just seems that opportunities to eat locally were minimal. So I feel this will be a treat."

They journeyed the short distance to the Seafood Shack on Main Street and easily found a parking place. Carl didn't think that was a good sign. He expected more people would be dining there. It was a good place.

After being seated at a table in the corner Carl breathed a sigh of relief. In just minutes, the place began to fill up. The young waitress asked them for their drink order, and while she went to the bar to fulfill their requests, they perused the menu. Ann quickly decided that since she was in a seafood restaurant, she would naturally order seafood. A halibut steak would seem to fit the bill. Carl preferred lobster but didn't want the fuss and mess. He agreed the halibut would be a good choice for him also. They put the menus down and awaited the arrival of their cocktails.

Karen and Tom sat at the supper table enjoying another favorable meal prepared by Karen. She was very proud of her cooking skills and never had much chance to practice them until recently. She thought she could get quite used to just staying at home and being a chef.

"How did the interview go?" Tom asked.

"I thought very well. We all agreed that my experience in the architectural arena was non-existent, but my business experience was a big plus. They said there were several other people interviewing, so they would notify me if there was to be a subsequent interview. When I got home this afternoon there was a message to call Turso Brothers Construction Company. Do you believe they want to interview me tomorrow? Their position is for a job at one of the construction sites across town. I'm not so sure it's my cup of tea, but I will go for the interview and see what happens."

"See, dear, you worried over nothing. Just one day and two interviews already. Let's toast." They picked up their glasses and toasted each other.

After sipping their cocktails and placing their orders, Ann and Carl relaxed at the table. Like a bolt out of the blue, Ann thought about Mary O'Leary. She asked Carl if he happened to remember her at the party in the Lincroft apartment that now seemed so long ago. Carl replied that he remembered her. "She had some part to play in your accident, didn't she?"

"Yes. She was a great comfort to me, a total stranger. I've dwelled so much on myself and Charles that I suddenly realized I have given her little thought since her death."

Before she started a guilt trip, Carl interrupted. "You lost your husband. Of course, that's going to occupy your mind. You have no reason to feel guilty."

"But Carl, the poor soul had no one. She spent a great part of her adult life at the cardinal's residence. Out of the blue, she took care of me and tended to me, a total stranger."

"I'm not telling you to forget her. I'm saying that the loss of one's spouse, as we both know, is a tough thing to get through. You were still in the early stages of grief over Charlie when she died. Remember, you did all that you could for her."

Ann sighed and said, "I know. I think I need to pray for her soul more frequently. I should not forget about her."

Carl grabbed her hand and held it in his. "That's what makes you a wonderful person. The very fact that you suddenly thought about her makes it obvious that you have not forgotten her."

Their appetizers arrived and they eagerly became engrossed in the meal. Ann thought that Carl was a good man and she did like him, but now she was thinking about how to hold him off. She certainly did not want him to know about her relationship with Harold. She knew that if she and Harold decided to fulfill their lives with each other, the stepping down of a cardinal would be front-page news. She knew that if she continued to see Carl, she would be leading him on. If she refused to see him, which she didn't want to do, he might figure out sooner than she wanted him to that something was going on with Harold. And as always, her love for Charles was still strong. She had to figure some way to juggle all of this and keep her sanity.

Carl put his fork down and took another sip of his drink. He looked at her and suggested they go out to the marina tomorrow.

He, at one time, had a boat there, but he had sold it after his wife's death. Ann began her juggling act, but it was easy this time. She had an appointment with the therapist tomorrow. She laughed and tried not to appear to be brushing him off. She informed him of her appointment, and she was thankful that he accepted her excuse without asking for a rain check.

Trying to keep things in a humorous vein, she chimed in, "I'm hopefully going to be able to get rid of this limp within the next few weeks. You'll have to bear with me." They continued to enjoy their dinner and discussed the upcoming conclave. Carl said, "Can you imagine if our friend Harold Farley gets elected pope?"

Although Ann scoffed at the idea, it did bring a whole new atmosphere to her relationship with Farley that she had not anticipated. "No," she replied. "I don't think it's a possibility. Americans never seem to have a shot at the papacy. I'm guessing that Fiorvante will get it. Anyway, he is the favorite."

They continued with their appetizers, and Ann changed the subject. She didn't want to entertain any idea that the man she was thinking she was in love with could ever possibly be elected. The fact that he was a cardinal was trouble enough. Ann talked to Carl about selling her apartment. She probed Carl to see if he could provide her with any new insights.

Their meals finally arrived, and the topics changed to more mundane things. They discussed among other things, many of the good parties that they had all enjoyed together. It was amazing to them just how much had happened. For Ann, it also brought back fond memories of the good times with Charles.

After their night at the Seafood Shack ended, Carl immediately drove Ann home. He escorted her to the door and told her to wait outside while he turned on the lights and checked the house. "You never know. I always like to be safe."

Ann thanked him and expressed her pleasure at his choice of restaurant. "As you said, Mr. Winstead, it was a great choice. I'm sorry Charlie and I never had the opportunity to go there."

He kissed her good night and as he walked away from the house, he felt so much stronger about their compatibility.

The next morning was an improvement from the day before in the city. Karen saw Tom off to another day of work. She hoped that she would receive a call from the Stern and Jackson Architectural Company. She went to her closet and began to select something appropriate for her interview with Turso Brothers Construction Company. She knew that apparel would not be an issue at a construction sight office, but she was going to the main office, and so she needed to dress up somewhat for the interview.

As the afternoon sun broke through a somewhat cloudy sky, Karen entered the Turso Brothers office. She felt comfortable in a tailored pair of slacks and a jacket. The receptionist greeted her and took her to the office of a Mr. Emery, the human resources manager. He stood and greeted her warmly as she entered his office, and he asked her to take a seat. He positioned himself behind his desk and addressed her. "Mrs. Kiely, I've looked over your résumé and find it to be very impressive. I feel certain you would have no problems. Of course, you are aware that this is a temporary position at our site across town. We feel that the job will last a little more then a year. I feel confident, however, that if things work out, we would be able to retain you. I feel it only fair to warn you though, that if we do retain you, it could be to another job site, then again, possibly here at our main office. Let me emphasize that none of this is guaranteed, but in looking at your résumé, the odds are good. If you accept our offer, I'm prepared to offer you a thousand dollars per week. Overtime, if necessary, would be at time and one half. Since you would be working in a trailer office, the dress code is extremely casual. Bear in mind that you will be at a field office."

She laughed with him and said, "So my clothes budget is close to minimal."

"That's so true."

Mr. Emery explained further company policies to Karen regarding holidays, vacation, hours, and other matters. "If you accept, we could use you as soon as possible."

Karen thanked him profusely and asked if she could have a day or two to think it over. She was especially fond of the casual dress code which would surely reduce her clothing budget. Her pay was far superior to what she had made at the cardinal's office. Thinking about it, she still preferred the job at the architect's office.

She continued to converse with Mr. Emery and asked him some questions. In a few more minutes, she shook his hand and again thanked him for his courtesies to her. She left his office and thanked the receptionist in the outer office and walked back on to the street. She headed straight to the apartment and said a small thank you prayer for the "dilemma" she was now facing. This was a great offer, but she still hoped to hear from the architects.

Upon her return to the apartment, there was a message on the phone to call Stern and Jackson. She wasted no time in dialing them. She was put through to Mr. Stern's office, and he told her that they felt she would be an asset to their firm. He informed her that they would like to have her come down to the office and discuss the position that very day. Karen was ecstatic and said she would be there in less than an hour. She hung up the phone and rushed to make herself a sandwich and just couldn't believe her luck. Two offers on the same day. *God is good*, she thought to herself. After her quick lunch, she changed to clothing she thought would be more appropriate for the interview. She took the short walk to the architectural office and was greeted by the young attractive woman at the receptionist desk. The young lady directed her to Mr. Stern's office. He greeted her warmly and told her that he was looking for a secretary. His present secretary was retiring, and she had worked for him for nearly fifteen years. Karen just saw her briefly when she entered Stern's office. He asked her to have a seat and he took a seat behind his desk. Stern laid out the job requirements. Surprisingly, it was not all that dissimilar to her duties with the cardinal. When Stern got to the area of pay, he told her they would start her at 850 dollars per week. He also explained the benefits, hours, and other aspects of the job. He informed her that it would be a salaried position and therefore not subject to overtime. He emphasized, however, that overtime was a rarity. After questions and answers, Karen asked for some time to think it over. Stern said he had no problem with that. He then took her to the outer office and introduced her to his present secretary, Jean. "I'll be here for a few more weeks and if you accept the position, I'll be happy to get you acclimated." Karen thanked them both and said she would get back to them shortly. On the short walk home, she again thanked God for her good fortune. *Not one, but two good offers. I'll discuss this with Tom tonight, and I'll ask for his help in making a decision.* She decided to pick up a bottle of champagne on her way home. This called for a celebration.

Ann went for her first session of therapy. The therapist assured her that she was healing faster than she or Doctor Lang led him to believe. "I'll have you back to normal in three sessions," he assured her. Then he laughed and said, "By the way, notice I didn't say how grueling those sessions would be." After discussing some of Ann's medical history, he took her into his examining room and began her first session. She thought that he didn't lie to her as the session turned out to be a tad more intense then she had planned, but she endured it. Her ultimate goal was to get rid of the limp. When the session finally ended, she had to admit she felt a little better about her gait. She scheduled her next appointment for the next week.

Karen greeted Tom with a hug and kiss when he came home and informed him of her good fortune. "Do you believe it? I was offered two jobs today just two days after I began my search." Tom was delighted with her enthusiasm. He became enthused with her as she rushed into the kitchen to uncork the champagne. "I bought this to celebrate. How can things be so good?"

"Because you are a good person and I'm so happy for you," Tom said as he grabbed her hand. He took the bottle of champagne from her and completed the task of uncorking. He poured the wine and they sat down and toasted. "Here's to a great life together. We've only just begun."

Karen just basked in the greatness of the moment and nary a thought of her "civil" marriage crossed her mind. "Let me tell you of my beautiful dilemma," she said.

"I've got all the time in the world," Tom replied.

"The construction job with Turso Brothers involves a bit of a commute across town and the hours are early, seven thirty in the morning until four in the afternoon. The pay is great, but it's only a temporary position. Mr. Emery informed me though that prospects were good for me to possibly be retained. A big bonus is that dress at a construction sight is not a high-budget item. Stern and Jackson called me in after lunch. They offered me considerably less money and also said I would be considered salaried so there was no chance of overtime pay. Clothes would be an issue here as it's obviously a professional office. One huge advantage though is proximity. Just a short walk from here."

Tom took another sip of champagne and agreed with her that it was a wonderful "dilemma." He put his glass down and looked at her. "Do whatever you like, honey. I'd go for the one you're most comfortable with. We are truly blessed in that money is not an issue."

She looked at him lovingly and said, "I just think the architectural office is more comfortable for me. I know it's less pay and dressier, but there is no commuter fare to pay. I am doubtful also about my ability to cope with a rough and tumble environment at a construction sight. As you say, honey, money is not an issue, so I think I have a feel as to what position I should take."

He interrupted her. "You're the one who wants to work, and so you have my blessing to do whatever your heart desires."

"Thank you, honey. I'll call Turso Brothers in the morning and thank them for their interest, and I'll call Stern and Jackson and tell Mr. Stern he has a new secretary."

With that decision made, Karen finished preparing their dinner. Tom again complimented her on her delicious cooking. It would be a good evening for the both of them.

Carl called Ann in the evening to see how her first session of therapy went. They joked about her limp and agreed that it would be a great thing to eliminate. Ann tried to prevent Carl's asking her out for a while, so to their conversation she interjected how busy she would be in the upcoming days. Not desiring to push him off completely, however, she agreed to dinner at the marina a few nights hence.

When he got off the phone with Ann, he sincerely hoped that he wasn't pushing too much. He did sense a slight resistance. He certainly didn't want that. He tried not to attach too much importance to her being busy because he realized she was still grieving Charles's loss, and she probably did have some major business to clear up. He liked Ann very much and was desirous that this relationship would blossom into so much more.

Ann had started reading a great detective novel, and so she went to the den and picked up the book. She proceeded from the point where she had left off yesterday. After one sentence, she put the book down and gave herself some quiet time as she relaxed in what was Charles's favorite chair. She hoped that she hadn't turned Carl off. She did like him, and she did enjoy his company. At the present time, however, she didn't want to encourage their friendship to be any more than that. She still harbored many doubts about her relationship with Harold. Could that relationship ever surmount the mountain of obstacles? She still mourned Charles's passing. She soothed her mind in possibly being able to sort all of that out when Harold returned. Until then, she had to continue the juggling act as best as she could. She wished for the conclave to be speedy so she could be reunited with Harold. She would then be able to sit down with him and decide their future. She struggled to restart her reading and get back into her book.

CHAPTER TWENTY-FOUR

The last five days of the interregnum were over. It was the first day of the conclave. Farley arose early and parted the drapes in his room to reveal another sunny day. He showered, shaved, and returned to his chair with his prayer book to begin his morning prayers. He actually asked his late friend in prayer to guide him in his choice of a successor.

He picked up a printed sheet of instructions that were left on his dinner tray the previous night and he looked them over again. On the sheet were the protocols for moving to the Sistine Chapel and back to the hotel. Silence was to be strictly observed as usual. A schedule of the balloting was also included, but it was said that exceptions must be planned for. They were advised to meet their escorts at eight in the morning. All were to proceed to the Sistine Chapel where the doors would be locked behind them for the day promptly at eight thirty. Lunch would be served in a small area to the rear of the Chapel. Since that area was too small to accommodate all of the cardinals, they would adjourn to that area in small groups. They would be allowed approximately one hour and fifteen minutes for lunch in order to accommodate all of the electors. Obviously it would not be an elaborate lunch, possibly a small sandwich and water or soda. He put the instruction sheet down and said to himself, *It will be what it will be.*

He was interrupted in thought by a knock on the door and realized breakfast had arrived. He opened the door and was greeted by Armstrong carrying a tray upon which rested two toasted muffins, juice, and coffee. Farley nodded a thank you and took the tray from Armstrong. He got up from his chair to get his pills from the bathroom and brought them back out to the desk now serving as his table. He swallowed his pills with the aid of the fruit juice.

While eating, he glanced at the protocols again and went through a self-imposed drill. Each day's session would begin at eight thirty. The door would be locked from the inside and outside. In case of an emergency, the Carmelengo, Fiorvante, would knock on the door three times and the outside lock would be opened by the Swiss guard stationed at the door. Fiorvante possessed the key for the inside of the door. A fifteen-minute prayer session would start the proceedings, except on the first day wherein there would be a brief election held to select the three tabulators who would assist Cardinal Fiorvante in the counting of votes. After the opening prayers, a period of meditation invoking the guidance of the Holy Spirit would ensue. They would then be called upon to write the name on the ballot as to their choice for Supreme Pontiff.

If the first ballot was inconclusive, the ballots would be placed in the stove and set on fire with a mixture of the chemical that would provide the color of black. This would inform the waiting crowds and the world that the first ballot did not choose a successor. At this time, a second ballot would be called for after another session of prayer and meditation. If no cardinal received the needed votes for election on the second ballot, they would break for lunch. After lunch, the third ballot would be taken. If no successor was chosen on that ballot, they would adjourn for the day and return to the hotel. If there was no conclusive voting on the third ballot, the escorts would observe the black smoke and know enough to proceed to the hallway outside the chapel to await the opening of the door and the release of the cardinals for the day. The same procedures would be in place on each succeeding day until a pope was elected.

As Farley continued to contemplate, a quick thought went to Ann. He put his mind at ease knowing he would soon see her again. He had been away too long. He knew he was in love with her, but he still loved his priesthood. He was especially content with the privilege of electing a new leader for the church. Then he gave a rather inane thought to the fact that Fiorvante and D'Angelo were busy making arrangements with the work crew in the Sistine Chapel preparing for the election. *I wonder how silent they were in this whole process.* He quickly realized that thoughts like that were foolish and counterproductive. He dismissed them and contemplated on the task at hand.

He started to think about the actual voting and how that would take place. The first three ballots required a three-quarters plus one majority. After the third ballot, a new pope would be elected with fifty percent plus one vote. He started to do the math. "Let's see. There were eighty-five cardinals eligible to vote. My understanding is that five of those men are not in Rome. Four are ill or incapacitated, and one was not allowed to leave his country for political reasons. We have eighty voting, so a new pope needs sixty-one of eighty votes. If we go to a fourth ballot and each ballot thereafter, a new pope would be elected with forty-one votes. That's a tall order. We have so many worthy candidates. For just one to get that many votes will probably take some time. I, personally, am leaning heavily toward Obiajunwa, but if he can't muster enough votes and the trend changes, I would look closely at Ortiz and Tessier. They are all good men but Obiajunwa has the edge on piousness. I still have a strong feeling, however, that in the end, Fiorvante will be our new shepherd."

After another period of meditation, Farley left his room to meet Armstrong down in the lobby. He felt guilty about leaving his tray on the desk, but he was assured that the maid would be able to handle the chore of disposal. Mayfield walked right behind him, and they got in the elevator together. When they got to the lobby, it was filling up fast. It seemed uncanny to see so many people gathered in one spot in complete silence. Only an occasional cough or clearing of someone's throat broke the silence. Farley noticed D'Angelo and Fiorvante standing in the lobby. He thought that they must have stayed in the hotel overnight after completing their arrangements at the Chapel.

When all had gathered, they began their journey to the Sistine Chapel. Cardinal Farley spied Mayfield and Spencer right behind him, but Josephson and Feeney were lagging far behind. Security was all around.

They finally arrived at the door of the Chapel. Eighty prelates and their escorts were in a single-file line down a long hallway. Farley was not too far behind so he was able to see the ceremonies at the door. The Prefect of the Papal Household, Monsignor Bella, presented the keys to Cardinal Fiorvante. He opened the door. He returned the outside key to the Swiss guardsman who would retain that key. Fiorvante possessed the key that would open and close the interior lock. When they exited tonight or sooner if a pope was elected earlier, Fiorvante would open the lock inside the door. He would then knock three times on the door and the Swiss guardsman stationed outside would unlock the outside lock. While the cardinals were at the hotel overnight, the Swiss guard would remain at the door to keep the Chapel secure. Farley was thinking about papal elections long ago when the electors were locked in the chapel until a pope was elected. Sometimes this would be for many days. These new procedures were a welcome change.

Gradually, the line of men entered the Chapel. Farley was amazed at how much work had been accomplished in the last few days. Lining each side of the Chapel were a chair and a desk for each elector with a canopy hanging over each chair. On the front of the canopy, a small but rather ornate name sign hung which identified the cardinal assigned to that place. Farley's chair was on the left side about four seats down from the front. He sat between Cardinals D'Angelo and Ainsworth. Everyone entered and took their proper places. When they were all seated, Cardinal Fiorvante ceremoniously locked the door from the inside. He tapped once on the door to let the outside guard know that the door was now secure from his side and he should proceed to lock the outside lock. Farley was too far away to hear the door lock from the outside.

He looked around the room and was in awe not only at the majesty of the room and the reverent silence, but also at the fact that he had a say in whom the next leader of the Roman Catholic church would be. What a magnificent privilege it was.

Fiorvante walked to the middle of the Chapel and stood there with a large card on which was written the oath of secrecy in several languages. Farley looked at his watch and it was only twenty past eight, so the program was off to an early start. After swearing everyone to secrecy, Fiorvante then explained the process for electing the tabulators. "We will elect by show of hands the three cardinals who will assist me at the altar in counting the ballots." After completing his charges to the electors, he walked up to the altar and picked up a list of all the voting cardinals. The first name he called was D'Angelo as he was in succession right after Fiorvante. Immediately, forty hands went up. That was half of the room. Only six more names were called before the three tabulators were chosen. As Farley watched this unfold, he thought these men might be the leading papal candidates since they were chosen so fast. Or he wondered if all just voted for the first few names called in order to save time. *We shall see*, he thought. The electors chosen were D'Angelo, Middleton, and Ortiz. Now he knew that the seat next to his would be vacant since D'Angelo would be moving up to the altar. Middleton and Ortiz joined D'Angelo and Fiorvante up at the altar.

When all three settled themselves at their positions to Fiorvante's right, Fiorvante called for everyone to stand for a moment of group prayer. At the conclusion of the prayer, he asked everyone to be seated for a fifteen-minute period of meditation.

When he completed his period of meditation, Farley gazed at his watch. It was now very close to nine thirty. He was aware that the actual voting process would take some time. Each cardinal, after voting, would bring his ballot up to the altar individually. When all ballots were placed into the chalice and all cardinals had returned to their seats, Fiorvante would start to pull the ballots one by one from the chalice. He would read the name aloud and hand the ballot to D'Angelo immediately to his right. D'Angelo would read the ballot again and hand the ballot to Middleton on his right. Middleton would verify the name and enter it on a tally sheet. Middleton would hand the ballot to Ortiz. Ortiz would pierce the ballot with a large needle attached to a length of heavy thread similar to twine. He would eventually "sew" all the ballots to the length of twine to be burned at the conclusion of the ballot session. After trivial thought given to this process, Farley pondered whether or not they would be able to complete two ballots prior to lunch. He knew, however, that everything was in God's hands.

Placed upon each desk was a small tablet upon which was written "Eligo in summum pontificem," Latin for "I elect as Supreme Pontiff." This was followed by a line upon which to write the cardinal elector's choice to be pope. Each tablet consisted of ten pages. Farley wondered what they would do if there were more then ten ballots. *I'm sure they have plenty of these in stock.* He laughed to himself.

Fiorvante placed the large chalice and the paten on the altar in front of him. Everything was ready for the first ballot. Fiorvante announced with great solemnity, "After thoughtful meditation, I humbly ask my brother priests to enter the name of the person you feel is best able to carry on the duties of the Chair of St. Peter." He repeated this in many different languages. Upon finishing this reading, he said he would begin to call for the electors to come up to the altar with their vote.

Farley was certain, after five days of intense meditation and prayer, that he was being led to select Obiajunwa. He did feel that Ortiz was a very able administrator, and Tessier had an outgoing nature, but Farley claimed in his mind that piousness was the number one qualification. He wrote the name Charles Obiajunwa on the line. He folded the paper and whispered a prayer to the Holy Spirit. *I pray that I have given this matter the proper thought. Continue to guide me as I elect a supreme earthly leader for your church.*

Five minutes had elapsed and Fiorvante asked if everyone had completed their voting. They all responded yes. He then began the roll call of electors. He began at the rear of the Chapel on the right side. Farley concluded that since he was on the left side and close to the front, he would be among the last to bring his ballot to the altar. Cardinal Wocinski from Poland was in the last seat on that side so he had the honor of being the first cardinal to bring his ballot to the altar. He solemnly walked up to the altar and stood in front. He held his folded ballot up over his head and then placed it gently on the paten. Fiorvante picked up the paten and slid the ballot from the paten and into the chalice. Wocinski returned to his seat and Cardinal Gamallo was next to come up to the altar. The process was repeated with each cardinal. Finally, it was Farley's chance to walk to the altar. He did as the others and held his folded ballot above his head. He then gently brought his hand down and placed the ballot on the paten. Fiorvante slid the ballot into the now almost-filled chalice and Farley returned to his seat. Since D'Angelo was already up at the altar, there were only two more votes from the floor. After those two votes, the four at the altar voted. Each one arose from his seat behind the altar and walked around to the front of the altar. Each followed the same ritual as all the other electors had. When Fiorvante walked to the front and placed his ballot on the paten, D'Angelo was the person to slide the ballot into the chalice. When Fiorvante returned to his seat, he called for another short prayer asking

God's blessing on them as the votes were tallied. The chalice was filled to the brim.

A bottle of water was provided at each desk, and so Farley quickly took a sip as the tabulators readied themselves. Fiorvante reached over to the chalice and pulled out the first folded paper. He read the name aloud. Charles Cardinal Obiajunwa. The ballot was handed to D'Angelo who again read out the name Charles Cardinal Obiajunwa. He handed the paper to Middleton who again verified the name and entered it on the tally sheet. Middleton handed the paper to Ortiz who pushed a needle through the paper followed by a strong thread that would collect seventy-nine more sheets. The next ballot was pulled from the chalice. Fiorvante called aloud his own name. Giaccomo Cardinal Fiorvante. *Only two ballots but no surprises*, Farley thought. The next five ballots pulled were all for Fiorvante. *Is it possible that we could elect Fiorvante on the first ballot?* Then a surprise.

Fiorvante opened the ballot and read the name Cardinal Harold Farley. *That I was not expecting*, a surprised Farley thought. He watched Ortiz put the needle through the ballot with his name on it. A number of different names were called and he now revised his concern about this being a one-ballot election. As they continued to tally the votes, Farley heard Tessier's name called several times. He was again surprised when he heard Spencer's name called. He was surprised that someone voted for him, as he was American, but was especially surprised that another American received a vote. Then he heard his name again. After more names were announced including Naguchi, Ortiz, and even Wocinski from Poland, Spencer's name was called again. Then, immediately following Spencer's name, Farley's name was called twice. He was becoming overwhelmed at the thought that some of his fellow prelates thought him to be worthy of succeeding Saint Peter. It was truly humbling. After continuing to hear different names, Farley now knew that no one would be elected on the first ballot. Surely no one had amassed sixty-one votes.

The names of those receiving votes continued to echo through the Chapel. The last name pulled from the chalice and read aloud was Giaccomo Fiorvante. Farley determined that Fiorvante was the front runner, something that offered him no surprise.

Ortiz had affixed the eighty ballots to the thick thread and Middleton announced the tally. Fiorvante indeed acquired the most votes at twenty-six. His favorite candidate, Obiajunwa, was second but with only fourteen. Farley thought Obiajunwa would have garnered more votes. The major surprise to Farley was next. Both he and Cardinal Tessier received ten votes. He considered Tessier to be a major contender, but now he was looking at himself to be in that position. He was becoming agitated. He was certainly not prepared for this. Cardinals Singh and Naguchi each received five votes. Surprising Farley even further was his friend Spencer receiving four votes. Ortiz received only three votes and that disappointed Farley. Ainsworth received two votes and Wocinski one vote. He harbored a trivial thought as to the fact that all the cardinals receiving votes, with the exceptions of Spencer and Wocinski, had just served on the marriage commission. Possibly the camaraderie in the past few weeks had an affect on their choice for supreme pontiff. He was also concerned that even though Middleton and D'Angelo were elected to be tabulators, neither received any votes. D'Angelo's lack of votes amazed Farley since D'Angelo was number two prelate to Fiorvante during the interregnum. *Not one vote.* Farley scratched his head. He was confused at the reasoning. He thought humorously, *I can't enter the mind of the Holy Spirit.*

Ortiz held all the ballots tied together on the length of thread. He clipped the thread and, holding all the ballots together in his hands, walked over to the stove. The stove was highly engineered to avoid problems that had occurred in previous conclaves. Although there had never been a fire in any of the previous conclaves, the chief improvement was related to fire and ventilation dangers. He opened the door of the stove and placed the ballots inside. He took the chemical jar with the black label and sprinkled the chemical on the ballots. He then lit the ballots with an automatic lighter. He closed the stove and returned to his seat.

There was a rather elaborate set of portable toilets set up in one of the rooms to the side and in the rear of the Chapel. Some of the Cardinals took the chance to avail themselves of the opportunity to use them at this juncture. Fiorvante announced that he would call for the second ballot shortly.

Out on St. Peter's Square, the crowd reacted to the dark gray smoke emitting from the chimney on the roof of the Chapel. Some thought it might be white and maybe a new pope was elected on the first ballot. But when there was no tolling of the bells of St. Peter's, it was apparent there was still no new pope. Another ballot was necessary.

Fiorvante called everyone to return to their seats. He waited a few more minutes to allow some stragglers to get to their seats. When they were all seated, he called for a fifteen-minute period of quiet meditation. The beautiful chapel surrounded them in complete silence. All felt close to the Almighty. In what seemed like less then fifteen minutes but was actually close to twenty minutes, Fiorvante announced that they were ready to vote again. He would allow another five minutes for the electors to make their choice. Farley looked at his ballot and read again, "Eligo in summum pontificem." On the line below that, he again wrote "Charles Obiajunwa." He folded his ballot and said a short prayer to the Holy Spirit thanking the Spirit for his counsel. In little more than five minutes, Fiorvante began the roll call. This time, he started from the rear of the Chapel but on the opposite side. Farley's walk up to the altar on this ballot would be almost midpoint in the casting of votes.

Again everyone walked up to the altar solemnly and placed their ballots on the paten. As Ainsworth arose from his seat next to Farley, Farley snickered as Ainsworth's stomach growled.

Farley looked at his watch and it was approaching twelve thirty. He knew that lunch would be after one in the afternoon. That was a long time from his coffee and muffins that morning. The water that they had at each desk wasn't doing much to alleviate their hunger. Ainsworth returned to his seat and Farley arose and approached the altar. On his arrival at the altar he held his head down, held his folded ballot over his lowered head, and placed the small sheet of folded paper solemnly on the paten. He returned to his seat and two more electors on his side of the room went to the altar with their ballots. Then it was the time for the cardinals on the other side of the room to begin to bring up their ballots. Cardinal Wocinski was the first on his side of the room to approach the altar since they were starting from the rear. Farley devoted the waiting time to prayer. He again uttered a prayer to his late friend, Clement, to guide him and the electors. At the moment, he was content with his selection of Obiajunwa.

When he had finished his prayers, he started to contemplate the outcome of this second ballot and what it might portend. He surmised that a lot of the names on the first ballot would not appear on the second. It would be a start in narrowing the candidates who were "papabili." It would bring them closer to the election of a new pontiff.

When everyone had placed their ballots at the altar, the tabulators and Fiorvante placed their ballots on the paten one by one, and Fiorvante tipped the paten to allow the paper to fall into the chalice. D'Angelo performed the task for Fiorvante. The chalice was again full. Fiorvante called for a prayer prior to the tally of votes.

Anticipation was abounding in the Chapel as everyone shared Farley's thought that this ballot would be more defining. Farley anticipated that Fiorvante would receive a stronger count as would Obiajunwa. He felt that he and Tessier would most likely fall by the wayside with the others receiving votes on the first ballot. But sixty-one votes were needed to secure the papacy, and he didn't think that either Fiorvante or Obiajunwa would be able to garner that many votes on this ballot. *We shall see*, he thought.

After the prayer, Fiorvante reached into the chalice and pulled out the ballot. He opened it and read the name, "Charles Obiajunwa." Farley became cautiously confident, but he knew there were a great many more ballots to be read. He listened as Fiorvante's name was called out on the next few ballots. Then to his astonishment, the name called was "Harold Farley." He took a deep breath and uttered to himself, *How can this be happening? I felt certain that my name would drop off after the first ballot. I am not prepared for this.* Obiajunwa's name was called again. That soothed Farley somewhat, but then he heard his name called again.

After all the names were read, it could be safely said that the list of candidates had indeed narrowed, but Farley was astonished that he was still on that list. Only four other names remained with his. Fiorvante received the most votes at twenty-four, but that was down two votes from the first ballot. That was surprising. Obiajunwa received eighteen votes on the second ballot and that was four more votes than on the first. What overwhelmed Farley now was that he and Tessier received fifteen votes each, and each received ten votes on the first ballot. The only other cardinal to receive votes on the second ballot was Ortiz who received eight votes. The field had probably narrowed itself down to these men, but there was no way of knowing that for sure. It was certainly possible that on a third ballot, there would appear different names. Farley gave some thought to some ancient conclaves that lasted for months. No one could receive the majority necessary for election. The bottom line for Farley was that he was still in the running and doing better on the second ballot. This was a fearful time for Farley. He never contemplated being "papabili." He had certainly heard it from his fellow priests and his friends, but he always accepted it as just banter. He relaxed and assured himself that things would change on the next ballot.

Ortiz again picked up the handful of ballots tied to the length of twine and again walked over to the stove. Exactly as he had done on the first ballot, he placed the ballots in the stove. He again took the jar marked with the black label and sprinkled it over the ballots. He lit the fire, closed the door, and returned to his seat.

Fiorvante called for still another prayer and then called for the electors to adjourn for lunch. They would convene in the small kitchen area set up at the rear of the Chapel in groups of twenty. The area was just too small to accommodate more then that comfortably.

Ann rose for the day and went to the kitchen. Marie had not yet arrived, so she prepared herself a cup of coffee and placed two slices of bread in the toaster. She turned on the television and tuned in to a broadcast of the papal election news. The smoke from the just-completed second ballot was just observed and it was definitely black smoke. The reporter advised those watching that there was some confusion after the first ballot as to whether or not a pope had been elected. The smoke was gray. But after a few minutes when the bells didn't toll, everyone knew that the chair of Peter was still vacant.

While Ann watched, she thought, *I feel I've been separated from Harold for such a long time. But soon he will be home and we can discuss what future, if any, we have together. Perhaps by my maintaining so much doubt about our relationship, I'm actually trying to find a way out. The defining thought etched on my mind is of Charles's death being so recent. Also, is it possible Carl came into my life at the right time? I truly love Harold but I continue to harbor so much doubt about a marital relationship with him. There are just too many impediments.* Ann stirred from her thoughts and took another sip of her morning coffee which was now too cold. She went to the kitchen, emptied the cup into the sink, and poured herself a new cup. *Back to reality*, she said to herself.

Reality brought thoughts of Mary O'Leary again. Ann knew that remembrances of Charles dominated her thoughts as well as her relationship with Harold Farley. Poor Mary had been given short shrift. Feeling guilty, she decided to call the Cathedral office that day and request some Masses for the repose of Mary's soul. *The poor woman,* she muttered to herself. *She gave up her whole life for the cardinal's residence. She was so kind to me. Having some Masses said for her is the right thing to do.* She finished her second and much better cup of coffee and went to her bedroom to prepare for the day. While she was getting dressed, Marie arrived and began her day in the kitchen.

Karen started her second day at Stern and Jackson that morning. Since it was so close to home, she was able to see Tom off to work and still have time to watch a little bit of the news before getting ready for her day at the office. She glimpsed the picture of the smoke coming from the Sistine Chapel while the reporter spoke about the papal election process. She wasn't surprised that after two ballots, there was still a church awaiting its new shepherd.

She did some cleaning up in the kitchen and then finished preparing herself for work. She was enjoying the feeling of being able to contribute, and she definitely enjoyed the short "commute" to work. She was very impressed with how helpful everyone was to her at the office, and how patient Jean was with her in explaining the various aspects of the job. Learning to navigate the office and locating certain files presented the highest hurdles, but she knew she would acclimate quickly. She thought about how one of the files she had to work with was a construction job being carried out by Turso Brothers. They were not happy about her turning down their job offer, but they knew it wasn't permanent and they respected her decision. She was feeling very good about herself and her marriage. Life was a joy.

Monsignor Beardsley showed up at the door to Bishop Reynolds's surrogate office. He directed himself to Reynolds and uttered, "Two ballots already and Harold still hasn't been elected." They both laughed.

Reynolds chimed in, "He better not get elected. I'll suddenly be in charge here and I'm going to quickly have to look to someone to take over my parish. Thank God my secretary has done a tremendous job in keeping me up to date at my own office, but I don't know how much longer I can handle my job and Harold's."

"Can I treat you to dinner tonight?" Beardsley asked with the hope of alleviating some of Reynolds's pain.

"Yes, you can. I'll look forward to it."

Beardsley told Reynolds he would meet him that night at their favorite restaurant and then walked out the door to the kitchen. He grabbed an apple from the table and started to walk out quickly when Marcia scolded him. "I saw that, Monsignor. That's stealing."

"I promise to pay you tomorrow." He laughed. He walked out the front door of the cardinal's residence toward his car down in the parking area. He munched on the apple as he walked. He didn't think it would look very well for him to be walking down the street biting into an apple, and so he was grateful that there were not a whole lot of people on the street. He arrived at his car and prepared to return to his parish. While driving, he thought about being Farley's spiritual advisor. He thought about his friend Harold Farley possibly being elected pope. He thought about Farley's relationship with Ann Lincroft. *When he returns, if he returns, he has to come to grips with this problem. What will he do if by any stretch of the imagination, he is elected pope? He is a good priest. She is a beautiful woman. I will remember them in my prayers.*

All the cardinals had availed themselves of the small kitchen area of the Chapel. As Farley expected, they were provided with an assortment of small sandwiches and water or soda. There were just a few sandwiches left over, and they were placed on one of the trays and covered with a plastic cover. Since no one was allowed in the Chapel while the electors voted, the remaining sandwiches and unused beverages would not be cleared from the kitchen until the cardinals adjourned for the day. They were deposited in the kitchen that morning as the cardinals entered the Chapel. Monsignor Bella, with the assistance of the Swiss guard, brought them in. If the third and final ballot of the day was not conclusive, Bella would remove the leftovers from the makeshift lunch room as the cardinals were exiting the Chapel. Fiorvante wouldn't lock the door for the night until all the cardinals and Bella had gone out from the Chapel.

Fiorvante waited patiently up at the altar for everyone to return to their seats. The tabulators were already at the altar and just two or three cardinals were yet to be seated. In just a few more minutes, they were all settled. Fiorvante asked everyone to rise for a prayer prior to starting the third ballot. Farley prayed with the other cardinals, and when the prayers ended, Fiorvante asked them all to observe the next ten minutes in meditation. Farley again asked for the guidance of the Holy Spirit and again imposed upon his late friend Frank for guidance. He did let a speculative thought enter his mind about this third ballot. *Will we hear more names or will it narrow down even further?* That was the question. *We will soon know.*

The time passed quickly and it was now time to vote. Farley looked at his tablet which was now down to eight sheets. He looked at the tablet and pondered. He still favored Obiajunwa. He did pick up some votes on the second ballot. His conscience convinced him to again write Obiajunwa's name on the ballot.

He tore the sheet from the tablet and folded it in half. He looked around the room and watched the other electors either writing or folding. Fiorvante was patient and gave them a few extra minutes. Most used the time for prayer.

Fiorvante called for the casting of ballots. The tabulators were in readiness. He called for the cardinals to approach the altar in the same manner, one by one, but this time he would start from the front on Farley's side of the Chapel. Since the seat next to Farley was empty, he would be the third elector to bring his ballot to the altar. As before, everyone walked solemnly up to the altar, raised the folded ballot up over their heads, and placed it on the paten. Fiorvante then tipped the ballot into the chalice. It took a little over an hour for all eighty to vote with Fiorvante voting last and D'Angelo tipping Fiorvante's sheet into the chalice. With all ballots filling the chalice, Fiorvante called for a prayer prior to the counting.

Upon the conclusion of the prayer, everyone took their seats to hear the counting of the ballots. The first paper pulled from the chalice bore the name of Fiorvante. This again was no surprise to Farley. He began to wonder as to how many ballots it was going to take to elect the man. But he still hoped that the conclave would look kindly on Obiajunwa. He was a holy man.

The next name to be read was that of Harold Farley. Farley immediately became anxious, but he knew many more ballots were yet to be counted. He sat and listened as Fiorvante's name was called several more times. He heard Obiajunwa's name just a few times and he wondered if Fiorvante was gathering too much momentum for Obiajunwa to overcome Fiorvante's lead. Then Farley's anxiety level started to rise as his name was called four times in a row. He relaxed a little when the name of Tessier was read. At this point it seemed as though the only cardinals in the room receiving votes were Fiorvante, Obiajunwa, Tessier, and him. Farley did some mental calculation, and so far there were no new names. In fact, it appeared that so far Ortiz had dropped off the list. At that point, he was looking at the reality that he was a major candidate for the papacy. Farley was definitely not prepared for this. He knew no one had amassed the sixty-one votes needed, but it looked as if the conclave would probably elect a pope on tomorrow's first ballot. Things could still change because now all the electors would have a full night to dwell on the subject, and after that much time, things could certainly change.

Middleton called out the tally. Twenty-seven votes for Harold Farley, twenty-five votes for Fiorvante, twenty votes for Obiajunwa, and eight for Tessier. Farley swallowed hard. He was dumbfounded. He was now in the lead. He took hold of himself and knew that he was far from being elected, but it appeared at this time to be a three-way tie. He tried to relax with the thought that with an entire evening to think, the cardinals could drastically change their minds the next day. At least he was hoping for that. But that also was a distinct difference from his thoughts only a moment ago that a pope would surely be elected by the next morning.

Ortiz gathered the string of ballots into his hands, walked to the stove, and again sprinkled the jar of chemical on the ballots, lit the ballots, and closed the door.

The crowd outside in the square was hoping by now that they would be greeting a new pope, but they were disappointed. The smoke this time was definitely black. They would have to return tomorrow and possibly even the next day. Just as the crowd had observed the black smoke, so did the cardinal electors' escorts. Aware that this was the third and final ballot of the day and there was no election, they proceeded to the Sistine Chapel to await the release of the cardinals for their return to the hotel. Armstrong managed to find his way close to the locked doors at the Chapel. He knew he was bound by silence, as was Farley, but he much desired to know what was going on in the conclave. He rested knowing that wouldn't happen.

Inside the Chapel, Fiorvante called again for prayer to close out the first day. He asked the electors to remain in place until he went to the rear of the Chapel and opened the door. He took the keys from the altar and slowly walked to the rear of the Chapel. He placed the key into the inside lock and ceremoniously opened the lock. He then hammered on the door three times. Farley watched all this but was too close to the front to hear the outside lock being opened. Although he didn't hear the lock being opened, he did see the door begin to open slowly from the outside. Fiorvante allowed Monsignor Bella and the Swiss guard to empty the kitchen first. When that task was completed, he called for the cardinals to proceed to the door and to meet their escorts. He encouraged them to continue to pray for guidance from the Holy Spirit. When everyone had exited, Fiorvante gave both sets of keys to the Swiss guard outside to keep overnight. Farley looked back and saw Fiorvante lock the door, place the keys in a specially sealed box, and hand it to the Swiss guard.

Farley quickly met Armstrong and the two returned to the hotel. Farley entered his room, hastened to undress, and avail himself of a shower and shave. He then got into some comfortable clothes. Before he picked up his prayer book from the dresser, he thought about the conclaves going back to the election of the first John Paul. The cardinals were locked in the Chapel until a pope was chosen. Washbasins and a cot were their only luxuries. *Now just how did they get the food in and out of there?* he pondered. Theirs was a much better situation. In another hour, dinner would be brought to his room. All the television sets were locked off as were radios. The room was certainly comfortable and the private bath was a definite plus, but some of the other aspects, especially the silence, were austere. He opened his prayer book and started to read. He read only one sentence and had to put the book down. It was just impossible for him not to have thoughts of Ann. He thought she was a beautiful woman, and he thought about living out the rest of his life with her as his partner. He also knew that he was now the leader in the polling for the church's shepherd. That thought surely traumatized him. He couldn't believe the faith his fellow prelates had in him. For the first time, he was terrified of the thought that he could possibly be the successor to Saint Peter. He was being forced to make a major decision. Since all previous conclaves were secret, as was the current conclave, he wondered if anyone elected to the papacy had ever declined to accept. Could he sublimate his love for Ann and accept the burden of Supreme Pontiff? *I'm still very far from having enough votes to be elected, he thought, but tomorrow's ballots only require forty-one votes to be elected. God help me, I beg you!* He opened the prayer book again, and this time earnestly prayed for guidance and help.

Ann had gone shopping for some incidentals. She returned to her house for lunch. She asked Marie to fix her a little something for lunch while she went to her bedroom and placed her purchases in their respective spots. She went back to the kitchen, and she and Marie engaged in conversation. Ann kept one eye on the television. There were reports that the third and final ballot for the day was inconclusive. The church was still without a leader. Ann had decided to wait until Farley returned to discuss selling her apartment which kept intruding on her thoughts. She had discussed it briefly with Carl when they were out for dinner, but she put more reliance on Harold's advice. She preferred his advice even to that of her lawyer. She decided she had no choice but to wait until the end of the conclave, which she was hoping would be soon, so she decided to put the apartment on the back burner for a while. She and Marie talked a little about the conclave and that kept her mind close to thoughts of Harold. She didn't let on to Marie that she was disappointed that the conclave was going into another day.

Farley was surprised at how good his dinner was. Now he really felt sorry for the electors in the conclaves of so many years ago. When he finished his meal, he placed the tray outside his door and noticed that the Swiss guard standing down the hall was yawning. *I guess he's bored with that job. All of us are behaving ourselves.* Farley closed the door behind him, and his fear of being elected renewed itself. *I don't think it's going to happen so I should just relax. I hope my outpolling of Fiorvante on the last ballot is not a trend.* He picked up the Bible in his room and opened up to the First Epistle to the Corinthians. He had no idea why he picked that, but he opened to that and decided to read it. He had a lot of time on his hands. The sequester was daunting.

The page he opened to was Chapter 7, Verse 32. It was staring him in the face. He read it slowly.

> I should like you to be free of all worries. The unmarried man is busy with the Lord's affairs, concerned with pleasing the Lord; but the married man is busy with this world's demands and occupied with pleasing his wife. This means he is divided.

He instantly felt the presence of the Holy Spirit. *Why did I just happen to open to that?* he thought. He went to Chapter 13, which he was very familiar with since it was so often used at a nuptial Mass.

> Love is patient; love is kind. Love is not jealous, it does not put on airs, it is not snobbish. Love is never rude, it is not self seeking, it is not prone to anger; neither does it brood over injuries. Love does not rejoice in what is wrong but rejoices with the truth. There is no limit to love's forbearance, to its trust, its hope, its power to endure.

He read further,

When I was a child I used to talk like a child, think like a child, reason like a child. When I became a man I put childish ways aside.

After a brief pause to gather himself together, he continued,

There are in the end three things that last: faith, hope, and love, and the greatest of these is love.

He couldn't believe that he had opened the Bible to Paul's letter. *I will possibly have to make a choice here. Is my love for Ann childish? And what about the case for an unmarried man and his devotion to his God? I have the possibility of being elected pope and to serve God in a way that is offered to very few people. I do love my God and my priesthood and how great an honor it would be to serve him as pontiff. My love for Ann is also intense, so am I willing to sacrifice a loving relationship with her to accept the papacy if it is offered?* He read the passages again and closed the Bible. Tears came to his eyes as he felt the presence of the Holy Spirit as never before. He had an entire night to think about this.

CHAPTER TWENTY-FIVE

After a fitful night's sleep, Farley arose to another day. In his mind though, it was not just another day. It could be the most momentous day of his life. He was trending ahead in the election. The sun shone brightly into his room, and it uplifted his spirits just a little. He was troubled by the totally unforeseen set of circumstances. He embraced the sunlight and thanked God for the gift of another day. He prayed fervently for the grace of God to accept whatever would come to him that day. He asked God to hold him up for he was weak. *Is the Holy Spirit directing me? Is a partnership with Ann never to be? If I am elected as Supreme Pontiff, I could still maintain our friendship, but it could never be what I desire it to be. Distance alone would prevent that. I will have to make a decision to accept or not to accept if elected. My love for God is also intense. Am I willing to give up my sexual love for Ann and accept this magnificent gift that possibly could be thrust at me? I have to. If the Holy Spirit truly works through the conclave and I receive the most votes, then I must accept. What will this mean to Ann? Why did I open the Bible last night to such a profound passage of the Word of God?* He continued in more formal prayer as he prepared for the day of voting. He was interrupted by a knock on his door. He knew that must be breakfast, but he had little appetite.

He opened the door and graciously accepted his tray from Armstrong. He closed the door and placed the tray on the desk. He went to the bathroom, took his medications from the cabinet, and returned to the desk. He sipped some juice to aid in the swallowing of his pills and settled in his chair to try and relax. He reached over, picked up the cup of coffee, and took a hearty gulp. He took a deep breath and reached over for a piece of toast. He knew he had to eat something since it would probably be close to one in the afternoon before he would be able to eat again. He struggled with the toast.

At eight in the morning, he left his room. Fully robed in red, he walked down the stairs to the lobby. He passed on the use of the elevator. When he arrived in the lobby and saw all the robed electors assembled there, he was again captured by the sacredness and seriousness of what was taking place. The silence in the midst of so many people in that area was awe-inspiring. It also terrified Farley. Armstrong quickly found him and shook his hand. The crowd started to move out of the lobby to the Sistine Chapel. Another day lay in front of them.

Would this be the day the world would greet a new pope? Farley turned around and fixed his gaze on Josephson and Feeney. Feeney gave him a very subtle thumbs-up. Farley acknowledged him with a smile, but inside he was in turmoil.

After crossing the Vatican grounds and enduring the rituals of opening the Sistine Chapel, they seated themselves at their appointed places. Fiorvante again locked the door from the inside and then knocked on the door so that the outside lock would be engaged. Fiorvante walked up to the altar and called up the tabulators who were chosen yesterday. When all in the room assumed their proper places, they joined with Fiorvante in the opening prayers. In Latin, on this second day, Fiorvante again asked all to swear to secrecy. When that task was completed, a fifteen-minute period of meditation was asked for. Again it amazed Farley to be cradled in the arms of this magnificent chapel, amid Michelangelo's masterpieces, in total silence. God's presence was truly felt. Farley's prayers sought support from the Holy Spirit in having to make the penultimate decision of his life, if he were to be elected. He quickly gave a thought to the story in the gospel concerning the rich man who asked Christ what he had to do to be one of his followers. Christ's answer was that he should give all he has to the poor and follow him. The man walked away. Farley did not want to be that man, but he so much desired Ann. He calmed himself by again realizing that he was no where near attaining the number of votes needed to be elected. No matter though; his life was fast approaching the point where he was going to have to make the most momentous decision of his life—choose between his love for Ann or his love of God. *I will watch this fourth ballot. I ask you Holy Spirit to guide me. Bless Ann, and I pray that any decision I make will cause no harm to come to her in any way. I pray that any decision I make will benefit my soul. I desperately need your help.* Farley drew a deep breath and looked at Ainsworth sitting next to him and smiled. Ainsworth smiled back at him. He then looked down at his tablet. He was still convinced that Obiajunwa was worthier than him to lead the church. He did have his doubts now that in the final analysis, Obiajunwa would be elected. He still preferred Obiajunwa over Fiorvante. Depending on how many more ballots would need to be taken, he would continue to vote for Obiajunwa until it got to the point where it would be of no use.

Fiorvante allowed five minutes for all cardinals to write their selections and fold their ballots. The actual casting of the votes would take place shortly. When it was time, the side opposite Farley was called up first beginning in the front. It would be a while before Farley would walk to the altar himself. Farley watched as, one by one, the electors walked up to the altar and placed their ballots on the paten. Farley's prayers were so intense that he felt one with God. When it was his turn to walk up to the altar, he felt as if he was awakening from a dream. He snapped back to reality and again went through the same ritual as he had done on the previous three ballots. He returned to his seat and returned to deep contemplation.

The sound of Fiorvante's voice calling them all to prayer roused him from meditation. After the prayer and after all were reseated, the counting began. The tabulators sat in readiness. Fiorvante pulled the first folded paper from the chalice and read, "Harold Farley." Farley became deeply emotional. His eyes filled and he shed a tear. "God, please put your arms around me and give me some sign that I am able and worthy to be the shepherd of your church."

The next name pulled from the chalice was Giaccomo Fiorvante. Farley relaxed a little, but he knew that there were still over seventy votes to be cast. He remained so deep in thought and prayer, that he found himself not paying a whole lot of attention to the names that were called. It was background noise, but he was somehow aware that only his name and Fiorvante's were being called with an occasional Obiajunwa.

All the names had now been called. It was time for Middleton to call out the tally. Farley was keenly aware that starting with this ballot, only forty-one votes were needed to secure the papacy. Middleton announced what Farley was dreading. He was still in the lead. He had received thirty-six votes—dangerously close to forty-one. Fiorvante received only one vote less at thirty-five. Obiajunwa received nine. Tessier dropped off on this ballot. It was now clear that it would be either Fiorvante or Farley.

As Ortiz gathered the attached ballots in his hand and took them to the stove to be burned, Farley looked down and tried to hide his emotions. He was crying. Ortiz mixed the proper chemical with the ballots, lit the fire, and closed the door to the stove.

The crowd outside in the square was again disappointed. No one seemed to think it would go on this long. It would be an hour, if not more, before they would see the results of another ballot. The smoke was clearly black. There was no doubt that the church was still without a leader.

After the first ballot of the day, Fiorvante called for a break. Ainsworth commented to Farley, in violation of silence, that the marriage commission they had served on seemed to have faded almost into oblivion. "That was our purpose in being over here, and now look at where we are." While dabbing at his eyes, Farley acknowledged him and had to admit that in the past few days he too had almost forgotten about the reason they were summoned to Rome some weeks back. It was an extraordinary series of events. He took a sip of water and dabbed at his eyes again. Ainsworth got up from his adjoining seat to use the rest facilities and left Farley sitting alone in his area. He and Fiorvante were virtually tied. Possibly either one of them would be pope on the next ballot.

Farley dwelled on the fact that he had never given himself any chance to be pope. It was simply too far off the radar. Clement was still fairly young and he was not much younger. It just never entered his mind. Now he was looking at the papacy as a very real possibility. He never gave a thought as to the name he would take as pope because he had never prepared himself to be in that position. He managed to calm himself, and he laughed a little when he thought, *How about Pope Harold? Seriously, I feel totally unworthy to take the name of Clement. I have always had admiration for Matthew. Perhaps I might use that name. Matthew was very progressive, but he always managed to keep Christ's church on track. But maybe God will let this chalice pass from me and I will be congratulating Fiorvante instead.*

He was roused from his thoughts by Fiorvante's voice calling everyone back to their seats to begin the next ballot. He called again for prayer and meditation. The quiet in the vast and holy Chapel was overwhelming and sacred. Time began to move too swiftly for Farley because it was now time to cast another vote. Farley bowed his head, and for the fifth time entered the name of Charles Obiajunwa on his ballot. He could not bring himself to vote for Fiorvante, and he definitely would not vote for himself.

Obiajunwa would again get his vote. He folded the ballot and held it in his now sweaty palm. In all his life, Farley had never experienced the tenseness that was now permeating his body and his spirit.

In just over five minutes, Fiorvante called up the cardinals starting with Wocinski at the rear. This was a repeat of the first ballot and would put Farley's walk to the altar as near last. Wocinski walked up to the altar and raised his folded ballot up over his head and placed it on the paten. Fiorvante raised the paten and slipped the paper off and into the chalice. Wocinski returned to his seat. Gamallo now proceeded to the altar at a very solemn gait and performed the same ritual.

It would be some time before Farley would go through this ritual, so he again went into deep thought. Strangely, Mary O'Leary entered his mind. He regretted his treatment of her through most of his tenure at the cardinal's residence. He had kept himself very distant from her. He didn't feel that he treated her badly, but he tended to take her for granted. He never allowed her to get close to him. In spite of this, she was as loyal to him as she was to his predecessor. Only when she became connected to Ann did Farley show her any closeness. He regretted it now. What dominated his thoughts at this moment was her life of sacrifice. She gave up marriage and family for her faith—a simple woman who displayed great faith. Could he do no less? Could he give up a life of marriage to Ann? His answer was fast becoming aware to him. Mary O'Leary was showing him the pathway to making his major decision. He would give up his life with Ann if elected. If Mary could surrender her desires throughout her life, so could he. She never knew on earth what effect her life would have on the history of the Catholic church. But her spirit was now aware of that impact, and she was extremely happy.

Awakening from deep thought, it was almost Farley's turn to walk up to the altar. He moved his attention to the rituals in the room. Ainsworth arose from his chair to bring his ballot to the altar, and he smiled again at Farley. Farley returned a smile and knew that Ainsworth had no idea of the anguish within him. When Ainsworth returned to his seat, it was Farley's turn. He walked up to the altar and went through the same ritual that he had practiced on the previous ballots. He returned to his seat and the remaining two cardinals seated out in the Chapel walked up and cast their ballots. Then the cardinals at the altar finalized the casting of votes for the ballot. The rituals completed, it was now time to hear the calling of the names.

Fiorvante first called for a group prayer and a very short period of meditation before calling for the tabulation of votes. Again the sacred Chapel was quiet and that silence terrified Farley.

The calling of names was now the next order of the day. Fiorvante pulled the first ballot from the chalice and read out the name "Harold Farley." He handed the ballot to D'Angelo, who again called out the name "Harold Farley." D'Angelo handed the ballot to Middleton who wrote the name on the tally sheet. Middleton handed the ballot to Ortiz who ran the needle through the first ballot. There was plenty of room on the thread for the remaining seventy-nine ballots. Would there be any new names on this ballot? That was highly unlikely. The anticipation in the Chapel was palpable. The next name called was again Harold Farley. Ainsworth again looked over at Farley and gave him a sign of approval. Farley again acknowledged him with a smile, but that was definitely a false front. Inside, terror filled his being. Fiorvante's name was then called, and surprisingly, Obiajunwa was called next. Farley prayed fervently to Jesus and even Saint Peter for strength. He felt himself to be a weak man, but his spiritual connection to Peter at that time reminded him that Peter too was a weak man. His eyes filled and tears coursed his cheek as he heard his name called again and again. If he was elected, would he accept? He had already made up his mind that he would, but if given a chance, would he refuse? It was true that so many years ago, Benedict XVI had resigned the papacy. Could he possibly accept the papacy only to submit his resignation at a later time? That was not an acceptable alternative. Again he wondered if in any previous conclaves, an elected candidate ever declined the election. Conclaves were secret, so he would never know. If he accepted, it would be for life. *I am so unworthy. Can I be a good pope? My fellow prelates seem to believe in me. I must believe in myself, and I must believe that Jesus will take my hand and help me. I'm sure Frank is smiling down on me and has forgotten our last moments together before he went to his eternal reward. I never saw myself ever in the throne of Saint Peter. Can I do this?*

All the votes were called out and Middleton announced the tally. Forty-three votes for Harold Farley, twenty-seven for Fiorvante, and ten for Obiajunwa. "Habemus papam," Middleton uttered. Everyone in the Chapel stood and applauded.

Fiorvante walked over to Farley's seat and lowered the canopy behind Farley. In the split second before Fiorvante addressed him; Mary O'Leary's courageous act of giving up a married life for her faith moved Farley to make his decision to do the same thing. At this most significant moment in Farley's life, he was inspired by the woman who had cared for his residence. A simple woman of great faith. Fiorvante looked at Farley and the room became silent. Fiorvante recited in Latin, "You have been elected by your peers to be Supreme Pontiff of God's church on earth. You have been elected to be the Vicar of Christ on earth. Do you accept?"

His eyes still brimming over, Farley answered, "Accepte."

"By what name do you wished to be called?" was Fiorvante's next question. Farley replied, "Matthew II."

Fiorvante glared into Farley's tear-filled eyes and shook his hand in congratulations. Fiorvante was totally aware of Farley's secret and that was disconcerting to Farley. At some point, he would have to find a way to salve Fiorvante's concerns.

Ortiz walked over to the stove for the last time. He placed the ballots in the stove with some straw and a different special chemical that would guarantee white smoke. He looked at the chemical jar carefully as at that moment he surely didn't want to cause black smoke. When everything was ready, he lit the contents of the stove. Fiorvante knocked on the door twice which was the signal for the Swiss guard to notify Monsignor Bella to quickly notify those at the Basilica to ring the bells.

One by one, each cardinal in the room approached Farley, embraced him, and assured him of their total fidelity. When everyone had returned to their seats, Fiorvante walked to the door again and this time knocked three times. He unlocked the door from the inside and the Swiss guard unlocked the door from the outside. While all the cardinals were up and milling about and exchanging conversation for the first time in six days, Bella and his aide moved into the kitchen and emptied the untouched food and drink that was to be for lunch. Bella looked into the Chapel and saw D'Angelo and Fiorvante standing with Farley and presumed Farley was his new pope. The cardinals began their procession to the Pauline Chapel for a period of prayer while Farley was escorted by Fiorvante and D'Angelo to the "room of tears."

When Harold Farley arrived in the "room of tears," he could not help but think how appropriate the name was. Having very little breakfast and no lunch, he still wasn't hungry. There was no time to think of hunger. He was overwhelmed and continued to dab at his eyes while the tailors scrambled for the right sizes for his papal attire. He knew he had to pull himself together to present a happy and comforting countenance when he went out on the loggia to greet the world.

Outside, the crowd on the square was practically frantic. They glimpsed the white smoke and began to cheer. When the bells of the Basilica pealed, the mood became electric. Their church had a new leader. They were aware that it would be some time before the new pope made his appearance. They were, however, enjoying the wait in anticipation of greeting their new shepherd.

Ann had just risen from her bed. She went to the kitchen for her morning jolt to reality. She quickly noticed how much better she was walking. She had another appointment with the therapist coming up, and she felt he would be pleased. She certainly was. After her first sip of the coffee which was a little too hot, she turned on the television. She was surprised to hear the reporters talking about the white smoke and the election of a new pope. She breathed a sigh of relief. *Thank God, Harold will be coming home.* She felt so much better. She kept her eye on the television as the camera panned the jubilant crowd waiting in the square. The reporters commented that it would be some time before the new pope appeared on the balcony. They mentioned that each of the cardinals had to pledge their fidelity to the new pope, and after that the new pope would be taken to the room of tears to be fitted with the papal cassock. She finished making her breakfast while glancing at the television. She didn't want to miss the appearance of the new pope on the balcony.

Karen and Tom were also glued to the television. Tom had to leave for work shortly, but Karen had the luxury of a job close to home. This was most helpful in allowing her to hopefully get a glimpse of the new pope before she left for work. The reporters were saying that they felt his appearance would not be for too much longer. They also expressed that they really had no idea. She felt proud about the fact that she was secretary for one of the people intimately involved in the conclave. Tom had to leave, so he kissed her good-bye and casually said to her, "Hope your favorite wins." She placed Tom's used dishes in the dishwasher and poured herself another cup of coffee. She turned up the volume and went to the bedroom to get prepared for the day. She kept one ear tuned to the television in anticipation of greeting the new Holy Father.

Reynolds had still not left his parish for the trip to the cardinal's residence and office. He was thanking God that the conclave was over for two reasons. First, the church had a new leader, and second, Harold would be returning soon. He could then get back to his own office and leave Farley to take care of Farley's business. Reynolds wasn't sure how long he could continue to do both jobs. He watched the television and decided to stay right there so he wouldn't miss the new pope being introduced to the world.

As the tailors fussed around Farley to get him fitted, he was composing himself, little by little. *Mary brought me to this hour,* he said to himself. *I have come to peace with myself and I thank you, Mary, for that. My dear Ann, please understand that this is what Christ asked me to do. I will always love you, but my intense love of God and his church compels me to sacrifice a life with you and give unto Christ what he asks.* He breathed a deep sigh and started to joke with the tailors. They feverishly endeavored to make him look his best for his first appearance to the world. His fellow cardinals had finished their prayer service at the Pauline Chapel and had come to the area of the loggia. Behind the door to the left, their new shepherd was being carefully groomed to greet them. Meanwhile, behind that door, his emotions were a roller coaster. He was still struggling to hold back tears of joy even though he had come to peace with himself. He felt that Jesus was giving him the strength he needed. He was ready.

Harold Farley, Pope Matthew II, emerged from the room amidst another round of applause from his fellow cardinals. Fiorvante walked up to him, embraced him, and again pledged his fidelity to him. He asked him in broken English, "Are you ready to give your first blessing, Urbi et Orbi?"

Farley took a deep breath and said, "Jesus is at my side and I'm ready."

Ann watched the television intently as the reporters noticed some movement behind the curtains of the window to the balcony. She thought this was a special time to be a Catholic. She was deeply moved by all the proceedings, not only of the past few days, but also right now in presenting a new pope to the world.

The curtains parted and the window was swung open. She observed people moving inside, but it wasn't clear enough to determine who they were. The crowd in the square roared. What a moment this was. Cardinal Fiorvante appeared on the balcony and that was a huge surprise. He was the favorite, but if he was stepping out now to introduce the new pope, it was a certainty that the results of the conclave were going to be a surprise. Ann gasped in surprise, also not expecting to see Fiorvante at this time. After all, Harold had assured her of that. The suspense was great as the crowd kept cheering and Fiorvante held up his hand to quiet them so he could make this highly anticipated introduction. Ann continued to watch intently and thought about the many papal elections she had lived through, and how each appearance of a new pope was a thrilling experience, not only for her, but for all the world's Catholics. It seemed as though it was life in microcosm. The sheer joy and anticipation of a new beginning in sharp contrast to the starkness of death, from a few days before, culminating in the funeral of Clement XV.

The news reporter could barely hide his excitement, as he knew they were now so close to a new pontiff. The camera moved in on Fiorvante as he said the words that would cause the crowd to cheer again with excitement. In Latin he blared "Habemus papam." As expected, the crowd broke into thunderous applause.

The square reverberated with cheering. In Latin and even with a thick accent and the deafening roar of the crowd, there was no mistaking the name: "Harold Cardinale Farley." Ann gasped again. She didn't even hear Fiorvante announce the name he was taking for his papacy, Matthew II. The reporter struggled to find any significance to his taking the name of Matthew. He assumed it meant that the new pope would continue the work of Matthew and his successor, Clement. Apparently no great changes seemed to be in the offing in a certain direction the church might take. He commented on the fact that Farley was the head of a delegation that was in Rome prior to Clement's death to study the issue of the annulment procedure in the Catholic church. By one vote, the committee voted to retain the annulment process as it had been in place throughout the history of the church. But the reporter was so much more excited about the fact that this was the first North American pope. "I'm sure the Catholics in the United States, Canada, and Mexico never thought they would see this day."

The crowd below waved flags and some even chanted "Viva il Papa" as Farley stood on the balcony. The priest, who was standing alongside the reporter, commented on what a great moment this always was for the church, "but our first American pope makes this so very special."

Ann was stunned. *I don't believe this—Harold.* She was suddenly filled with remorse for ever thinking about marriage to a priest, especially a priest that was thought so well of to be elected to lead the Catholic church. *God took care of that arrangement,* she thought with a forced humor which exhibited itself as a result of shock. It was real, however. She was looking at Harold as he stood out on the balcony with his arms outstretched, embracing his flock. *I can't adjust to this,* thought Ann. *I...I can't believe it.*

She continued to watch as the man she loved greeted the crowds in Latin, then English, and to the sheer delight of the Italians, in Italian. Farley had heard about how well the first non-Italian pope, John Paul II, had blessed the crowds in Italian and how well he was received by that gesture. After all, the pope is also the Bishop of Rome. After Clement's reign as an Italian pope, Farley wanted to endear himself to the Italians. They loved it. At this moment, the whole world was his.

As Ann continued to watch, she realized that their relationship was over. She did not want to allow herself to feel selfish. She was happy for Harold and was very content to know that she was a close friend to the pope. She assured herself that he wouldn't be out of contact with her completely, but certainly their time together would be almost infinitely less than it had been just a few short weeks ago. Ann was religious enough to accept God's will. Lord knows she had done so much of that these past few months. It took every bit of fortitude she could muster. *Each of us must now start a new life.*

After giving his blessing, "Urbi et Orbi," he once again embraced the crowd and then retreated behind the windows. They were then closed and the curtains were drawn. On the television, they replayed his introduction to the world. Ann turned it off and cried.

When Farley reentered the room, he gathered again with his fellow cardinals. He was told that the chefs at the Domus Santa Marta were preparing a festive meal for the cardinals and their celebration. This was welcome news as none of them had eaten since breakfast. There was abundant camaraderie. Cardinal Singh came up to him and told him, "I warned you that you were papabili." They both laughed. Obiajunwa walked over to him, and Farley had all he could do to keep his oath of secrecy. He wanted to tell him that he had supported him in every ballot. Farley truly admired the man's humility and holiness. Instead, he embraced him and he told him of his great admiration of him. Obiajunwa gently smiled and expressed his support in whatever he was asked to do. Amidst the laughter and warmth, Farley had a deep moment of thought. *"Thank you, my God. Thank you, Frank. Thank you, Mary. My dear Ann, I will always love you. I pray that you will accept the will of God. You will always be in my prayers."* He continued to work the room, and they all started to make their way to the hotel. Farley eschewed the papal car for the short walk and accompanied his brother cardinals. The era of Matthew II had begun.

Karen couldn't believe it. "I was once his secretary," she said, beaming. Suddenly, she realized that at that early stage of her job, she had better not be late for work. She dressed in a hurry. She was ecstatic. She couldn't wait to tell her fellow employees the good news. She realized, of course, that they probably already knew, but she wanted them all to be impressed that she was, at one time, his secretary. On her way to work, she wondered if she would ever have any direct contact with him again. Then she gave some thought to perhaps his convening of a new marriage commission. Some day, there might be the possibility of her marriage being blessed by the church. She loved Tom, but she still desired the blessing of her church. In spite of that, it was a great day.

Reynolds was at once ebullient and dumbfounded. His phone rang and it was his friend and Farley's spiritual advisor on the other end. Beardsley excitedly greeted Reynolds with, "Do you believe it? God bless him." Of course, Beardsley was one of the few people who knew of Farley's dilemma. He felt confident that Farley would concentrate on being a great pope and that his relationship with Ann would be over. The sheer logistics involved in maintaining a relationship with her were insurmountable.

Reynolds replied to Beardsley, "Where does that leave me? Now I'm permanently in charge of a parish and the diocese. I was sort of looking forward to a one-job situation."

Beardsley responded, "Maybe Pope Matthew's first order of business will be to appoint an auxiliary for you. Then you can name him to your parish. In any event, I am so very happy for our friend Harold, and this is a great day for our country and our diocese. Just think of the media attention you'll be getting now that your archbishop is the pope."

"No doubt about that. Seriously, I'm very happy for Harold. Let's remember though that he's looking at formidable obstacles in his road ahead, and I'm looking down a similar road in our diocese."

Beardsley interjected, "Have confidence in yourself. You're already doing a great job." Then he laughed and said, "Who knows? Maybe I'll be appointed your auxiliary."

Reynolds laughed. "Harold wouldn't do that to me."

Marcia and Jane were together in the kitchen of the Cardinal's Residence. They were overjoyed. They both snickered about how little time they spent with Farley in their brief term of employment at the residence. They both wondered if Reynolds would be taking over as their permanent boss. Both of them liked him, but had no idea, at this point, where they stood. They were just enjoying the moment.

Ann had to put on a happy face before Marie arrived for the day. *How much can I take? First, my beloved Charles was gone from me, and now my beloved Harold. I know the relationship would have been tenuous due to its many obstacles, but I positively felt that discussion with Harold would have smoothed things over. I did think we had*

possibilities. She sighed. *How my God is testing me.* She composed herself and hastened to her bedroom to prepare for the day. She was in shock, but she intended to put up a good front for Marie.

When Marie arrived, she could hardly contain her excitement. She yelled upstairs to Ann, "I can't believe that someone we know so well is the pope. This is so wonderful."

Ann was on her way downstairs, struggling to smile and show enthusiasm to Marie. She said to Marie, "I wonder if we'll ever see him again? His road has definitely taken a new turn." She looked at Marie and sighed. "I am happy for him." Marie began her chores in the kitchen thinking to herself that Ann didn't seem all that enthused. That was puzzling to her in light of her close friendship with Farley.

Ann walked into the den and saw the book she was trying to finish still lying on one of the tables. *It appears as though I'm never going to finish that book.* While looking at the open book, it suddenly occurred to her that she hadn't heard from Carl yet. *I'm surprised that he hasn't called.*

Carl was very enthused at seeing Farley as the pope. He had been in his company so many times with the Lincrofts. He wanted to call Ann and share what must be a happy day for her, but he was afraid he was becoming too pushy. He definitely wanted a relationship with Ann, but he felt he didn't want to push the envelope. He sensed some resistance from her. He made up his mind he wouldn't push any further, and so he sipped on a cup of coffee and read the morning paper. He resisted the strong urge to call her.

Ann picked up the book and again tried to resume where she left off, but she just couldn't concentrate. *I wonder why Carl hasn't called. I hope he's all right.* She picked up the phone and dialed his number.